The Stubborn Kind

By: Jessica Terry

THE STUBBORN KIND

First edition. November 10, 2023.

ISBN: 979-8988003656

Written by Jessica Terry.

Much appreciation to any and everyone that showed me support as I banged out another story from this universe of characters (which I *love*).

My family, friends, readers, Wordmakers (love those Night Owl write-ins), anyone who has shared my posts on social media or hyped me up in any way, all of you...I love and appreciate you more than I can say. Thank you for continuing to rock with me.

Prologue

....

"NATALIA, I CAN'T BELIEVE you've managed to put up with my stubborn, pain-in-the-ass brother for ten years," Roland Bell joked, holding up his glass of Moet. "Now I'm glad I didn't bet any money on how long y'all would last like I was tempted to."

Natalia laughed as she held onto her husband E.J.'s waist. "I'm glad you didn't, either."

"Now, if we're talking about y'all making it *another* ten..."

"Shut up, Roland," E.J. grumbled, glaring at his little brother though there was a hint of amusement in his eyes. "Just make your toast and stop trying to be funny."

"I think I'm doing pretty good, considering everybody is laughing."

E.J. moved towards his little brother, but Natalia tightened her hold on him, placing a hand on his chest. Everyone knew E.J. wasn't really angry, though. The brothers were just messing with each other as they usually did.

"You just wait until you and Lovey's anniversary," E.J. teased, referring to his giggling sister-in-law who was standing near her husband.

"Whatever." Roland grinned. "But for real, though, y'all, I'm so happy for you two. I had a feeling when Natalia came into the picture years ago that you had found your one, despite how much you two tried to run from it at first. I'm glad you quit playing and locked her down, brother."

E.J. gazed down at Natalia, biting his bottom lip. "You and me both."

Natalia almost forgot they were in a room full of people; she had an instant urge to straddle him for looking at her like that. Even after ten years of marriage, he could still turn her on at the drop of a hat.

She reached up and slid her fingers around the back of his neck, bringing his face closer to hers. "You just wait until we're alone, mister," she whispered, her lips grazing his ear.

"Don't act like I won't put everybody out right now and take you where we stand. 'Cause you know I will."

Natalia did know. And part of her wanted him to. She was officially turned on to level ten.

But she told herself to calm down and planted a kiss to the side of his neck. "Later."

"Hey, y'all cut that out," Desiree Mashburn, a friend that Natalia had met through Lovey and had grown very close to over the past couple of years, spoke up. "I recognize that look."

"I bet you do," her hulk of a boyfriend Lorenzo teased, holding her hand firmly in his huge one. She just winked at him and playfully bumped him with her hip.

Silently telling himself to stop acting mannish, E.J. slid an arm around his wife's shoulders and looked around the room full of their loved ones. They were in the private room of his and Roland's club, 845, and even though he wasn't known for being the most sentimental man in the world, his usual granite heart couldn't help but be softened at the occasion. He'd never even considered getting married before he met Natalia, and now there they were, ten years in and still as into each other as they were during the first.

And E.J. was especially excited because hitting the ten year mark meant that Natalia would finally grant him what he'd wanted since the beginning. And he had every intention of collecting right away.

"It means a lot to me that you all are here for us tonight," he said to everyone, his eyes sliding around the room. "And I think I can speak for my wife when I say that we love and appreciate everyone in here. I know I wasn't gung-ho about a party at first-"

"*Major* understatement," Roland muttered.

"But I'm glad that my wife and my brother...and my sister-in-law...*and* my employees, talked me into it."

Everyone laughed. It had taken all that convincing to get E.J. to relent, because he had initially just wanted to celebrate with Natalia privately. And usually once E.J.'s mind was made up about something, nobody but the good Lord himself could make him change it. But this was one time he was glad he gave in.

"I'm glad we wore him down because this is awesome, having all of you here," Natalia commented, her fingers linked with her husband's. She grinned up at him. "Ten years married is a big deal, especially nowadays. And there's gonna be many more because I'm damn sure not giving this fine man up for anything or anybody."

"I know that's right, girl!" someone called out.

"You know I'm all yours," E.J. assured her, his dark cheeks warming at her statement. He loved when she said stuff like that. "This became a life sentence as soon as I slid that ring on your finger. There's no going back."

"For life," Natalia happily concurred, her grin widening even further. She untangled their fingers and hooked her pinky with his.

He winked at her. "For life."

The party went on for a while longer, everyone drinking and mingling and eating from the catered spread that was beautifully displayed near the bar. E.J. hung with his brother and a few other men, his eyes drifting over to his wife, who stood across the room with Desiree, Lovey, and Lovey's sister, Liz. He watched as she laughed loudly at something Desiree said, throwing her head back, her freshly done shoulder-length blunt-cut hair swinging. His gaze slid down her body, admiring the white strapless dress she wore that hugged every curve. Her bronze skin popped in that, and it had taken all E.J.'s restraint to not tackle her when she emerged from the bathroom in it before they left the house.

Though he *did* back her against the wall and kiss her senseless. Her supposedly kiss-proof lipstick didn't stand a chance.

"Man, can you stop eye-stripping your wife for two seconds?" Roland admonished with a smile, nudging his arm.

E.J. smirked and shook his head, his attention still across the room. "Nope."

"That might be our cue, fellas," Roland announced to the other men. "I think this party is a wrap."

He wasn't wrong. In the next ten minutes, people were getting their coats and bidding their final 'happy anniversaries' and congratulations. Since Natalia had already arranged for the invited employees to be on post-party clean up duty, she and E.J. wasted no time rushing out to his black Mercedes, lunging for each other as soon as they were inside. They made out like horny teenagers for several minutes before finally coming up for air, panting and unsatisfied.

"Hurry up and get us home," Natalia ordered, licking her lips as she eased a hand up his hard thigh. "I can't do what I want to do to you in the front seat of this car."

"I have a backseat," E.J. teased, though he immediately started the engine.

"You know I love me some car sex, but we're gonna need space for this. So step on it."

Grinning, E.J. peeled out of the parking lot, glad their house was only fifteen minutes away.

"I hope you tossed out the rest of those condoms," he commented, glancing over at her as he smoothly navigated the wheel with one hand. His other was clamped in hers as she nibbled on his fingers. "'Cause we're making babies tonight."

Natalia managed to keep her face even despite the instant anxiety that washed over her and cooled most of her arousal. She should have known E.J. wasn't going to forget about the promise she'd made to him. He'd wanted kids right after they married, but she managed to convince him to wait ten years before they started trying. She'd prayed that over that time, he would grow to be as satisfied with it just being the two of them as she was and let go of the idea, but clearly, he was ready to cash in that raincheck.

Not wanting to spoil the mood by telling the truth, she made herself continue to nibble on his thick fingers as her mind whirled on how she was going to get out of this. Not sex with E.J.; she was always down for that. But the part about making babies? She wasn't ready to take her finger off the pause button on that part.

But she knew her husband would explode if she admitted it. She'd made him wait ten years, after all.

"You just focus on breaking our orgasm record," she made herself say, hoping a challenge would take over as first and foremost in his mind. E.J. almost never backed down from a challenge. "I believe our personal best is seven."

"Challenge accepted, baby." He winked at her as his foot pressed harder on the accelerator, breaking speed limits to get home.

Chapter 1
Two months later

• • • •

NATALIA'S SKIN TINGLED as she rolled her hips, groaning as E.J.'s hands slid up and grabbed her breasts. Darkness cloaked the room and little was spoken outside of whispers and hisses of pleasure. It was barely five o'clock in the morning and Natalia was no early bird, but she loved morning sex. And she knew it was now or never for that if she wanted any before E.J. went to the gym. So she slammed down her alarm, grabbed a breath mint strip from the nightstand drawer, and stroked her husband's dick until it was stiff and ready for mounting.

"Baby..." E.J. whispered, smoothly pushing up into her. Natalia loved the way he moved.

"Yes, baby..."

"I'm close...*fuck*, I'm almost there..."

Natalia groaned as she braced her hands on his pecs and worked her hips faster, waiting for the right moment. When the back of E.J.'s head dug into the pillow and a loud guttural growl erupted from his throat, Natalia hopped off of him and slid her mouth over his hardness, just in time to catch all his sperm-laden juices. Since he had gotten rid of their condoms and she hadn't had time to sneak a diaphragm in, she had no choice.

E.J. cursed loudly as she sucked him off, his hand gripping the head scarf still covering her hair and his hips lifting off the bed. She didn't stop until he gently pushed her off of him, and she could only hope that he was too drained for another round.

"You good?" she asked, grazing her nails along his inner thigh.

"Mmm-hmm." He graced her with a lazy smile. "I'm more than good."

"That's what I wanna hear."

"I noticed you got off me again before I came, though. As much as I love you sucking my dick, I can't put a baby in you through the throat."

Natalia was glad the room was dark because her smile immediately faltered. "I know, but..."

Sitting up, E.J. turned on the bedside lamp. His post-coital easiness was now replaced with a knowing frown. "But what, Natalia?"

She sighed. "E.J., come on, let's not. We just had a good time."

"We did. But that doesn't mean I don't notice what you're doing."

Her eyes dimmed guiltily. "What are you talking about?"

"I'm far from stupid. You think I haven't noticed how you've done every creative thing you can to avoid me coming inside you? Changing positions, sucking or jacking me off, claiming you wanted to do some kind of tantric sex bullshit..."

"E.J."

"You've made me come everywhere else but inside you more times in the last two months than you have in ten years. You were always worried about it getting in your hair, but now you apparently love me unloading on your face. You think I don't know what you're doing, Natalia?"

Natalia should've known he would've figured it out. E.J. was nobody's idiot. And just because they continued to ravage each other didn't mean his mind would get clouded to the obvious. The only other option would have been to stop sleeping with him altogether, which absolutely wasn't happening.

Or she could've just been straight with him.

Pushing herself up, Natalia righted her head scarf and faced her naked body to his, folding her legs underneath her. The expression on his face dared her to tell him anything but the truth.

"Fine," she finally relented. "I'll admit that I'm still not ready to start trying to get pregnant."

Even though he'd already sensed that, his annoyance flared upon hearing it. "Why?"

"I've told you; I'm not ready for things to change. It's just the two of us and I love that."

"Yeah, I love it, too, but you knew from the beginning that I wanted to have kids. And you *said* that's what you wanted, too."

"I know..."

"Were you lying?"

Well....

Natalia knew she needed to tell him the truth. But if she did, all hell would break loose and she knew it.

"Can you just give me a little more time, baby?" she pleaded instead. "I know it's asking a lot..."

"I've given you ten years."

"I know. But being somebody's mama is a big deal and I'm still trying to wrap my head around it-"

E.J. slid off the bed, cutting his eyes at her. "Right."

"I'm sorry, baby, but not everybody is ready for this at the same time."

"Like I said, it's been ten damn years. I was patient and didn't hound you because you were singing this same song after we got married, and now you're giving me the stiff-arm again. So don't expect me to be understanding right now."

She started to respond, but he walked into the bathroom, having no more words for her. She eyed his dark strong muscular body until it was out of sight, then flopped onto her back on the bed. That hadn't gone well at all.

The shower in the bathroom came on, and Natalia hoped that E.J. would have calmed down enough to talk to her by the time he was finished. She grabbed her phone to check the time, then rolled over and waited. E.J. always worked out first thing in the morning, but Natalia didn't have to be at work for another four hours.

When she heard the shower turn off, she hopped off the bed and rushed into the kitchen, hurriedly grabbing his shaker cup and the tub of pre-workout powder out of the cabinet. She filled the cup with the appropriate amount of alkaline water and added a hefty scoop of the fruity pre-workout mix into it, having seen him do it enough times to know how he liked it. Screwing on the top, she vigorously shook the cup with one hand and slapped the top back onto the tub with the other, hastily pushing it to the corner of the counter before heading back to the bedroom. E.J. was grabbing a tank top out of the drawer, his body still glistening with droplets of water. Natalia hated that he was mad at her because she ached to take him again right then.

My GOD this man is sexy, she thought to herself for the millionth time.

"Here, baby," she offered as she approached, holding the shaker cup out to him. "I fixed your pre-workout for you."

He glared at her for a moment before slipping the tank top over his head. "Thanks. You can just set it right there." He jutted his chin at the dresser as he yanked the drawstring on his sweats, tying it.

Doing as asked, Natalia bit her lip anxiously. Her hand tentatively grabbed his arm. "Can we please talk?"

"I'm good."

"Stop, E.J. You're pissed at me. We shouldn't leave things like this."

"What's to say, Natalia? You made yourself clear when you told me you weren't ready to have my baby."

"Th-that doesn't mean I don't love you, though, or that I *never* want to...look, I just don't want you to shut down on me and then we go around here avoiding each other for days. That's no way to handle things."

"You've got a lot of advice for someone who wasn't straight up about what she didn't want."

Natalia's mouth opened, but she had no response. He was right.

E.J. continued getting dressed before grabbing his workout bag from the closet and snatching the shaker cup from the dresser. He didn't say a word as he stalked out of the room, then Natalia heard the front door open and slam shut moments later.

Dejected, Natalia climbed back into bed. She hated when E.J. got upset with her, even more so when she'd brought it on herself. If she had just been honest with him from the beginning, they wouldn't be in this position.

But she feared that they wouldn't be together at all, hence her assuring him that she wanted kids as much as he did. He'd made no secret of how much he wanted to be a father, and Natalia thought he'd break up with her if she didn't share his baby-enthusiasm. Maybe he wouldn't have, but she hadn't been willing to take that chance.

Burying her face in the pillow, Natalia hoped that she hadn't made a mess she wouldn't be able to clean up.

· · · ·

HAVING RESISTED THE urge to call out of work, Natalia sat in her office at MODCode, the tech company where she worked, staring at the multiple computer screens. She had a pile of things to do but her concentration was shot.

A meeting maker popped onto the screen of her laptop, and she groaned. The last thing she felt like doing was sitting through a stand up, where everyone gave updates on whatever they were working on. Especially when she knew her bosses were eventually going to call for volunteers for the headache of a project that was coming up. They'd made it clear they wanted Natalia in on it, but she'd resisted because it would involve a lot of overtime and while she liked being a software engineer, she didn't like it *that* much. She was just thankful that volunteering was an option because at the tech company where she worked right out of college, it would've just been assigned to her whether she liked it or not.

"Hey, Natalia," her coworker Sandy greeted as Natalia trudged out of her office, iPad in hand. Sandy's was right next to hers. "I love that skirt."

Natalia was always overdressed compared to her coworkers. Sandy was in jeans and a long-sleeved tee while Natalia was in a skirt and a fitted blouse. She usually wore heels, even though they almost always came off as soon as she got to her desk, and she kept a pair of flats in her bag. She just figured if she had to be cooped up all day, she could at least look good doing it. Natalia's style had always leaned more towards dressy than casual.

"Thank you," Natalia smiled. "I wish it had some pockets so I could sneak some mini bottles of Jack in there to put in that nasty coffee. I'm gonna need to stay awake during this bullshit."

Sandy giggled. "I so agree with you. You would think that they could spring for decent coffee around here. It's not like they can't afford it. Everything else around here is pretty much top notch."

"Yeah, well. As long as they keep the money I earn flowing to my paycheck, I don't care what they do with the rest of it."

"I'm with you on that one."

They entered the conference room where everyone else was still trickling in and making small talk. Natalia noticed the assortment of doughnuts, and she wasted no time grabbing two of them, opting for a bottle of water instead of trying to choke down the usual bitter coffee. A whole bottle of flavored creamer and a bucket of sugar couldn't save that stuff.

Once everyone was getting settled around the large conference table, Natalia glanced around the room curiously before leaning over to Sandy. "Savannah isn't here today?" she whispered, referring to their immediate superior.

"Oh, didn't you hear? She's gonna be out for a while. She had a miscarriage last night."

"Oh..." Natalia righted herself in her seat, though she now felt like she was buzzing. Her trembling hands slid between her thighs and the cushioned chair as she tried to gather herself. She and Savannah got along fine but they were hardly friends, so Natalia couldn't understand why she suddenly felt tears stinging her eyes. It wasn't like Savannah had asked her to be the baby's godmother or anything. All Natalia had planned on doing was getting her a gift card.

So why was she so shaken up?

The meeting kicked off and Natalia half-listened to the progress updates, about the new software programs that were being implemented and all the tests that needed to be applied, and everything else that needed to be done, and she fought to keep at least some of her attention on what they were saying. Her mind was on Savannah, but mostly on E.J. and the house full of tension that she knew was going to await her when she got home. Knowing her husband, he'd have very few words for her for the next few days, and Natalia wasn't looking forward to the cold shoulder. She knew she was wrong for how she'd handled the whole baby issue, but she wished he wouldn't shut down on her just because he was pissed. That was no way to live.

And she knew she could forget about sex any time soon. Since E.J. knew she was avoiding any conception attempts, he wasn't going to indulge her any rolls in the hay. Natalia almost groaned out loud at the thought.

She heard her bosses make their call again for volunteers to take the lead and head the new projects, and her hand eased into the air almost on its own. Several people looked shocked at the action, including Sandy. Natalia wasn't always the first to go above and beyond. She usually just did what she was assigned to do and called it a day, not interested in impressing anyone. She liked her job, but that's all it was to her; a job. There were more important things in her life she wanted to spend the rest of her time on.

But there was no need for her to rush home every night if her husband was just going to act like she wasn't there.

"Wow, Natalia, this is a pleasant surprise," her manager, Humphrey commented. "I thought we might have to bribe you to get in on this."

Natalia forced herself to join in on the chuckles that surrounded her at the joke. "Yeah, well...if you all can promise to get some better coffee in here to keep me going while I camp out in front of my computer for hours on end, then I'm all in."

"Hell, *done*," Humphrey immediately agreed. "If that's all it takes, we'll get specialty coffee flown in here."

"Some Dunkin' Donuts or Starbucks will be good enough."

"It'll be here tomorrow. Thanks for volunteering, Natalia."

"Sure."

Several people around the table shot her grateful looks; they had been unreasonably stubborn about getting better coffee in the office for a while, for whatever reason. But since the work was so important and tedious and there was a lot riding on it, they were apparently willing to bend if it meant having someone willingly take the lead. It was going to mean a lot of early mornings and late nights, and that wasn't something most people jumped at.

Once the meeting was over, Natalia went back to her office, planning to bury herself in work until it was time to leave for the day. She wasn't thrilled about all the work she had just signed up for, but at least she'd have something to occupy her time and thoughts other than being in the doghouse with E.J.

Unfortunately, she wouldn't even have that to lean on like she thought. A couple of hours after the morning meeting, she got an email from Humphrey saying that someone more experienced had stepped up to take the lead, and due to the importance of the project, they were going with them. Natalia was both relieved and insulted, but she just expelled a long sigh and asked to be kept in mind for anything that might be coming up, banging on the computer keys a little harder than necessary as she typed.

"Well, there goes that," she muttered to herself, mindlessly looking over the items on her desk. Her office wasn't huge but it was sufficient, and it was times like this that she was glad to no longer be in the cubicle that she'd been stuck in when she first started at ModCode. The way things were structured there, most of the newer engineers worked in the cubicle hub while the more senior ones got graced with offices, however small and unimpressive they were. No one cared that much because they worked from home most of the time, anyway. Natalia tended to get cabin fever, though, so she often went into the office more than her associates, just to get out of the house.

Since her door was closed, she checked to make sure she didn't have another meeting she'd forgotten about and then leaned back in her desk chair, closing her eyes and hoping the solution to fix things between her and E.J. would drop into her mind.

But she knew that nothing short of telling E.J. that she was ready for a life of snugglies and diapers and lullabies would stop the attitude he had towards her. If only she was.

• • • •

WHEN IT WAS TIME TO leave work, Natalia was in no hurry to head home, even though she knew E.J. probably wasn't there yet. He and his brother Roland owned two night clubs as well as having some other business ventures, so he usually got home after she did most nights. E.J. mostly took care of the back end stuff at the clubs, handling most of the business side of things, while Roland took lead of the front end, overseeing the nightly events and working with any promoters. E.J. did interviews and met patrons when needed but rarely made himself seen on the club floors; he had no interest in partying or socializing. He was just focused on the business and making sure everything was how it should be, and that all the numbers were going in the right direction.

He hadn't even called or texted her all day. Usually he sent her a few messages checking on her, seeing how her day was going, flirting with her. But Natalia dejectedly looked at her phone, seeing none of that. She started to call him but changed her mind; even if he answered, he wouldn't be happy to hear from her like he usually was. Natalia didn't want to hear that.

So she called someone else, hoping they were free.

"Hey, girl," Desiree answered, to Natalia's relief. "What's up?"

"Hey. Not too much; about to leave work. Are you busy?"

"Not really. Just getting my to-do list together for tomorrow and scheduling these social media posts. Lorenzo is working late so I'm trying to keep myself occupied by doing stuff I should've had done already."

"You got time to meet me somewhere? I need a drink."

"Bad day, huh? I feel you, but you know I'm not gonna let you drink and then try to drive home after that. Unless you plan on getting an Uber or something."

"Ugh...all right, well we can just go somewhere and pig out, then. Rocky's is still open."

"Now you're talking my language. Some fried seafood is just what I need after dealing with all this."

"Bet. Can you meet me over there in thirty minutes? Is that enough time?"

"Twenty is enough time. All this stuff will be here when I get back."

"See you in a bit, then."

Natalia had renewed energy as she headed towards the hole-in-the-wall seafood spot that she and Desiree loved so much. The owner Rocky was a friend from college and he always got her order going as soon as he saw her walk in the door, since he knew what she liked. Natalia loved that.

Thanks to traffic, Desiree beat her to the restaurant. She was concentrating on something on her phone, but she put it down when she saw Natalia walk in, standing from the table and greeting her friend with a strong hug.

"It's good to see you, girl," Desiree commented, retaking her seat. "We haven't hung out since you and E.J.'s anniversary party."

"Yeah." Natalia was glum as she took the seat opposite Desiree, waving at Rocky across the small restaurant. "It's been a minute."

Noticing the change in demeanor, Desiree sat forward, concerned. "What's going on?"

"Things are kinda jacked up at home right now," Natalia admitted, not in the mood for pretense. "E.J. is pissed at me."

"Why?"

"Because I'm not ready to start popping out babies like he is."

"Oh wow," Desiree sat back in her seat. "I mean, I guess I can understand him not being thrilled about it, but to get pissed at you over it? He must feel pretty strongly."

"He does. And I'll be honest and admit that I might've led him to believe that I was more willing to be a mother than I really am. I love kids, but I love it being just me and E.J. more. I'm good with how we are now."

"I thought he was, too, seeing as how you two have been married ten years now."

"Well...that's on me, too. He wanted to knock me up the first year, but I managed to get him to agree to give me ten with just the two of us. That seemed like a lifetime when he agreed to it and I guess I thought he'd change his mind, or whatever. I should've known better than that, though."

Desiree eyed her. "You're really *that* against having kids?"

"It's just not as high on my wish list as it is E.J.'s. I love *other* folks kids; but I saw how it was with my mama trying to raise me and my brothers and sisters...we were all she worried about, especially after my dad died. She practically had no life of her own because we took up so much time and energy. I don't want that to be me and E.J."

"Girl...you have *seven* brothers and sisters. That's a lot on *two* parents, let alone one. Hell, you know I have three sisters, myself, and we were a handful for my folks. But y'all just having *one* baby-"

"Won't be enough for E.J.," Natalia interjected. "I already know he wants more than one."

"And he refuses to budge?"

"You know E.J. doesn't budge. But he's more upset about me not being straight up with him, which I know I should have. I just..." Natalia plunked her chin into her hand with a sigh. "It's just kind of a mess right now."

"I wish I could tell you how to fix it. You know I'm the last one that needs to be giving out relationship advice; this is more of a Lovey area. But I *can* say that you should just make sure you don't hide anything else from him from here on out, even if it's something he'll get upset about. I know as well as anyone what it's like to be on E.J.'s shit list."

"True enough."

E.J. had written Desiree off after she dated his brother Roland, dumped him, wormed her way back in once he started taking an interest in Lovey, and then suggested they share him. She then proceeded to sabotage Lovey to try to win Roland's affections, which was even more scandalous considering she and Lovey had been best friends since they were practically kids. It took a while for her to win everyone's forgiveness back, and E.J. had been one of the last people to come around.

Once their orders were ready, they proceeded to tear into their fried seafood dinners, the subject mercifully changing to how things were going with Desiree's event promotion business, and the progression in her relationship with her man Lorenzo. Natalia was floored with how sprung Desiree was over him, given how anti-monogamy she used to be.

They'd been talking and eating for almost two hours when Natalia's phone rang. She sat up straight when she saw it was E.J. calling.

"You okay?" Desiree asked, noticing how anxious her friend suddenly looked.

"Yeah...it's E.J." Natalia ran a hand through her hair and adjusted her sleeveless top.

"You know he can't see you, right?"

"Shut up." Natalia cleared her throat as she answered her ringing phone. "Hey."

"Where are you?" E.J. immediately asked.

"Having dinner with Desiree."

"Having dinner where?"

"At Rocky's."

"I was worried when I got home and you weren't here, and I didn't have any messages from you. How come you didn't let me know you weren't coming straight home?"

"Figured you wouldn't care. You didn't have anything to say to me after our disagreement this morning and I haven't heard from you all day."

"Natalia," E.J. sighed, his voice losing its earlier edge. "Babe, regardless of whether I'm upset at you or not, I still need to know you're all right. You're my wife and I love you. Us arguing doesn't change a damn thing about that."

Natalia felt like she could melt right there in her seat. The smile on her face was so wide it made her cheeks ache, and Desiree just softly chuckled and shook her head, sensing her friend was being sweet-talked.

"I love you, too, baby," Natalia softly replied.

"Come home, Natalia. It's getting late and there's a thunderstorm coming; I don't want you out driving around in that at night."

Natalia felt warmed that E.J. was showing such concern for her despite how angry she knew he still was. But then, she shouldn't have been surprised, as E.J. might've been stubborn but he wasn't petty. "Okay. I'll be leaving in a minute."

"You haven't been drinking, have you?"

"No. Desiree wouldn't let me."

"Good. Thank Desiree for me then bring your ass home."

If it had been *any* other man, Natalia would have gone off until their ears bled. But coming from E.J., she was already getting up from her chair and ready to break all the speeding laws getting home to him.

"Fight over?" Desiree teased as Natalia hurriedly put on her jacket and gathered her things.

"I don't know but I hope so, 'cause that man...whew!" She hurried for the door, waving over her shoulder. "Bye girl!"

Desiree just laughed, watching through the window as Natalia practically ran to her car.

Chapter 2

. . . .

E.J. ADJUSTED HIS LEGS as he sat on the floor with his eighteen-month-old nephew, Xavier. The smile hadn't left his face ever since Roland and Lovey dropped him off a couple hours earlier so they could have a much-needed date night. Even though getting his anxious sister-in-law to actually leave Xavier with him wasn't the easiest.

"I've got him, Lovey," E.J. patiently assured her as she planted her third set of goodbye kisses to the top of her baby boy's head. "You gave me all the necessary instructions; plus this isn't my first time babysitting. You have nothing to worry about."

"It's just that it's still a little hard for me to leave him, that's all," Lovey whined, standing as Roland gently started to pull her back towards the door. Again. "It's not that I don't trust you, E.J..."

"I get it; I'm not taking it personally." E.J. picked Xavier up, tickling him and making him squeal with giggles. That seemed to put Lovey at ease a little. "Go have a nice evening; me and little man here are gonna have more fun than you, though."

"Thanks for watching him for us, man. Come on, babe," Roland urged, putting his arm around his wife. "The sooner we leave, the sooner we can come back and pick him up."

"All right. Love you, my baby!" Lovey cooed to Xavier as Roland pulled her out the door. Once they were finally out, E.J. closed the door behind them, chuckling and shaking his head.

E.J. couldn't remember the last time he'd had more fun. 'Soft' was never a word that usually described him, but when it came to Xavier, he was pure mush. He loved babysitting his chubby-cheeked nephew, who had his and Roland's dark coloring but Lovey's features, and it only made him want some children of his own that much more. Thinking of that made him remember how Natalia was still refusing to take her foot off the brake when it came to starting their family, but he forced that out of his head. He just wanted to enjoy the time with his nephew.

"Ball!" Xavier exclaimed, holding his little arms out as he pushed a blue plastic ball towards E.J.

E.J. rolled the ball back to his nephew, getting rewarded with a huge smile displaying his budding teeth. It didn't matter that they had been doing the same thing for at least twenty minutes; E.J. was having just as much fun as Xavier was.

His cell phone rang and E.J. reached over and grabbed it off the couch. He shook his head when he saw who it was.

"He's fine, Lovey," he droned. It was the second time she had called.

"Did he eat yet?" There were voices and street sounds in the background and E.J. figured she had stepped outside (again) to call him.

"I'm just about to feed him now."

"You checked his diaper, right? Make sure you clean him really good because he's prone to diaper rashes, and-"

"Lovey, will you come back in here?" Roland's voice called out.

"Just a second! I'm...checking my voicemail."

"You and I both know that's not what you're doing."

E.J. chuckled. "I promise you, we're fine, sis. We've been having a grand ol' time rolling the ball across the floor, and I chased him around the living room about a hundred times."

"Yeah, he *does* love that," Lovey replied, the smile in her voice evident.

"To answer your question, yes, I checked his diaper, and he's been thoroughly cleaned. I'm gonna feed him this organic stuff you left for him and then we're gonna get down with some of these picture books until he tuckers out."

"Okay. Thanks so much, E.J. We shouldn't be too much longer."

"Take your time."

E.J. proceeded to get Xavier fed, then they curled up on the couch so E.J. could read to him. Natalia came home, instantly smiling upon seeing little Xavier curled up on her husband's lap. E.J.'s shirt was clutched in his tiny fist, and Natalia couldn't resist fishing her phone out of her purse and taking a picture of them.

"Hey," she whispered, putting her purse on the stuffed armchair and joining E.J. and a dozing Xavier on the couch.

"Hey." E.J. glanced at her briefly before going back to reading.

Natalia noted now soft and soothing E.J.'s voice was, and how tenderly he was holding Xavier. Occasionally he would lean down and press his lips to the top of the baby's head, and Natalia couldn't help but be touched. And if she was honest, a little turned on. She had no doubt that E.J. would make an amazing father.

"Can I hold him?" she requested, holding her hands out.

Glancing at her, she almost expected him to refuse because it was clear he didn't want to, but he eventually relented, slightly turning towards her. Natalia leaned forward and gently lifted Xavier off of E.J.'s lap, placing him on her chest, where he instantly snuggled up to her. He sighed and Natalia melted, leaning down to inhale his irresistible powdery scent as she closed her eyes and sank further into her seat.

E.J. watched her but said nothing. A pang shot through him at the thought that they could have a child of their own but she was denying them the pleasure. She clearly liked kids. And while he knew that liking them and wanting the lifetime responsibility for one were two different things, he still hated that she was so resistant to them having a family of their own.

More to the point, that she had told him she wanted what he wanted, made him wait ten years, and now she was changing her tune.

Neither E.J. nor Natalia tried to engage in conversation; they were both content to just sit and watch Xavier sleep, Natalia's hand lovingly rubbing his back and E.J. lightly stroking Xavier's tiny hand with his finger.

To E.J.'s slight disappointment, Lovey and Roland came back a little while later to pick Xavier up.

"He didn't give you any trouble, did he?" Lovey asked after she hugged Natalia.

"No trouble at all. We had a great time," E.J. replied.

"Thank y'all again for watching him for us," Roland commented, stuffing Xavier's toys into his diaper bag. "Lovey and I needed a kid-free evening. Even if she *did* spend half of it talking about Xavier or calling you to check on him."

"Well, I couldn't help it," Lovey defended, rubbing her cheek against Xavier's before gently putting the still-sleeping baby in his car seat. "I'm not at the point where I don't mind being away from him yet."

"I understand that," E.J. assured.

"My sister was the same way when she had her daughter," Natalia commented. "She'd be blowing my phone up whenever I babysat, checking on her every ten minutes. But you'll get more used to it soon enough."

"I guess *we'll* never know how that is, though," E.J. muttered, looking at the opposite wall. He didn't want to be snide but he couldn't resist. "Apparently all we'll ever *be* is babysitters."

The three of them looked at him in surprise. Natalia cleared her throat and tried to force a smile at her in-laws, who were curiously glancing back and forth between her and E.J.

"Baby, I think that's a conversation for another time, huh?" She slid an arm around his waist, noticing how he immediately stiffened at her touch. "Nothing is set in stone, as far as that."

E.J. cut his eyes at her but didn't respond.

Natalia looked at their guests. "Y'all want something to drink or anything?"

"Oh nah; we should get going," Roland immediately replied, giving E.J. another curious glance before leaning down to get the car seat. "It's getting late and we need to get this little man to bed."

"Thanks again for babysitting," Lovey added, following Roland to the door with a gentle hand to his back. It was clear they could sense the tension in the air. "You two, um, enjoy the rest of your night."

Once they were alone, Natalia turned to E.J. with a frown. "Was that really necessary?"

"What? Telling the truth? Still not trying to do that, huh?"

"Dammit, E.J..." She ran her hands down her face. "Regardless, I wish you hadn't brought them into our issues. You clearly made them uncomfortable, with how they ran out of here."

"Like you weren't telling Desiree everything the other night while y'all were out."

Unable to deny that, Natalia threw her hands up. "Well, hell, I had to talk to somebody. *You* weren't talking to me."

"The time to talk would've been ten damn years ago when you were lying to my face about wanting to have kids. Or any time *since* then." E.J. faced her, folding his arms. His eyes bored into hers. "But you basically led me on for our entire marriage, letting me think we were on the same page about something that's a major deal when we weren't. All those times I'd go on and on about how I looked forward to us starting our family and you just sat there nodding and cosigning, *knowing* you didn't mean that shit. But *now* you wanna talk, huh?"

"E.J., baby...okay, look, I know I was wrong for not being totally honest about where I stood on the whole parenting thing. At the time, I thought it was a deal-breaker and I wasn't trying to lose you."

He just looked at her.

"It's just that I don't want our lives to be all about kids," Natalia continued, running a hand through her hair and dropping onto the arm of the couch. "Once the babies come, everything changes. And I love how things are now; just you and me."

"How long did you think you could keep this up, Natalia? When you started all this, did you not expect for me to want us to actually follow through with having kids like we talked about? 'Cause I'm sure you're not delusional enough to think I'd forget."

"No, not *forget*...I guess I hoped you'd love how things are with us as much as I do.'

"I do love it but that doesn't mean it can't get better." He dropped his arms, his expression softening slightly. "I've always wanted to be a father, Natalia, you know that."

"I do. And I'm so sorry that I didn't feel I could be straight up with you back then." She went over to him, taking his hands in hers. "I still think that we can make the best of this, though. Little Xavier is adorable, not to mention the kids my siblings have. We can just be the cool aunt and uncle that they wanna hang with to get away from their parents. We can love on them, spoil 'em and then send them home. In a lot of ways, that's even better, right?"

"No," he immediately retorted, pulling his hands from hers. "That is not *better*. Being an uncle is not a consolation prize for me."

"So, what do you wanna do, then?" Natalia asked, unable to hold her agitation any longer. "How are we gonna get past this?"

"You tell me. You're the one who changed up the program."

"So, what, we're just gonna go on with you pissed at me indefinitely?"

He shrugged, sliding his hands into his pockets.

"Fine." Natalia started towards the stairs, but suddenly stopped and whirled around. "For the record, I'm sorry for lying to you. But I *don't* think I should have to apologize for not wanting to have kids. Just because I'm a woman doesn't mean I owe that to anybody, including you."

An incredulous frown distorted E.J.'s handsome face. "I never said you did. But you know what you *do* owe me, though? Honesty. That's the main thing I thought we had between us but I was clearly wrong about that, too. So you can save the woman empowerment shit, 'cause *you're* the one that put us in this position, not me."

"But *you're* the one that refuses to deal with it and move on."

"Oh, so I'm supposed to just get over it, right? My wife has been lying to me for over ten years and I'm supposed to just brush that off? Would *you* do that if I misled you like you did me? I'll go ahead and answer that for you," he forged on when Natalia opened her mouth to answer. "*No.* You wouldn't and we both know it. You'd be cussing me out until the Lord came back. So don't try to make me out to be wrong just because you are."

"That's not what I'm doing, E.J.!"

"The hell it's not. You're trying to turn this around on me and make yourself look like some kind of victim. 'Ooh big bad E.J. wants to have a kid, how dare he'. Yeah, you can keep that bullshit."

"Oh my god..." Natalia took a step back. "Are you serious with this??"

"I'm all the way serious. So just like you don't feel you have to apologize for not wanting to have kids, I don't have to apologize for wanting to."

They faced off, each glaring and unyielding. Natalia wanted nothing more than to somehow resolve this so she and E.J. could get back to the wedded bliss they were basking in before, but it looked like they were at an impasse. And since neither of them were willing to budge, there was no telling what was going to come of it, and that scared her.

Would he leave her over this?

The thought cooled her off and turned her agitated frown into a worried one. But before she could ask him to assuage her fears, he stormed past her and up the stairs, not saying anything else to her for the rest of the night.

Chapter 3

• • • •

"SO WHAT WAS UP WITH that last night?"

E.J. didn't look up from the pages he was looking at, even though he hadn't been able to concentrate on them. "What?"

"Don't play me, brother," Roland admonished, leaning against the wall in the office of their club, Barfly. It was the first club they opened together before they expanded to 845 and business was better than ever, despite their initial struggles. "The little comment you made to Natalia about the baby thing?"

"It's nothing for you to worry about."

"I'm not trying to get in your business. But I saw the look on your face when you said it. If you have something on your mind you need to get off, I'm here. That's all I'm saying."

His body had tensed all on its own, and E.J. slapped the papers onto the desk and leaned back in the chair, rubbing his eyes. "She lied to me."

Frowning, Roland pushed off the wall and perched himself on the corner of the big black desk. "She lied to you about what?"

"About wanting to have kids. Back when we were dating, she said she wanted them as much as I did. But it turned out to be all bullshit."

"For real? I'm surprised by that; I've always known Natalia to be a straight shooter."

"Yeah, well. She wasn't about this."

"Why would she lie, though?"

"Apparently she thought I'd dump her if she was honest."

"Well, would you have?"

E.J. shrugged. "I don't know, honestly. As much as I was into Natalia, I'd like to think I wouldn't have just broke it off just like that."

"You sure?" Roland quirked a challenging brow. "*You* wouldn't have broken it off if she said having kids was off the table, knowing how much you wanted them?"

Noting the inflection, E.J. quirked his own brow. "What are you trying to say?"

"Come on, man. You're stubborn. And you're quick to cut people off. If Natalia had told you that she didn't want any children before y'all got married, there probably wouldn't have been a wedding and you know it. You'd have ended it right then."

Knowing there was some truth to his brother's words, E.J. defiantly shrugged and folded his arms across his strong chest. "Regardless, I shouldn't just be finding out about this ten years in. She made me wait all this time knowing good and well she had no intention of giving me the family I want. So if you're about to tell me I need to get over it, you can save it."

"No, I'm not gonna say that. She was definitely wrong for lying and not being straight up with you all this time. What I *am* saying, though, is you should try to cut her some slack. Maybe find out *why* she doesn't wanna have kids."

"I know why. She said she likes it being just us. And that she doesn't want us to get consumed with parenthood."

"I mean, I get it. Kids change everything. Lovey and I are *still* getting adjusted to the reality and responsibility of parenthood. It's a big deal."

"I know it is. That doesn't scare me in the slightest. I don't run from stuff just because it's difficult."

"But that's *you*, brother. Not everyone responds the same way, or wants the same thing. It doesn't make them wrong."

"Maybe not, but lying does. Every time I think about how she looked in my face and told me she wanted what I wanted, then begged me to put it on the shelf for *ten damn years* knowing nothing was going to change, it just pisses me off more. I'm just...I'm angry but I'm also hurt that she would play me like that."

"I don't think she was intending to play you, though, man. I get why you feel like that, and I'm not gonna act like I wouldn't feel some kind of way if I were in your shoes, but it sounds like she was just scared of losing you and did something foolish because of it. At the end of the day, though, Natalia is still your wife. Y'all have been married ten years and you've been happy together. I'd just hate to see that end over this."

"Is this where you tell me I need to just forget what I want, forgive her, and move on?"

"Definitely not. What you want matters just as much as what she wants. I'm saying that the situation is what it is, and you're gonna have to find some way to deal with it. Deal with that anger you're feeling because it's not gonna just disappear on its own."

E.J. nodded thoughtfully as he tapped his thumb on the arm of his desk chair. "Wish I knew how to do that."

"And I wish I had the magic solution to make it all better but unfortunately, I don't. Talk to your wife and work this out, man. However you need to."

Everything in E.J. wanted to do exactly that but he didn't know how. He hadn't gotten to where he could think about the situation and not have his blood boil. He felt betrayed, and that wasn't an easy thing to get past.

They went on about their morning, with Roland leaving to go handle some things at 845 and E.J. doing inventory and hosting the daily staff meeting, as well as joining some conference calls about some potential collaboration opportunities. He also looked over the applications of the people coming in about the bartender position later in the day. He would usually delegate a lot of that to his manager, Casey, but he needed to keep his mind occupied. Sitting alone anywhere, even if he was working ,would just lead to him doing more stewing over the mess his marriage was currently in.

It was mid-afternoon before E.J. decided to take a break and get something to eat. The protein shake he'd had after his morning workout had done all it could, and his stomach was growling.

"Casey, has Hive made it in yet?" Hive was their chef.

"He got here a while ago. They're back there getting prepped. Need him to make you something?"

"Yeah. I haven't eaten in hours."

"What else is new?" Casey joked, flashing her dimpled smile. E.J. couldn't help but chuckle, because he knew he had a bad habit of getting so consumed with work that he didn't eat for long stretches. Natalia was always getting onto him about that. "I'll have him whip something up for you, boss. Anything in particular?"

"Nah. He knows what I like. Whatever he makes will be fine."

"Consider it done."

"Thanks, Casey." E.J. was thankful to have such a dependable employee that he could trust on his payroll. Casey had been with him and Roland since the beginning, and after they promoted her to manager of Barfly, she'd been a huge help in taking some things off their plates.

Casey headed back to the kitchen and E.J. checked a message on his phone, leaning against the bar. He felt a tap on his shoulder and turned around curiously. A woman stood there, her smile brightening.

"You're E.J. Bell, right?"

"I am. And you are?"

"I'm Selina Murray. I'm supposed to interview with Casey for the bartender job, but I'm a little early."

E.J. glanced at his watch. "It's a little after two and your interview is scheduled for three-thirty."

"Okay, I'm a *lot* early. I was hoping to get a chance to meet you."

"For?"

"Well, I..." She stepped closer. "I hoped we could get to know each other better. Get really acquainted, you know, especially if we're gonna be working together."

E.J.'s expression didn't change but he recognized the glint in Selina's eye. Women hitting on him was nothing new; it was almost a daily occurrence for both him and Roland since they opened Barfly. And while he never entertained it any other time, he definitely wasn't in the mood for it today, especially from someone trying to become one of his employees.

"I think you need to just focus on your interview with Casey before worrying about getting acquainted with me," he told her.

"But you're the boss," she pressed, her brown eyes sweeping up and down his body. "And maybe this is a little out of line, but I'm *so* attracted and impressed by everything I know about you...I couldn't help but come in here and shoot my shot."

Looking her straight in the eye, E.J.'s voice was strong when he said, "If you're here for any other reason than to pour drinks, you might as well leave now. That's the only thing you can do for me."

Her expression faltered for a second but she recovered, leaning in slightly. "Are you sure about that?"

"*Yes*, bitch, he's sure."

E.J. whirled around at the sound of Natalia's angry voice. He hadn't even heard her come in, but there she was, standing there looking sexier than he wanted to admit and ready to tear this Selina woman apart. She was as protective and possessive of E.J. as he was of her.

Selina apparently recognized the look because she immediately took a couple steps back, fear taking over the flirtatious expression she'd worn moments before. "Oh..."

"Yeah, *oh*." Natalia moved towards her, but E.J. placed a hand on her arm. He knew his wife wouldn't hesitate to pounce on this woman if he let her. "You picked the wrong one, sweetheart. This is *my* husband, and I don't share. So you need to take your thirsty ass on somewhere, and not let me see you sniffing up on my man again. 'Cause I'm throwing hands on sight if I do."

"I...I didn't know he was married," Selina weakly defended, her eyes flitting back and forth between them. E.J. didn't buy that for a second. "But I still want to work here-"

"Damn that," Natalia negated before E.J. had a chance to respond. "That's not happening."

"What's going on?" Casey asked, alarmed, as she returned from the kitchen.

"Selina Murray just removed herself from consideration for the bartending position," E.J. informed, his hand still holding Natalia's arm. He could almost feel the heat of her anger bouncing off of her. "Apparently she thought it was a good idea to come and hit on me before her interview and wasn't aware that I'm a married man who doesn't fraternize with employees or anyone else other than my wife. So now, we're going to wish her a good day and escort her out."

"*I* don't wish her a good day," Natalia grunted. "I hope she gets hit by a fucking truck."

"Natalia!"

"Selina, you need to leave," Casey stated. Her voice was strong but E.J. could see the hint of amusement in her eye at Natalia's statement. "That's totally inappropriate and we don't go for that here."

"So you're trying to tell me you've never noticed how fine this man is??" Selina asked Casey as she started to usher her towards the door. "Unless you're just not into men, there's no way you haven't. And I'm not buying that someone *that* gorgeous is faithful to one woman, I don't care what-"

"You must not think I'll tear your ass up! Keep talkin'!" Natalia exclaimed, yanking away from E.J. and rushing towards her. She evaded E.J.'s grasp as she dropped her purse and went straight for Selina, sending the woman running and screaming. Natalia literally chased her to the door until E.J. caught up with her, grabbing her by the waist and lifting her off the ground to carry her back inside. Natalia's eyes stayed on the door to make sure Selina didn't come back in.

"We'll be in my office, Casey," E.J. informed, still holding his fuming wife as Casey handed him Natalia's purse. He could tell she was trying to hold back a laugh at that whole scene, and was sure it would be discussed by the few employees that had been there to witness it as soon as he was out of earshot. "Give us a minute, okay?"

"No problem, boss."

E.J. finally set Natalia back on her feet when they were halfway across the main floor and heading towards the hallway leading to the office. They didn't speak as they walked side by side, each of them buzzing with the raw emotion from what just happened as well as the still-unresolved issue between them.

E.J. slammed the office door behind them a little harder than necessary, locking it as Natalia threw her purse onto the chair in front of the desk. They stood there glaring at each other, chests heaving, before an invisible switch was flipped and they lunged. Natalia threw herself into E.J.'s arms, her legs encircling his waist as they kissed hungrily and sloppily. His muscled arms squeezed her as he backed her against the nearest bare wall, one hand hurriedly unbuttoning his pants and pushing them and his boxer briefs off his waist. When he reached under Natalia's skirt and literally ripped her lace panties off her, she released a loud breathy groan, her arousal shooting through the roof.

He wasted no time sliding inside of her, biting his lip when he realized just how wet she was. Natalia's nails dug into his shoulder as her head went back, allowing E.J. to slide his long tongue up the length of her neck as his thrusts fell into rhythm. Natalia braced a hand against the nearby bookcase, already feeling like she was gonna explode.

She turned her face back to his and he immediately captured her lips, sweeping his tongue against hers. The kiss went as deep as his thrusts, and Natalia's arm clamped even tighter around him, taking everything he was giving her.

Sex at work wasn't something E.J. usually did but at the moment, he didn't care about anyone possibly hearing them through the office door. He was the boss, it was his club, and if he wanted to have angry sex with his wife against the wall in the middle of the day, that was his business. He knew nobody would have the balls to say anything to him about it, if they did happen to hear them.

"I love how you fuck me when you're mad at me," Natalia whispered, her lips brushing his.

"Yeah?"

"Yes..." Her breath caught in her throat as E.J. pushed all the way inside and held it there. Her eyes closed and her hand slid up the back of his neck to grab his head, shuddering violently. "Oh my god, yes..."

"I don't like being mad at you, babe." E.J. resumed his strokes, now going even harder than before. Natalia screamed, which only urged him on. "I want us to get past this."

"Me, too," she panted, feeling the orgasm building. She wanted to cry at both how good he felt inside of her and at hearing him say those words. She just hoped it wasn't the sex that was making him say it. "And we will. For life, right?"

His eyes landed on hers and he was reminded of just how much he loved this woman. In that moment, he almost didn't care about the issue they were dealing with and wished to high heaven he could hang onto that, even if he knew he couldn't. "For life."

In the next few moments, Natalia was orgasmic-yelling curses so loudly that E.J. had to clamp a hand over her mouth, still thrusting as he released inside of her, growling into the crook of her neck. Natalia just held onto him tightly as the pleasure washed over her, both of them trying to get their breathing under control.

E.J. gently withdrew from her and stepped back, easing Natalia back to her feet. He ran a hand down his face, trying to regain his composure. She stood with her eyes on the floor, looking stunned for several moments before finally righting her clothes. When she looked up at E.J., he was already eying her as he buttoned his pants. She wasn't able to read his expression; he was the master of keeping a poker face while she had always been the emotional one.

"Are we okay?" she finally asked him. "Or at least, *will* we be okay?"

"I want us to be."

"Really?"

"Yes, really. I'm not sure how, but...we'll figure this out."

She almost wanted to faint with relief. As strongly as she felt about the whole baby issue, the last thing she wanted was to lose her husband over it.

"I love you, E.J. More than anything."

He looked at her so long that she started to think he wasn't going to say it back, but he suddenly reached out and yanked her to him by the wrist, causing her to squeal with surprise. His eyes roamed her pretty bronze brown face as he held her close to him, her hands resting on his chest. "And I love *you*."

Grinning, Natalia grabbed his face and brought it to hers for a kiss, eagerly sliding her arms around his neck. She hoped he was right and that they were able to figure things out, because she hated the tension between them. The whole reason she had come to the club in the first place was because the silent treatment was driving her crazy, and she figured cornering him at work was her best bet at getting him to respond to her. But when she saw that other woman pushing up on him, she lost it. Natalia didn't play when it came to E.J., and problems or not, he was hers.

"Can you give me some time?" she whispered between kisses, still holding the back of his neck. "About the whole kid thing? I've been doing a lot of thinking since last night-"

"Don't tell me anything else you don't mean, Natalia," he warned, easing back slightly and looking right into her eyes. "I don't need to be pacified."

"I'm not pacifying you, E.J. Saying stuff I didn't mean is what got us into this. I'm sincerely rethinking the idea of having a baby; seeing you with little Xavier last night did something to me. You'll make an amazing father, baby. The thought of getting to see you like that with a child of our own...it made me feel good and I started thinking maybe my mindset about all this is off. I'm just asking you to be patient with me."

E.J. eyed her, not knowing what to think. He wanted to believe her, but he couldn't help but wonder if the post-sex high mixed with the desire to get back on his good side was making her say these things.

Choosing to take her at her word, he just nodded and brushed her bangs out of her eyes. "All right."

They came together in a tight hug, the uneasiness about their future still enveloping them both just as tight.

. . . .

IT WAS THE LAST THING he felt like doing, but E.J. had agreed to swing by his cousin Jay's house to hear some business idea he had come up with. E.J. already knew the chances were high that he wouldn't be interested, but he agreed to listen just because it was family.

"Edible toilets!" Jay exclaimed once E.J. was seated in his sparsely-furnished living room. His arms were held out dramatically, and he was looking at his cousin as if he was waiting on him to join in on his enthusiasm.

E.J. hated he had even gone over there. "What?"

"Edible toilets, man! Come on, you've *gotta* feel me on this one!"

"Jay..." E.J. tried to keep his patience in check. "You've come at me with some crazy ideas you wanted me to invest in, but this is the absolute stupidest yet. Who in the world would want an edible toilet? How would that even work?"

"See, you're thinking about toilets people sit on and pee in. I'm talking about party centerpieces."

"That doesn't make it sound any better. It's just more ridiculous."

"It's not! Look, they can be made of any kind of cake you want; you know folks make cakes to look like anything nowadays, and they look mad realistic, too. Or maybe even candy. Guests can eat from it."

E.J. sighed and looked at his watch. "Man-"

"*Or* it could be used as a punchbowl. Think about the fun this could be at frat houses, or even as gag gifts! Nothing wrong with a good novelty item."

"And you actually think people would want to eat something that looks like what they take a shit in?"

"That's the genius of it, cuz; *nobody* would think of this shit!"

"Pun intended, huh?"

"What?"

E.J. just shook his head, unable to resist chuckling at Jay's confused expression. "Nothing, man. Go ahead."

"Huh. Well, it would draw attention just because it's so different!" Jay continued, his excitement resuming. "You know folks share stuff on social media or buy it just out of curiosity; think of all the crap you've seen on infomercials back in the day, and those shows that talk about them now. It'll be popular just because it's oxymoronic."

E.J. wondered who had helped his cousin with this little presentation, because Jay did not use words like *oxymoronic*.

"Jay, even if I could ride with you on the whole shock value thing, I just don't think it would be profitable in the long run," E.J. concluded, standing. "Even if some people were initially curious about it, eventually the novelty would wear off. You'd be out of business in a year, if that."

"Nah, nah. Not if we keep it fresh with a bunch of side items. Melt-in-your-mouth candy toilet paper. Cotton candy toilet brushes. White chocolate toilet fresheners. Spray that's in a cleaning bottle but it's actually peppermint."

"Just stop, man," E.J. held up his hand, laughing because he couldn't help it. His cousin had imagination; he'd give him credit for that much. "Let's say I wanted to entertain this...idea of yours. What do the numbers look like?"

Jay's grin flattened slightly. "Numbers?"

"Yes. How much would it cost to make all of this? *Where* would you make all of this? Can't see you establishing production in this two-bedroom apartment, not to mention, you can't even bake. So if you're not doing it yourself, who would you get to do it and how much would that be? How much do you plan on selling it for? What would your profit margin be? Have you even thought about how and where you'd sell it?"

"I'd sell it direct, from my own website."

"So you know how to set up an e-commerce site, because if not, that's just more money you'd have to pay someone else to do for you. Not to mention maintaining it, *and* the inventory, *and* handle shipping. And speaking of inventory, would this be something you make per order, or would you try to make them in bulk? If so, where would you store all that? Hell, do you even have a *name* for this business?"

Clearly stumped, Jay tugged on the front of his t-shirt. "I hadn't gotten that far yet."

"Gotten that far? Man, this is basic stuff. If you haven't considered any of this, how would you seriously expect me to put any of my money into it? How much do *you* even have to get it off the ground? I don't suppose you have some kind of prototype."

"Prototype?"

"Dammit, Jay... yes, a prototype. Like a model of what you're trying to get me to invest thousands of dollars in? You don't even have a picture of it or a presentation or anything; for all I know, you just thought of this shit this morning and called me over here. Have you applied for a patent?"

At his cousin's blank expression, E.J. just shook his head, looking amused as he headed for the door. "I'm out, man. Tell your mama I said hello."

Heading out to his car, E.J. kicked himself for wasting his time. Jay was far from the first family member trying to pitch a big idea to him or Roland, trying to get them to fork over some money. E.J. had yet to hear an actual viable idea. And apparently, he was supposed to just jump in and support them because they were hyped about whatever their brainchild was, regardless of how little business sense it made. E.J. promised himself he was going to stop being polite about entertaining these 'pitch meetings.' Jay wasn't even a close cousin.

"Edible fucking toilets," he muttered, starting his car. "At least this one was funny."

He headed home, hating that he still had some work things he needed to look over when he got there. He would've loved to turn his mind off, but he'd promised Roland he'd check out the merchandise mockups their business manager had sent over, and the projections Desiree had drawn up for a series of events she wanted to put on at Barfly.

When Natalia's car was missing from the garage, he wondered if she was out with one of her girls. He hoped she wasn't avoiding him again. They'd only semi-reconciled in the few weeks since their romp in his office, but he was trying to ease up on the anger and put that energy towards figuring out a resolution. She had asked for more time on the baby issue, and he didn't know what it was she needed to figure out, but he wasn't going to pressure her. He didn't want to force or cajole her into parenthood; it needed to be something they were both fully on board with.

Once he got inside and put his things down, he called Natalia to make sure everything was all right.

"Hey, baby," she greeted him after a few rings. "You home?"

"Yeah. Where are you?"

"I'm still at work."

E.J. glanced at his watch with a frown. "Why are you still at work? It's after nine o'clock."

"I know, but I got assigned to a new project and it's gonna take a lot of overtime. There's a fucking mountain of back-end development that needs to be done for this operating system. I thought I mentioned it."

"No. You didn't."

"Sorry about that. But yeah, this is how it's gonna be for a couple weeks, probably. Especially since we had to re-do most of what had been done already."

"And you can't do any of that work from home?"

"Maybe some of the time but usually, I'll need to stay here. It's just less distractions. Plus, there are security concerns for this particular project, and all that."

"Hmm." Something seemed off to E.J.; he didn't think she was flat-out lying, but he sensed there was more to it than she was telling him. Natalia had made no secret of how she had zero desire to do anything that required extra hours in the office, and she hadn't mentioned being considered for any projects like this. He didn't believe it was just dropped on her without warning; that wasn't how they usually did things at ModCode. Usually people volunteered for projects that required tons of overtime on top of their other work, from what she always told him.

Choosing to leave it at that, E.J. just replied, "All right, then. What time do you think you'll be home?"

"Shouldn't be any more than an hour, hopefully. I'll text you when I'm on the way."

"Okay."

They ended the call, E.J. realizing after the fact that they hadn't exchanged 'I love you's' like they usually did. But he told himself it was no big deal; it was understood, even if it wasn't said.

He took a quick shower and made himself a sandwich before going to his home office, sighing as he woke up his laptop. His eyes weren't on the screen when it lit up, as he was checking the security cameras for the clubs on his phone. He was glad to have trustworthy employees to leave in charge, but he still liked to keep an eye on things when he wasn't there. His managers would absolutely let him and Roland know if anything major or urgent were to come up, but he always liked to see for himself when he wanted, for his own peace of mind.

When he finally turned his attention to his computer screen, he was surprised to see that there was a web page already opened. Natalia had her own work space at home but sometimes still used his computer so he didn't think anything of it, but before he could close the page, he started taking note of what it consisted of. His brow furrowed almost to the point of pain when he saw the page full of web search results. His skin flamed when he read what had been typed into the search bar:

'How to cause a miscarriage.'

Chapter 4

• • • •

NATALIA HADN'T FREAKED out like this in years.

The little romp with E.J. in his office had been amazing, but it wasn't lost on her that he hadn't been wearing protection, and she didn't stop him from coming inside of her. And since it wasn't planned, she had no diaphragm in, and she didn't love using those, anyway. At the time, it was the last thing on her mind. But when her period didn't show up when it was supposed to, she thought she was going to lose it.

She hadn't mentioned it to E.J., because she knew he'd likely just get excited about the possibility of her being pregnant. Even though she had sincerely begun to reconsider her stance on having babies and requested patience from E.J., she wasn't ready for this. Getting pregnant now was not what she wanted, and she prayed every day to see blood when she went to the bathroom.

Though she'd felt terrible about it, she even looked up what she could do to cause a miscarriage, if it came to that. The very thought sickened her, but she'd rather do that than go through a whole pregnancy and give birth to a baby she wasn't sure she wanted. She'd like to think she'd get used to the idea and learn to love it, but what if she didn't?

It was part of the reason she hopped on the project at work; another opportunity rolled around a couple of days after her period was supposed to have shown up, and Natalia went to Humphrey and all but begged to be put on it.

Thankfully, he granted her wish and didn't switch things up later like he did the last time.

"You know you're wrong for not telling E.J. about all this," Desiree admonished while Natalia was visiting her one night. E.J. thought she was still at work. "I know about it but he doesn't?"

"I just don't want to upset him," Natalia defended with a sigh. She smoothed her bangs from her head, resting her forehead in her hand as she sat on Desiree's couch. "He would've gotten all excited if he thought I was pregnant, and it would've been a big issue if I wasn't."

"But you turned out not to be pregnant, right? So how come you couldn't tell him when you found that out?"

"Because then he'd be pissed at me for keeping it from him in the first place. And we're just getting back on speaking terms again."

"So you think keeping more secrets is the answer? Look, girl," Desiree said, nudging Natalia's bare foot. "You know I've got your back. And I'm damn sure no relationship expert. But even *I* know that stuff like hiding a pregnancy scare from your husband and faking like you have to work late just to avoid him aren't good signs."

"I wasn't faking. I *was* supposed to work late tonight but there was some kind of system issue, so we just wrapped it up early. We have to be back in there stupidly early in the morning, though, to make up that time. Damn it."

"Hey, don't complain now. You volunteered for that, remember?"

Natalia's hand dropped. "Since when are you Team E.J.? I thought *I* was your girl."

"You are, but I keep it real. Just like you'd do with me. You know good and well you'd be telling me off if I was trying to pull this kind of stuff on Lorenzo."

Natalia couldn't deny that. "I guess."

"Not being straight up is what got ya'll where you are now. Don't make it worse." Desiree took a bite of the red velvet cake she was holding on a plate in her lap. "You sure you don't want some of this? Mama made it this morning."

"Oh, your mama made that? Hell yeah. I thought it might've been another one of your man's vegan desserts."

"Don't be hating on my man's desserts. He knows what he's doing with those, but sometimes I just want the regular, fattening version."

"That's what I want. I'm about to get me a big ol' slice, too."

Natalia hung out at Desiree's for a while longer, with them eating and watching *Love it or List it*. Knowing she couldn't avoid going home forever, though, Natalia eventually made herself get ready to leave. Desiree reminded her about her upcoming birthday party, urged her to talk to her husband, and pushed her out the door.

She felt ridiculous. Natalia was actually nervous about going home to her husband, and all because she couldn't bring herself to be honest with him yet again. As if she shouldn't have learned her lesson from the last time her dishonesty came back to bite her. Natalia had never been shy or one to bite her tongue. But E.J. brought out a different side of her; he was the first man she was actually submissive to. One thing they had in common that she always loved was that neither of them took any shit, but when it came to this whole baby issue, her usual spine of steel had turned into cardboard.

It wasn't like E.J. would blame her for turning out not to be pregnant. That wasn't on her. But the relief she felt over there being no baby cooking in her belly would surely be a point of contention. Regardless, she should be able to tell him how she felt, whether he got upset or not.

So why was her car heading to the movie theater instead of home?

It was getting late and she knew E.J. was expecting her. She had already responded to his texts that he'd sent while she was at Desiree's with short, vague responses. It burned her that she was being such a punk.

The horror movie she watched did little to take her mind off of things. E.J. had sent a couple more texts asking where she was, and she knew that she was just digging her hole deeper. Before the movie was even half over, she got up and left, telling herself to get a grip.

"Ugh, why does he wanna have kids so bad, anyway?" she groaned to herself, plunking herself in the driver's seat of her Porsche Macan. Her frustration flared. "Why am I not enough?"

Her brain was twisting the narrative so that she was as irked with E.J. as he was with her like a clown making a balloon animal. Her husband could be frustratingly stubborn, like his way was the only way. Yes, she'd been wrong for lying to him. But everything didn't have to stop now just because of it.

Her mind was racing down this path almost as fast as she was racing down the road, and she was surprised when her phone rang. She loosened her grip on the steering wheel and lightened up on the accelerator, not needing a speeding ticket on top of everything else.

Breathing a sigh of relief that it was her brother calling and not E.J., she touched the button on the HD display on the dashboard to answer. "Hey, Frankie."

"You know I don't like when you call me that," her brother Franklin barked. Natalia chuckled. "I can gladly start calling you by *your* middle name, if we're going there."

"Fine, you big baby. What do you want?"

"I need you to get your sister before I kill her."

"What did Kira do now?" Natalia had three sisters, but she didn't have to ask which one he was talking about. Kira was definitely the problem child among the eight of them.

"She sweet-talked my wife into loaning her some more money after I already told her ass no. Money we were setting aside for something else."

"Well I hope you're as mad at your wife as you are at Kira, 'cause that was stupid of her. She's not new to Kira, either."

"True, but Kira lied to her about what she needed it for, talking 'bout she was having surgery. And you know my wife can be too nice, always wanting to take in strays. We can't pass a homeless person without her digging in her purse, or some cat wandering around that she wants to adopt."

"I'm aware. Amazing that she married your grumpy ass."

"Yeah, like your man is a ray of sunshine," Franklin grumbled. "*Anyway*, now Kira is camped out in my living room and I've already told her she's outta here in the morning. Did you know she quit *another* job?"

"I can't keep up with all her nonsense."

"Even Mama wouldn't let her come stay with her. Kira is the baby so if Mama won't even tolerate her, she must be good and fed up."

"Especially since it's mostly Mama's fault that Kira is so spoiled. Since Daddy died not too long after she was born, Kira always got a pass on her shit."

"Yeah, well, her passes are about used up, looks like. You know it's only a matter of time before she shows up at *your* house."

"As if. You know E.J. isn't having that."

"Oh well. Maybe this will force her to grow up, finally, if we all quit bailing her out. I suggest you talk to her; you're one of the few she'll actually listen to."

Natalia sighed, not in the mood to deal with her childish sister yet again. Even if Kira straightened up, it would only be a matter of time before she started acting crazy again.

"Fine," she droned, not looking forward to it at all.

"All right. In the meantime, I'm gonna have yet another talk with my gullible wife and try to get some of the money she loaned Kira back."

"Hmph. Good luck with that."

They ended the call as Natalia pulled up to her house. Her mind was so consumed with her sister's foolishness that she'd temporarily forgotten about why she was so apprehensive to come home in the first place, or the frustration she'd managed to scrape together. But when she walked in and saw a frowning E.J. leaning against the arched entrance to the kitchen, she forgot all about Kira.

"Where have you been, Natalia?" he demanded, no preamble in sight. His arms were folded tightly across his chest. "And don't try to tell me you've been working all this time."

Not having the energy to deflect, Natalia sighed and slid her coat from her shoulders. "No, I wasn't."

"So?"

"I *was* supposed to work late but there was a system issue, so we ended up leaving earlier than planned. Then I went to Desiree's...then a movie."

"Hmm." Pushing himself off the wall, E.J. slid his hands into the pockets of his sweatpants. "Funny that I don't remember you mentioning any of that during the several times I called or texted you."

"I know. I'm sorry about that, but I'll admit that I wasn't in a big hurry to come home."

"And why is that?"

"Because..." Natalia ran her hands down her face and took a fortifying breath that didn't quite do the job, "I didn't know how to admit to you that I thought I might've been pregnant and didn't say anything to you about it."

E.J.'s expression didn't budge. He didn't look surprised in the least. "No kidding."

Momentarily stumped, Natalia cleared her throat. "I'm not, though."

"Yeah, I figured as much. How did you do it?"

"What?"

"How did you kill our baby?"

She gasped. "E.J.!"

"What's the astonishment for? Were you or were you not researching ways to do just that?"

Natalia's eyes slid closed, wanting to slap herself for being so stupid. She must have forgotten to close the internet browser on E.J.'s computer.

"Baby..." she hedged, holding her hands out as she dared to take a few steps towards him, despite the fire in his eyes. "I can explain that."

"Please do."

"I was just...my period was late and I freaked out. I was only looking at that stuff just in case."

"Just in case? So if you actually did turn out to be pregnant, you really would have tried to get rid of it on purpose without a word to me?" He slapped one hand to his hard chest, his angry expression giving way to a hurt one. "Do you have *any* idea how I felt when I saw that, Natalia?"

She felt like the worst person alive. "I..."

"Believe it or not, I could understand you being freaked out at the possibility of being pregnant, babe. It's a big deal. But that's something we could've – and *should've* – worked through together. But once again, you kept the truth from me. And once again, I'm wondering what the hell kind of marriage we really have."

Tears streamed down Natalia's face at his words. It hadn't occurred to her the effect all of her secrets could really have on things; that it would make her husband feel like he couldn't trust her. All she had been worried about was her own feelings. The part about E.J. being affected in her one-sided decisions hadn't entered her mind, other than knowing he'd be angry about it whenever he found out.

But what she saw on his face now was pure hurt, and it wrenched her heart.

"I'm so sorry," she whispered. She hurriedly crossed over to him, clutching his shirt in her hands. She sniffed as she looked up at him, the glassiness in his eyes making her chest ache. "Baby, I...I guess I didn't consider things from your side. It would've been *your* baby, too, and...I..."

"You didn't care about that, clearly." E.J.'s voice was flat as he stood staring at her, almost in a new light. "It's all about what *you* want. Or don't want. I don't even get the courtesy of getting updates about what's going on with you at work or where you really are when you're not here. So I guess I shouldn't be surprised, huh?"

"No! That's not how it is!"

"That *is* how it is!" he roared, startling her. He pushed her hands from him. "One thing I never worried about in all our years together was if I could trust you or not. But now-"

"You *can* trust me, E.J.! Please don't start doubting me over a couple of errors in judgment."

"Errors in..." His voice trailed off as he shook his head in amazement, sarcastic chuckles peppering the air around them. He pivoted away from her, his hands swiping down his face. "Did you seriously just say that?"

"I'm not a terrible person, E.J." Natalia swiped at her own tears before folding her arms around her waist. "I made some bad decisions; I'll own that. But outside of this baby issue, I've been a damn good wife to you. You're lying if you say I haven't."

"Nah, I'll leave all the lying stuff to *you*." All amusement or tenderness left his voice, leaving nothing but a menacing growl. "Up until a couple months ago, I thought I'd hit the jackpot when it came to who I chose to spend my life with."

Her breath hitched. "And now you don't?"

"Now that you're making a habit out of keeping things from me? Kinda hard for me to hang onto that, Natalia."

She couldn't remember the last time she'd been more hurt. Natalia didn't know how they had gone from the bliss of celebrating ten years of marriage just a few short months ago to him questioning if he should've married her at all.

"So what do you wanna do?" she made herself ask after several tense moments. "If you're starting to question the kind of woman I am..."

E.J. glared at her, eyes narrowed and breaths deep and measured.

"Do you wanna separate?"

Natalia had to force the question out, because she was afraid of his answer. What if he did? That was the last thing she wanted, but she knew better than anyone that E.J. only had so much patience. And he only gave so many chances. Her being his wife might've allowed her more leeway than others, but not much.

E.J. took his time responding, and Natalia's knees weakened with every second that ticked by. She didn't know if he was actually considering her question or if he was just torturing her, but she prepared herself for the worst.

"No."

Natalia's head whipped towards him, eyes wide. "Wh-what?"

"We're not separating," he verified, his voice slightly louder. "*I* don't run just because things get tough."

It was a clear jab at her, and not even an inaccurate one, but Natalia still took offense. She'd only suggested that because she thought it was what he wanted, not because she was trying to run from their issues.

Knowing she was in no position to defend herself on that point, though, she just pursed her lips and wiped the fresh tears that had flooded her face at the thought of having to separate from him with one hand and swiped the other through her hair, leaving her bangs askew but not caring. "All right."

It was on the tip of her tongue to thank him, but her own stubbornness was having a flare-up. So she just brushed past him into the kitchen, hearing his footsteps stomping up the stairs moments later.

She yanked open the refrigerator but made no move to grab anything; she just stood staring at the contents, ignoring her stomach gently reminding her that she hadn't eaten in a few hours, and that was just some cake at Desiree's. This latest argument with E.J. had drained her of any energy she had to prepare anything, so she trudged to the pantry to see what she could grab and eat. Settling on a pack of saltines, she flopped down at the kitchen table and chomped on the dry crackers, pouting.

Natalia had always had a bad habit of letting her emotions run her, often speaking or acting first and then thinking second. It had gotten her in trouble many times growing up. She thought she'd gotten better about it, but apparently not. When she considered that she'd actually looked for ways to get rid of her own child if she turned out to be pregnant, she winced in both shame and embarrassment. What kind of person did that, regardless of the reason? She knew for a fact that her mother Florence never wanted eight children that were rather close in age, but as she revealed to Natalia several years earlier, she never thought about terminating any of her pregnancies. Her father loved having a big family, and Florence acquiesced to make him happy. And she certainly couldn't have foreseen her husband dying suddenly and leaving her to raise them all by herself. Of course she loved them dearly, but if left up to her, she would've stopped at two or three, tops.

Even though she wasn't as amicable about having kids as her mother had been, Natalia knew that one thing she definitely had in common with her was not being a punk. Florence had always taught her and her siblings to be strong enough to face the music when they'd made a mistake, and be woman or man enough to take whatever consequences their decisions came with.

And to respect people they claimed to care about enough to be honest.

Somehow Natalia had gotten away from that. And now things between her and the man of her dreams were hanging by a thread because of it.

Leaving the remaining crackers on the table, Natalia grabbed a bottle of water and quickly chugged it, moistening her dry mouth. She headed upstairs, hoping E.J. was still awake, though she wasn't totally sure what she'd say if he was. She just wanted to say or do something to push them past this tense phase they were in.

E.J. was sitting shirtless on the side of the bed, rubbing lotion on his elbows. He barely glanced at her as she entered the room. Undeterred, Natalia wordlessly went into the ensuite, shimmying out of her clothes and taking the quickest shower possible, wanting to catch E.J. before he went to sleep. Hurriedly drying off and slathering on the peach-scented body butter she knew E.J. loved, she grabbed one of his tank tops and slid it over her head as she padded across the now-darkened room, sliding into bed. Hesitating only briefly, she wrapped her arms around him from behind, placing a kiss between his shoulder blades.

"I'm sorry," she whispered. She pressed her cheek against his warm skin. "I really am."

He didn't respond for several moments and Natalia wondered if he'd heard her, but a warm surge of hope shot through her when she felt his hand grab her arm.

"I know."

"I'm gonna earn your trust back, baby." She ran her lips up and down his spine. "I promise. All this bullshit I've been doing lately...it was wrong. And so unfair to you; I realize that. Just...*please* be patient with me. Because I can't lose you, E.J."

His abs clenched under her hand, and Natalia pulled her bottom lip between her teeth. Tingles began to take over her body; despite the circumstances, she still couldn't help reacting to being so close to him. They hadn't made love since they ravaged each other in E.J.'s office at Barfly.

Her breath quickened when he turned to face her, resting his head on one arm while the other pulled her closer. His eyes roamed over her face.

"You didn't wrap up your hair," he quietly observed.

"I don't care."

"You'll be fussing in the morning."

"E.J..."

His finger trailed underneath her chin. "I'm still here, babe. Because I *want* to be here. But you know how I feel about secrets..."

"I know..."

"We *have* to be able to trust each other."

"You're right."

"I want us to get off this treadmill we're on. Maybe we can go to counseling, or...something. I don't know. But I'm willing to try to work through it; I need you to work with me."

Her hold on him tightened. "Absolutely."

He leaned his face towards hers, and she eagerly met him the rest of the way, pressing her lips to his. Her hand grabbed his face, wasting no time sending her tongue searching for his. The air filled with their long sharp intakes of breath as his fingers gripped her tighter. He was returning her kiss, to her mild surprise and delight, and she eased her leg over his, hooking it around his hip and pressing him closer. Her arousal began overtaking everything, her hips beginning a slow grind against him.

"I've missed you," she whispered between kisses, drawing a sharp intake of breath when she felt his hardness twitch against her. She reached between them, grabbing him and earning a tortured groan. "Get inside of me. It's been too long."

He clearly wanted her; she could feel it in his kiss and pressing between her legs. But his hand stopped hers when she began sliding his boxer briefs down over his hips.

"Maybe we should cool out," he suggested, his voice gruff. Natalia could see his jaws clenched with forced restraint.

She blinked in confusion. "Why?"

"We're out of condoms. And I don't want to have to pull out."

Her mouth fell open, not expecting that. "You don't have to worry about that, baby."

"Why don't I?" He leaned back slightly. "You on birth control again?"

"No! I wouldn't do that without telling..." Her voice trailed off at his quirked brow. She sighed. "I'm not on birth control. You know those didn't agree with me. And I'm not wearing a diaphragm. I just want you to make love to me."

"And I want to. But I need us to get to where you don't panic every time I come inside you."

"E.J.-"

"I love you." He placed a lingering kiss to her lips, quieting her, before gently easing her leg from his and rolling onto his back. He rubbed his eyes with his fingertips before releasing a long, tired breath. "Let's just go to sleep."

He turned his back to her, leaving Natalia laying there stunned and bewildered. E.J. had never resisted her before then. It was almost as bad as him shutting her out altogether.

Forcing herself not to cry, she made herself get up and trudge to the bathroom so she could wrap her hair.

Chapter 5

• • • •

E.J. WAS FRUSTRATED, both sexually and emotionally.

He and Natalia were on speaking terms at least, but things were strained. She almost seemed to walk on eggshells around him, which wasn't like her and he hated to see it. One thing he'd always loved about his wife was how fiery she was; she didn't bite her tongue and was quick to check anyone she felt was disrespecting her. That was hot to him.

But she also never liked for him to be upset with her, even if she had to challenge him on some things. And try as he might, E.J. was having a tough time getting past the surges of anger he felt whenever he thought about her plotting how to get rid of the baby she thought she might've been carrying. He didn't know when it happened, but Natalia had gotten a little too comfortable keeping things from him, and he couldn't stand for that. He didn't hide things from *her*, uncomfortable or not. He deserved the same courtesy.

"Hopefully I'll be wrapping things up no later than eight tonight," she told him one morning, putting the cap back on the mascara she'd just applied. He had just gotten back from his morning workout and she was getting ready for work. "I'll let you know if it'll be later than that."

E.J. threw his hoodie into the clothes hamper. "All right."

"You know what you want for dinner tonight?"

"Nah. I'll probably get home before you so I'll start something. Whatever."

"I put that salmon in the refrigerator."

"That's fine."

The conversation petered out as E.J. prepared to get in the shower. Natalia eyed him, missing the playful banter they used to have in the mornings, or any other time. They were always best friends as well as husband and wife, and she hated all of this awkwardness. If only she could turn back time.

Not wanting to leave things in such a tense state, Natalia hung around until E.J. got out of the shower, not caring that she'd likely be a little late to work. She was already going to be working overtime, so they'd just have to get over it.

"How come you're still here?" E.J. asked, surprised to see her sitting on the bed when he emerged from the bathroom a little while later. A towel hung loosely around his waist. "Something wrong with the car?"

Natalia had to force herself not to think about the deliciousness she knew was under that towel and keep her mind on what she'd stayed to talk to him about. Her heel began bouncing all on its own, in reaction to having to restrain herself when she *really* didn't want to.

"No, the car is fine. I stayed because I wanted to see if you wanted to go out tomorrow night."

He looked at her, his hand on the drawer he'd been about to pull his underwear from. "Really?"

"Yeah. We haven't had a date night in a while. Since the anniversary party, really. That was over four months ago, which is way too long, baby."

E.J. hadn't realized that long had passed since they'd been out together. They usually tried to have date night at least once every couple of weeks.

"True," he agreed. "Aren't you gonna have to work, though? Thought you had to do all this OT now for that project."

Again, Natalia hated that she'd volunteered for that. Another example of letting her emotions fuel her decisions and not thinking beyond whatever she was feeling in the moment. She should've known she'd regret having to commit so much extra time. "Let me worry about that. If you can make the time, so will I."

The corners of his lips quirked up, causing her hopeful smile to spread. He wasn't immediately brushing her off, which was a great sign.

"That sounds good," he agreed, grabbing a pair of boxer briefs from the drawer before pushing it closed with the side of his fist. He then leaned against the dresser, his right hand grabbing his left wrist. "And I know just where we should go, too."

Her smile spread into a grin. "I love it, whatever it is."

His own smile grew as his eyes softened, gazing at her like he used to before all this drama started. "Glad I can make you happy."

"For almost twelve years now. I've never been happier."

Amusement twinkled in his eye. "Even the first six months or so when we were just fooling around?"

"With each of us proclaiming to anyone that asked that we didn't want anything serious?" Natalia chuckled, shaking her head. They'd both been stubborn from the beginning. "Yeah, even then. We might not have locked each other down yet, but I damn sure looked forward to seeing you more than...anyone else."

They shared a long look, the smiles still lingering on their lips. Natalia fought to keep her face even and her emotions in check, not wanting to be the one to break the good vibes they finally had going between them. She forced her near slip of the tongue out of her mind.

"I'm looking forward to it, babe," E.J. said, his voice holding a tenderness that warmed Natalia from the inside. He sucked his bottom lip between his teeth and the warmth turned into a raging fire. "I can't wait."

She stood and kicked off her green patent leather heels. "I can't, either."

E.J.'s eyes never left her as she sauntered over to him, taking the boxer briefs from his hand and tossing them to the floor. "You won't need those yet."

She heard his intake of breath when she yanked the towel from his waist. "Natalia-"

"Hush." She placed a finger to his lips. "I know what you said the other night. And I get it. But you're not gonna keep walking around me half-naked and expecting me not to enjoy your fine ass *at all*." Her other hand began stroking his length, enjoying seeing the pleasure float over his face as his eyes slid closed. "Can I enjoy you for a minute, baby?"

She was already sinking to her knees, swirling her tongue around his tip. E.J. groaned deeply, his hands gripping the edge of the dresser.

"All the minutes you want," he granted in a hoarse whisper, his hips beginning to slowly thrust as he looked down at her.

"Oh, you shouldn't have told me that."

They both ended up being late to work.

• • • •

"WE NEED TO TALK, BROTHER."

E.J. blinked as Roland entered the office at 845, where he'd been standing at the window. The office was bigger than the one at Barfly, which was basic and had no windows, and E.J. often liked to stand and watch the passing traffic or passersby when he needed to clear his head.

Or like now, when he couldn't keep his mind on what he was supposed to be doing.

Natalia had given him the best head of his life that morning, making him a whimpering, weak-kneed mess. And of course, there was no way he was going to let her break him down like that and not return the favor, especially with how smug she was looking. As soon as he had a minute to recover, he'd snatched her down to the floor, pushed up her skirt, and clamped her legs around his shoulders while he used his tongue and fingers to make her lose her mind. And when she tried to crawl away, her made her pay for trying to get away from him by savoring her beautiful breasts, which had always been super-sensitive. Once he finally made himself leave her alone, she didn't get up off the floor for a good ten minutes.

"E.J?"

Turning, E.J. ran a hand down his face and silently admonished himself for acting like he'd never gotten any. As good as his time with Natalia had been earlier, he was at work now. *Focus*.

"Yeah." He cleared his throat and moved back over to the desk, giving a brief glance to the monitor showing all the security camera footage. "What's up?"

"Something has come up that we need to seriously discuss."

E.J. looked at him, frowning. "What's wrong?"

"Oh, nothing is *wrong* at all." Roland dropped a folder onto the desk and folded his arms, an anxious smile on his lips. "This is a great way to start the day, I'd say."

E.J. opened the folder, looking at the top page. The furrow between his brows deepened the more he read. He looked up at Roland. "Is this for real?"

"Absolutely."

"When did this come about?"

"Just yesterday. He approached Casey over at Barfly, and she called me at home. I met them over there around six o'clock last night."

"And why the hell am I just hearing about it? Why didn't y'all call me?"

"I wanted to vet it first. Part of me thought it was some bullshit, but it's legit. Ned checked it out and everything."

Ned was their attorney. E.J.'s temper simmered at learning about this *after* his subordinate and someone that he kept on retainer, but he made himself keep his cool. It wasn't the most important thing.

Carlton Barber, a billionaire who'd made his fortune in commercial real estate and technology innovations, was apparently interested in buying Barfly and 845. E.J. was familiar with him, though they'd never met, and knew he owned several entities, including a telecommunications company and a professional hockey team. E.J.'s eyebrows shot up when he saw the amount of money being offered.

"I know, right?" Roland commented, reading the look. He grabbed the dark gray cushioned chair in front of the desk and dropped onto it, resting his elbows on his knees and looking at his brother excitedly. "I for sure thought I was dreaming when I saw that number."

"It's pretty substantial; can't deny that."

"Substantial? Bro, even split in half, that's life-changing money. Like, we wouldn't have to worry about a damn thing anymore, money-wise. It's more than just *substantial*. Barber wants to have a meeting with us ASAP to discuss."

"And I guess by the way you're practically vibrating that I don't have to ask what way you're leaning on this."

"I mean, can you blame me? Look at the number again."

"I saw it the first time. And it's generous but what's throwing me is how eager you are to accept. We opened these clubs with the sweat off our backs and you're ready to just give them up the first time someone tries to throw some money at us?"

"When it's *this* much money, I'd be a fool not to consider it. And you would, too."

E.J. eyed him. "Have you told Lovey about this?"

"No. Wanted to talk to you first, see where your head was at."

Closing the folder, E.J. leaned back in his chair. "Not interested."

Roland's eyes bucked. "Excuse me?"

"I'm not selling my clubs."

"*Our* clubs. And it's not like I *want* to sell them, either; I love what we've built. But there's no way I can just ignore an offer that would set my family up for life. Especially if the terms are fair."

"I didn't see any terms notated in here."

"That's why we need to take the meeting, man. Let's at least sit down with him and see what he's talking about. If the particulars are fair, then we have something to work with. If he's on some bullshit, then we tell him to keep walking and go on about our business."

"Have you thought about what this will mean for our employees? We employ a lot of people. What if he wants to get rid of all of them and bring in his own staff? Hell, what if he wants to tear everything we've done down to nothing and start over?"

"He could just open his own clubs if he wanted to do that. Clearly, he likes what we have going on here. And as for the employees, that's something that could be discussed in the meeting. You know we'd make sure they're taken care of, either way."

E.J. drummed his fingertips on the desk, pondering his brother and business partner's words. Yes, it was a lot of money. But that wasn't enough to sway E.J. Owning those clubs and running them with his brother meant something to him; being able to provide a way for people to make a living, namely other Black people, gave him a sense of pride that couldn't be bought.

But he also knew it wasn't just his decision, as much as he wanted it to be. And if Roland thought it was worth entertaining, then E.J. knew he had to at least go through the motions of hearing what this billionaire had to say.

Then he'd say no.

"Fine, we'll have the meeting," he finally said. "That's all I'll say right now."

"That's all I expect right now. I'll call Ned and get it set up."

"Let's do it soon and get it over with. I don't want this hanging over our heads forever."

Roland shook his head but didn't comment. He just stood and strolled out of the office.

E.J. glanced at the folder once more before pushing it away and waking up his computer. He hated the idea of wasting time entertaining this whole notion of selling his clubs, because it absolutely wasn't going to happen. If it would appease his brother, though, then he could sit through a short meeting. But his mind was already made up.

• • • •

E.J.'S DAY ENDED UP being longer and more stressful than he anticipated, thanks to an issue with their liquor supplier, two employees calling in sick, and a mistaken double-booking at 845 for the coming weekend, which infuriated him. After he chewed out the manager for that mindless mistake, he had to smooth things over with the party that had been booked second, thankfully managing to get everything worked out even though it took some clever rescheduling and promises of free bottles and appetizers.

By the time E.J. called it a day, all he wanted to do was take a long, stinging-hot shower and park it on the plush couch in his den to listen to an audiobook or his favorite meditation station. He'd love it if Natalia would give him one of her amazing hot oil massages...even better if she did it wearing nothing but those lace bra and panty sets she had a thousand of.

Imagining this made him remember what they did before work that morning, and the tightness in his traps eased while the aching in his groin increased. It did something to him when she got aggressive like that; as much as he loved taking the lead most of the time, the way she yanked his towel off and slid to her knees in her pretty green silk blouse and gray skirt, her red lips wrapped around him as she looked straight into his eyes...

He adjusted himself in his driver's seat with a frustrated grunt. Part of him hated that he had temporarily declared sex off limits; he didn't like that any more than Natalia did. But he'd meant what he said; he didn't need her freaking out every time they made love without protection, which he was past tired of using. But Natalia had tried several different forms of birth control and the side effects always messed with her, she didn't love wearing diaphragms, so they were still using condoms like they were when they were just dating, which E.J. felt was ridiculous. He shouldn't have had to look at another condom ten years into his marriage, especially since they were both healthy. But Natalia always insisted, so he acquiesced.

Of course, had he known the real reason she was so insistent...

Feeling himself getting riled up, E.J. forced out a few deep breaths and told himself to chill out. He was in no way over what Natalia did, but walking around angry all the time wasn't going to fix anything. If they were going to make it work between them – and he was determined they would –

he'd have to do his part towards dealing with the frustration he was still harboring.

Natalia wasn't home when he got there, but she had already let him know she wouldn't be, especially since their bedroom floor shenanigans made her late that morning. E.J. heated up one of the pre-made meals of teriyaki salmon, broccolini and mashed cauliflower that he kept on hand for the nights neither he or Natalia felt like cooking, then ate while he got caught up on the news before taking his shower. Remembering the agreement they'd made earlier for a date night, E.J. took advantage of having the house to himself to get started planning it, feeling the tingles of excitement wash over him when he pictured Natalia's face when she saw where they were going. He already couldn't wait.

Thankfully he didn't have to wait long. Natalia kept her word and managed to get off work at her regular time the next night, allowing them to enjoy their evening together. When E.J. pulled up to Roll n' Groove, a small local skating rink, Natalia looked at him with a curious glint in her eye.

"Wow, I haven't been here in a minute," she commented. "Not since..."

"Our first real date," E.J. finished for her, taking her hand and kissing it. "The night I brought you here was when I knew I wanted to lock this in and make you mine. And I damn sure wanted to be yours."

She grinned, her eyes glistening. "Oh, E.J. This..." She caressed his face with her free hand. "This is *so* sweet of you."

"I remember actually being nervous when we pulled up," he recalled, looking off to the side with a chuckle. "Part of me thought you would shut me down. But I was gonna ask you regardless." His eyes turned back to hers. "I had already started thinking of you as my woman."

"And I'm glad you did. Because I was claiming you as my man in my head. But every time I thought about mentioning anything about us making things official, I imagined you telling me what I didn't wanna hear. That would have been humiliating."

"Thankfully we were both on the same page." He kissed her hand again, letting his lips linger on the soft skin. He turned it and inhaled the faint scent of the Dior perfume on her wrist, unable to resist a small groan. "It's been me and you ever since, babe. And I don't want that to change."

"Neither do I," Natalia quickly concurred. She scooted as close to him as the seats would allow, letting her hand slide down to his neck. She'd always loved his neck, of all things; the perfect proportion to his gorgeous face, the dark chocolate skin that was like candy to her, the strong adam's apple. She especially loved the effect it had on him when she licked and sucked on it, especially that spot right underneath his ear...

"Babe?"

"Huh?" Natalia realized she'd been sitting there gazing at him, and felt her cheeks flush a little. It amazed her that she still felt like a schoolgirl with a crush around E.J. at times.

He was looking at her as if he knew exactly what she'd been thinking; she could see the mischievous glint in his eye. "Feel free to hold that thought until we get home."

She bit the corner of her bottom lip as her eyes grazed over his face. "You better believe it."

Giving one last press of his lips to her hand, he gently brought it down between them before releasing it. "So, shall we skate?"

"Baby, as much as I love the idea, I'm not exactly dressed for it," Natalia commented, looking down at her sleeveless red dress and pumps.

"Yeah, I know. Check the backseat."

Glancing behind them, Natalia noticed the duffel bag which she suspected contained a change of clothes for her. She looked at him with a grin. "I should've known you'd think of everything."

"Of course. So let's get it going."

They headed inside, hand-in-hand. Natalia headed to the bathroom to change into the leggings and baby tee E.J. brought for her while he got their skates, then they headed out onto the rink together, which was strangely empty.

"Where is everybody?" Natalia questioned, glancing around as E.J. helped her onto the rink. "I know it's a weeknight, but..."

"I wanted us to be alone," E.J. replied, linking his fingers with hers. "It's just us and the DJ out here."

She gasped. "You seriously rented out the entire rink?"

"You remember how we kept having to dodge all those kids on our date that night? I didn't want to be bothered with that. I needed it to just be you and me tonight."

Everything in her wanted to jump into his arms right then and she hated that she didn't trust herself in roller skates enough to do it. It warmed her all over that he would do that for her, for them.

And it was on the tip of her tongue to make a comment about how he apparently liked it being just the two of them, but she kept it to herself. She wasn't about to ruin the vibe.

Just as they did on that night years ago, they sailed around the rink together, sometimes with E.J. turning and skating backwards while he held her hands firmly in his. He was so smooth, the way he moved and glided on those skates. Natalia admired his agility now as much as she had back in the day, especially since he was skating backwards without even glancing behind him. It was just another thing he was effortless at.

"Can you still do that spin you did that night?" he asked her. "You went right there to the middle of the floor-"

"And almost fell on my ass," Natalia laughed, shaking her head. "Nah, I don't think I'm in the mood to make a fool out of myself tonight, thank you."

"You *didn't* fall, though," E.J. reminded her. His eyes softened. "I caught you, remember?"

Her smile faded slightly as she got caught up in his gaze. Their speed had slowed to almost nothing and the DJ was teasing them for skating slowly through a rap song, but neither of them cared. They'd slipped into their own world.

"I do remember," she practically whispered.

It was that moment all those years ago, when E.J. saved her from busting her ass, that Natalia knew she'd always be safe with him; that he wouldn't let anything happen to her. And she wasn't wrong. She had always prided herself on being independent, and she was. But E.J. was the protector that she never even thought she needed. And as she learned, it didn't diminish how strong she was in the slightest.

E.J. tugged her hands, pulling her to him and wrapping her in his arms. His lips overtook hers, and she let them. She fully gave into the kiss as her arms slid tightly around his neck, wavering only slightly on her skates as she made out with her husband in the middle of the roller rink like horndogs. It wasn't until the DJ started playfully making kissing noises around them that they finally broke apart, laughing as they glanced around before resting their foreheads against each other.

"I think we're putting on a show out here," he commented, tweaking her chin.

She grinned. "I don't mind it."

"Yeah? Well let's crank it up, then."

Natalia shrieked as E.J. grabbed her around the thighs and hoisted her over his shoulder before she could blink. He took off as if she weighed five pounds, his arm clamped across the backs of her thighs, zooming around the rink. Natalia was laughing as much as she was screaming, her hands gripping the back of E.J.'s shirt and her hair flapping over her face.

"Had enough?" he called out, speeding up slightly.

"I didn't challenge you to this!"

"No?"

"No!"

"Just tell me you've had enough and I'll stop."

"Hey, I'm just riding...I can last as long as you can!"

"You sure about that?"

E.J. did an abrupt spin, causing Natalia to feel like she was going to slide off his shoulder. She screamed and held onto him tighter, even though she knew in the back of her mind that he wasn't going to let her fall. "E.J.!"

"Need me to stop? Can't take anymore?"

"If I throw up on you, it's your own fault."

That made him slow down some. "Like you would risk getting any of that in your hair."

"You'd just have to wash it for me in the shower."

"We'd have to *get* to the shower first, and I don't want that in my car, so..." E.J. cruised to a smooth stop, giving Natalia's behind a pat before gently setting her back to her feet. "I'll let you have this one...as long as you let me have this dance."

Natalia realized they were at the center of the rink, and the lights around them lowered as the center spotlight beamed down on them. Then the light switched to green and strobe lights began circling around them, as the music switched to "Stay" by Jodeci.

Her jaw dropped. "Baby!"

"Come here." He pulled her to him, sliding his arms around her waist and burying his face in the crook of her neck.

Natalia tried to keep her tears in check as she held onto him as tightly as he was holding her, one hand resting on the back of his head as they swayed to the music best they could on their skates. Her heart was surging in her chest; it almost scared her just how much she loved this man.

Especially since she knew he was still feeling some kind of way about the lie she told him not to mention the pregnancy scare situation, and the whole baby issue was still in limbo, but he was making this kind of effort to keep them going. Most men would've left it up to her to mend things, seeing as how she'd been the one to mess up. But E.J. wasn't like most men. In that moment, she almost would've agreed to anything to make him as happy as she was right then.

Time seemed to stop as they danced through a couple more songs, with them sharing occasional kisses and loving whispers. Natalia was in no hurry for the moment to end, but eventually E.J. eased back, smiling down at her.

"You good?"

Her smile widened. "I'm better than good."

"I know you're ready to eat by now so come on."

He took her by the hand and led her towards the edge of the rink, throwing an appreciative wave to the DJ as they sailed by. By the time they were seated at one of the tables clustered along the side of the rink, a couple of employees were heading over to them with trays of chili lime chicken wings, truffle mushroom pizza, and fried cauliflower bites. Fruit-infused sparkling water accompanied the food.

"Wow, they surely have stepped their game up with the food," Natalia marveled, looking at everything in amazement.

"You think this came from here? I had this brought in," E.J. informed, spreading a napkin over his lap. "This place isn't exactly known for its cuisine."

"Oh my god. You have *no* idea how much I love you right now. I wasn't gonna complain but I was surely in no mood to eat their nasty pizza."

They chuckled as they proceeded to dig in, tearing through the food. E.J. couldn't keep his eyes off his wife's face, loving how utterly happy she looked. This was what they needed; it had been a while since they'd had fun like this. It wouldn't solve all of their problems, but it was a reminder of why they were so good together and what drew them to each other in the first place.

Once most of the food was gone, Natalia wiped her hands on a napkin and looked at him with a playful glint. "So what's next?"

"We can head home. It's getting kinda late."

"Okay. But..." She swung her legs over the bench and stood, then took off towards the rink. "Not before we have one more race!"

With no hesitation, E.J. pushed away from the table and chased after her, maneuvering around the tables and practically leaping back onto the rink. Natalia was a pretty good skater but he gained on her quickly, and they engaged in a race that lasted several more laps, complete with plenty of laughter and loud trash talk.

Once they were finally tuckered out, they got ready to leave, both taking a moment to thank the manager and the DJ. Natalia held onto E.J.'s arm the entire ride home, still floating from their evening. When she'd suggested a date night, that had been the last thing she was expecting; she figured they'd just go out to dinner or something. But E.J. had blown her mind again.

As soon as they were through their front door, Natalia grabbed his shirt before he could head towards the stairs, jumping into his arms.

"Thank you for tonight, baby," she smiled at him. She tucked some hair behind her ear before going in for a kiss. "I love you *so* much...this has been an amazing evening."

"I'm glad you enjoyed it." His hands slid up and down her back.

"What do you have planned for us for the rest of the night?"

His eyes narrowed playfully. "I'm sure you're asking because you have something in mind."

"You better believe I have something in mind."

Returning to her feet, Natalia grabbed his hand and led him upstairs straight to their bedroom, pushing him onto the bed and climbing on top of him, pulling her shirt over her head and tossing it to the floor before crashing her lips onto his. The heat escalated quickly as they tongued each other down, her hands clawing at his clothes and his touching her everywhere they could reach as they rolled around on the king-sized bed.

"Get naked," she ordered in an impatient whisper, grinding against him. "We have some things to do."

"Oh yeah?" E.J. pushed onto his knees and literally ripped his t-shirt off, making Natalia's face contort with almost pained desire and her panties flooded. "Like what?"

"Like you getting this..." She gave a light grab to his crotch, earning that guttural groan that she loved so much, "Inside of this."

E.J. drew in a sharp intake of breath when Natalia laid back and began playing with herself. His body began to burn as he watched her red nails teasingly rotating on her clit, sliding between her folds, and to his delight, going between her lips. Their eyes were locked the whole time, and E.J. was granite-hard and literally aching with desire.

As much as he didn't want to kill the mood, he felt he didn't have a choice but to remind her of something.

"We're out of condoms."

She smirked, apparently having anticipated this. "No, we're not. I got some more. They're already in the nightstand."

Some of E.J.'s fire cooled, just slightly. He didn't know how to feel about her going out to get more condoms after he had thrown their last batch out. Nothing had changed with either of their stances on the baby issue and he knew that, but it still bugged him.

Telling himself to get over it, he wordlessly leaned over and retrieved the condoms from the nightstand, slapping the drawer closed a little harder than necessary. He could feel Natalia's eyes on him as he ripped the wrapper open and rolled the condom on, and he tried to ignore it just like he tried to ignore that he wasn't as hard as he was just moments before.

Natalia felt the shift in the air but she tried to keep the heat up on her end, her fingers still working between her legs and her hips undulating. She'd only gotten the condoms to eliminate the concerns when they made love, which she knew were hers. She also knew E.J. hated having to wear them, but she hoped that he would focus on them being together and ending their amazing night on a good note instead of that.

"Come here, baby," she whispered when E.J. seemed to be taking his time getting on top of her. The condom was on but he seemed to be frozen in place. "What's wrong?"

"Nothing." It came out in a grunt, and not the good kind. Nevertheless, he crawled over to her, saying nothing as he pushed her hand out of the way and entered her. His hips began to move, but his eyes were beside Natalia's head and not on her like she wanted.

"Baby...E.J." She grabbed his face with both hands, turning his face to hers and waiting for his eyes to follow. "Look at me."

His brown eyes darkened as they stayed on her face, turning so intense and focused that it almost made Natalia nervous. She pulled him down for a kiss, caressing his face and hoping to get him back to the mood he was in before she mentioned the condoms.

But after several more moments, it was clear that wasn't going to happen. She sighed, dropping her hands from his body.

"You might as well stop," she declared, frustrated. She crossed her arms over her bare chest. "There's no point in us doing this if you're not into it."

"I'm doing it, ain't I?" E.J. barked, frowning. "How are you still not satisfied?"

"Are you serious? Because you're clearly just going through the damn motions, not putting any kind of feeling into it. You're barely looking at me; you're not even saying anything. Why would I want sex from you like that?"

"What does it matter? I'm wearing the stupid condom so you don't have to worry about getting knocked up with my baby. I'd think you'd be happy with that."

Her mouth falling open momentarily, she leaned up on her elbows, matching his frown. "So, what, you're just appeasing me now?"

"You can call it what you want to. But you know good and damn well I don't like wearing these. I shouldn't *have* to wear these. I want to feel you; all of you. And I can't do that with these fucking condoms, I don't care what it says on the box."

"I cannot believe you're doing this right now," she muttered, shaking her head. "We were having *such* a nice evening..."

"Me??"

"Yes, *you*, E.J. Everything was perfect and as soon as I mentioned that I'd bought some condoms, your whole mood changed. So it damn sure wasn't me."

"Look," he sighed, running a hand down his face. "I have been trying to do my best to deal with this situation and not focus on the elephant in the room, but at *some* point, we're gonna have to make some decisions, Natalia."

"And that has to be right now, while you're still inside of me?"

"I tried to stay in it; I did. But I can't help that this bothers me."

"So this is how it's gonna be? We can never have sex again like we've been doing all these years just because I don't wanna have your damn baby?"

His face hardened before she realized what she'd said. Her frown melted into remorse as she grabbed his arm, but he yanked it away from her, extracting himself before pushing off the bed.

"E.J., I didn't mean that!" She scurried off the bed.

"Yes, you did." He went over to the dresser, yanking some pajama bottoms from the drawer.

"That was a fucked up thing of me to say; I'm *so* sorry!" She briefly covered her mouth with her hands before reaching for him again. "I didn't...I was just upset. Please, E.J...."

"Please, what?" he snapped. "You made it pretty clear. I thought this was something we were gonna work through together but clearly, there's nothing I can do. I'm apparently *never* getting the family I want; got it."

"Wait, is that was this night was about? You buttering me up to try to get me to change my mind?"

He shook his head as he pulled the pajamas over his hips, giving a sarcastic chuckle.

"This night was about us," he stated, stepping forward and looking down at her intently. "Getting back to *us*. I didn't have an ulterior motive. And I'd think you'd know me well enough by now to know that I don't play games."

Her frown eased.

"Yes, I want us to have a child; create a life together. I've dreamed of it since before we got married, Natalia. But I'll be damned if I'm gonna try to trick you to do it. The fact that you would even think that says a lot."

"It's just..." Natalia was at a loss for words. She absolutely knew E.J. didn't play games; it was one of the things she'd always loved about him. "I just don't know what to think right now. All of this...it's a lot. I wasn't kidding when I told you I'd think about us having a baby-"

"Well, you apparently haven't thought about it *too* much, seeing as how your opinion clearly hasn't changed." He turned to leave.

"E.J., don't shut down on me like this. Let's deal with it."

"We'll deal with it. But I can't look at you right now. I'm going to sleep in the guest room."

"I don't want you to do that. I want you in here with me."

"That's all right. Wouldn't want to risk doing anything that might result in you getting pregnant with my *damn baby*, right?"

Before she could say another word, he walked out.

Chapter 6

· · · ·

"NATALIA, WHERE IS YOUR head at tonight?"

Startled, Natalia looked over at Desiree, then at Lovey, as if she'd forgotten they were there. "Hmm? What?"

"What's wrong with you? You've been zoned out ever since you got here."

"Oh...yeah. Sorry about that." Natalia sighed. "I've got some things on my mind. Y'all mind if I finish this?" She held up the bottle of chardonnay that she'd brought over to Lovey's, where they were congregated.

Desiree and Lovey glanced at each other before Desiree shrugged a shoulder. "I mean...I thought you brought that for all of us but, hey. Do you."

The words were barely out of her mouth before Natalia drained the rest of the bottle, not bothering with the glass in front of her. She plunked it down on the coffee table in front of her, then flopped against the back of the couch with a long sigh.

"Natalia, what's the matter?" Lovey asked, leaning forward with a concerned expression. "You haven't smiled since you got here."

"Don't have a whole lot to smile about at the moment," Natalia muttered.

"Why do you say that?"

"Because I keep putting my foot in my damn mouth and messing things up with my husband. You'd think I'd learn when to hush by now."

"Uh-oh...what did you say?" Desiree asked.

"Hold that thought; I need to go check on Xavier real quick," Lovey requested after hearing some murmurings on the video baby monitor. She stood and hurried upstairs, coming back a couple of minutes later. "He's still asleep; was just stirring. Now, what's going on, Natalia?"

Natalia recalled her latest argument with E.J. after their date a couple of nights earlier, wincing when she got to the statement that had set her husband off. She was still kicking herself.

"Ouch," Desiree muttered.

"You actually said that?" Lovey confirmed, as if she didn't want to believe it.

"It just came out; I didn't mean it," Natalia defended. "At least, I didn't mean to say it like *that*. Y'all should've seen the look on E.J.'s face...he was pissed but I know that cut him, too. He's barely been able to look at me since."

"Yeah, I can imagine hearing your wife tell you she 'doesn't want to have your damn baby' would be a gut punch."

"Thanks, Desiree."

"I'm just saying."

"We've all said things in anger that we didn't mean," Lovey assured, reaching over to rub Natalia's arm. "I'm sure E.J. understands that. Just apologize; I'm sure you can work this out."

"Lovey, girl, I've apologized a hundred times. He's not trying to hear it."

"Could that be because he knows you really *did* mean what you said, even if it came out harsher than you wanted it to?" Desiree offered. Her fluffy natural hair framed her face in a defined twistout style. She used to be the queen of wigs but she eased back on them after she started seeing Lorenzo, saying she realized she liked being her natural self with him. "If we're keeping it real, you said exactly what you've been saying all this time."

"Yeah, but there's something to be said for timing," Lovey jumped in before Natalia could. "*And* tone of voice. It was a tense situation about an extremely sensitive subject for E.J. Even if it wasn't a secret that she doesn't want children, the *way* she said it..."

"I get that, but getting in his feelings isn't going to change anything," Desiree countered. "As tough as E.J. is, he should be able to take some candor."

"Come on, Desiree. If Lorenzo said something harsh like that to you, are you trying to say that you wouldn't care at all? You'd just brush it off?"

"Maybe not, but I wouldn't waste time giving him the silent treatment."

"Really? I seem to remember you crashing our guest room when you and he had a fight a few months ago," Lovey reminded with an arched brow. "*And* you wouldn't take his calls. It wasn't until he came over here after you that you finally stopped being stubborn."

"Well...we're not talking about me right now. This is about *Natalia's* big mouth."

"Again, thanks a lot, Desiree." Natalia sat up in her seat, grabbing the bottle she'd already forgotten she just drained, then sucked her teeth when she realized nothing was in it. "Can we go for a drink somewhere? This wasn't enough wine."

"Roland should be here in a little bit so he can stay with the baby," Lovey replied, glancing at her watch. "We can go when he gets here."

"I just wish I knew what to do to make things better," Natalia groaned, sliding her hands through her hair. "E.J. and I are just stuck in this place where neither of us wants to budge. And he's insisted that he doesn't want us to separate and wants us to work it out, but...how? Unless one of us changes our minds..."

"Are you *that* against having children?" Lovey asked. "Like, dead-set against it?"

"I wouldn't say *dead*-set. I've been considering it recently, especially after that last time we watched Xavier. I still look at the picture I took of the two of them and can't help but grin my ass off every time. E.J. would make an amazing father and I know that."

"But you have to want to be a mother, too," Desiree stressed, poking her friend's shoulder. "I get that you want to make your man happy but what you want matters just as much as what he wants."

"I know that. I wouldn't have a child just to appease E.J. It's just..." Natalia clawed her hands, trying to convey her point. "Every time I think I'm on board with it, it's like there's something in my head that comes and blocks it. I don't know what it is. I actually love the *idea* of having E.J.'s babies. I think I'm just...scared."

"That's totally understandable," Lovey assured her. "I was thrilled when I realized I was pregnant with Xavier, but I was still terrified. Being a mother is a huge responsibility."

"Yeah, but I don't think that's what has me freaked out, though. I'm sure that if I were to wind up pregnant tomorrow, once we had the baby, I could be a good mother. Hell, I watched my mama raise eight kids practically by herself. I had to help out a lot after my dad died, so I know I could do it. I think I'm more worried about how things would change between me and E.J."

"I mean, yeah, things will be different, but that's not necessarily a bad thing. Having a baby in love can bring you even closer. It certainly did for me and Roland."

"But what if it doesn't, though?" Natalia countered, looking over at Lovey with eyes pleading for solutions. "I'm worried about us getting so consumed with the baby and everything about it that we drift apart. That's the last thing I want."

"Then you put in the effort so that doesn't happen," Desiree advised. "Look, I don't even know if I want kids myself. But you've seen my parents. They're still all over each other after four grown daughters and four grandchildren. Because they committed themselves to keeping things hot between them; they knew that they'd be no good for us if they let their relationship go stale."

"True," Natalia mused, slightly encouraged. "Your folks *are* some horndogs."

"Shut up. But true."

"I went over there last month and heard them fooling around in the laundry room," Lovey chuckled. "I think I was traumatized for a minute."

"You? Hell, I can't even *count* the times I've caught or heard them getting it in," Desiree retorted. "It almost doesn't even faze me now. Though I still don't wanna see it."

Roland came home a few minutes later, and after Desiree and Natalia waited patiently for him and Lovey to stop making out like they hadn't seen each other in months, the ladies headed out to a nearby bar. Natalia wasted no time ordering a round of shots, though Desiree warned her she was stopping her after three rounds.

"When did you get to be such a stick-in-the-mud?" Natalia muttered, grabbing one of the shot glasses full of Patron.

"You don't need to be getting hammered; that's not gonna fix anything," Desiree fussed. "Plus, you have to work tomorrow."

"It's Friday."

"Remember that extra work you volunteered for to avoid your husband? You said that requires weekends."

"Damn it." Natalia drained the shot, wincing. "I wonder if it's too late to un-volunteer."

"I tried to tell you. Oh, before I forget, y'all are still coming to my birthday party, right?"

"Girl, stop. You know we're gonna be there."

"Are your men gonna be there with you?"

"Roland will," Lovey replied. "Though I admit I had to do a little enticing."

"E.J. will, as far as I know," Natalia informed. "But don't be surprised if something 'suddenly comes up' and you don't see his face in the place."

Desiree's eyes widened slightly. "Well, damn. I thought he and I were cool now."

"I wouldn't take it that personally. He's in a mood these days, with all of our drama going on. But hopefully things will be a little better between us by the time the party rolls around."

Just then, Desiree's phone rang and when she glanced at the screen, a huge grin shot across her face.

"Must be Lorenzo," Lovey surmised with a smile, taking a sip of her merlot.

"Lemme talk to my boo real quick; I'll be back," Desiree commented, grabbing her phone and stepping away. Lovey and Natalia shook their heads, amused.

"She is too gone," Natalia chuckled.

"Girl, he's had her since their first date. I've always told her it would just take the right man to change her mindset about relationships but she wasn't trying to hear me. I have a lot of fun teasing her about that."

"What do you think it'll take to change *my* mindset about this baby thing?" Natalia asked, pushing the empty shot glass around with her fingertips.

Lovey put her glass down on the high tabletop, looking at her sympathetically. "I wish I knew, sweetie."

"Just tell me what to do. You know I trust your advice more than damn near anyone else's."

"If I could give you the perfect solution, you know I would. I want nothing more than to see you and E.J. work this out. But this is something that you have to figure out with him; only you two can determine what's best for your relationship."

"Ugh. It's like, I know that and it makes perfect sense, but...still. I just want things to be all good in my house again."

"I know." Lovey placed a warm hand over hers. "If it means anything, I'm praying hard for you both."

"It definitely does. I'll take all the help I can get."

"Oh shit...Natalia? Natalia Gaines, is that you?"

Freezing momentarily, Natalia hoped that voice didn't belong to who she thought it did. Her eyes widened as she looked over at Lovey, who was looking at the man standing behind Natalia with a curious frown.

"I'm back," Desiree announced breathlessly, bouncing back to her spot between Natalia and Lovey. She glanced at their visitor, then at Natalia, noticing her freaked-out expression. "Who is this?"

Snapping out of it, Natalia silently told herself to get it together before turning around. A six-foot maple brown-skinned man stood there smiling at her, his right dimple just as prominent as ever. His dark gray eyes roamed over her appreciatively.

"Dane," Natalia greeted, forcing politeness. "And my last name is Bell now. Don't act like you don't know."

"Oh, damn. Still married, huh?"

"Damn straight." She turned to her curious friends. "Y'all, this is Dane McKenzie. My ex."

"Ohh..." Lovey and Desiree sang, their expressions clearing with realization.

"Dane, these are my girls Lovey and Desiree."

"Nice to meet you ladies," Dane smiled and nodded at them before turning his attention back to Natalia. "I just cannot believe I'm running into you like this, Natalia. It's been a minute."

"Yeah, it has. What have you been up to?"

"I'm still in hotel management, plus I own a couple of barbershops now. I just moved back to the area."

"Cool."

"You know Pops still asks about you. He was campaigning hard for us to make it happen long-term. He actually cussed me out when we broke up. Even though I tried to tell him it wasn't *my* fault."

Natalia tried not to squirm under his pointed glare. "Well, hey. Things worked out like they were supposed to. I'm happy where I'm at and you're apparently doing your thing."

"Yeah, but that doesn't mean I have everything I want," Dane commented, eying Natalia intently. The desire was evident. Desiree subtly nudged Lovey in amusement. "Now that I've run into you, how 'bout we stay in touch? Maybe we can hang out or something."

"I don't know about hanging out but I suppose we can stay in touch," Natalia commented, to her friends' shock. "My number is still the same."

"You'll have to unblock me," he noted with a smirk.

"I guess so, huh? All right. Just don't mess up your privilege and be calling me at unreasonable hours. Or else *I'll* be cussing you out, too."

"Wouldn't be the first time." Dane winked at her before finally tearing his eyes away, looking at her stunned friends. "Y'all enjoy the rest of your evening. I'll be hitting you up soon, Honeybun."

"Don't call me that," she retorted, but he had already turned and walked away, pretending not to hear her. She just shook her head before turning back to her friends, who were looking at her incredulously.

"What?" she asked.

"Did you actually just give another man your number?" Desiree marveled.

"No, I did not. He already had it. I just said I'd unblock him."

"But why was he blocked in the first place? Does E.J. know about him?"

"He knows he exists. They've never met. And as for why Dane was blocked...that's a long story."

"Natalia, do you really think it's a good idea to be engaging with your ex?" Lovey asked carefully. "Especially with everything you're going through with E.J. right now?"

"Damn, y'all act like I agreed to meet him over at the Marriott. All I said was that we could keep in touch."

"I get that, but still. Are you saying that E.J. wouldn't care about it at all? Would you want him conversing with his exes?"

"No," Natalia replied quickly, a slight frown marring her face at the thought. "But I trust my husband. And he trusts me."

"Why did you and Dane break up?" Desiree asked.

"That's another long story. But let's just say we weren't on the same page about some things."

"Hmm."

Natalia noted how Desiree was averting her eyes as she sipped her Ciroc. "What, *hmm*?"

"Sounds familiar, is all I'm saying."

"Girl...the situation with Dane is not the same as what I'm going through with E.J. Trust, nothing is going to happen between Dane and me. I don't need to fool around with bench riders when I've got the MVP at the house."

"All right then, MVP. Just be smart, is all I'm saying."

Natalia sucked her teeth dismissively, picking up her shot glass. Then she noted the concerned look on Lovey's face, as if she could already foresee something bad happening. It gave Natalia some pause, but she brushed it off. If she was sure of nothing else, she knew she'd never let anything happen between her and Dane. E.J. was it for her.

To her relief, the subject changed to other topics. Desiree recalled how her last couple of events had gone, and Lovey vented about the headaches of managing the accounting firm she worked at, though she was quick to insist that she still loved it. Natalia lamented for the umpteenth time about volunteering for all the extra work like she did, not particularly enjoying it. If she was honest with herself, being a software engineer wasn't exactly her life's passion.

"What would you rather be doing?" Lovey asked her.

"I don't even know, to be honest," Natalia admitted. "This is what I went to school for and I *like* it, but I'm not amped about it like I was when I first started...now it's just something to do. I hate being stuck behind a computer for most of the day, mostly only interacting with people on Slack or Zoom calls. And there are *so* many damn meetings! If I lost that job tomorrow, I don't even think I'd care."

"Are you looking for something else?" Desiree asked. "I don't know if I could do something everyday that I didn't enjoy. That's why I went into business for myself."

"I'm not, but maybe I should be. You two love what you do, E.J. and Roland are killing it, running those clubs..."

"Speaking of that, that offer they got was something else, wasn't it?" Lovey marveled. "I couldn't believe it when Roland told me how much that billionaire was willing to give them for the clubs."

Natalia frowned. "What are you talking about?"

"E.J. didn't tell you? Carlton Barber wants to buy Barfly and 845. And for a very generous amount of money, too."

"Carlton Barber, really?" Desiree exclaimed. "Damn, that's major."

"Yeah, it sounds like it." Natalia grabbed another one of the shot glasses and tossed it back, wincing as it went down her throat. She slammed the glass back onto the table. "E.J. didn't say anything to me about it."

"Oh..." Lovey looked apologetic. "I'm sorry..."

"Not your fault."

"If it means anything, E.J. was against it, from what Roland told me. Maybe that's why E.J. didn't mention it; if left up to him, there wouldn't be anything left to talk about."

"Yeah." Natalia appreciated Lovey trying to make her feel better, but it wasn't helping. It stung that E.J. hadn't told her about something so major, regardless of whether he was interested in the offer or not. That was something he'd usually tell her about as soon as he got home the same day, if he didn't call her first. What else was he keeping from her?

. . . .

NATALIA WAS TIRED AND grumpy. Tired because she'd stayed out with Lovey and Desiree longer than she should have, and grumpy because she was working on a Saturday. It didn't matter that they had gotten the good coffee or brought in breakfast; she didn't want to be there.

Work was the last thing on her mind. She'd gone home the night before with every intention of asking E.J. about the buyout offer, if for no other reason than to get him back talking to her, but he was already asleep when she got home. She considered waking him, but thought better of it. He'd only be irritable and certainly in no more of a hurry to open up to her.

Sighing, she adjusted her headphones and tried to turn her attention back to the code she was supposed to be troubleshooting. She had meetings coming up with the developers that she needed to be ready for, and wasn't about to risk not having her stuff together. So she managed to put thoughts of her marital issues aside and concentrate.

Around lunchtime, she trudged back to her office after getting yet another cup of coffee, closing her door behind her. She wished she could go home but she had a couple more hours of work to do, especially since there were some bugs found in the first rollout of the gaming software they'd been working on, not to mention a list of features that needed to be added. Just the thought of it made Natalia want to throw something. Some of the team was working from home but Natalia had chosen to go into the ModCode office, hoping that being there would keep her mind off of her issues with her husband. Clearly, she'd been wrong on that.

Before diving back into her work, she decided to call E.J. They'd barely spoken that morning, even though he'd been up when she left. It was mere forced pleasantries, along with Natalia letting him know what time she thought she'd be home. He gave a simple one-word response, barely looking at her before leaving the room. Natalia knew he'd likely be out and about himself, and she knew it was the weekend that he spent time with the young men he mentored.

Thinking positively, she dialed E.J.'s number, plastering a smile on her face as if it would bring her good luck.

"Yeah," E.J. greeted, his voice gruff.

"Hey, baby. You got a minute?"

"Not really. What is it?"

Trying to tamp down her hurt, Natalia forged ahead. "I hope that we can sit down and talk when we both get home later on."

"About?"

"What do you mean, *about*? You know what I'm talking about, E.J. You said we were gonna deal with what happened the other night and you've barely even looked at me, let alone anything else."

"Maybe because when I look at you, I remember what you said."

"I put my foot in my mouth; I get it. And I've apologized. Just how long do you plan to keep punishing me?"

"I'm not..." He sighed. "Natalia, I don't have time for this right now. Was this all you called me for?"

"You need to *make* some time, E.J. This is ridiculous. You can't just shut me out whenever I piss you off."

"Maybe you need to quit pissing me off, then."

"*Or* maybe you need to quit being so stubborn when I do. You act like you never make mistakes."

"I know I do. Don't act like you're any quicker to get over it than I am. You're the damn queen of holding grudges."

"Not against *you*, I'm not. And you know that."

"Whatever. Like I said, I don't have time for this. We're gonna have to talk later."

"Fine, E.J. But I'm gonna hold you to that. I'm sick of this silent treatment bullshit."

"Well, join the club, 'cause I'm sick of a lot of shit, too. Bye."

He hung up, and Natalia resisted the urge to call him right back to ask him what he meant by that. But she decided to leave it alone, knowing nothing productive would likely come from it, that's if he even answered the phone.

Natalia put in a few more hours of work before she was finally able to leave, thankfully getting too busy to obsess over her and E.J.'s problems. By the time she left, part of her hoped E.J. wasn't home yet. She just wanted to turn her mind off and relax, and not have to worry about being cloaked in their ever-present tension.

She had just gotten home and was about to dig into the takeout meal she'd gotten from Rocky's when she got a call from her sister, Kira. Sighing, she debated whether she wanted to answer the phone or not. Her little sister usually brought nothing but headaches and Natalia already had her fair share.

Ultimately, though, she picked up the phone. "Yes, Kira?"

"Well, damn, hello to you, too."

"What do you want, liar?"

"You must've talked to Franklin," Kira muttered.

"Yeah, I did. You know that's some foul shit, lying to his wife about needing surgery so she'd loan you some money."

"Look, I was desperate. And Franklin put a stop on the check she gave me, so it's not like I got anything out of it."

"It shouldn't have happened in the first place, Kira. Scamming your own family was a bitch move."

"I know, I know. But don't you even want to know what I needed the money for?"

"Not really. What are you calling me for? I'm sure you know better than to come to *me* asking for money, I don't care what story you've come up with."

"You're always so mean to me."

"I'm hanging up."

"Wait!" Kira called out, knowing Natalia would do exactly that. "I'm sorry. I really do feel bad about taking advantage of Dandria like that. I'm sincerely trying to straighten up."

"Uh-huh. You found a job?"

"I have some feelers out."

"Why don't you go back to school?"

"No need until I figure out what it is I wanna do. I'm still trying to find my niche."

"And in the three schools you've enrolled in and dropped out of, none of those were your niche?"

"No. And I know you're being sarcastic right now, but not everybody automatically knows what they want to do with their life. It's not like you came out of the womb wanting to be a web designer."

"I'm a software engineer, you donut hole."

"Whatever. You think you could help me? Maybe give me some advice?"

"I've tried that, Kira. You know you don't listen to anybody. Or you start stuff and then get bored and quit before finishing anything. You're twenty-two years old; you're gonna have to grow up. Even if that means just getting whatever job you can until you figure out what your passion is."

"Ugh. You mean like fast food or retail?"

"I wasn't implying those, but so what? It's honest work that pays, Kira, which is what you need right now. You don't have to work there forever. And you're in no position to be picky."

"You think E.J. would be willing to talk to me? Doesn't he mentor teenagers or something?"

"Yeah, but he talks to young men who don't have any other male figures in their lives. *You're* problem is that you want everything to be handed to you."

"Yeah, that's what Mama said, too. But she told me I'm on my own, just like everybody else. I get that I need to figure some things out for myself but it would be nice to have some support from *somebody*."

Natalia's frustration softened, despite herself. Kira might've been immature and spoiled, but she wasn't a terrible person. And she *was* still her little sister.

"Where are you staying?" Natalia asked her.

"With a friend. I'm not sure how much longer that's gonna last, though. I think they want their couch back."

"All right, Kira. I'll do what I can to help you out, but I'm telling you right now, I'm not putting up with any of your bullshit. You can't just brush off whatever I say because it requires too much effort or you don't wanna hear it. And I swear, if you even *try* to screw me over-"

"You don't have to worry about that. I've learned my lesson," Kira quickly insisted. "I really appreciate this, sis. So how much are you gonna give me?"

"Ha! Nice try. I said I wasn't giving you any money and I meant that shit."

"Hmph."

They talked for a few more minutes before Natalia ended the call, having no more energy for it. She promised she'd get back to her sister soon enough, though she still wasn't sure exactly what she felt like doing for her. Kira wasn't always the easiest person to help.

But maybe figuring that out would give her something else to focus on besides E.J., which was another situation she didn't quite know what to do about. Clearly, something was going to have to change, and soon. Because there was no way they could keep going like this.

• • • •

"YOU DON'T WANT ANY more pizza, Mr. B?"

E.J. shook his head. "Nah, man. Two slices is my limit. I'm not seventeen anymore like y'all."

"Please," Nigel, E.J.'s mentee, scoffed. "You're built like a statue. You can eat whatever you want."

"Plus you work out every day," Teddy, his other mentee, chimed in. "Do you even *have* any body fat?"

E.J. chuckled. "I'm pushing forty, fellas; it takes more effort at my age."

"I need you to train me, Mr. B. If I had all your muscles, I'd be *set*," Nigel commented, flexing his meager bicep. "Is that how you got your wife?"

E.J. always wanted to be honest with his mentees, but he was in no hurry to admit that he and Natalia were basically just sex buddies for months before they decided to get serious. He didn't think that was the best example to set. "Not exactly."

"My girl and I have been together for almost a year now," Nigel commented. "She's already started dropping hints about the M-word."

"Already??" Teddy marveled.

"She said her parents have been together since they were in sixth grade and that's the kind of thing she wants, too."

"What about you?" E.J. asked Nigel. They were hanging out in the small conference room in the community center that was close to where the boys lived. It was a forty-minute drive for E.J., but he didn't mind. Especially since he knew their mothers were working and weren't always able to pick them up or drop them off. The center was within walking distance of the apartment complex the boys lived in, but E.J. usually went and got them and took them home afterwards. "Are you thinking about that kind of stuff already, too?"

"I don't know. I'm kinda young for that."

"Yeah, true. It's certainly nothing you need to be rushing into. You think you'd want to get married one day, though?"

"Eventually, yeah. It would be nice to have the kind of family I didn't have growing up, with both parents taking care of the kids. My dad leaving and hardly keeping in touch showed me what *not* to do. I wanna be better than him."

"And you can be. But you need to make sure you're the best version of *yourself*, though, so you can be the best for your family. Part of that is taking the time to educate yourself, get some life experience, make a plan for what you want to do with your life."

"You always knew you wanted to be a club owner?" Teddy asked.

"I knew I wanted to be an entrepreneur; I don't like taking orders from anybody else. And I wanted to be able to help my community by providing jobs."

"Maybe I need to do that, 'cause I don't like anybody telling me what to do, either."

"I had to work up to that, though," E.J. informed with a chuckle. "I worked a regular job for a few years after I graduated college to stack my money. When the opportunity to buy the building where Barfly is in now came up, my brother and I jumped at it. It took a while to get it going and make it successful, but we just kept grinding 'til we got there."

"And now y'all have two clubs. That's tight. Are y'all gonna open any more?"

E.J. automatically frowned upon remembering how Roland seemed a little too eager to sell the clubs they had, but he told himself to chill out. "We don't have any plans for that right now, but we do have merchandise that we sell on our site, and we're working on our own alcohol and sauce brands. We have some other things in the works, but we don't want to do too much at once and take on more than we can handle."

"I wanna be like *you*, Mr. B," Nigel commented, jutting his finger at E.J. "You're jacked, you've got all these successful businesses, you have a wife that's fine as fu-"

"Watch it," E.J. warned, his eyes narrowing.

"Sorry," Nigel shrank in his seat a little. "Didn't mean to be disrespectful; just saying Ms. Natalia is fire, that's all."

"That she is. But there's some stuff you still shouldn't say."

"Yes, sir."

"Did you two finish those college applications?" E.J. asked, changing the subject. He wasn't eager to talk about his wife at the moment. "You had some essays to finish, right?"

"Ugh, I hate that they make us do all that," Teddy grumbled, reaching for his backpack. "I don't have a computer at home, so I wrote mine out. I'll use the computer at school to send it off once I get it like I want it."

"Yeah, I need to do that, too," Nigel concurred. "I finished mine last night. Could you take a look at it, Mr. B? I'm not the best writer. Mama read it last night and she said it was good, but she says that about pretty much everything I do. So I can't really go by her."

E.J. chuckled, holding out his hand for the notebook Nigel was pulling from his bag. "Some mothers can't be totally objective. Mine was the same way. I had to go to my dad to get the real about stuff."

"Yeah. It's cool how she always wants to hype me up but sometimes I just need someone to tell it like it is. That's why I appreciate you, Mr. B."

"Me, too," Teddy chimed in. "My mama works two jobs so she's always tired, and I don't wanna bother her when she's home 'cause I know she needs to rest. It's good to know I can call you when I need to. You even make time to come to my games sometimes."

"And to my parent-teacher conferences. Mama said she still wants to make you a pie for when you went with me that time she had to work late."

"That's what I'm here for, fellas," E.J. commented, his chest warming. It did his heart good to know he was making a difference in their lives. "I've been in your lives since you were freshmen and I'm not going anywhere; couldn't love you more if you were my own sons."

The boys grinned and ducked their heads. E.J. knew how they felt about him, even if they were too bashful to say it.

E.J. proceeded to help the boys with their college essays, then took them to get something to eat (since they were both hungry again despite the pizza they'd had earlier) before dropping them off at home. He felt renewed, as he usually did after he spent time with his mentees. They meant a lot to him, and he wished he could spend even more time with them than he did.

The realization that Nigel and Teddy were likely the closest he would get to having sons of his own saddened and angered him, though the sadness was first and foremost. He always wanted kids; his own father had been a prime example for him before he passed, and E.J. looked forward to marrying the woman that he would raise his tribe with. Everything in him believed that was Natalia. But of course, that wasn't the case anymore.

He still couldn't believe she actually thought he'd change his mind about wanting children. Sure, he loved their life together as it was. But to him, children would only add to that happiness, not dull it. Ever since he found out the real deal about Natalia's feelings about parenthood, he tried to see things from her side; to at least try to understand her point of view. While he saw where she was coming from, he still didn't agree with it. Yes, things would change if they had a baby, but since when was change a bad thing?

It was still taking all of E.J.'s strength to get past the fact that she had actually considered – *researched* – getting rid of the baby she thought she might've been carrying. And instead of telling him she thought she might be pregnant, she avoided him. He'd just started coming to grips with how she flat-out lied to him, and had been throughout their entire marriage. His blood boiled whenever he let himself focus on that.

Realizing he was gripping the steering wheel so hard his knuckles were starting to hurt, he forced out a few deep breaths. Every time he thought he was ready to start to move past it, something would happen to remind him just why he was so furious. If this were anyone else, he would have cut her off without a second thought. But Natalia was the person he loved more than anything or anyone. And that's also why her betrayal cut him so deep.

A sudden chiming broke him out of his thoughts, and the notification of a text from Natalia flashed across the screen on his dashboard. He sighed, already feeling drained.

Hesitating, he went ahead and called her back, reminding himself to at least try to be cordial.

"Hey," he greeted upon hearing her voice.

"Hey," she replied, her voice filling his car via the Bluetooth. He briefly closed his eyes at the familiar stirring in his gut. Just because he was mad at her didn't mean she didn't still affect him. "Are you still with the boys?"

"I just dropped them off. Headed home."

"Okay. I'll probably get there not too long after you. Um, I've been thinking about our...situation..."

E.J.'s jaw clenched.

"And I think a change of scenery would be good for us. We should take a vacation."

His lip curled. "Not trying to sound like an asshole here, but how is a vacation gonna fix what we're going through?"

"It wouldn't *fix* it, but maybe it can give us some renewed focus. Maybe we need a refresh. And we're overdue for one, since we haven't been anywhere in a few years."

"I get that and maybe if we didn't have this dark cloud over us right now, I'd be down with it. But nothing is gonna change about our situation just because we go to the beach."

She sighed. "Don't be sarcastic, E.J."

"I'm not being sarcastic. Am I wrong in what I said? Will us going away together make either one of us change our minds about what we want or don't want?"

"Maybe not, but it could help us better figure out what to do about it and where to go from here. If we can get away from work and all of our other distractions and just focus on *us*-"

"What else have we *been* focusing on? It's just been us for ten years, remember?"

"In our house, yeah, but don't act like you haven't been working to build your businesses with Roland during the bulk of our marriage. And don't get me wrong; I had no problem with that. I totally support you, and I'm proud of everything you've done. What I'm saying, though, is that we should take some time where there's no clubs, no work projects, no obligations to think about. Just you and me. I'm not saying the solution would just magically fall out of the sky once we got there but it couldn't hurt to try."

"And what if we go on vacation and come back with nothing changed? Then what?"

"Then we try something else. How 'bout you try thinking positively, E.J.?"

"Oh, believe me, I've *been* doing that. I'm still here, aren't I?"

There was a pause. E.J. could feel his heart thumping in his chest, and his hand had resumed its death grip on the steering wheel. He dragged his bottom lip between his teeth and tried to calm his shallow breaths.

"You've thought about...*not* being here?" Natalia finally asked, her voice missing its usual fire.

He didn't want to admit it, but he wasn't going to lie. "It crossed my mind once or twice. I meant what I said about not running, and wanting to work things out. But as angry as I was-"

"I don't want you to go anywhere, E.J. That's why we need to try to do everything we can, to avoid that."

E.J. stayed quiet, his eyes locked on the road in front of him.

"E.J....baby, I'm *sorry* for causing this rift between us." The anguish in Natalia's voice was evident. "I so wish I could go back and make better decisions. And I wish I could get past the hang-up I seem to have about having kids. It has nothing to do with you or us; it's all in my own head."

"Natalia...what am I even supposed to say to that?"

"I don't know. I...I just want to make sure you know where I'm coming from. And that I'm sincerely trying to figure it out."

"And in the meantime...what?"

"In the meantime, we do our best to respect each other's positions. I'll try not to say any more dumb shit and you try not to shut down on me when you get upset."

"It's..." E.J. ran a hand down his face. "It's not like I'm enjoying this, Natalia."

"I know. I get it. That's why I think we need to go away together, though; I really do think it would do us some good. Sometimes clarity comes with new surroundings."

"Even if I thought it would help, this isn't the best time to be taking a trip, anyway, with everything we've got going on. I've got stuff with the clubs, you've got your work stuff, not to mention-"

"E.J., there's always gonna be *something*. You're always so worried about work that you don't let yourself have any fun. I'm sure Roland can hold things down for a few days, just like you did when he was on his honeymoon. And as for me, I'll have some more free time in a couple of weeks."

"Hmm. I don't know."

A few moments passed before Natalia spoke again. "Fine, E.J. It was a suggestion that I really think will help us, but if you don't agree, whatever...I can't force you. I just want you to think about this, though."

"What?"

"If we can't even make time to go away for a measly weekend now, what do you think it would be like with a baby in the house? This is exactly the kind of thing I was afraid of, and we don't even have any kids yet."

E.J.'s back straightened. "Yet?"

"Don't read too much into that. But I meant it when I said I was trying to work through this. I need you to work with me. At some point, we both have to stop being so stubborn and move forward." She released a long breath. "I'm gonna go. I'll see you at the house."

She hung up.

Chapter 7

• • • •

"WHAT TIME IS THIS DUDE supposed to be here?" E.J. asked, glancing at his watch.

"Two o'clock. For the fifth time," Roland droned, pouring himself some water from a glass pitcher. They were in the banquet room at 845, waiting on Carlton Barber to arrive for their meeting. "And he's not late, so you can stop looking at your watch."

"And where is Ned?"

"He'll be here, man. Will you chill out?"

"I have other things I need to be doing. Plus, I'm not happy about being roped into going to Desiree's birthday party this weekend."

"I'm not thrilled about that, either. But I'm sure it won't be that bad."

"It'll be more fun than this bullshit you have me doing today."

Roland lowered his glass from his lips, giving an admonishing glare. "E.J. You need to come up off this attitude before they get here. Are things not any better between you and Natalia?"

E.J.'s frown automatically deepened. "No."

"Damn, really? Not at all?"

"No progress worth mentioning. As soon as it seems like we're making a step or two forward, something knocks us back. I don't know what the hell needs to happen to get peace back in my house again."

"Is this still just about the baby issue or has something else come up?"

"No, the baby issue is plenty."

"Why don't you try getting a dog?"

"That's not a substitute for a child to me."

"No, but it could be something to love on."

"I don't want a damn dog."

"Okay, then. Why don't you go to counseling?"

"*That's* something we should do. 'Cause trying to figure things out on our own surely isn't getting us anywhere."

"I'm trippin' that you two are still at odds, though. You and Natalia have always been as thick as thieves; hell, I looked to y'all as an example for *my* marriage."

"I'm flattered, brother, and once upon a time, I would've been proud of that. But Natalia and I aren't to be emulated. We clearly don't have the marriage I thought we had."

Roland looked over at his big brother, noticing the seemingly ever-present furrow in his brow and the tightness in his movements. E.J. had been snippy all morning and Roland knew he still wasn't on board with the idea of selling their clubs, but he also knew that his marriage woes were probably taking precedence over everything for him.

Before Roland could reply to E.J.'s comment, Ned, their attorney, breezed into the room in his usual tailored suit and fresh haircut. Right behind him was Carlton Barber and a couple of other men, who were introduced as his lawyer and his business manager. E.J. didn't bother trying to remember their names.

"Let's get right down to why we're here, gentlemen," E.J. ordered once they had all exchanged pleasantries and were seated around the long dining table. "I'm sure we all have more things we need to get on with today."

Roland frowned at him but Carlton Barber smiled, crossing his arms over his chest. He was in his mid-fifties, but could pass for ten years younger, his papersack brown skin practically free of facial hair or blemishes. "Not about the bullshit. I respect that. All right, then. We're here because I've wanted to venture into the nightclub arena for a while now, and I love what you Bell brothers have built with Barfly and 845. I want in."

"So you want to come in and take over after we've done all the work, huh?" E.J. replied before Roland could, crossing his own arms and looking the billionaire square in the eye. "Because I already know you aren't interested in any kind of partnership. You don't just want *in*; you want it all."

"Of course," Carlton replied without hesitation, holding up a hand when his business manager opened his mouth to speak. "Don't mistake, Mr. Bell, I respect the hell out of everything you and your brother have done. And I'm sure you're probably wondering why I don't just start my own entities from scratch."

"Why don't you?"

"Because after discussing it with my team, it would be a better business move to take on businesses that are already thriving and have an established clientele rather than building from the ground up. I've done a lot but when it comes to this arena, my name doesn't mean much. I don't just buy businesses and fall back; I'm very hands-on. And once my team looked into the numbers, I was even more convinced. I have no problem admitting that I'd prefer to hit the ground running rather than try to build up steam from nothing."

"I get it. But one thing I'm concerned about is what would happen *after* the sale, should we get to that point," Roland commented, ignoring E.J.'s glare. "We don't want you coming in here, doing a sweep and bringing all your own people in, leaving the folks that have been rocking with us from the beginning and are part of the reason we're so successful out in the cold."

Carlton glanced at his associates before turning his light brown eyes back to Roland. "Understandable."

"Of course if we were to sell, we'd have no say in how you ran things. But that's a definite factor in our decision."

"And I'd personally like to know what other changes you're planning on making," E.J. added, barely hiding the edge in his voice. "Speaking for myself, *I'm* proud of what we've done here. And the offer of money doesn't make me forget about the reputation we've established or the impact we have on this community. And regardless, our names would still be associated with Barfly and 845, and I don't want that to sour because we sold out to someone who didn't give a damn."

Roland was seething but fought to keep his ire in check, not only at E.J.'s combativeness but also at the slight dig he took at him, implying that money was enough to make Roland forget about everything they'd built. He knew he had to wait to address it, though; they couldn't appear divided in front of Carlton Barber.

The other men in the room glanced at each other as E.J. and Carlton continued to stare each other down. It was clear that E.J. wasn't impressed or intimidated by this man, and wasn't going to make anything easy on him.

Finally, Carlton spoke. "Mr. Bell, I'm sure you've checked into my background as much as I've checked into yours. So you undoubtedly know that my compassion is almost as vast as my bank account. I'm not a monster; I'd never just come in and kick all of your employees out the door like it was nothing. Everyone currently working here would have the opportunity to keep their jobs."

E.J. quirked a brow. "The opportunity?"

"I'm not going to lie to you and act like I wouldn't make *any* changes. I would put my own stamp on things in some way. We'd absolutely take the time to sit everyone down and discuss where we're trying to go and if they feel they can align with that. If they choose to leave, so be it. But if they want to stay on board for the new era of Barfly and 845, they'd be more than welcome to do so."

Roland glanced at E.J., whose expression showed no indication of what he thought of Carlton's words.

"So Mr. Barber, the offer you've presented to us is all-encompassing, correct?" Ned spoke up.

"All-encompassing. I'd take over all operations, building leases, licenses...everything. Once everything is finalized, the Bell brothers would have no further dealings or ownership whatsoever. Though I would hope they'd remain as patrons."

Roland could almost *feel* the heat emanating from his brother beside him.

"What timeline are we looking at?" Ned asked.

"Ideally, I'd like to have this finalized before fourth quarter kicks off, so we can really dig in at the top of Q1.

At the same time, though, I totally understand that this isn't an easy decision and I don't expect it to be made without significant thought. I'm not trying to put my foot on your necks, here. So take whatever time you need."

Roland nodded. "That sounds fair enough."

"I'll say, though, that I really do want these clubs, and – call me spoiled – I've gotten pretty used to getting what I want," Carlton added with a smirk and a shrug of his shoulder. "So I'm more than willing to sweeten the pot if it means nudging you towards a decision faster."

He nodded to one of the men beside him, who slid a leather folder across the table to Ned. Once Ned opened it and scanned the contents, his eyebrows shot up to his razor-sharp hairline. He wordlessly slid it over to Roland, who felt like his stomach dropped out of his body when he read the new buyout offer. He had to resist the urge to rub his eyes, because that amount of money had only appeared in his dreams.

Roland managed to keep his expression neutral, though, as he turned the folder where E.J. could better see it. E.J. eventually glanced down at the number in front of him, and if he was pleased with the increased amount, he showed no signs of it. His hard expression stayed locked in place.

E.J. was no more tempted than he had been when this meeting began. He loved money as much as the next man, and he wouldn't deny that the offer was generous. But how generous it was made him suspicious. Carlton seemed a little too eager to buy them out, and E.J. didn't believe that things would be as smooth and seamless as he tried to make it seem.

"We'll get back to you on this," he stated, closing the folder and standing from his chair. Clearly, the meeting was over.

Getting the message, everyone else followed suit, mumbling their thanks and wishing each other a good rest of the day. Roland and E.J. talked with Ned for a few minutes before he had to head out to another meeting, with Roland assuring him they'd be letting him know which way they were leaning.

"I'm not *leaning* anywhere," E.J. commented once they were alone. "I'm flat-footed where I'm at. Ten toes down."

"Yeah, I gathered that," Roland grunted, his frustration evident in how hard he closed the door behind Ned. He turned and faced off with his brother. "So that's why you were looking all evil and taking shots at me?"

"I didn't say anything that wasn't true. You can call it taking shots if you want to."

"Look, man," Roland forced himself to take a breath and run his hands down his face, "I don't want this to put us at odds. We can disagree but we don't need to be turning on each other."

"If you chose to take what I said personally, that's on you, brother. But I didn't want there to be any confusion about where I stood on things. And let's not act like I didn't say from the jump that I wasn't interested, anyway."

"Well, I *am* interested. I know you don't wanna hear that, but I am."

E.J. shook his head. "Just like that, huh?"

"You heard what he said; he assuaged the main concerns we had, regarding our employees. *And* he upped the offer.

Get mad about it if you want, but I'm not willing to just walk away from that like it's nothing."

"We've been doing this long enough to know that nothing is as easy as it looks up front. He's making it seem like everybody from both sides are just gonna hold hands and skip off into the sunset like one big happy family with no headaches or hiccups whatsoever, and I don't buy it."

"The man said there would be changes, E.J. We'd have to expect that, anyway."

"And of course, he was ambiguous about that. 'Changes' could mean anything."

"We can't very well agree to take all that money and still expect to approve every single thing he might think to implement if we sell to him."

"Why can't we? We own this shit, don't we?"

"Dammit, E.J., will you quit being so damn stubborn? Think about something other than what *you* want and don't want for once?"

"Oh, what, now I'm selfish? This man is offering way more money than the clubs are worth for a reason. Why are you so eager to give in to this?"

"Because. I have a wife. We have a son now and we're trying to have more as we speak. And I want to be home with them and see them grow up instead of working all the time."

Roland noticed the break in E.J.'s hard expression at the mention of kids; he could see the hurt flash across his eyes before he turned his head away. Some of Roland's own frustration eased a bit.

"Like I said, man, I love what we've done," Roland continued, placing a hand to his chest. "And I *am* proud of it. But it doesn't come before my family. And this deal could set me, Lovey, and our kids up for life. Maybe that doesn't matter to you but it does to me, and that's not a bad thing. There's more to life than all this, brother."

He turned and headed for the door, leaving E.J. to think about what he said. But he knew his brother well enough to know that it would take a lot more to sway E.J. from his stubborn stance.

E.J. did consider Roland's words. And despite Roland mentioning his growing family feeling like a kick in the gut, E.J. made himself shut off the personal part of his brain and look at it from a business perspective. On the surface, the terms seemed fair enough. His employees would seemingly be taken care of. And of course, there was the money. It would be too easy to just take the money and run.

And do what, though? E.J. was never one to just sit around and do nothing with himself. He could only tolerate so much traveling. He'd likely start another business, because he knew the itch to build something else would get too intense to resist. He could do it alone if he had to, but one thing that he loved so much about his businesses was that he was running them with his brother. Starting something else without Roland just wouldn't feel the same.

It was because of that fact that E.J. also felt a little betrayed. Roland used to be as on fire for the empire they were trying to build as he was, but now his focus had shifted and E.J. couldn't help feeling slighted. He could almost feel the resentment growing inside of him like a vine climbing up a wall.

Natalia's words about kids changing things rang through his head. He certainly hadn't forgotten their conversation where she pointed out the impact children would have on their already busy schedules, especially considering they apparently didn't have time to take a vacation, according to E.J. He had brushed it off when she said it, but now it was knocking at his remembrance like an annoying neighbor.

Shaking his head, he glanced at his watch and snatched the folder with Barber's offer off the table before heading out of the room. He didn't have any more time to think about something that, as far as he was concerned, was never going to happen.

· · · ·

THE NIGHT OF DESIREE'S party rolled around, and E.J. was anything but amped about it. He didn't still hold a grudge against Desiree, but he wasn't in the mood to help her celebrate her birthday.

But, he'd given his word that he would go, and he liked to do what he said he was going to do. So he grudgingly got dressed, already telling himself that he'd give it a couple of hours, tops.

Natalia eyed her husband as he pulled a white Henley over his head, feeling her whole middle constrict when he mindlessly pushed up his sleeves to put on his watch. She had never been so turned on by someone's forearms as she was when she got with E.J., and she had to make herself turn away and gather herself. She was still miffed at him for being so dismissive of her vacation idea, and she wasn't ready to let go of that just because he aroused her without even trying.

Part of her had expected him to back out of going to the party altogether, but she didn't let her hopes get too high over it. E.J. was a man of his word, so it would have taken a sincere conflict for him to not go. That corner of her heart that would always swoon for him regardless was giddy over the fact that they were essentially going on a date, even though they were barely speaking and hadn't even touched each other since the night of their latest disagreement. They slept in the same bed, but kept to their respective sides. When they were in the kitchen or bathroom or den together, they moved around each other with patented stubborn choreography. Natalia didn't love it, but she was temporarily out of energy for trying to get back into E.J.'s good graces.

"You ready?" E.J. asked her when he finished getting dressed.

Natalia finished putting on her gold hoop earrings and grabbed her purse from the bed. "Yeah."

They headed to the party, which was being held at Desiree's boyfriend Lorenzo's house. Quite a few people were already there; Lovey and Roland, Lovey's sister Liz, Desiree's parents and three sisters and their husbands, and other friends and associates. E.J. and Natalia entered, side by side but not touching, and Lovey rushed over as soon as she saw them, smiling excitedly. Roland was behind her, but with notably less enthusiasm.

"It's so good to see you two!" Lovey exclaimed, giving them both warm hugs. She stepped back, her smile widening. "Y'all are coordinated and everything; that's so cute!"

Natalia and E.J. glanced at each other. Her white sleeveless top and dark jeans indeed looked like it was supposed to match E.J.'s own white shirt-dark jean combo, but it wasn't intentional. Neither of them had even noticed that until Lovey pointed it out.

"Yeah, how 'bout that," Natalia made herself comment, trying to sound playful but not quite pulling it off. Lovey must have noticed because her smile dimmed slightly. "Hey, Roland."

"What's going on, sis?" Roland stepped forward to give Natalia a hug, but his pleasant expression faded when his eyes flitted to his brother. "Hey, man."

E.J. barely lifted his chin in acknowledgement. "What's up."

Lovey looked back and forth between them in surprise. The tension was evident. She'd never seen them be so distant towards each other. Natalia just shook her head.

"Where's the birthday girl?" she asked, brushing her bangs from her eyes.

Lovey looked like she was still trying to decipher what was going on between her husband and brother-in-law. "She was in the kitchen, last I saw her."

Natalia's phone lit up before she could walk off, and she cast a brief glance at it before tucking it back into her purse. She looked over at E.J. and his eyes were fixed on her. Swallowing, she made herself turn and walk off to find Desiree. Lovey looked after her, concerned.

"Okay, what's going on with you two?" She wasted no time asking the brothers, her brown eyes pinging between them. "You're barely even looking at each other."

"Natalia and I are fine, Lovey," E.J. grunted, already checking his watch.

"All evidence to the contrary, but I was talking about you and Roland."

Roland sighed. "It's nothing for you to worry about, babe."

"I'm not trying to pry. But I hate seeing the two of you like this. Please don't tell me you're letting the buyout offer cause a rift between you."

"It's just a rough patch. We'll work it out."

Both Roland and Lovey turned hopeful eyes to E.J. He hated being put on the spot, and it didn't do anything to help his mood.

"We'll get through it, eventually," he made himself say. "I'm gonna go find something to drink."

E.J. was glad that there were so many people milling around Lorenzo's spacious living room and getting lost in the music and their relative conversations, because he could fade into the background without much notice. He wasn't feeling festive at all but he didn't want to be a grouch to everyone, so he tried to stay to himself as much as he could. He did make himself at least go and wish Desiree a happy birthday and thank her and Lorenzo for having him, since he *was* in the man's house.

"Thanks for coming, E.J.," Desiree commented with a grin. Her hand rubbed Lorenzo's, which was splayed across her stomach as he stood behind her.

"You're welcome. I have to admit I forgot to get you a gift, though."

"Natalia just gave me one; said it was from the both of you."

E.J. should've figured Natalia would've thought of that. He felt a tiny bit of relief, because he realized how it looked for him to show up empty-handed. But he honestly hadn't thought about it until he got there. "I'm glad. Hope you like it."

"I appreciate any gifts but really, I'm just happy to be here with my man and all my family and friends," Desiree commented, smiling up at Lorenzo. He kissed the top of her head and pulled her closer to him. "I don't have anything to complain about and after the last couple of years I had, I'm just grateful for that."

"Well...good." E.J. glanced around, hating the awkward feeling that had a grip on him at the moment. His eyes darted around the room and landed on his wife in the far corner, looking at something intently on her phone as she mindlessly sipped from the glass of champagne she held in the other. Her thumb moved around the screen, apparently replying to a message, and E.J. couldn't help but wonder who it was that had her so enthralled.

Desiree got pulled away by one of her sisters, and E.J. and Lorenzo made small talk as everyone continued to enjoy themselves. E.J. was already wondering when they could leave, though, since they'd made an appearance, given their gift and spoken to the birthday girl. Roland was obviously steering clear of him, which burned his gut almost as much as Natalia doing it. E.J. didn't know when he had become the bad guy.

"You good, man?"

His eyes snapped to Lorenzo. "Yeah. Why do you ask?"

"'Cause you're looking like you want to murder someone."

Trying to neutralize his expression, E.J. tried to take a calming breath. It was then that he noticed the ache in his jaws from so much clenching and he ran a hand absently over them. "My bad."

"Hey, we all have those days. Hopefully you can get past whatever it is that has you so balled up. I'm not gonna try to get in your business but I'm here if you want an impartial ear."

Giving a curt nod, E.J. muttered, "Appreciate it," before taking a long sip of his water. He liked Lorenzo all right, but he wasn't about to confide in him. There were only two people he really opened up to and both of them were giving him a wide berth at the moment.

A little while later, Desiree's parents, Elyse and Darius, called for everyone's attention so they could say a few words to their second-born, and then Lovey gushed about how much she valued their almost lifelong friendship. Then her sisters Dori, Dana, and Diamond all joined in, with things quickly shifting from love fest to good-natured roast. Desiree laughed along with everyone else at all of their playful jabs, reveling in all the attention.

"Y'all know I'm gonna get you back for this, right?" she warned with a grin, playfully shaking her index fingers at her giggling sisters. "Just wait until *your* birthdays roll around."

"I just won't invite you," Diamond commented with a shrug, then shrieked when Desiree tossed a balled-up napkin at her. Everyone laughed around them. "Brat!"

"Ooh, if *that* isn't the pot calling the kettle black!" Desiree exclaimed. Looking around the room, she pointed a finger at her little sister. "Y'all, don't let her fool you. She was always scheming to get her way just because she's the youngest. I hope that daughter of yours runs you ragged!"

"Whatever!"

The laughter was still filling the room when Lorenzo wrapped his strong arms around Desiree from behind and lifted her, drawing a yelp from her that melted into a wide grin as he briefly buried his face in the crook of her neck.

"Is it my turn now?" he asked, setting her back to her feet and turning her to face him, grabbing her hands. He glanced at her sisters. "Or do you ladies need to get some more digs in?"

"We're all right for now," Dana replied with a wave of her hand. "You can go ahead."

"Thanks." Lorenzo chuckled as he turned his attention to his girlfriend, looking down at her with a loving smile. "Can you believe it's been almost two years since we got together? Did you think we'd last this long?"

"*I* damn sure didn't," Diamond muttered.

"Shut up!" Desiree tossed over her shoulder before turning her eyes and smile back to Lorenzo. "I had my doubts at first because of all my hang-ups but I'm glad I was wrong. You came in and changed the game for me, baby."

"You had my attention from the first moment I saw you. And I still don't have eyes for anybody else."

"You'd better not," Desiree teased, grabbing the front of his shirt and shaking him, though he didn't move. The man was like a boulder.

"I appreciate you trusting me and allowing me in here." Lorenzo gently tapped a finger to her chest. "It's something I don't take lightly because I know what you've been through. You're everything to me, Desiree. You know that, right?"

"I do. And it's definitely mutual."

"I'm glad to know that. Because I've been thinking about this for a while and the more I do, the happier it makes me. And really, it took everything in me to wait until tonight."

Desiree looked on curiously as Lorenzo motioned towards one of his friends standing nearby, who stepped forward and handed him a black velvet bag. A few gasps went up around them as he pulled out a red ring box, and the cheers began when he lowered himself to one knee. Desiree actually screamed, taking a tiny step back as her hands flew to her mouth.

"Desiree," Lorenzo flipped open the box to reveal a two-carat emerald-cut yellow diamond ring, which only drew more gasps and cheers, not to mention several phones being lifted to capture the moment. His eyes stayed fixed on Desiree, though, as he gently grabbed her left hand and kissed it. "There's not a doubt in my mind that I want to spend my life with you. I want to give you everything, including my last name."

"Lorenzo..." Desiree's free hand drifted to her heaving chest. Her face looked stricken.

"Will you marry me?"

A tear rolled down her face as her hand squeezed his. Natalia stood nearby with Lovey, both of them grinning excitedly as they anticipated her answer, their arms locked as they practically bounced with anticipation. When Natalia scanned the room for E.J., even he wore a small smile, apparently unable to maintain his sour mood through this touching scene. When his eyes met hers, she winked at him before turning her attention back to her friend.

Several moments passed and Desiree still appeared frozen in place, staring at the ring cradled in Lorenzo's large hand. People began to glance at each other curiously with every silent second that ticked by, and Lorenzo's gaze went from lovesick to concerned.

"Babe," he urged, gently shaking her hand. "You okay?"

"No," Desiree finally whimpered, her voice a mere squeak.

Standing to his full height, Lorenzo grabbed her shoulders, looking at her with a concerned frown. "What is it? What's wrong?"

"I meant no...to your first question."

Realization flashed across Lorenzo's face and he recoiled as if she'd slapped him. His hands fell from her. Desiree looked up at him pleadingly as his nostrils flared in mounting anger. Everyone around them was absolutely dumbstruck, their eager phones now lowered.

"I see." His voice sounded as angry as it did pained, and he snapped the ring box closed. That seemed to yank Desiree out of her momentary trance, and she reached for him.

"Lorenzo, I-"

"No, you made yourself clear," he snapped, evading her touch. "Message received."

He turned and stalked out of the room, and Desiree, apparently realizing what she'd just done, covered her horrified face with her hands before running after him.

"Lorenzo!"

Moments later there was a loud door slam, and the sounds of Desiree and Lorenzo's loud voices going back and forth. It wasn't clear what they were saying, but it was perfectly clear who was pissed off and who was begging for forgiveness.

Natalia couldn't believe what she'd just seen. She looked over at Lovey, whose fair brown skin was flushed. Her eyes glistened with unshed tears.

"What the hell just happened?" Natalia muttered.

"I'm still wondering if I'm dreaming or something," Lovey admitted.

"Did you know he was gonna propose?"

"I didn't, but I figured it was coming eventually. And I would've bet anything that she would've accepted when he did. You've heard her talk about what kind of wedding she wanted them to have; she's crazy about Lorenzo. I wonder what happened."

"I don't know..." They paused as the voices from the back of the house got even louder. "But it sounds like our girl is already regretting it."

Needless to say, the party was over. Everyone started to file out, still shell-shocked at what they witnessed. Lovey and Desiree's family insisted on hanging back to make sure Desiree was okay, and Lovey promised to call Natalia once she found out what was going on.

E.J. and Natalia headed home in stunned silence, processing the night's events. Natalia looked over at him, curious as to what was on his mind.

"That's was crazy, huh?"

E.J. nodded, his eyes still on the road. "It really was."

"I wonder why she said no. Desiree is head over heels for Lorenzo."

"Apparently not *that* much, seeing as how she turned him down."

"I have to believe she didn't really mean that. You saw how freaked out she got. It looked like she already wanted to walk that back."

"Who knows?" E.J. shrugged a shoulder. "Hopefully they can work it out, but I don't know a lot of men that would stay with a woman after she shot down their marriage proposal."

"Lorenzo is reasonable; I can't imagine he'd just straight dump her over this, especially if she has a good reason."

E.J. shrugged again, having nothing else to say about it. They rode in silence for a few more moments before he spoke again. "So who was that that kept hitting you up all night?"

Natalia should've known he would notice that. Just like she knew that he wouldn't accept some passive answer. And not being honest had gotten her in enough trouble.

"It was Dane."

He frowned. "Why does that name sound familiar?"

"Because it's my ex. The one I was with before you."

After pulling to a stop at a red light, E.J. turned hard eyes to her. "And why is he calling you?"

"I ran into him a little while back and he asked to keep in touch," Natalia commented, trying to sound casual despite the fact that her hands that were stuffed under her thighs were shaking. "No big deal."

"Hmm." The light turned green and E.J. jammed down on the gas, causing Natalia to lurch forward. "So y'all are kicking it again or something?"

"No, E.J., it's nothing like that. I told him we couldn't be hanging out."

"But you can talk?"

"E.J..." She leaned her head against the headrest. "Don't blow this out of proportion. But since we're on the subject of talking, how come you didn't talk to me about this buyout deal from Carlton Barber?"

His lip automatically curled in a snarl. "It's not a *deal*; I haven't agreed to a damn thing."

"Still. That's pretty major and you never said one word to me about it."

"You getting cozy again with your ex isn't even in the same ballpark as me not talking about an offer I have no intention of accepting. The only reason I was entertaining it at all was because Roland was so interested."

"He is, really? He'd be willing to sell the clubs?"

"It's too much money for him to ignore, he said. And with him and Lovey trying to..." His jaw clenched briefly. "With them trying to have more kids, he wants to be able to focus on them instead of work."

Natalia didn't miss the change in his voice, and resisted the urge to place a hand on his thigh. They weren't arguing for the time being and she wanted to keep it that way. "It's that much money?"

"Yeah. It's a lot."

"And you're not interested?"

"No," he replied without hesitation. "I'd rather work to earn it on our own than have some entitled rich dude come in and buy up everything we've built. It means too much to me."

"I can understand that," Natalia replied, giving him a soft smile. "And I definitely respect it. How much is Barber offering, though? I know you don't want to accept, but I can't help but be curious. Especially since it kind of affects me, too."

E.J. glanced at her as if he hadn't considered that. "I wasn't trying to be shady. Maybe part of me thought you'd try to get me to accept it, too, and I wasn't trying to hear that."

"I love money. But I'd never try to pressure you into selling what you've worked so hard to build. Especially if I knew you were dead-set against it."

A few quiet moments passed before E.J. finally told her the latest figure Carlton had brought to the table. Natalia jutted forward in her seat, hair flying as her head whipped around to him. Her jaw was practically in her lap.

"Are you messing with me?" she verified incredulously.

Shaking his head, E.J. simply replied, "No."

"I didn't think it was going to be *that* much..."

"You gonna start pressuring me now, too?"

"No...I mean, I'd be lying if I said I wouldn't be thrilled if you accepted it. But I understand why you don't want to. I still wish you'd told me about it, though."

"It's not like our communication is top-notch right now." E.J. turned onto the street leading to their house, smoothly guiding the wheel with his left hand. "This wasn't really front and center on my mind, with all our other shit we're dealing with."

Natalia started to comment, then they arrived at the house and she was reminded of yet another example of their poor communication, and this one was all on her. She cursed under her breath, already knowing E.J. was going to be furious.

It didn't take him long to notice what she was kicking herself over, and his scowl was on full blast when he killed the engine and turned towards her once they were pulled into the garage.

"Why the hell is your little sister sitting on our doorstep? With *suitcases*??"

Chapter 8

• • • •

E.J. COULDN'T BELIEVE that Natalia had invited her sister Kira to stay with them without running it by him.

The last thing they needed was a houseguest. Even more than that, a houseguest that was a spoiled brat.

E.J. liked Kira all right, but mostly because he wasn't the one that had to put up with her. He was very well aware of her apparent refusal to grow up, crashing on folks' couches and borrowing money instead of getting a job and making her own way. He had no respect for able-bodied people who expected everything to be handed to them, and that was Kira.

"You wanna tell me why I'm the last to know that you invited her to come stay here?" E.J had demanded to Natalia once they were in their bedroom the night they got home from Desiree's birthday party. Kira was downstairs. "Why would you do that?"

"I know I should've told you," Natalia commented, holding her hands out to him. "I guess it slipped my mind."

"Slipped your mind?"

"I told her I would help her and when her friend put her out, she didn't have anywhere else to go. It was either give her some money or let her stay here, and the money thing wasn't happening."

"There's a third option. She can get a damn job and take care of herself."

"She's gonna get a job. I already told her she's not about to be crashing here indefinitely doing nothing."

"So how long is she gonna be here?" E.J. asked, not caring if Kira heard him. It was clear he hadn't been happy about her being there from the moment they got home. "And what about when we're both at work? She's just gonna be here by herself all day?"

Natalia's hands dropped. "You act like she's some kind of criminal."

"I don't put anything past her. So I hope she has somewhere to go when we're not here."

"E.J."

"Don't 'E.J.' me. Be grateful I'm not kicking her out altogether. I told you, this is not the time for us to be having houseguests."

"Maybe it would be good for us to have some kind of buffer, because it's not like it's been exactly pleasant around here. We've barely talked in days."

He frowned, her words registering. "So it *didn't* slip your mind; you invited her here on purpose."

"Maybe I did," she sighed. Her eyes challenged his. "She can keep me company while you're acting like I'm not here."

"Wow." He chuckled wryly. "So it's like that, huh? All right, then."

He stalked out of the room, having no more words for her.

"Uggghhh!" Natalia practically screamed, fisting her hair in both hands as she bent over at the waist, the frustration overtaking her. If it wasn't one thing between her and E.J., it was something else. Now he had just another excuse to be pissed at her.

It didn't help that Kira wasn't trying very hard to be the ideal houseguest. She stayed up late, blasting the television or her music (until Natalia would curse her out), she constantly raided their pantry and fridge, and she wasn't exactly neat. It took all of E.J.'s restraint to not throw all of her things outside and send her out after them.

But even that wasn't the worst thing. Kira had another tendency that E.J. had a particular problem with.

"Good morning," Kira greeted early one morning as E.J. was preparing to go to the gym.

E.J. turned from where he was mixing his preworkout at the kitchen counter to see Kira saunter in wearing nothing but a thin camisole and boy shorts. Skimpy clothing was the norm for her, though E.J. noticed that it was significantly more so when it was just the two of them. When Natalia was around, Kira was in regular t-shirts and shorts or leggings.

"Hey," he grunted, turning back to what he was doing. He hated that he was alone with her, though Natalia was upstairs still asleep. "Why are you up so early?"

Kira shrugged, joining him at the counter. "Heard you in here; thought I'd come and speak."

She was standing too close for E.J.'s liking, so he moved away. "You job hunting today?"

Her smile flattened a little. "I was going to check out some things online, yeah."

"How many places have you applied to?"

"Umm, a few. Still waiting to hear back."

"I look forward to hearing about the progress you've made later on today," he said pointedly, screwing the cap back on his shaker cup and flipping the hood of his hoodie onto his head, since there was a light rain falling outside.

"Sure..."

"And if you're going to eat up my damn food, you need to clean up after yourself. I know Natalia washed those dishes you left last night and that's the last time she's gonna do that for you." He stopped and glared at her. "Understood?"

"Sorry. Yeah, understood."

E.J. left without another word, wishing she would be gone when he got back but knowing better.

It didn't help things that Natalia was still putting in a good amount of overtime at work – and she still had a myriad of excuses as to why she couldn't or wouldn't work from home - which only meant more time that he was in the house alone with Kira. He'd meant what he said about not leaving her alone while they weren't there, but when he was, Kira was a little too eager for his attention, always finding an excuse to follow him to his office or the den or wherever he was. He was trying his best not to be rude to her, since she was his sister-in-law. But if it was up to him, he'd put her out and not give it another thought. Especially since she didn't seem to be in any particular hurry to get her act together so she could move out on her own.

"E.J., I'm fixing some hot dogs," she called out from the kitchen one night. Natalia hadn't gotten home yet. "You want some?"

Rolling his eyes, E.J. reminded himself to be polite. Or at least, polite enough. "No."

"You sure? They the all-beef ones."

"I don't eat hot dogs."

A beat passed before she muttered, "No wonder you're so fine."

"What you say?"

"Nothing."

There were several instances of this where Kira would make a flirtatious comment or let her eyes linger a little too long, or 'accidentally' touch him. E.J. would call her on it and she'd always insist that it was unintentional. And of course, she was still sauntering around in her revealing outfits.

E.J. was in his office when she appeared in the doorway, gently knocking on the door.

"I'm busy," he barked, eyes still fixed on his laptop.

"I just need a second."

When is Natalia coming home?? E.J. wondered to himself, releasing a sigh. He sat back in his chair, looking at her with forced patience. "What is it?"

She grinned and strolled into the office, her light brown braids falling over her shoulder. Stopping at his desk, she perched her hands on the edge and leaned over, her bare right foot rubbing the back of her left leg and her breasts jutting from her sports bra. She was wearing that and cutoff shorts that might as well have been underwear, they were so short. E.J.'s eyes stayed on her face.

"I wanted to let you know I have an interview tomorrow," she informed, leaning a little further over the desk. She pulled her bottom lip between her teeth as she eyed him. "At one of those fashion stores in the mall."

"Congratulations."

"You proud of me?"

"Ask me that again after you actually get the job."

"I'll do my best."

"Good." E.J. stopped short of reminding her that she was on limited time in his house. He was only home as much as he was recently because Natalia pleaded with him to be, not wanting to leave Kira to wander around the city all day while they worked their long hours. And since Natalia was working so much overtime, E.J. was on babysitting duty, which was what it felt like.

Kira lingered at his desk as E.J. resumed what he was doing. When she hadn't moved after several moments, he glanced up at her, clearly bothered. "Was that it?"

"I..." Kira hesitated, seeming to lose whatever nerve she had the more she looked into E.J.'s impatient expression. "You know what, never mind. I'll leave you to your work."

He just grunted in acknowledgement, and she turned on her heel and dragged out of the room, as if she was waiting for him to stop her.

Once she was finally gone, E.J. glanced at the time and grabbed his phone. This was ridiculous.

He called Natalia and was surprised she actually answered; she hadn't been the easiest to reach since Kira came to stay with them.

"Hey."

"When are you coming home?" E.J. demanded without preamble.

"Why? What's wrong?"

"What do you mean, why? I'm sick of having to babysit your damn sister, that's why. You're the one that invited her to stay here yet you're conveniently gone more now that she is."

"That's just how it happened, E.J. It's not intentional. There were a bunch of changes to the new software we'd been working on for this client and the deadlines were tight, not to mention my having to help out on some other stuff. But I do want to let you know that I appreciate you rearranging things so you can be there with Kira when I'm not."

"Uh-huh. Look, I'm gonna let you know; I don't like being here alone with her. My patience is wearing thin on all this."

"I wish you would make more of an effort to get to know her. She's not a bad person. She just needs some guidance."

"She's an adult. Maybe if y'all stopped babying her-"

"E.J., is she anywhere near you? Can she hear you right now?"

"I don't give a damn if she can hear me or not. It's not a secret that I'm not thrilled about her staying here. I could see if she was trying to be helpful in any way she can, but she's not even doing that."

"I know she can be a pain to live with sometimes, but if I didn't believe she was sincerely trying to get her act together, she wouldn't be in our house. You know I don't have much more patience for her shit than you do."

"It's easy for you to say that 'cause you're not the one that's having to..." He stopped himself, rubbing his eyes. "Are you about done at work?"

Natalia took her time answering. "Actually, I'm not at work right now. I got off about an hour ago. I'm at Desiree's."

"Excuse me?"

"She's still really messed up over what happened at her birthday party and I was worried about her. Lorenzo hasn't been talking to her-"

"And I sympathize, but we've got our own problems, Natalia. And how come you didn't say anything to me about going over there? It seems like you're trying to find any excuse you can not to come home."

"I'm just trying to be here for my friend, E.J., that's all."

"I get it. And I'm not trying to be insensitive. But it could be said that Desiree brought that on herself when she rejected his proposal in front of everybody. I don't see what she's so distraught for if she doesn't want to marry him, anyway."

"E.J.!"

"What?"

"Just because she...look, I'll be home as soon as I can"

"That could mean anything. I need specifics."

"Damn it...within the hour, all right?"

"Don't be getting frustrated with me. You're not the one stuck here watching after a twenty-two year old against your will."

She sucked her teeth. "Bye, E.J."

E.J. hung up the phone, hanging his head and clasping his hands behind his neck. He wished he was eager for Natalia to come home because he missed her, but if he was honest, it was mostly because he was tired of dealing with her sister by himself.

By the time Natalia got home, Kira had slipped a hoodie over her sports bra, and was camped out on the couch in the living room, streaming things on Netflix and eating from a shareable-sized bag of Skinny Pop. A blanket covered her lower half, so it was a toss-up if she was still wearing the skimpy shorts or not.

"We need to talk," E.J. announced to Natalia as soon as they were alone in their bedroom. "Straight up, your sister has to go."

Natalia groaned, kicking off her shoes. "Can we not do this right now?"

"This isn't just because I don't want her here. She's getting a little too comfortable, being inappropriate with me."

Her eyes snapped to him. "What do you mean, inappropriate?"

"She flirts, Natalia. Not to mention how she's always walking around in next to nothing when you're not here."

"I wouldn't think too much of it, E.J." Natalia moved over to the vanity and started taking off her earrings. "Kira has always been a big flirt. Let her tell it, there's not a man she can't get."

"And that's fine with you? You have no problem with her flirting with your husband?"

"I didn't say all that. She's not stupid enough to act on it, is all I'm saying."

"I don't care. I'm not gonna keep being uncomfortable in my own house. So either you talk to her and tell her to get it together or I will. And I don't think you want me to do it."

"No, no. I'll take care of it."

The next afternoon, Natalia worked from home so E.J. could go handle some things at Barfly. Natalia felt it was a little silly that they couldn't leave Kira alone in the house, but E.J. was unyielding on it. And Natalia figured if Kira would lie about needing surgery just to get some money, she didn't deserve a lot of leeway.

"Let's talk," she told Kira as soon as she heard her get up. E.J. had already left. Natalia entered the guest room where Kira was staying without invitation and perched herself on the queen-sized bed. "It's important."

"Okay..." Kira eyed her warily as she rested her back against the headboard, adjusting the scarf covering her braids. "What's up?"

"Just what is it you're trying to do with E.J.?"

Kira's eyed widened slightly. "What do you mean?"

"He said you've been a little too flirtatious with him, and you walk around here damn near naked. And I know you, so I know he's not lying."

"I mean...I don't know." Kira hunched her shoulders. "I'm just messing around. It doesn't mean anything."

"You need to cut it out. Now."

"Is he upset?"

"What do you think? You're already on thin ice and this isn't helping any. And while we're at it, you need to help out around here more. I didn't let you come here to be a freeloader."

"Okay, okay."

"And just know, if you were any other woman, I'd be beating your ass right now. But don't think because you're my sister that I'm gonna let you have some kind of free pass on getting comfortable with my man. That's not gonna fly."

"You know I wouldn't do that," Kira insisted. "Everybody knows E.J. is committed to you. Although..."

Natalia's brow lifted. "Although what?"

"Well, I couldn't help but notice that you two haven't kissed or hugged since I've been here. At least, *I* haven't seen it. And you two used to be all over each other."

Pursing her lips, Natalia's eyes dropped to the bedspread. "E.J. and I are going through some things right now."

"Like what?"

"I lied to him about wanting kids. It's just been downhill since he found out about that. That's the main thing."

"Wow. Are you two gonna split up?"

"No," Natalia immediately replied. "We're not. We said we were gonna work things out but it hasn't exactly been smooth sailing."

"I didn't know you don't want kids but I can't say I'm surprised to hear it. You're not exactly the most nurturing person."

"Excuse me? You're saying that to the only sibling that was willing to take you in? *And* who convinced their husband to let you stay?"

"I'm just saying-"

"Let's drop it." Natalia stood from the bed, Kira's words still stinging. "What time is your job interview today?"

Kira eyed her sister, sensing that she had hit a nerve but not exactly sure why. What she said wasn't intended to be mean but it was true; Natalia *wasn't* the most nurturing person. Kira could recall several times during her childhood where she would hurt herself or be upset over something that happened to her, and Natalia would basically tell her to get over it and move on. She was different with other people's kids, cooing and cuddling and being the softie she never was.

But when it came to those she was actually responsible for, that went out the window.

Keeping all this to herself, though, Kira simply replied, "Three o'clock."

"All right. You gonna need a ride?"

"No, thanks. I got it."

Natalia left the room without another word.

Kira's words stayed on Natalia's mind for most of the day. Not only about her not being nurturing but about Kira's observation of her and E.J. They hadn't been affectionate at all, not just with their bodies but even with how they spoke to each other. There was no tenderness, no playfulness, no terms of endearment. They were cut-and-dry conversations. Natalia had let herself sink so deeply into her frustration with E.J. that she stopped actually trying to fix their issues, and she suspected the same was the case with her husband. If there was one thing they had in common, it was how stubborn they were.

So when E.J. got home later that evening, she was waiting on him in their bedroom. He entered the room looking confused.

"What's wrong?" she asked him.

"Kira is downstairs cleaning."

She chuckled. "I had a little talk with her earlier. She's trying."

"Hmm. Did you talk to her about the other stuff too, with the flirting?"

"I did. I told her to cut it out."

"I guess we'll see if she listens to you. I don't wanna have to hurt her feelings."

"Nobody wants that. But I don't wanna talk about Kira right now. Can you come here?"

He looked at her, clearly surprised. "Why?"

"Damn, E.J. Have we really gotten this bad? Now you're hesitating when I ask for a hug?"

His face clearing, he tossed his keys to the dresser and turned to her. "We haven't been doing a lot of that lately."

"We haven't been doing *any* of that. And it's a shame. We're drifting apart, E.J. With every day we go without talking or touching or addressing what's going on between us, the rift between us just gets wider and wider. And...that scares me. I don't want that."

He moved closer to her and looked into her hopeful brown eyes. "I don't want that, either."

"So can you kiss me? Touch me? I know that's not gonna fix everything, but-"

His finger pressed against her lips before he grazed his hand through her hair, admiring her beautiful face. His chest tightened with how much he missed her now that he was holding her in his arms. They'd been in the same house the whole time, but like she said, they'd just been going through the motions, ignoring each other along with their issues.

Unable to resist anymore, he lowered his face to hers, moaning as soon as their lips met. She immediately responded to him, gripping his shirt before sliding her arms around his neck. Their tongues stroked against each other, deeply and languidly, enjoying being together like this again. They traded moans as they inched towards the bed, E.J. ending up on top of his wife and her legs lifting around his waist.

They rolled around, their hands and lips roaming and their bodies deliciously grinding together, forgetting about everything else. It just felt so good to be together like this that it didn't occur to them that their bedroom door was still sitting wide open.

So neither of them noticed Kira peeking around the doorway, her bottom lip between her teeth, watching them.

Chapter 9

• • • •

"WHEN ARE WE GONNA QUIT playing and hash this out?"

E.J. figured this call was coming sooner or later. He and Roland hadn't talked much since the meeting with Carlton Barber, outside of regular work stuff. That wasn't like them and E.J. knew they needed to get past it.

"I have to take care of some stuff but I should be at Barfly in a couple of hours," E.J. informed.

"All right. I'm at 845 but I'll be over there."

By the time he was face-to-face with his brother again, E.J. had convinced himself to try to keep an open mind and not be dismissive of Roland's stance. Even though E.J. was firm in his position, he knew Roland had a right to feel however he felt, regardless of whether E.J. agreed with it or not.

"So what are we gonna do about this?" Roland asked once he showed up later, joining E.J. in the office at Barfly.

"I'm not sure, since I'm sure neither of us has changed our position."

"I already know you haven't. And I haven't, either."

"And this is what Lovey wants, too?"

"She hasn't given her opinion, actually. She just said she'd support whatever we decided to do."

"Hmm."

"Why, what did Natalia say? Or have you even told her about it?"

"Technically, I didn't, but she still found out. Likely by your wife. I have a feeling she wouldn't be mad if we accepted Barber's offer but she said she understood why I don't want to."

"So we're still at an impasse, then," Roland surmised, sitting back in his chair.

"Look, man..." E.J. looked off to the side as his mind whirled, "If the main thing is you needing more family time, you know you can just take a leave of absence. That wouldn't be a problem at all."

"So then everything would fall on you."

"I can handle it."

"E.J., I don't get what's so wrong about taking this money," Roland expressed. "If anything, it should be a compliment; Carlton Barber doesn't get involved with bullshit. If he thinks highly enough of what we've got to offer *that* much money, it must mean we've got something good, here."

"Exactly, and I want to keep it going. Yeah, it's cool to be wanted, but I knew that we had something great already. By the long lines that stretch down the street every night waiting to get in here, by the packed dance floors and hustling kitchen and drained bars, by the waiting list to reserve spaces at both spots, by the thousands of reviews we have on social media. Not to mention the people that have been working with us since day one that tell me how much they love working here. I *know* our shit is on point. And nobody can buy that."

Roland sunk in his chair slightly. "If I could have it both ways, I would. As much as I love what I do here, I'm not gonna lie; I'm happiest when I get home to my wife and son."

"So, what, you don't want to work; you just want to sit at home and make babies forever?"

"Here it comes," Roland shook his head with a wry chuckle. "E.J. the asshole. I was waiting on it."

"What? I think that's a valid question. Because all I've heard is how you want to stay home; I haven't heard anything else."

"Maybe I *do* want to chill for a while. We've been busting our asses for years, not to mention my few years in corporate America before we got Barfly open. Then I got married and became a father back-to-back, all while we were opening 845. It's been a years-long whirlwind and I thank God for it every day, but I need a minute, man."

E.J. eyed his little brother, hearing the fatigue in his voice for the first time. It hadn't occurred to him how hard they'd been going for so long. It didn't bother E.J.; he loved it. He thrived on the grind.

But Roland wasn't him. He was far from lazy, but he enjoyed downtime as much as he enjoyed working. He liked to close himself off at home and just sit and watch sports or movies, doing nothing productive for stretches of time. That wasn't something E.J. could relate to.

"I get it," E.J. finally replied, his voice even. "I'm not trying to be insensitive and if I sound like I am, I apologize."

"Thank you. I know we're not built the same. We're just in different phases of our lives, man. Neither of us are wrong but we need to figure out how we're gonna move forward. Barber is gonna need a decision eventually."

Tenting his fingers under his chin, E.J. sat back in his seat as he eyed his brother and business partner. Several quiet moments passed before he finally spoke again. "What if I buy you out?"

His eyebrows shooting up, Roland marveled, "What?"

"I'll buy you out. Then you can take the time to be home with your family and do whatever else you wanna do."

"You're serious?"

"Do you know me to joke a lot?"

"So if you buy me out, whose gonna help you run all this?"

"I'll run it myself, but it's not like I won't have any help. If I decide to bring someone else in down the line, I'll cross that bridge when I get to it."

"So...I'd just be *out*?"

E.J. frowned, confused. "I thought that was what you wanted."

"It's not the same-"

There was a knock on the door, surprising them both. They glanced at each other before E.J. turned his eyes to the security monitors. When he saw who was standing at his door, he groaned.

"What?" Roland asked.

"I don't have time for this shit," E.J. muttered. He looked towards the door. "Come in!"

The door eased open and Casey entered, followed by Kira, who was all smiles.

"I'm sorry to disturb you two; this young lady said she's your sister-in-law?" Casey verified to E.J. "She expressed it was pretty urgent. I tried to call back here first but your phone is on Do Not Disturb."

E.J. told himself to keep his cool; biting Casey's head off for disturbing him anyway wouldn't change anything. Kira could've been anybody and she just escorted her back to his office based on nothing but her word.

Making a mental note to have a talk with Casey later, he grudgingly nodded. "Yeah, she's my sister-in-law. Thanks, Casey."

A look of relief flashed over Casey's face as she quickly left the office.

Kira was standing there grinning at E.J., both hands clutching her purse in front of her. Her tight jersey dress was a departure from what he usually saw her in, and he wondered (hoped) she was heading to another job interview or something else that would get her out of his house.

"What are you doing here, Kira?" E.J. finally asked when she didn't say anything for a few moments.

"Oh! Sorry..." Kira giggled. E.J. wondered if she was high. He knew she had an affinity for CBD gummies, from some of the trash she'd left in the living room. "Guess I lost my train of thought, there."

"Okay..."

"I'm sorry to just drop by like this but I was out doing some more job hunting and thought I should stop by here."

"For what?"

"Because...it occurred to me that maybe I could just work for *you*." She flashed a smile that likely had gotten her what she wanted in the past, but E.J. was unfazed. "There *has* to be something I can do in one of your clubs, right?"

Resisting the urge to laugh at the ridiculousness of the request, E.J. glanced over at Roland, who was looking at Kira strangely. "You hear this?"

It was then that Kira noticed the other person in the room; she'd been fixated on E.J. the entire time. When she turned her eyes to Roland, they widened as her smile faded like water down a drain. "Oh..."

"Don't I know you from somewhere?" Roland asked, the curious squint still in his eyes.

"Uhh, I don't think so. I've been told I just have one of those faces." Kira ducked her head and turned away, suddenly in a hurry to leave. "I just realized I need to be somewhere in a few minutes. Sorry to bother you. I'll see you at home, E.J."

E.J. looked over at Roland after Kira scurried out. "What the hell was that?"

"She's staying with y'all?" Roland asked, his finger aimed at the door.

"Yeah. Not that I'm thrilled about it. But she's Natalia's little sister, so..."

"I get that she's family and I don't wanna be disrespectful, but...be careful of her in your house, man. That's all I'm gonna say."

"No, that's *not* all you're gonna say. What does that mean, be careful of her in my house? Where do you know her from?"

Roland started to respond when his phone rang. When he glanced at the screen, he told E.J. to hold on a second before he answered the call.

"Hey, babe."

E.J. just sat back in his chair and waited while Roland talked to his wife. He needed to know what was behind that warning about Kira. E.J. knew she was spoiled and lazy but that was the worst he'd heard about her; he couldn't imagine Natalia bringing her into their home if there was something worse than that.

Roland shot out of his seat, heading for the door with the phone still pressed to his ear. He glanced at E.J. "I'll get at you later, man. I need to roll."

"Is everything all right?" E.J. asked, alarmed.

"It's something with Xavier; Lovey's freaking out. I'll catch you up later."

Roland rushed out the door, leaving E.J. curious and worried. He hoped his nephew was all right.

E.J. tried to get back to his work, but now his mind was clouded with concern about little Xavier, Roland's warning about Kira, and his impromptu offer to buy Roland out of their businesses. He sat back in his seat and rubbed his eyes. In that moment, he felt like he needed a break, too.

• • • •

NATALIA HADN'T WANTED to bring Kira along with her when she met up with Lovey and Desiree, but she was whining so much about none of her friends having time for her and how bored she was sitting around the house that Natalia relented just to shut her up.

"It turned out to just be an ear infection," Lovey was saying, glancing down at Xavier as he played on the floor with Kira. They were all gathered at Desiree's. "I feel a little silly now for how panicked I got."

"It's understandable; that was your first time dealing with something like that," Natalia assured her. "Every first-time mom has done that at some point or another, I'm sure."

"It was so sweet, though, how Roland rushed right home when I called him about it. When I got pregnant, I was worried about us both being so busy and how that would affect things, but he's really made the effort to make sufficient time. Sometimes I actually have to tell him to go to work."

"He loves his boy. Y'all are trying to have some more, right?"

"Absolutely," Lovey blushed, taking a small bite of her fruit salad.

"That's her bashful way of saying she and Roland are getting it in every chance they get, trying to put a bun in that oven," Desiree translated with a roll of her eyes. "It's like they're trying to win a contest."

"I'd enter that," Kira joked as she continued playing peek-a-boo with Xavier. "Sounds like a fun competition."

"Pretend your job search is a competition, 'cause that's all you need to be worried about," Natalia ordered, shaking her head. She was a little snippy due to Kira getting on her nerves so much recently, always asking for spending money and having excuse after excuse why she kept bombing her job interviews. And Natalia had caught Kira eyeing E.J. once or twice when she thought no one was looking. Of course, Kira denied it when Natalia called her on it.

Kira just sucked her teeth but didn't comment, her momentary frown turning back into a grin as Xavier climbed into her lap.

"Are you feeling any better, Desiree?" Lovey asked her. "You and Lorenzo are talking again, right?"

Desiree's expression grew somber and she began anxiously rubbing her arm. "Yeah. But it's really strained. He's still pissed at me and was even talking about splitting up for a minute."

"And you don't want that?" Natalia verified.

"No! Y'all, I am still *so* in love with Lorenzo...I had to damn near beg him to stop talking about us breaking up. And when have you known me to beg a man for anything that didn't involve food or sex?"

Kira laughed and Natalia nudged her with her foot, even though she was trying to hold back a smile, herself. Lovey's face was turning red from trying to hold hers in.

"So I have to ask this, girl...why did you turn down his proposal, then?" Natalia asked.

"I...I don't know," Desiree whimpered. "In the moment, the thought of it all just freaked me out. I've never wanted to get married...well, not in years, I haven't. That's just where my mind automatically went when he asked."

"And you're feeling differently now?" Lovey asked. "Because really, if you two don't want the same things, then it might just be best to let him go. It can't work in the long-term."

"I don't want to let him go. Lorenzo is it for me. I tried to explain to him that I panicked in the moment and that it doesn't mean I don't love him; when he asked, my mind flashed through all the bullshit I've been through with men and it paralyzed me. But I was regretting it as soon as I saw that look on his face."

"What did he say when you told him all of that?"

"He said he understood. But I know he's still hurt. And probably embarrassed. I wish I'd known he was going to propose in front of everybody like that."

"It was a surprise, Desiree," Natalia reminded her, amused.

"I'm not good with surprises. Clearly."

"I think you two can work this out," Lovey stated, placing a hand on Desiree's knee. "But you need to make sure you're completely honest with him going forward about where you are with things. If you're having fears or doubts, let him know."

"And if you don't think you want kids, make sure you're straight up with him about *that* now, too," Natalia added. "Trust me, you don't want those issues."

Lovey and Desiree looked at her sympathetically while Kira just shook her head, holding Xavier's tiny wrists as he danced around in front of her.

"I'll just say it; I don't know what your problem is, sis," she stated. "I can't *wait* to have kids."

"It's not for everybody," Lovey commented.

"Yeah, but Natalia should have thought about that *before* she married a man that she knew wanted a family. And anyway, who knows how she'd feel if she gave him what he wanted? She could change her tune."

"But what if she doesn't?" Desiree spoke up. "What if she had the kid just to appease E.J. and then ended up resenting the child *and* him? That's a recipe for disaster."

"I just believe a woman should do anything possible to make her man happy," Kira replied with a shrug. "As long as it's not anything crazy. Otherwise, why are you even together?"

Natalia thought about her sister's words as the ladies continued to go back and forth. She didn't believe a woman should have a baby just to please her man, but Natalia's resistance wasn't about not wanting to be a mother. It was more about what being a mother would do to her and E.J.'s relationship. But the truth was, she had no way of knowing what would happen, and her fear was causing more damage to their relationship than having a child probably would. It was a fact that hadn't occurred to her until that moment.

When she and Kira were headed home, Natalia didn't have a lot to say as Kira went on and on about how cute little Xavier was. She looked over at her sister, who was clearly deep in thought.

"You mad about what I said?" Kira asked her.

"No. You're entitled to your opinion."

"You disagree, though."

"It doesn't matter, Kira. I already know I've handled this situation all wrong. It's on me to figure out what to do about it."

"You think E.J. would leave you? If you keep refusing to get pregnant?"

Natalia winced. "He said he wouldn't."

"Hmph. Well, I hope you come to your senses. You've got a good man. One that a whole bunch of women would gladly pop out as many babies as he wants for. I know E.J. loves you and everything and he's trying to stick to his commitment, but...a man can only take so much."

"Whatever. I'm not taking marriage advice from someone who hasn't been in a relationship longer than a *Real Housewives* season."

Kira sucked her teeth and started scrolling on her phone, but her words stuck in Natalia's mind, despite herself. She believed E.J. when he said he didn't want to leave her over all this, but everyone had a breaking point. If he ultimately decided that he couldn't get past her deception, then what? What if a baby was something he just couldn't let go of?

Tears were stinging her eyes at the mere thought of losing E.J. Natalia knew she couldn't let that happen.

As soon as she got home, she tossed out the rest of the condoms.

Chapter 10

• • • •

E.J.'S MUSCLES BURNED as he finished his last set of chest presses, pushing more weight than usual. He had a lot of tension to work off and looked forward to feeling the delicious soreness later.

Sitting up on the bench, he wiped his face with a towel before reaching for his water jug, taking a long swig. He had a long day ahead of him, and he needed this intense workout to clear his head. He'd been admittedly grouchy given how up-and-down things had been with Natalia, not to mention the disagreement with Roland over the buyout offer and having an unwanted houseguest, along with the general headaches that came with running multiple businesses.

"E.J.?"

He glanced up, barely registering the woman that addressed him. "Yes?"

"Oh my god, how are you? It's been so long!"

He started to brush her off as he usually did when women did the pretending-to-know-him game, but then he realized he knew that voice. He looked up again, and his frown cleared when he recognized who was grinning down at him. "Lyric?"

"And here I was thinking you forgot about me," she commented amusingly. "Which would've been pretty insulting, considering we were together for over a year."

"Sorry about that." E.J. stood, receiving her light hug. He smiled at her. "Damn, it's been a minute. What's been going on with you?"

"I'm still in the journalism field. I'm hosting a new lifestyle show, plus my blog and podcast are both doing really well."

"Glad to hear that. Congrats."

"Thanks. I'll admit I already know you're killing it with entrepreneurship. Barfly is the spot to be, especially on the weekends. And my parents rented space at 845 for their anniversary party."

"Yeah? I didn't know that."

"Well, you never met them; we didn't get to that point since they were living out of state at the time," Lyric reminded with an easy smile. There was no resentment to be found in her tone or her expression. "Wow, I just can't believe I'm running into you like this. You look as great as ever."

E.J. could say the same about her, although he didn't. Her tawny brown skin was just as dewy as ever, and she always looked like she was ready to shoot a toothpaste ad. When she ran a hand over her ponytail, E.J. noticed that her black hair had grown significantly since he last saw her. And the black sports bra and leggings showed off what great shape she was still in.

"I appreciate it," he replied.

"You got married, right?" she verified, glancing at his left hand.

"Yep. You?"

"I did, but it didn't last long, unfortunately. He didn't turn out to be who I thought he was; I don't do well with people keeping secrets from me and he was the king of that."

Of course E.J.'s mind automatically went to Natalia. A frown started to form but he quickly cleared it; he didn't have time to hop back on the weights because he'd worked himself back up. "I hate to hear that. Well, Lyric, I need to get going; I've got a lot going on today that I need to get a jump on."

"Still the workaholic machine, huh?" Lyric chuckled. "Some things never change. I respect it, though. Keep in touch with me; I'm on social media under my maiden name. Maybe we can meet up for drinks or something. With your wife, too, of course."

"I don't know about that, but it was definitely good to see you. Take care of yourself, Lyric." He gave her a small nod before turning and heading to the locker room.

By the time he'd showered and dressed, the encounter with Lyric was forgotten. He headed straight over to 845, diving into the list of things he had to do for the day as he chugged the protein shake he'd brought with him. His tension eased as he buried himself in work, making notes to go over with Roland later.

When two o'clock rolled around and he still hadn't seen or heard from his brother, E.J. wondered what was going on. They were supposed to go over some things with their business manager about their merchandise, and they needed to hop on a call with their social media manager. And he and Roland never finished their discussion about E.J. buying him out of the businesses.

After E.J. finished booking Barfly's entertainment for the next couple of months, he smiled as he looked over the things they had in the works. Barfly was still jumping, so much so that they decided to open it one more night a week. Desiree did a great job hosting events for them, keeping things new and fresh with a variety of themes and bringing in the occasional celebrity guest to host parties. 845 was more exclusive and upscale, only being open three nights a week. It catered to a different demographic than Barfly, which was more laid back. It was a challenge balancing the two but E.J. loved it. He and Roland had really made a name for themselves in the industry; barely a day went by without them being approached to partner with this influencer or that brand or some other company, or for an interview.

Checking the time, E.J. finally called Roland, an impatient frown already forming.

"What's up, man?" Roland answered.

"What do you mean, what's up? Where are you?"

"I'm at home."

"Why, you sick or something?"

"No..."

"You know I don't care if you work from home but it would be nice if you let me know. We had shit to do today."

There was a pause. "I see you forgot."

"Forgot what?"

"It's me and Lovey's anniversary, man," Roland reminded him, his voice biting. "I told you a while back that I'd be spending today with my wife."

His frown vanishing, E.J. closed his eyes, kicking himself. "Damn, man, my bad. That *did* slip my mind, I admit."

"See, this is what I'm talking about. All you think about is work. Do you even remember when your *own* anniversary is?"

E.J. scoffed, though he *did* have to take a moment to think about it. "Of course I do."

"One day you're gonna realize that it's okay for other things to come first sometimes," Roland told him. "Doing what you love is all good. But when are you gonna let yourself enjoy what you've been working so hard to build? Is everybody supposed to wait while you keep chasing the bag? Life is to be *lived*, man. Loosen the hell up."

E.J. was still holding the phone moments after Roland hung up, his words sinking in. He recalled Natalia saying something similar to him. He hadn't gotten that bad...had he?

• • • •

THE REST OF THE DAY went on, but E.J. didn't have the same vigor that he had when he started it. He was pretty much just going through the motions.

Forgetting his brother's anniversary made him feel terrible. He'd been team Lovey ever since she came into the picture, and especially when she and Desiree were vying for Roland's affections. Roland had never been happier than since he'd been with Lovey, and it bugged E.J. that such a special day slipped his mind.

More than that, though, the whole situation with Natalia was like a siphon to his mental energy. Things were okay since the night they semi-reconciled and fooled around some, but they were *just* okay...their issues were still lurking in the shadows, waiting to start blaring again.

E.J. knew they wouldn't really be able to move forward until they came to a final conclusion about the baby issue. While he respected where his wife was coming from (or at least tried to), he didn't know if he could ever agree to never having kids. There wasn't a scenario where he saw himself being okay with that. He didn't want to get to where he resented Natalia for denying him something he truly wanted. And thankfully, she knew that, so they made an appointment with a marriage counselor. It gave E.J. a modicum of hope that they were taking steps forward instead of just going around in the same circle that had been making them dizzy for the past few months.

When E.J. finally got home that night, he was mildly disappointed to see that Natalia wasn't home. She'd said that she was coming to the end of the project she'd been working so much on, and would likely beat him to the house. Apparently not, though.

He was sending her a text letting her know that he was there and was looking forward to seeing her when Kira came knocking. E.J. had almost forgotten about her.

"I'm so glad you're back," she expressed, releasing a dramatic sigh as she removed her magenta-colored puffy jacket. "It's been a *stupid* day."

E.J. wasn't sure how to respond to her day being *stupid*, so he just grunted. "Sure."

"I thought Natalia would be home by now."

"You and me both."

"Hmm...that's interesting."

E.J. stood from where he'd been peering inside the refrigerator and glanced at her. "What's interesting?"

Kira pursed her lips for a moment, then shook her head. "Nothing," she chirped, giving him a wide smile. "I'm gonna go change clothes real quick."

She skipped out of the room and E.J. squinted after her, then shrugged and went back to deciding what he was going to eat. By the time he was finished heating up some chicken and spaghetti squash and taking a seat at the kitchen table, Kira was bouncing back into the kitchen wearing some tan leggings that looked like they were painted on and a cutoff shirt. Her silver belly ring gleamed as she approached him.

"Mind if I join you?" she asked, grabbing some chips out of the pantry.

He did, but E.J. was trying not to be rude. "Knock yourself out."

She took a seat opposite him at the table, loudly opening the bag and crunching on the sour cream and cheddar chips. E.J. tried to ignore her as he proceeded to check emails on his phone.

"Whatcha doin'?" Kira asked, leaning over slightly and peering at his phone.

"Kira," E.J.'s eyes were still on his phone screen, "You should know me well enough by now to know I don't care for small talk."

"Oh, sorry. Guess I'm just one of those people that hates sitting in silence. Can't help it, I guess."

"Well, try harder."

"I did want to ask you again about the job thing, though," Kira persisted, somewhat hesitantly. "I know we got interrupted when I went to your office. How didn't I know that Roland was your brother?"

"No idea, 'cause damn near everybody else does. Speaking of that," E.J. finally looked up at her, "Why did you run out of there like you did when you saw him? How do y'all know each other?"

"Oh, well..." She stuffed her mouth full of chips and shrugged. "You know how it is."

"I don't like the coy game, either, Kira."

"We just had an unfortunate meeting, is all. It's really not that interesting of a story. Plus it was years ago. Can we get back to the part about me working for you?"

"Nothing to talk about there. I'm not hiring you."

"Awww. How come??"

"Because your work history is shit, Kira. You've never even been at a job longer than six months. And from what I've heard, you're not exactly a model employee when you have one."

"But I'd be different for you," she insisted, pushing the bag of chips aside and looking straight into his eyes. "Maybe I didn't care anything about any of those people but...you're different. I wouldn't let you down."

"It shouldn't matter who it is, Kira. If you take on a responsibility, you should have enough pride in yourself to go one hundred with it."

"You're right. You're absolutely right. And I *swear*, if you gave me a chance, I'd be all in. I'd do anything for you, E.J."

Her gaze at him softened before she caught herself, tucking some braids behind her hear and tracing circles on the table with her long nail. "Not everybody can say that."

His eyes narrowed and he started to ignore that statement, but couldn't. "And just what do you mean by that?"

"You know I love my sister," Kira began, her eyes still on her twirling finger, "But once she digs her heels in about something, that's it. And – don't cuss me out for this – she's *not* gonna change her mind about babies. I told her she was being stupid, but you know how stubborn she is. All I'm saying is...*I'm* not like her."

His face hardening, E.J. stood, tossing his fork onto his half-eaten food. "You really need to stay in your lane, Kira. Don't let yourself get too comfortable."

"Just trying to help." Kira eyed E.J. as he stomped to the sink and scraped his uneaten food down the garbage disposal. When he started to head out of the room, she blurted, "Where did she tell you she was tonight?"

Pausing, E.J. turned. "Excuse me?"

Standing, Kira rolled up the bag of chips and pushed her chair under the table, taking her time. She sauntered over to him, looking up at him and standing a little too close when she said, "Just ask her who she was with this evening. You know, whenever she makes it home."

She continued out of the room, leaving him standing there to fume about what she said.

Chapter 11

. . . .

NATALIA KNEW MEETING up with Dane probably wasn't the smartest idea.

They'd been in casual contact ever since they ran into each other at the bar, which she didn't feel bad about since E.J. knew about it and it wasn't anything inappropriate; they were all text conversations that centered mostly on jokes, generic topics, and the occasional memory from their past. Whenever he tried to get too personal, she shut him down; she had no interest in getting close to Dane again.

What she didn't let herself consider was why she was even bothering with him at all. They didn't end on the best of terms, and she had long since moved on. She'd held a grudge against him for years – hence the block – but she had E.J. now so she figured she could leave the past in the past. Communicating with Dane was just something to do.

But then he started talking about them meeting up, and she immediately refused, but Dane had always been persistent. He insisted that he had no ulterior motive; that he just wanted to have a drink as friends. Against Natalia's better judgment, she agreed.

Of course, E.J. thought she was working, and the thin thread of dread steadily weaved through her the entire time she was with Dane. Natalia knew she should've let E.J. know where she really was, and the fact that she didn't made her uneasy. It wasn't lost on her that this was yet another thing she was hiding from her husband, and she wondered when she'd gotten so comfortable doing that. That never used to be her.

"You look like you've got a lot on your mind," Dane commented from across the table. They were at a hole-in-the-wall spot on the edge of town, at Natalia's suggestion. "What's wrong?"

Natalia looked at him and shook her head. "I shouldn't be here."

"Why?"

"Because you aren't my husband. And the man who is doesn't know where I am."

"You should've told him, then. Must be a reason you didn't."

Her eyes narrowed. "Meaning?"

"Maybe you're not as over me as you thought," Dane stated smoothly, sipping his beer while his eyes stayed on her. "You wouldn't be here if you didn't want to be and we both know it."

"Just because I'm having a damn beer with you doesn't mean I want to hop on your dick, Dane. Don't read more into it than it is."

"As much as I love the thought of you hopping on my dick, that's not what I'm talking about. How we ended...things were left up in the air. That never sat right with me and apparently it didn't with you, either."

"I'm over that."

"Really? So you never think about how you went behind my back and aborted our baby, then dumped me in a fucking email?"

Some of her frustration cooled when she looked at him. "I apologized for that."

"*In a text*. You refused to see me in person. Which I think I deserved because I certainly didn't want you to get rid of our baby like you did. Hell, I was making plans to get a bigger place so you could move in with me."

"I told you I wasn't trying to just shack up. We were going back and forth about the marriage subject and you weren't exactly all for it."

"So what? That doesn't mean you had the right to make that kind of decision without me. I was excited about having a baby with you, Natalia. And you took that from me."

The guilt that Natalia had managed to suppress over the years came roaring back. Leaning across the table, she touched her hand to his. "I'm sincerely sorry about that, Dane. At the time, I just couldn't see having a baby with a man that didn't want to marry me. But you're right, I shouldn't have just...that was foul of me, to have that abortion and then shut you out. Maybe it doesn't matter after all this time but I really do hope you can forgive me."

His hand grabbed hers. "I *have* forgiven you, Natalia. That's why I was so happy when I ran into you. I was pissed about that situation for years but I never stopped missing you. I *still* miss you."

She tried to ease her hand away but his grip tightened. "Dane-"

"I want you back."

Recoiling, she sputtered, "Wh-what??"

"You heard me. I've been comparing every woman I've been with over the years to you and none even come close, despite the foul shit you did. I can't even tell you how many nights I laid in bed and ached that you weren't there with me."

"You've lost your mind," she scoffed, snatching her hand away. "I'm not leaving my husband for you. There's no way in hell."

"Stay with him, then. I don't mind being your side piece."

"Are you high??"

"I've never before said that to another woman but I'm willing to take what I can get of you, Honeybun. I still love you."

"I'm not your damn Honeybun anymore, Dane. And I'm not a cheater, either."

"Natalia-"

Her phone rang with E.J.'s special ringtone, and Natalia grimaced. Of course he would call when she was somewhere she had no business being.

Grabbing the phone, she looked at Dane and pressed a finger to her lips before answering. "H-hey, baby."

"Hey." His voice sounded strange. "Where are you?"

"I'm just...out at a bar."

"What bar?"

"Just having a drink after work-"

"I'm gonna run to the bathroom, baby," Dane announced loudly, making sure E.J. could hear him. Natalia's eyes bugged before she practically turned red from anger, giving him a murderous glare. "I'll be right back."

"Who the hell was that??" E.J. demanded, his voice rising.

Natalia couldn't believe she'd been so stupid. Again. Cutting her eyes at Dane's retreating back, she sighed. "That was Dane. He asked me to grab a drink after work-"

"And you chose not to tell me about that, huh? I thought you were working. Had no idea you were sneaking off with your ex."

"It's not like that, baby. We're in a public place having a beer, that's it."

"Why didn't you tell me where you were going, then?"

"I..." Natalia knew she had no defense for that. "I should have."

"And he called you 'baby.' What the fuck was that?"

"He was being an asshole because he knew it was you on the phone. E.J., baby, I *swear-*"

"Get your ass home," E.J. growled. "*Now.*"

Natalia knew she was in trouble. She should've known agreeing to meet Dane was going to bite her in the ass.

"I'll be there soon," she muttered, hanging up and draining the rest of her beer. It was the only one she'd had so she knew she'd be fine driving home, though she wished she could get something stronger to steel herself for the storm that she knew would be waiting on her when she walked through the front door.

Dane came strolling back to the table as Natalia was putting on her coat. "Where are you going?"

"Home," she bitingly replied, not even looking at him.

"Just like that? We're not finished with our conversation."

"Oh, we're absolutely finished, asshole. You knew good and well what you were doing, calling me out like that."

He sighed, stepping closer to her before she shot him a warning glare. "I'm sorry about that."

"No you're not. You did that on purpose and it was petty as shit. So I hope you're happy. And I hope it was worth whatever satisfaction you got from it 'cause it damn sure won't be happening again. Consider yourself re-blocked."

"Come on, Natalia-"

"Shut up! I apologized for the shit I did so we officially have nothing else to talk about. Go to hell."

She turned and stormed out, the sound of her heels clicking against the concrete floor partially drowning out Dane calling after her.

The ride home was tauntingly short, as she made every green light and there were almost no cars on the road. Natalia knew that E.J. was furious, and he had a right to be. She surely would've been if he'd gone out with his ex without telling her, no matter the reason. She knew she wasn't doing a very good job of winning his trust back with stupid decisions like this.

The yelling started almost as soon as she was through the door, and they went back and forth for several minutes, with Natalia pleading her case and E.J. lighting into her for yet another deception. Arguments were nothing new for them lately but she was actually fearful of what would come of this one; Natalia didn't think she'd *ever* seen E.J. so angry.

"What the fuck are you doing going on dates with your ex, Natalia?"

She tried to gather words that wouldn't dig her hole any deeper. "I know I should've told you where I was going but it was *not* a date. Dane and I just had some things that needed to be hashed out, that's all!"

"Like?"

"Just unresolved shit from when we broke up. I haven't thought about it in years but apparently he has. It wasn't anything even remotely romantic."

"You'll have to forgive me if I'm having a hard time buying this, seeing as how you seem to have a habit of keeping things from me lately." E.J. stood with his arms folded, looking at her as if he was trying to figure her out. "I don't know what's happened to us but...this isn't it. What we have now isn't the kind of marriage I want, Natalia."

Her stomach dropped at his words, and she pressed a hand against it, feeling suddenly unsteady. "What does that mean?"

"It means I don't feel like I know you anymore," E.J. replied, evident pain in his voice. "One thing I always loved about you was your candor. Hell, you used to *over*-share. But now I never know what's going on with you or what to believe. We're supposed to be able to trust each other."

"I..." Natalia blinked back tears. "I don't have a defense for that. I've made some really bad decisions these past few months. And I'm sorry for that, baby; I truly, truly am."

"You keep apologizing but I don't see anything changing, Natalia."

"E.J. I'm...you have to know that this hasn't been a picnic for me, either. My head has been so jumbled up lately that it has me doing stuff I wouldn't normally do. But please know that I love you as much as I always have. And I want nothing more than for us to come out of this together."

"Right," he scoffed, actually rolling his eyes.

She reeled. "Why are you saying it like that?"

"Where are the condoms?"

"What?"

"There's nothing wrong with your damn ears. Where are the fucking condoms that you insisted on getting that used to be in the nightstand? I looked earlier and they're all gone. And I know *we* haven't used them."

"Oh my god..." Natalia had temporarily forgotten she'd thrown those out and didn't tell him. "E.J., the only dick I've had or want is yours. I am *not* cheating on you. I swear on my daddy's grave I'm not!"

His shoulders relaxed, but only a little. "So where are they, then?"

"I threw them out."

"Why?"

"Because..." She walked over to him, placing her hands on his chest. "I've been thinking about things and I realized what my issue was, as far as having kids. I love what we've had going on so much that I was afraid of anything changing it. It would be easier if I could see into the future and be assured that things would be just as good or better, but I can't."

His eyes studied hers as if he was deciding whether to buy her explanation or not. "So you're saying you're ready to start trying, then? You want to have a baby now?"

"I...I *wanna* be ready..."

"Fuck!" He exclaimed, his head falling back as he backed away from her, crossing his arms over his eyes. "Is anything *ever* easy with you?"

"Me? What about *you*, E.J.?"

"Excuse me?"

"I know I'm not the easiest to deal with but you sure as hell aren't, either."

"How did this get to be about me?"

"You want honesty so here it is. I love you, but being your wife can be overwhelming because your expectations are so damn high. Not to mention, the only person you hang with outside of me is Roland."

"So?"

"E.J., baby, you don't have any other outlets. And since Roland has gotten married and had a baby, more of that focus has fallen on me. And it can be a lot."

"I can't believe this shit," he muttered incredulously. "Now I give you *too much* attention? A minute ago you were talking about how scared you were about things changing, now you're complaining about how they currently are. Which one is it, Natalia?"

"I'm not complaining. It's..." She pressed her hands to her face, momentarily stumped for words. "You don't get it."

"No, I don't. Somehow we went from you explaining why you were sneaking off with your ex without telling me to me being to blame for it, like I'm the damn bad guy. It sounds like you're deflecting. Again."

"I'm not deflecting, nor am I blaming you for my dumb decision to see Dane. I fully owned my shit. And now I'm telling you about yours. You wanted candor, right? Well, I'm telling you that you need something outside of me or work to focus on sometimes. A hobby or *something*. You're just so rigid and disciplined and generally speaking, I love that about you but, baby...you hardly even laugh anymore." She looked at him, her eyes pleading for understanding as her hands fell to her sides. "I can't remember the last time I heard you laugh. Do you realize that?"

"What have I had to laugh about lately, Natalia?"

"Even before, E.J. You've never exactly been lighthearted or easygoing."

"And that makes me a bad person?"

"I didn't say that. I wouldn't be so head over heels for you if that were the case. But we all have room for improvement; I know *I* do. And I'm just lovingly telling you that you do, too. It's not about me trying to take the heat off myself." She moved over to him, leaning up and kissing his lips. "If we're gonna be better together, we need to keep working on ourselves individually. Please let your guard down and listen to what I'm saying."

She briefly pressed her hand to the side of his face for a moment before walking past him to the bathroom, leaving him standing there pondering.

• • • •

IT WAS PAST E.J.'S usual bedtime but he couldn't sleep. The conversation with Natalia was heavy on his mind.

He sat in his darkened den, his head leaned against the back of the couch. The TV was on showing the news, muted. E.J.'s eyes were on the screen but his mind was on what his wife had told him. Her words had been steadily sinking in ever since she left him standing in the middle of their bedroom.

It never occurred to him that his personality was such a point of contention for her. He knew he demanded a lot of other people but it had nothing on what he demanded from himself. To hear that she felt overwhelmed with him was humbling. He hadn't been arrogant enough to think he was without flaw, but this was the first time Natalia had brought this to his attention. Even if she was deflecting some, it didn't mean it wasn't valid.

Especially since he could recall his ex-girlfriend Lyric saying something similar when they were together. He'd dismissed it at the time but now it made him wonder.

Sitting forward, he rested his elbows on his knees and drug his hands down his face before hanging his head. The confliction between his anger at Natalia's deceptions and his own apparent part in things felt heavy on him. Was he somehow to blame for the state their marriage was in? He wanted to take any ownership he was due, but try as he might, he couldn't twist things to make himself at fault for her lying to him years ago about wanting to have a baby when she didn't. Even if she was afraid of his reaction, he still deserved to know the truth about that.

Thinking about all of this was agitating him. He dropped to the floor and did push-ups until his arms and chest burned, but the frustration about the situation remained. A hundred crunches didn't help, either.

He grimaced at the sound of the television in the guest room and Kira laughing. He so wanted that woman out of his house. But he then wondered if maybe he was being unreasonable about that, too. He wasn't the picture of maturity at twenty-two, either. Maybe he could be more patient, which wasn't something he was usually good at.

But he thought about how things had been since he found out about Natalia's lies and he figured he'd been *more* than patient when it came to that, because it hadn't exactly been uphill since and he was still there. He wanted to work things out. Didn't that count for anything?

Snatching his phone, he called the one other person he knew would be straight up with him.

"E.J., what's up?" Roland asked, his voice low.

"I'm sorry about calling so late," E.J. droned, easing himself back onto the couch. "I need to talk, if you have a minute."

"Yeah, of course. Give me a second." There were some rustling sounds and E.J. figured Roland was moving to another room. "Okay, what's going on?"

"I didn't wake you, did I?"

"Nah, I was up. You know I'm a night owl. I was just in bed reading. Lovey is asleep so I came downstairs. I'm surprised *you're* up, though."

"Yeah, I've got a lot on my mind. This might seem out of the blue, but...am I difficult?"

Roland paused. "In what way?"

"Just in general. Am I hard to deal with?"

"I mean, yeah, you can be. But I've certainly been around worse. Why?"

"Because Natalia said something tonight that got me thinking about my part in all this shit we're in now. Then it made me remember something Lyric said back in the day..."

"Wow, there's a name I haven't heard in a while."

"I never think about her. Our split was amicable but once we were over, I moved on. But I happened to run into her the other day at the gym and after Natalia said the stuff about how I can be hard to live with and that it's hard being my only outlet-"

"Your only outlet?"

"Yeah, she said that I don't have anything to focus on other than her. And work, I guess. Especially now that more of your time is going to your family, all that energy is going to her. Which is apparently a bad thing since I'm not the life of the party. Oh, and I have super-high expectations."

"You saying you don't?"

"No, but it's not like I'm expecting perfection. *I'm* not perfect. But when my wife keeps lying to my face, am I not supposed to get angry about that?"

"I would. You deserve honesty from your wife, no doubt."

"Thank you!"

"*But* we've also established that you're stubborn, brother. And you tend to think your way is the only way, and God help whoever doesn't fall in line with that. You can cut people off like it's nothing and that can be intimidating to people that care about you."

"You think I do that, huh?"

"Man, what did you just say about Lyric? You *never* think about her. Y'all were together for a while, and you didn't even have a falling out, but yet it's almost like she quit existing to you. I can see how Natalia would be afraid of the same thing happening to her if you got fed up enough."

"Well, she's not doing much to help prevent that, with how she keeps messing up."

"Man, that happens. We all do stupid shit. But this marriage thing is supposed to be for better or for worse. I'm not defending her mistakes but you're not the easiest person to make mistakes *with*. Once you feel wronged or betrayed, it's hard as hell getting back on your good side."

E.J. started to retort, but paused. He thought about the situation with Desiree's mistreatment of Roland and Lovey a few years earlier, and how he was the last one to forgive her, even though he hadn't even been directly involved in it. And he knew he had a tendency to shut down when he got pissed off, but that was his way of avoiding doing or saying something he'd regret. He never claimed it was the best way.

"Could this also be referring to the situation with the buyout?" he eventually asked.

"It could," Roland admitted. "You're taking it personally that I'm interested in the offer when it really isn't even about you. Regardless, we're always gonna be brothers, whether we're running those clubs together or not. I wouldn't let that come between us, but you would. You *have*."

Knowing Roland had a point, E.J. cursed under his breath. "Guess I can't deny that."

"It's okay for plans to change sometimes, man. Believe me, I get your reasoning for not wanting to sell. In a lot of ways, I'm right there with you. And I know we need to make a decision, but I'll take some more time to think about it, 'cause I want to respect your position as much as I want you to respect mine. In the meantime, maybe it wouldn't hurt for you to find a hobby or something, and I'm not talking about listening to those dry audiobooks and Ted Talks."

"Maybe that's what I consider enjoyable."

"Man, do something mindless sometimes. Something that serves no purpose other than it makes you laugh or feel good."

E.J. tapped his fist against his knee. "Natalia said she couldn't remember the last time she heard me laugh."

"I believe it. Hell, getting a grin out of you is an achievement. I've said it once and I'll say it again; loosen up."

"You've given me a lot to think about."

"Dig that. And I'm proud of you for even getting to the point where you're considering your part in everything; that's progress."

"I appreciate it."

"And know this, E.J.; even though I'm married with a baby, it doesn't mean I'm not still here for you. We're *always* gonna be tight, man. Don't forget that."

That made E.J. smile. "Good to know. I actually needed to hear that."

"Get some rest; it's late. Love you, brother."

"Love you back."

E.J. hung up, feeling a little better. Getting some clarity on what he needed to work on within himself gave him a strange sense of relief. It was going to be a challenge, but he didn't run from those.

He groaned when he saw how late it was, knowing he only had a few hours before he needed to be up to go to the gym. Pushing himself off the couch, he turned the television off and trudged out of the room, the tiredness finally catching up to him.

After double-checking all the doors downstairs and making sure the security system was set, he headed for the stairs. When he passed the guest room, he could hear Kira's voice, apparently talking to someone on the phone. He didn't think anything of it until he heard something about a plan coming together. E.J. wasn't inherently nosy, but his suspicion radar was immediately going off. He paused at the door, leaning closer to listen over the sound of the television she had going.

"I know, but I can't help it," she was saying, then there was the sound of a soda can being opened and some rustling of the bedsheets. "He's just...he does something to me; makes me get all outside of myself. And she doesn't even appreciate what she has."

E.J. didn't want to assume she was talking about him, but he recalled all of her flirting and revealing outfits that seemed to disappear whenever Natalia was around, not to mention her comment about being willing to do anything for him. He'd skimmed over that at the time but now he couldn't help but wonder just what she'd meant by that. Maybe she wasn't just talking about trying to be his best employee.

"I *will* have him," Kira's declared, her voice rising slightly. "You can believe that."

Chapter 12

• • • •

BARELY FOUR HOURS LATER, E.J. was back up and getting ready for the gym, though he was uncharacteristically dreading it. Lack of sleep had him grumpy.

It didn't help any when Kira came bouncing into the living room where he was packing his duffel bag. She was dressed in workout clothes.

"Going to the gym?" she asked.

He eyed her, resisting the urge to point out what a dumb question that was. She knew he was going to the gym; he went at the same time every morning. "Yeah."

"Mind if I join you?"

E.J. straightened to full height, looking at her. He hadn't forgotten what he'd overheard through her door a few hours earlier. Part of him wanted to ask her about it while the other part told him it was nothing. And confliction frustrated E.J. almost as much as lack of sleep. "Why?"

"Figured it would be good to switch things up; maybe a good workout will help clear my head for job searching."

"You've had at least three interviews since you've been here and you've apparently bombed them all."

"I was just nervous. But I'm getting better at what to say and what not to say."

"It shouldn't be that hard, Kira."

"I'm still new to all this. But I told you, I'm gonna get it together. I'm gonna make you proud of me."

His mind automatically going to what he overheard earlier, he demanded, "Exactly what do you mean by that? Why is it so important for me to be proud of you?"

The question momentarily stumped her. "Uhh..."

"Are you trying to make something happen between you and me?"

"What? No!" Her voice rose to an almost squeaky level, and she started chuckling nervously. "Wh-why would I do that? You're married to my sister!"

"So all the flirting and the revealing clothes mean nothing, huh?"

"I'm proud of my body."

"And the flirting?"

"It's harmless. I flirt with everybody."

"I'm just being clear that if you have anything on your mind about you and me being anything other than in-laws, you're deluding yourself. I'm a one-woman man and that woman is Natalia. Not you or anybody else has a shot in hell with me."

He could see something flit across her face at his statement. "I get it, E.J. All I meant by what I said earlier was that I respect you and how you move; your hustle is something serious. And you're mad successful. I could learn a lot from you; that's all."

Choosing to leave it at that even though he didn't totally believe her, E.J. lifted the hood of his hoodie over his head. "All right."

"I still want to go with you to the gym, though, if I can," Kira blurted before he could walk off. "I need to get a good workout in. I swear I won't bug you."

It was on the tip of his tongue to deny her again but he remembered the recent declarations that he needed to loosen up, and finally relented. "Fine. Hurry up and let's go."

She grinned and ran to the guest room to get her things. They left a few minutes later, with E.J. initially having no intention of saying much but figuring it wouldn't hurt to try to get to know her better.

"What were you in school for?" he finally asked after whirling through a mental list of questions.

"Nursing."

"Why'd you quit?"

She shrugged, looking out the window. It was still dark outside. "Realized it wasn't what I really wanted to do. I only tried it 'cause my friends were."

"What is it that you like to do?"

"Good question."

"It takes some people longer than others, sometimes."

"Exactly." She cast a grateful glance at him. "Folks just say I'm making excuses when I say that. Calling me a spoiled brat. Or that I'm lazy. Truth be told, my family really doesn't know me as well as they think they do."

E.J. regretted trying to strike a conversation. He was feeling awkward, not knowing what to say, and it made him uncomfortable. Which annoyed him.

They rode the rest of the way to the gym in silence. Kira kept her word and went off to work out by herself once they were inside, to E.J.'s relief. He went on about his workout, firing up an entrepreneurial podcast to listen to as he warmed up on the treadmill. He put Kira and her issues out of his mind as he got geared up to push some weights.

He zoned out as he worked his chest and triceps until they screamed for mercy. Sweat poured from his face, stinging his eyes as he did a fourth set of tricep dips on the bench. His muscles were on fire, but he gritted his teeth and pushed forward, refusing to stop until he was done. When he finally was, he pushed himself onto the bench, sitting and panting slightly. He plucked his towel from his waistband and swiped it over his face before tossing it over his shoulder, giving himself another few seconds to rest before standing.

"You're putting in some serious work this morning."

E.J. looked over his shoulder, the automatic frown at being bothered already in place, then he recognized who was speaking to him. His face cleared as he turned with a small smile.

"Hey, what's going on, Lorenzo?"

Shrugging a huge shoulder, Lorenzo wiped his hands on his own towel before he and E.J. touched fists. "Just getting this workout in before I get my day started. I was just wrapping up when I saw you over here."

"I didn't see you come in."

"You were focused on what you were doing. As was I, which is why I didn't see you at first, either."

"You usually come to this gym?"

"Yeah, but it's usually at the end of the day. I just knew I wouldn't have time later on so I'm getting it in early."

"I feel that." E.J. was mildly curious about where things stood between Lorenzo and Desiree after she declined his marriage proposal, but not enough to ask. He wasn't nosy and also, he didn't know Lorenzo well enough to pry into his personal life like that. "It's a must for me to do mine first thing. Gets my mind right for the day. Plus, I have to go see my boys tonight."

Lorenzo's brows lifted curiously. "Your boys?"

"Yeah, the ones I mentor."

"Yeah? I do that, too. Was just with them last night; took them to get fitted for their first suits. You should've seen how proud they were; stylin' and profilin'."

E.J. chuckled, inspired. He made a mental note to take Teddy and Nigel for suits, since he was quite sure they didn't have any. They always wore plain button-down shirts and khakis for any occasion that called for them to dress up. "Every man should have at least one. I'm gonna do that for my boys, too."

"This might make me sound like a sap, but it's really amazing how much I've grown to love those boys. It's gonna be tough for me when they graduate and go off to school; I can only hope they'll still keep in touch."

"Nothing sappy about that, man. I feel the same way about mine. I'm just glad I can play a positive role in their lives, especially since their dads aren't around."

"Same."

They continued to talk for a few minutes, E.J. temporarily forgetting about the tight schedule he usually kept himself on in the gym. He'd been around Lorenzo several times; he was an old friend of Roland's who moved back to the area a couple of years earlier and then started dating Desiree. But they never exchanged more than casual greetings or minimal conversation. Surprisingly, E.J. found that he didn't hate talking to Lorenzo at all.

When Kira sauntered over, E.J. almost asked her what she was doing there; he'd totally forgotten she'd come there with him.

"Aren't *you* a big hunk of caramel," she flirted, clear lust slanting her eyes as she gazed up at Lorenzo. "Don't I know you from somewhere? Like every fantasy I've had since I was twelve?"

E.J. rolled his eyes as Lorenzo chuckled. "I'm flattered, but I'm also spoken for."

Kira looked to E.J. "Did you tell him to say that?"

"No need for me to do all that," E.J. replied. "This is a grown man who can speak for himself."

"Hmph." Kira turned her attention back to Lorenzo, sliding a hand behind her neck and jutting her breasts forward. "I wouldn't mind being your little secret. You'd never have to worry about me saying anything about it."

"*I'd* mind," Lorenzo wasted no time replying. "And my lady Desiree would, too. More than that, though, a pretty young lady like yourself shouldn't be so willing to settle for being a side piece."

"Wait, Desiree??" Kia marveled, her hand dropping to her side. "You're the one she shut down when you asked her to marry you? And you're still with her??"

"Kira, that's enough," E.J. interjected as Lorenzo's eyes narrowed slightly. "You're way out of pocket right now."

"I was just saying-"

"Go away. Now."

Sucking her teeth, Kira stomped off, muttering something about women having men they didn't appreciate and how unfair it was.

"Sorry about that," E.J. said, glancing at Lorenzo. "That's my wife's sister. She can be a little childish."

"So I see." Lorenzo shrugged, flashing a good-natured smile. "But it's all good. It's already forgotten."

The men chatted for a couple more minutes before they each needed to get going. E.J. rounded up Kira and they headed out, Kira still pouting over Lorenzo's rejection. They were barely out of the parking lot before E.J. let her have it.

"What the hell was that?"

She looked at him, feigning alarm. "What do you mean?"

"Don't do that."

Sighing, she shrugged, playing with the ends of her braids. "I saw a fine man and was shooting my shot."

"And questioning why he's still with Desiree?"

"Well? I think that's a valid question. Would *you* have stuck around if Natalia had said no when you asked her to marry you?"

E.J. wouldn't have and he knew it, but this wasn't about him. "Regardless, you overstepped with that. It's like you don't know anything about tact."

"I'm sorry. But it's hard being around all y'all when I don't have anybody for myself. I'm sick of being single."

"I empathize but...still."

"Is it so wrong for me to want what Natalia and Desiree and Lovey have? Men who are fine as hell and make good money and treat them like queens? Why wouldn't I want that for myself?"

"Didn't say you couldn't."

"Maybe you could fix me up?" Kira excitedly suggested, turning towards him in her seat. "You *have* to know some men that are about their business that would be good for me."

"I know plenty of fellas. None good enough to be trying to set them up with anybody."

"Oh, come on..."

"And I think you need to be more worried about getting yourself together instead of getting a man."

"Why can't I do both?"

"What do you even have to offer anybody, Kira? And don't try to tell me anything about your body or some sexual bullshit. Real men require more than that."

"So you don't know anybody closer to my age that's on the come-up, too? We could build together."

"Forget it," E.J. stated with finality. "If you want to be hooked up, ask your sister or somebody else. I'm not getting involved in your love life."

Plunking against the back of her seat, Kira sulked the rest of the way home.

Natalia was in the kitchen making eggs when they got back to the house. She was clearly surprised to see them walk in together, and looked after Kira curiously when she went straight past her towards the guest room without even speaking.

"Um, I'm not sure what I want to ask about first," Natalia stated as E.J. locked the door behind him. "What's wrong with her or why you two are coming in here together."

E.J. shrugged. "She asked to go to the gym with me."

"And you just agreed?"

"Didn't really want to. But I'm trying to make an effort to be nice to her. And I only agreed after I made sure we were on the same page."

"The same page about what?"

"I just wanted to make it clear that she was wasting her time with all the flirting and shit."

"Wow." Natalia turned off the stove and grabbed a plate from the cupboard. "I'm glad to see that you're making an effort with her. I know she can be a pain in the ass but really, she just has more maturing to do. She's not a bad person."

"I know." E.J moved over, gently taking the plate from her hand and placing it on the counter before turning her to face him, his hands on her waist. He could see the wariness in her eyes as she looked up at him, lightly resting her hands on his chest.

"I just want you to know that I heard what you said last night," he told her. "About how difficult I can be to live with...I didn't realize I was that bad. I'll try to be better."

"Baby..." Natalia palmed the side of his face, pride surging through her. "Thank you so much for that. And please know that I love you regardless of what flaws you have. You are still the number one person in the world to me."

He couldn't help the smile that appeared at her words. "Really?"

"Of course!" She moved closer, grabbing the other side of his face as she gazed at him in amazement; she was still so amazed by him. "I know we're both stubborn as hell but, E.J...I'll *never* stop loving you, I don't care how much you get on my nerves. I can't see my life without you right next to me."

The emotion hit him right in the chest. He pulled her to him and wrapped her tightly in his arms, and she went willingly, not caring that he was still in his workout clothes. She stood on her bare toes and squeezed him around his neck, resting her head on his shoulder with her eyes closed. It meant a lot to her that he wasn't just dismissing her concerns because he disagreed with them, as a tiny part of her feared he would do. Him doing his part to fix things only renewed her resolve to do her part.

"How hungry are you right now?" E.J. asked, his lips brushing the side of her neck.

"If we're talking food, maybe a seven. If we're talking what I *hope* you're talking about, fifteen."

E.J. grinned before easing back, taking a lingering kiss before standing up straight and looking at her. "I was just thinking that since I have to get in the shower anyway, and it doesn't look like you've taken yours yet, that we could save some time and take one together. I'll try not to mess up your hair. But, if you want to have your eggs first-"

"Damn my hair and damn those eggs." Natalia grabbed his hand and headed out of the kitchen towards the stairs, E.J. following her with a wide smile. "I have shower caps."

"You don't care about being late for work?" he asked her once they were in their bedroom and she was pulling his clothes off his body. He pushed her mint green silk bathrobe from her shoulders, loving that she was naked underneath. He hissed at the sight. "'Cause I'm gonna take my time."

"I want you to." Her voice was breathless as he yanked her around and pulled her against him, her back to his chest, and one hand cupped her right breast and fondled the nipple with his thumb while the other made magic between her legs. "Oh god, yes, E.J..."

"Tell me you want all of it. All of *me*," he whispered against her neck, growling as she began winding her behind against him. "I need to know I can go all the way with you, baby. If I can't, stop me now."

"Don't you dare stop," she breathed, grabbing the wrist of the hand that was between her legs as if to keep it in place. Her head fell back against his hard chest as her voice melted into a whimper. "I want everything, E.J...no restrictions. I need you, please..."

"Say no more." He picked her up and carried her to the bathroom, giving her exactly that.

Chapter 13

• • • •

NATALIA WANTED TO THROW a party.

The project she'd volunteered for had finally wrapped, after seemingly countless hours. The client was happy and so were her bosses, and Natalia was glad they were pleased, but she was even more glad to be done with all that. She was looking forward to getting back to her normal schedule and not having her nights and weekends sucked up with coding and testing and meetings. She'd surely learned her lesson about trying to use work to avoid problems at home.

"Hey, Natalia, you got a sec?"

Glancing up from her computer, she looked up at her manager Humphrey hovering in the doorway of her office. "Yeah, sure. What's up?"

Entering the small space, Humphrey grabbed the back of the chair in front of Natalia's desk, his belly protruding over the edge a little. His dark eyes peered at her through his thick glasses. "I just wanted to let you know we appreciate you stepping up on this project, putting in so many extra hours. You did a great job."

"Thanks, Humphrey. I appreciate that."

"And I also wanted to let you know we've got another big one coming down the pike soon; even bigger than this one was. We're finalizing this client acquisition and they have two systems that need to be built practically from scratch, so there's a crapload of coding that needs to be done, not to mention everything else. It'll require more overtime but if we nail it within the desired timeframe, it'll also mean a sizeable bonus for all involved. I wanted to give you a heads up, since you did so well on this one. You interested?"

Natalia wanted to ask if she could get the bonus without working any overtime, but she figured he wouldn't appreciate that little quip.

"I'm not sure; I'll need to think about that one," she admitted. "When do you need to know?"

"I'm gonna be announcing it to the team at the next meeting, then it'll be up for grabs. So if you want in, I can fill you in on the particulars."

Natalia chewed her lip. Part of her wanted to just decline and be done with it, but she wasn't one to just discard sizeable bonuses just like that.

"Honestly, I'll need to talk it over with my husband first," she told him. "He didn't love all the overtime I had to do on this last project."

"I get that." Humphrey stood straighter, brushing his wispy hair out of his face. "That's part of the reason I'm divorced now; the wife said I was putting this before her and she got sick of it. So now it's just me and the cat."

Natalia was uncharacteristically stumped, not wanting to say anything inappropriate. She just sat there with a tight smile, waiting for him to change the subject or get out of her office.

"Well, anyway," Humphrey exclaimed, finally snapping out of the trance he seemed to temporarily fall into. He patted the back of the chair before turning to leave. "Let me know in the next day or two."

"Sure thing."

Natalia tapped her pen against her desk. She didn't want to hide behind work anymore, especially now that E.J. was making such an effort. And it wasn't like she just loved spending so many extra hours working, stuck behind her computer or sitting in on mind-numbing meetings. She'd much rather be home with her husband, especially if he was going to keep putting it on her like he did the morning before in the shower.

Her legs pressed together under her desk as she remembered how he had her back against the marble shower wall, stroking into her until her voice was actually raspy from moaning and talking and screaming so much. The way he moved...there was never any hesitancy when it came to E.J.'s lovemaking. He knew what he was doing, he knew what he wanted, and he made it known. Natalia often wanted to pinch herself that she got all of that beautiful Black man to herself for life.

Her mind was still on her husband when she met Lovey for lunch a couple of hours later. Lovey smiled cautiously when she saw the faraway look in her friend's eyes.

"I recognize that look," she teased as they were seated at their table. "Things are better between you and E.J., I take it?"

"Girl..." Natalia playfully fanned herself, drawing a giggle from Lovey. "That man, that *man*."

"I can relate. His brother does the same thing to me."

"We married some fine-ass men, didn't we? I tell you, Lovey, just *thinking* about E.J. had me closing the door to my office and pulling out the silver bullet I keep in my desk."

Lovey's face immediately flushed and Natalia laughed loudly.

"I guess this is more of a Desiree-type conversation, huh?"

"Hey, I'm no stick in the mud," Lovey insisted, brushing her long brown hair from her face. People usually mistook it for a weave because of its length and fullness but it was all hers. Just like they assumed she was biracial because of her light skin, but she was quick to correct and let them know she was Black. "I might not be as...*outspoken* as Desiree but I enjoy sex as much as the next person. Especially with Roland; I swear he has spoiled me for any other man, not that there could ever be anyone after him. Though I can't say I've gone so far as to pleasure myself in my office."

"You don't know what you're missing." They gave their drink orders to their server, with Natalia going ahead and ordering some teriyaki salmon bites as an appetizer. "Speaking of Desiree, where is she? I've been trying to call her."

"Oh, she and Lorenzo went out of town this morning," Lovey informed with a grin. "He surprised her with a little impromptu getaway. Had her bag already packed and everything. You should've heard how giddy she was when she called to let me know."

"I bet. I'm so glad it seems like they're back on track."

"Yeah, Lorenzo was hurt and his pride was bruised but I think he believed that Desiree's reaction to his proposal was more about fear than not wanting to spend her life with him, just like she said. He loves her enough to be patient with her."

"She hit the jackpot, then, 'cause there's nothing like a man that doesn't run at the first bump in the road. I wouldn't be surprised if they come back hitched."

"Anything is possible, though I know she'd want her family to be there and for her dad to walk her down the aisle. Though if you asked her, she'd probably try to say it was because she had to sit through her sisters' weddings and her parents' vow renewal so they'd need to do the same for her."

Natalia laughed. "Yeah, that sounds like something she'd say."

They proceeded to get caught up on each other's mornings as they nibbled on their appetizer and waited for their entrees. When Lovey couldn't resist showing off the latest pictures of little Xavier, Natalia gazed at her chubby-cheeked nephew, her smile turning wistful.

"Nothing like being a mother, huh?" Natalia mused, giving Lovey's phone back.

"Nothing." Lovey grinned at the image of her baby. "I was already happy with Roland but I've been over the moon since Xavier was born."

"I think I'm ready to see what that's like."

Lovey's eyes snapped up. "What? You've changed your mind about motherhood?"

"I really have."

"What changed your mind? E.J.?"

"Actually, no. His stance was firm but he also refused to pressure me about it. I realized what my issue was; it wasn't about not wanting kids. It was about how having them would change things between me and E.J. I'm so happy with how things are now that I was scared to death of it changing, especially remembering how my mama struggled with all of us."

"That's understandable."

"But I had to realize its two different situations. My dad passed unexpectedly and left Mama with eight kids to raise by herself; of *course* she was going to struggle with that. She didn't plan on being a single mother. E.J. would be right here with me as we raise our *one* child, at least until we decide to have more. And yeah, things will change, but I had to get it out of my head that that's a bad thing. Once I did, I actually started to get a little excited about having E.J.'s baby."

"Oh my god, that's so wonderful!" Lovey squealed, reaching over and grabbing Natalia's hand. "I bet E.J. was thrilled."

"Honestly, he was a little wary. I think he felt I was just saying what I thought would make him forget why he was so pissed at me; you know, get back on his good side. But once I tossed out our condoms and let him raw dog it in the shower, he knew I was serious."

Their server came back just in time to hear the tail end of Natalia's statement, and his face turned as red as the tomatoes in Lovey's salad. He quickly deposited their plates on the table and hurried off, leaving Lovey about to hurt herself from laughing.

"You probably traumatized that poor man," she hissed across the table as she picked up her fork.

"Please," Natalia waved a hand. "He's a grown man. I'm sure he's heard worse."

Lovey shook her head as she drizzled strawberry vinaigrette over her salad. "So you and E.J. are officially trying to get pregnant, then?"

"Kinda unofficially; we haven't flat-out said it. But I told him there were no more restrictions. I even downloaded one of those apps to track when I'm ovulating and all that kind of stuff. I've been picturing the look on E.J.'s face when I tell him he's finally knocked me up."

"Look at you; seems like somebody has caught baby fever."

"Maybe a little bit."

"I'm *so* happy for you two, Natalia. This is so exciting; Xavier is going to have a little cousin to grow up with. I hope things work out as well with this buyout offer the guys are still battling over."

Natalia cut into her steak. "Neither of them are budging, huh?"

"Doesn't seem so. At least they're talking again, though. Roland keeps insisting that he'd be fine to sell the clubs but I don't really buy it."

"No? But you'd be happy with him having more time to spend with you and the baby, right? Especially since you're trying to have more kids now?"

"I like the idea of it, but I'm thinking more long-term than Roland is. He might be good with it at first, but eventually he'd realize just what he did and will regret selling. I'm sure of it."

"Wait," Natalia cocked her head, her fork halfway to her mouth, "So you *don't* want them to sell?"

"I don't think they should, no. Yes, it's a lot of money and it's extremely tempting, but I care more about my husband's happiness. Roland may not think so now, but he'd be kicking himself down the line, money or no money."

Natalia nodded thoughtfully as she chewed her food. She hadn't been asked for her own opinion on the subject but if she were, she would have told E.J. to sell with the quickness. Money like that didn't come along every day, and Natalia would be able to quit the career she'd grown indifferent to and spend her time doing what she wanted. She and E.J. could travel. When they had a kid, they'd be able to give them loads of quality time, which was a luxury she didn't have growing up since her mother was busy working multiple jobs to provide for her and her siblings. As far as Natalia was concerned, E.J. and Roland could start up more businesses down the line, if they really wanted to.

But she knew how adamant E.J. was on the subject, and she wanted to support him. They weren't hurting for money. And there was no telling what kind of eternal funk E.J. would be in if he acquiesced and gave in to make her happy or to appease his brother.

This was still on Natalia's mind when she headed back to the office after lunch. So much so that she almost didn't notice Dane sitting in the lobby.

"Natalia."

"What the hell??" Natalia jumped, her hand flying to her chest. She glanced at the receptionist and back at Dane, who looked a little too amused at having startled her. "Dane, why are you here?"

"I need to talk to you, if you have a minute."

"I don't."

"Natalia, it'll just take a couple of minutes. I tried to call, but turns out you weren't kidding about the re-block."

Pursing her lips, Natalia resisted the urge to say what she really wanted to say. It was bad enough that the receptionist had a front row seat to their conversation as it was.

"Fine," she forced through gritted teeth, turning on her heel and heading for the entrance to the main offices. She waved her security badge in front of the sensor and yanked open the door. Thankfully, no one was around to see them going into her office alone, since most of her coworkers were working from home that day and the upper level offices were on the other end of the floor. "Three minutes."

Once they were inside her office with the door closed, Dane got right to it, knowing Natalia meant business about the time limit.

"I wanted to apologize to you for what I did that night at the bar, when your man called," he said. He gently grabbed her arm before she could retreat around her desk, turning her to face him. "That was foul of me."

"And childish. And petty."

"Fine, yeah, all of that. I thought about it later that day and was kicking myself; we'd *just* gotten back on cool terms and I messed it up. I don't want to be on the outs with you again, Natalia."

"Dane," Natalia sighed. "Look, let's just leave well enough alone. It's been years. The past is over with. I apologized for what I did. But I don't think us trying to be friends at this point is a good idea."

"Good, 'cause I'm not just trying to be your friend." He stepped closer.

She didn't budge, refusing to let him think she was running. "So clearly your ridiculous proposition wasn't a part of your apology. Do you always throw yourself at married women?"

"I'm not acting like it's an honorable request. But that's how much I miss you."

"Well, then I suggest you make good use of whatever pictures of me you have left. Hell, have a doll made in my likeness, for all I care. You can do that thing that I never let you do and get no complaints."

"You remember that, huh?" His eyes dropped to her lips. "I *knew* you thought about me."

"Remembering stuff I did in the past doesn't mean I want to repeat it, Dane. Is this all you came here for?"

"I still love you, Natalia." He reached out and grabbed her waist, pulling her to him. She gasped, shocked at his nerve. Her hands pushed at his chest. "And I want you. Think of it as a way of making things up to me."

"Have you lost your damn mind?? Let go of me!"

"Honeybun, please..."

"Dane, I *swear*, if you don't-"

She squealed when his lips crushed onto hers. He tried to wrap his other arm around her and slide his tongue into her mouth when she stomped his foot with her stiletto heel then punched him square in the jaw.

"Augh *shit*, Natalia!" Dane yelled, hopping on one leg while holding the side of his face. He glared at her incredulously. "Did you really just punch me??"

"You had no business putting your damn hands on me, Dane! I told your punk ass that I wasn't stepping out on my husband with you or anybody else and you try to stick your fucking tongue down my throat?? If I had a bat I'd be beating you like a piñata right now!"

"Natalia-"

"Shut up and get the hell out of my office, and do *not* come around here or me again! Now hop your ass out the door before I call security!"

His face hardened as he gingerly returned his throbbing foot to the ground and moved his jaw from side to side a couple of times as he stood up straight.

"No need for all that," he finally conceded, holding up a hand. "I'll go. But since we're talking about making calls, maybe I'll make one, myself. Does your man know everything about when you two got together?"

Her eyes narrowed. "Excuse me?"

"Don't play. Does Mr. Bell know that you were still technically with me when you started messing around with him? I heard about the two of you sneaking around town before you finally sent me that kiss-off email. What, was he helping take your mind off the abortion you snuck and had? Does he even know about that?"

Natalia forced herself to keep her game face on, even though her insides felt like they'd been coated with ice. E.J. *didn't* in fact know about the overlap in her relationships with him and Dane. It wasn't until after E.J. asked her to make things official that she finally sent Dane that email.

And as for the abortion...that was another secret she'd kept from her husband, having told herself it wasn't important, even though she knew better.

"Maybe I'll stop by Barfly or 845 and see if he's there," Dane continued, sensing he'd hit a nerve Natalia was too stubborn to admit to. "I happen to know he's usually there during the day; he doesn't seem big on the partying. Whenever I ask if he's around when I'm hanging there at night, they always say he's gone."

Natalia's hands balled. "Are you fucking *stalking* my husband?"

"That's an ugly word, Honeybun. A man should always keep an eye on his competition. It's not stalking. I've always wanted to meet the man that managed to snatch the notorious Natalia Gaines off the market. He must be something else, huh?"

"Dane..." Natalia reached for her letter opener, gripping it in her fist.

He noticed and immediately backed up, not putting it past her to use it. "I'm gone. You know how to reach me if you change your mind...or if you suddenly find yourself single again." He smirked as he turned and limped out, closing the door behind him.

As soon as he was gone, Natalia dropped the letter opener to the floor. She pressed one hand to her churning stomach and groped for her chair with the other, lowering herself down into it on shaky legs. She never thought about how she dated E.J. while she was still technically with Dane, because she and E.J. weren't official yet. But she knew he still would've liked to know; in fact, he had flat-out asked her if she was seeing anyone else during that time and she said no. Even though she had shut Dane out, she hadn't broken up with him yet because she was still conflicted over the abortion. E.J. was part of how she made herself feel better, which was why she wasn't interested in anything serious at first.

She couldn't believe that she was sitting on yet another secret from E.J. He had just gotten past her meeting up with Dane without telling him. Now she had to worry about Dane following through with his threat just as her marriage was finally back pointing in the right direction. He could've been bluffing, but he might follow through just to get back at her for rejecting him again. Natalia knew that if E.J. found out from anyone other than her, he'd explode.

Briefly putting her head in her hands, she grabbed her phone and tried to call E.J., but he was in a meeting. Her paranoia kicked in, making her wonder if Dane had somehow made it to his office that fast and was telling him everything, though she knew that wasn't possible. Natalia wanted to find her husband right then and tell him about all this, but her calendar reminded her that she had meetings coming up, and she knew she couldn't miss them just because she needed to save her ass with her husband.

As soon as they were both home later that night, she'd tell him. She could only hope Dane didn't beat her to him.

• • • •

E.J. *was* in a meeting, but it wasn't with Dane. It was with local R&B singer Slinky, who wanted to reserve 845 for her listening party. She loved 845 and had insisted that it was her first choice, and was willing to pay top dollar to rent out the whole establishment.

"Thank you *so* much, Mr. Bell," she gushed as they were wrapping things up. She and her manager stopped just outside of the office, turning to face E.J. with big smiles. "I'm hyped already about this party."

"I'm glad to hear that, Sarah," E.J. replied, addressing her by her real name. He refused to call a grown woman *Slinky*. "We're glad you chose us for such an important event."

"There are a lot of clubs in this city but I always knew that I wanted to come here, even if I had to shell out a few extra dollars to do it."

"You mean the *label* had to shell out the extra dollars," her manager corrected.

"Whatever," Slinky waved dismissively. "I insisted. This is a big deal. And you and your brother are doing your thing around this city, not to mention how damn near every person I see working for you is Black. And I have yet to hear about y'all trying to screw anyone over or gouge folks out of their money just because you could, which happens too much around here. With all the charity work stuff I read y'all do, too? Trust, you'll have my support as long as you're in business."

E.J. bowed his head gratefully, unable to resist a proud smile. "That means a lot, to hear you say that. We've worked really hard to get to this point and to hear that it matters so much to our community is what it's all about."

"Oh, it absolutely matters. The first time I stepped foot in Barfly and your brother Roland treated me like a VIP without even knowing who I was? I was all in."

They all chatted for another minute or so before Slinky and her manager had to rush off.

E.J. went back into his office, almost in a daze as he crossed over to his desk. Slinky's words had touched him. It was an indication of the impact they'd made in their city, and that people actually gave a damn about what they'd worked so hard to build.

Even though E.J. was more back-of-the-house when it came to the businesses, he was still eager to personally meet his patrons and was more than glad to do interviews or meet guests who requested it. He'd just been a guest on a popular podcast the day before, discussing his and Roland's entrepreneurial journey. That was important to him, to be accessible. He didn't think Carlton Barber would be the same way.

When he finished everything that absolutely needed to be done for the day, E.J. got ready to head home. He was looking forward to seeing Natalia and spending the evening with her. She had thrown him for a loop with her revelation about why she thought she didn't want to have kids, and that she felt she was past it now. He'd been waiting for her to start freaking out since their unprotected shower romp, but she hadn't. E.J. was excited that she was coming around, but something still warned him not to get his hopes up too high too soon.

His plans to get home were halted when he got into his car and it wouldn't start. He'd driven his old Maxima because his regular car needed an oil change and he hadn't had time to take care of it. Cursing under his breath, he glanced up at the interior light and his head fell against the headrest, remembering he'd turned it on when he arrived to read something on his phone that morning and apparently forgot to turn it back off. Boneheaded mistake.

Getting out of the car, he slammed the door and pulled out his phone. He called AAA to come give him a jump, but they wouldn't be able to get to him for almost an hour, and he was too impatient to wait for that. He stalked back inside the club to ask if any of his employees could help him out, but none of them had jumper cables. E.J. started to say they could use his, then he remembered he'd put his set in Natalia's car in case she needed them and hadn't gotten any more yet.

"Damn, I'm slippin'," he muttered to himself, heading back outside. He tried to call Natalia, but she was way on the other side of town helping her mother with something she needed unexpectedly; she offered to come get him but he didn't want to pull her away from her mother. Roland didn't answer. Practically vibrating with frustration, E.J. went to what felt like his last resort.

"Hey, E.J.!" Kira answered brightly.

"Hey," he grunted. "Look, I need you to help me out with something."

"Really? Me??"

He tried to keep his patience in check. It wasn't her fault his car battery died. "Yes, Kira."

"What do you need me to do?"

"Do you have any jumper cables?"

"What's that?"

"Jesus...look, my car won't start so I need you to grab the spare keys to my Mercedes that's in the drawer in the kitchen by the refrigerator and come over to 845. I'll just have to come back for my car 'cause my ass forgot to get another set of cables."

"No problem. I'm gonna put my shoes on now and head out; I should be there in twenty minutes."

"Thanks, Kira." E.J. sighed with relief. "I appreciate it."

"Told you I'd do anything for you. See you in a minute."

She hung up before he could respond, but he told himself to let the comment go. He'd already made it clear to Kira that nothing was going to happen between them, so he wasn't going to read too much into it. Flirting was one thing, but he was sure she knew better than to actually try anything with him.

True to her word, Kira was pulling up to 845 a little under twenty minutes later. She was grinning as she put the car in park and got out.

"Told you I'd get here fast," she proudly greeted, spreading her arms wide.

E.J. didn't know if she was expecting a hug or not, so he pretended she wasn't. He just nodded and stepped around her, going to open the door on the passenger's side.

"Thank you again," he said, holding the door open. "Let's go on and go; it's been a long day."

"Hmm." Her arms dropped as she turned to face him. "Is your car gonna be okay here?"

"Yeah, this area has around-the-clock security. I'll come back and take care of it tomorrow."

"Okay."

She rounded the car and slid into the passenger's seat, eying E.J. as he closed the door for her. Once he was behind the wheel, she immediately asked, "Can we stop and get something to eat? All I've had today was snacks."

E.J. refrained from reminding her they had actual food in the house she could have cooked. He figured getting her some grub was the least he could do, since she'd bailed him out. "What you want?"

"Taco Bell."

Biting his tongue yet again, E.J. just nodded and pulled out of the parking lot. What she liked was her business but he hoped she didn't expect him to join her, because he didn't mess with that. He hadn't had Taco Bell since he was in high school.

Once they went and got her food (which E.J. had correctly figured he'd end up paying for), they headed home. Kira had started to break into her tacos as soon as the bag hit her lap but E.J. wouldn't let her eat in the car. So she just hummed along with the Jill Scott song that was playing, rocking in her seat.

"E.J., do you ever wonder about alternate situations?"

"What?"

"Like, how things would be now if you'd made different decisions back in the day."

"Oh. Not really, no."

"Really? I always think about stuff like that."

"Seems like a waste of time to me," E.J. said with a shrug. "What's now is what it is. I'd rather spend my energy focusing on reality than what-ifs."

"I guess..."

"And you can drive yourself crazy, agonizing over what you could've done and didn't."

"True. I know I spend too much time thinking about stuff I should've done differently."

"Energy that could be better used for how your life is now."

"Right. So let me ask you something...what's one thing you really want right now that you don't have yet?"

E.J. wondered if she was trying to bait him into discussing his and Natalia's baby situation with her, because a child was definitely at the top of his wish list. He refused to get into that with Kira, though.

"Jumper cables."

Bursting out laughing, Kira playfully swatted his arm. "Silly!"

He couldn't resist a chuckle.

"You know what I mean, though. There isn't anything you *really* want right now?"

His eyes on the road, E.J. hunched a shoulder in thought. "I'm pretty happy with my life the way it is. I'm blessed to have all that I need and most of what I want. There are some business ventures I want to explore in the near future."

"How come you never got into modeling?"

He grunted, glancing at her as if she was joking. "For what?"

"Because you're freakin' *gorgeous*. No disrespect," she quickly added, holding up a hand. "I'm just sayin'...anybody with eyes can see it. You'd probably make a grip in music videos."

That was certainly a first for E.J. He'd been complimented on his looks plenty but had never heard that.

"Thanks for the compliment. Modeling was never something I considered getting into, though."

"I don't know why. I know I thought that's what I wanted to do, for a while."

"Hmm."

Several quiet moments passed before Kira spoke again, eying him. "Aren't you gonna ask me what it is that *I* really want right now?"

He hadn't planned on it, but figured what the hell. "Okay, what?"

The *last* thing he expected was to feel her hand in his lap. The car jerked slightly as he pushed her hand away from his crotch, not believing she had just tried him like that.

"*Have you lost your fucking mind??*" he yelled.

"I'm sorry; I couldn't help myself!" She slapped a hand over her mouth, apparently realizing what she'd done. "It...I wasn't even planning on doing that!"

"Yeah. Right."

"E.J., please don't be mad at me! It didn't mean anything-"

He glared at her before swinging the car to the side of the road, jamming his foot on the brake and sending her lurching forward, clutching her bag of food.

"Get out."

"Huh??"

"Get the hell out of my car, Kira."

"Are you serious??" She screeched, eyes bugged. "It's dark outside!"

"I don't give a fuck. If you're bold enough to grab my dick after I already told your ass I'm not going there with you then you should be good to handle whatever comes up. Get. *Out*."

She had tears in her eyes but E.J. didn't care. He was furious and it was taking all his restraint not to *really* hurt her feelings.

Kira glanced around before easing the door open, moving slowly as if she expected him to change his mind. But he just sat there seething.

"Hurry up!"

She had barely closed the door before E.J. screeched off, leaving her standing there. He glanced in the rearview, seeing her figure get smaller as he got further down the street.

Chapter 14

• • • •

"SORRY I MISSED YOUR call earlier. What's going on?"

E.J. sat on the couch in the den, having just got home a few minutes earlier. He was still fuming from what Kira had just tried in his car when Roland returned his call. "Don't worry about it; it's taken care of now. But I still need to ask you something, though."

"What's up?"

"You had started to tell me how it is you know Natalia's sister Kira that day in the office and we got interrupted. I need to know now. Why did you give me that warning about her?"

"Oh yeah, that." Roland sighed. "I know this guy that used to date a former friend of Kira's. Kira was staying with her for a while, and he said she would flirt with him when he went over there, getting a little too close to him and stuff when her friend wasn't looking."

"Sounds familiar," E.J. muttered.

"Then she started saying stuff about them doing threesomes, but insisted she was just playing. And when her friend started getting suspicious, Kira tried to say her man wasn't her type and she wasn't even interested in him. Which turned out to be complete bullshit considering what she ended up doing."

"What did she do?"

"She snuck and took dude's used condom out of the trash after him and her friend finished getting busy, and stupidly tried to impregnate herself with his sperm."

"Stop. Are you serious??"

"No lie. And then her friend found a hidden camera that Kira had put in her bedroom; so whenever they were getting down, Kira was watching it on her phone. Her friend kicked her ass and then kicked her out."

"What the..." E.J. was floored. He processed Roland's words as he leaned back on the couch, running a hand over his hair and expelling a long breath. All this time he just thought Kira was immature and spoiled; but turned out she was grimy, too.

"And you're *sure* about this?" E.J. felt compelled to confirm. "This isn't just some gossip shit; it actually happened just like that?"

"Dude swore on it. Plus, he actually had a video of his girl confronting Kira, and Kira was on there apologizing for everything. Not that it mattered because she still got her ass handed to her. That was how I recognized Kira when she came to the office; he showed it to me a while back. And Kira recognized me because I had run into the three of them when they were out together one night, and I happened to hear the woman warning Kira to stay in her lane and not try anything with her man. Kira actually tried to shoot her shot with me but when I shut that shit down mid-proposition, she tried to say she was drunk and didn't mean it."

"I'll be damned." E.J. wondered if Natalia knew about all this, but figured she probably didn't. Kira wasn't the type to be forthcoming with her indiscretions. Natalia probably wouldn't have even let Kira stay with them if she knew this story.

"Yeah, your sister-in-law is on some shit."

"That ain't even the half of it, brother. She just tried to make a move on me in the car."

"What?!"

"She tried to say she wasn't thinking but I wasn't going for that, especially since I had to check her about her flirting and shit already a while back. I put her out of my car."

"Bro, you need to get her out of your house ASAP. I know she's family, but-"

"Oh, I'm way ahead of you. I already decided she was out of here. As soon as she gets back, she's packing her shit."

"You told Natalia yet?"

"Not yet. But best believe-"

"Emeril Jamal Bell! *Get your ass out here!!*"

"What the hell?" Roland asked. "Is that Natalia?"

"Yeah." E.J. stood from the couch. "I'm guessing she knows I made her sister walk back. I'll talk to you later." He hung up without waiting for a response as he strolled out to the living room to find a crying Kira standing next to his wife, who was breathing fire.

"What?" he droned, unfazed by her anger.

"You actually put my sister out on the side of the road *at night* and made her walk because y'all had a disagreement??" Natalia screeched. "What if I hadn't been nearby when she called me, huh?"

He actually laughed, which only incensed Natalia more.

"Oh *now* you've got something to laugh about?" she marveled. "You think this shit is funny??"

"A disagreement, huh? Is that all she told you?"

"She said you disagreed with something she did and then put her out, even though she apologized!"

"That's an interesting spin on her grabbing my dick. I certainly *disagreed* with that."

Natalia froze for a second as Kira's sobbing turned to bug-eyed panic. She clearly hadn't thought ahead to E.J. telling Natalia the actual truth. Either that, or she thought Natalia wouldn't believe it.

Slowly turning to her sister, who was already stepping back with her hands held up, Natalia's eyes narrowed as she began closing in on her.

"Is that true?" she asked menacingly. "And I *dare* you to lie."

"It wasn't...I didn't mean..." Kira stumbled over her words before she stumbled over the edge of the couch, falling on top of the bag of Taco Bell that was hanging from her wrist. She tried to scramble to her feet, but Natalia stood over her, ready to pounce. Kira looked absolutely terrified as she looked up at her sister who was so furious she was turning redder by the second. "You're just gonna automatically take his word-"

"Did you put your hands on my husband?" Natalia asked plainly. "Yes or no."

Kira knew trying to skirt the truth was pointless. She'd already tried that and it only got her so far.

"Yes."

It was the tiniest whisper, but it was all the confirmation Natalia needed. It was barely out of Kira's mouth when Natalia pounced on her, punching and pulling braids. Kira screamed, trying to fend her off but Natalia was not to be denied.

"You must've forgot that I don't play!" Natalia screamed, her fists still pummeling her sister's body. "I bring you into my house and you do this shit?? You betray me like that?!"

"I'm sorry! Natalia, stop!" Kira screeched as Natalia's fist landed square on her jaw. "Please, E.J., help me!"

"Don't you dare say his name, bitch!" Natalia immediately ordered, picking Kira's limp body up long enough to sling her against the wall before resuming her beating. "I'll knock out every tooth you have if you even *look* at him again!"

"I'm your sister!"

"I don't give a *fuck*! You didn't think about that when you were trying to get with my man, did you?? I won't even know your *name* after this!"

E.J. finally went over and grabbed Natalia by the waist to pull her away, figuring he needed to step in before she killed the woman. It wasn't easy, though, because Natalia wasn't through making Kira pay. She kicked at her whimpering sister, the adrenaline flooding her body and making her stronger than a bull.

"Come on, baby, you made your point," he tried to tell her, picking her flailing body up and turning her away from Kira. He eyed his beaten sister-in-law over his shoulder as he slid a calming hand up his wife's neck to caress her face. "Babe, it's over...try to calm down, okay? I'm right here with you."

Natalia's chest was still heaving as she glared at Kira, who was trying to pick herself up off the floor, gingerly touching her beaten face. E.J. kept an arm braced around his wife's back, keeping her in place because he had no doubt she'd shoot back across the room for more if he let her.

"I'm so sorry..." Kira repeatedly whimpered, wincing in pain as she tried to stand. Her hand was holding her left rib, which Natalia had undoubtedly punished with her kicks. "I just want what you have and I got carried away...I guess I hoped-"

"Shut up!" Natalia warned, making a move in Kira's direction and trying to pry E.J.'s arm from her, but it wasn't budging. She sucked her teeth in frustration. "Don't piss me off more by trying to explain yourself. There's nothing you can say to me to justify that, Kira. Nothing!"

"I get that I messed up, but-"

"No, there's no *but*! You fucked up and I'm *done*! I'm done making excuses for you, done trying to help you, done *period*! And to think I had actually gotten your ungrateful ass a job! Well, you're gonna need it because you have ten minutes to get your shit and get out of my house!"

Kira's mouth fell open, and E.J. noticed she had a busted lip, and her eye would probably be swollen shut by the morning. He felt no sympathy for her, though. She brought it on herself. "Where am I supposed to go?"

"You think I care?"

"Natalia!"

"Let me go, E.J.!" Natalia yelled, fed up, pushing again against E.J.'s arm.

"If I let you go, you'll try to kill her and you know I hate getting anything on my walls. So no." He looked over at Kira, who actually tried to turn on a pitiful puppy dog expression for him. This girl never learned. "Kira, last time. Get your shit and get out. Otherwise, I *will* turn her loose on you again and if I do, you're on your own."

Defeated, Kira limped towards the guest room, her bag of now-smushed food still hanging from the wrist of the hand gingerly touching her busted lip while the other cradled her injured rib. She was still sniffling and sobbing pitifully.

"Hurry up!" Natalia yelled after her. Anger was still coursing through her so furiously that her skin trembled and was actually hot to the touch.

"Breathe, baby," E.J. instructed, pulling her to him and smoothing the back of her hair. "Calm yourself down."

"I cannot believe her!" Natalia exclaimed, her face in his chest.

"Me, either. But...part of me isn't even that surprised, I hate to say." He figured it wasn't the time to go into what Roland had told him about Kira. He'd wait until Natalia had calmed down to divulge that information. "My gut was telling me I couldn't totally trust her."

"I'm sorry she did that to you," Natalia muttered, sniffling as she swung her head up to look at him. Her eyes were glassy with tears that represented her anger as well as her disappointment. Her hands gripped the sides of his shirt. "I'm sorry for letting her stay here, I'm sorry for trying to convince you to give her a break, I'm sorry for everything."

"Hey, she's your sister. You wanted to think the best of her; I get that. And you aren't responsible for her actions so none of this is on you. You did everything you could for her; *she's* the one who messed it up."

As ordered, Kira was limping out of the house in the next few minutes, laden with her bags. She sat crying in the driveway until a white car eventually came and picked her up, taking her away.

"Where do you think she's gonna go?" E.J. asked once she was gone. They were seated on the living room couch, her head on his chest. "And don't try to tell me you don't care."

"I *don't* care. At least we didn't send her away with nothing; she's got her nasty-ass tacos to eat on the way there."

E.J. found that humorous even though he knew he shouldn't have. "Babe, come on."

"Come on, what? Hell, I'm surprised you're worried about it. You never wanted her here in the first place."

"No, but she's not *my* sister. And I tried to give her the benefit of the doubt."

"Hmph. We've all made a career of doing that. Well, I won't make *that* mistake again."

They sat in silence for a few moments, E.J. rubbing her shoulder.

"Hey," he eventually said softly, giving her a squeeze.

She looked up at him. "Yeah?"

"I know you're still feeling some kind of way about that whole scene, but I need to let you know that it means a lot that you believed me when I told you what happened."

Her frown was slight. "Why wouldn't I believe you?"

"Because she's your sister and I know how it can be with family sometimes. Some women might have questioned what I did to provoke or encourage her, or try to get me to let it go. It just...it means a lot to me that you had my back with that."

"Of course I did," she assured, her expression clearing. "I know you wouldn't lie to me about something like that. And I don't put much past Kira; I knew she had a crush on you, even though she tried to say she didn't. I guess I just wanted to believe that she'd respect me enough to keep it in check."

"It's too bad she didn't. But at least that's behind us now and we can get back to focusing on us." He took her face in his hand, leaning down to give her an appreciative kiss. "And maybe this isn't the best time to bring this up, but I'm excited about what the future holds, as far as our family. I admit I was wary when you said you were ready to start trying to have a child, but I had to check myself; I know you wouldn't tell me that if you didn't mean it. Not after the shit we've been through already these past few months."

"Absolutely not."

"I get why you were concerned, baby, but please know that I'm going to do everything I can to make things even better for us once we have our child," E.J. promised, the hand still cupping her face tightening in conviction. His eyes bore right into hers. "I know this is still a big step for you and I don't want you to regret anything. I'm still gonna work on myself, as far as what you said, and make sure we still make plenty of quality time for each other. It just feels good to not have any more secrets hanging between us."

Her body clenched at his words. He was looking so sincere and earnest that tears came rushing to Natalia's eyes, though she rapidly blinked them back.

Mistaking her tears for happy ones, E.J. took her lips again, this time more impassioned. He moaned against her lips, his body leaning into hers. She held onto his wrist and accepted the kiss, loving his words but hating the ones she knew she still had to say to him.

Now on top of her, E.J. lifted her legs higher around his waist as he deepened their kiss. Their breaths and moans between kisses intensified as they began pulling at each other's clothes. E.J. didn't have the patience for them to take the time to get totally naked, and he was glad she was wearing a dress. He reached underneath and yanked her panties to the side, caressing her folds that were getting wetter by the second.

"Oh my god, E.J..." she breathed, her brick red nails digging into his shoulders. Her back arched as she opened her legs wider for him, wanting him to have all the access he needed. Her brain screamed for her to stop this and tell him what she needed to tell him, but her body was steadily drowning that out. "Yes..."

She bit her lip when he eased two fingers inside of her, then released a gut-scraping moan when his thumb began strumming her clit. Her eyes opened just in time to see him pull the top of her dress down with his teeth as his free hand lowered the strap down her shoulder.

"I need you, Natalia," he whispered against the lace covering her breast. He licked the nipple through the fabric before his teeth pulled that out of the way, too. She shuddered and gripped him tighter when he helped himself to her bare breast, circling the areola with his tongue. "You ready for me?"

"Yes, baby," she groaned, her hips steady grinding against his hand. Her outside leg dropped to the floor before clamping around him, then back to the floor, her foot hitting the hardwood with a thud. It was almost like she didn't know what to do with herself, she was so turned on. E.J. always drove her crazy. "I'm all the way ready."

Breaking contact just long enough to push his pants and briefs down, E.J. wasted no time getting inside of his wife, the pace revving up within the first few strokes. He leaned up on one arm as he moved inside her, his other hand lightly gripping her neck, which she loved. Natalia met his rhythm, their familiarity with each other adding to the pleasure. In a time that was far too short for either of them, they were careening towards an intense climax that had them both screaming loud enough for their neighbors to hear.

"Shit!" E.J. panted before Natalia pulled him down for a sloppy kiss.

"That was amazing," she muttered against his lips between kisses, holding his chin to keep him in place. "Damn, I love you so much..."

"I love you, too." He squeezed her thigh. "And I love that I can come inside of you now as much as I want."

"You wanna do it again?"

"Hell yeah."

They worked themselves back up to round two, this time with Natalia straddling E.J's lap. She loved the freedom of not stressing over the climax and if the condom did its job or not, and part of her wanted to make love to her husband until her limbs turned to dust to make up for lost time.

But, that nagging voice that wouldn't leave her alone reminded her that she could only use sex as a distraction for so long. At some point, she was going to have to tell E.J. about Dane and the abortion. He deserved to know, and she needed to unburden herself; it'd been worrying her since Dane came to her office days before. He might have been bluffing about contacting E.J. himself, but he might not have been; he could be waiting until he thought Natalia had let her guard down before he sprung it on E.J. out of the blue. Natalia knew she couldn't risk that; if E.J. found out from Dane and not her, there would be hell to pay and she knew it.

I'll tell him tomorrow, she promised herself, closing her eyes as E.J. tightened his arms around her and licked the spot on her neck that made her weak. Her arms encircled his neck as she leaned back and enjoyed it. Then he lifted his hips and began slowly thrusting into her, and all thoughts left the building. All she cared about was matching his strokes and getting him to scream her name again. *I swear, I'll tell him tomorrow.*

But when E.J. woke her up the next morning by putting his head between her legs, Natalia's plan was stalled again. What he was doing felt too amazing to stop, and she clutched the back of his head through the sheet, fully awake and buzzing with arousal. E.J. had been insatiable since the night before, not being able to get enough of her. Their orgasm record had been officially surpassed.

"*Fuck*, E.J., yes!" she screamed, her thighs clamping his head and her back arching off the bed. Her hand clawed the padded headboard as she came down off this latest orgasm, her skin so sensitive that she jumped at the slightest touch. E.J. took his time extracting himself, loving how she responded to him.

"You are so sexy," he whispered, trailing his tongue up her stomach as his hands gripped her still-heaving breasts. "Gotdamn, Natalia..."

"E.J..."

"Can you take the day off today?" He slid his tongue through the valley of her breasts to her neck, then kissed her as he eased his body between her legs.

Her eyes eased open. "Why?"

"So we can spend the day together."

Her lips parted in amazement, momentarily stumped for words. E.J. still planted soft kisses around her open mouth, his fingers brushing her damp skin as he tucked the hair that had escaped her bonnet behind her ear. "Are you serious?"

"I'm absolutely serious." He gazed at her, the obvious love in his eyes both warming her and reheating the guilt that she'd managed to put on ice the night before. "It's been too long since we've done that."

"You don't have meetings or something that you have to be in today?"

"I'll call Roland. And we have managers. It's nothing that they can't handle. You're more important to me than those clubs, babe. You know that, right?"

She nodded, getting choked up. Though not for the reason E.J. probably thought she was.

"I love you, Natalia," he told her. He rested his forehead to hers as his hand held the side of her neck. "I never want to take you or us for granted."

Tears slid down her face as she clutched his forearm. "Baby-"

"Wait, let me say this, okay?" He leaned back to look at her, his expression firm but pleading. "I know you didn't change your stance on us having a baby just to appease me, but it still means so much to me. It hits me right in the chest whenever I think about it. And whatever it takes, I'm gonna do my damndest to make sure you don't regret it. My being a father won't take away from me being your husband. I *swear*, baby. Tell me you believe that."

Full-on sobbing now, Natalia nodded, feeling like she didn't deserve this beautiful, strong man on top of her. Here he was pouring out his heart and willing to make whatever concessions she needed, with no idea that she still had secrets she needed to let him know about. Her heart ached that she was going to have to break it to him, but she knew she did.

"E.J., I...that means the world to me. And I *do* believe it. I know you love me enough to do everything you're saying and more." Her eyes squeezed shut as she buried her face in the crook of his neck. "I don't even know if I deserve you."

"Why would you say that?" He rubbed her arm that had slid around his neck, kissing her shoulder as she cried what he mistook for happy tears. "Babe, we've both made mistakes but we're on the right track now. I don't wanna dwell on the past. It's a clean slate, all right?"

Her cries just got louder upon hearing that, and she knew she couldn't wait any more. "Before I let you declare that, there's something that needs to be addressed first..."

"You still want to go on that vacation? Let's plan something for later this month or next; hopefully I've put a baby in you by now so I want us to get at least one trip with just us before we expand our family."

Every word he said only made her feel worse, so she eased her hand over his mouth. "I love that idea, but let me say this first, okay? I need to get this out."

His eyes turned curious, but he nodded in agreement.

Her hand drifted to his sculpted shoulder as she tried to summon both the words and the strength to say them. "Baby, there's something that happened years ago that I didn't tell you about; I told myself it was because it didn't matter but the bigger part of me was just afraid. But I know that's no excuse."

His brow furrowed.

"I need you to know that I recognize how wrong I am for keeping this to myself all these years, and I'm not going to make any excuses. Um...when you and I started fooling around, before we became official, I was still...technically with Dane."

Pushing himself up slightly, his eyes narrowed as he processed what she said. "I thought you said you were single. I specifically asked you."

"I know you did. And in my head, I was. I knew I was going to break up with Dane; I just hadn't pulled the trigger yet."

"So why couldn't you have just told me that so we could've waited until you did?"

"Because I wasn't trying to risk you meeting someone else and forgetting about me. I knew I wanted you, even if I wasn't ready for a full-on relationship at that point. I figured it was harmless enough since what we had was casual-"

"If we hadn't had that conversation, I might buy that," he interjected, his frown deepening. "But I flat-out asked you if you had a man, Natalia. And you looked me in my face and said you didn't."

"I know, E.J., I know." She quickly grabbed him when he tried to get off of her, and he surprisingly didn't resist. She felt hopeful. "And like I said, there's no excuse; I should've been woman enough to be straight up."

"Okay, so you overlapped us. I don't love hearing that but I'm making myself stay calm about it; it's not as bad as the *other* lie you told me back then."

She winced at his words, and hoped what he said about a clean slate still applied. "I'm sorry."

"Were you still with him when I asked you to be my woman?"

"I...again, technically yes. But I ended it with him that same night. There wasn't a doubt in my mind who I really wanted and it *wasn't* Dane."

"What took you so long ending it with him, then?"

Natalia wondered if he could hear her heart pounding, because it felt like it was going to burst out of her chest. "Because I was still feeling a little guilty."

"About?"

"About..." She took a deep breath. "The baby I had aborted without telling him."

It took a second, but her words finally hit home. She could see the change in his eyes as he looked at her, and she wondered if this was finally it; the final straw that sent him packing.

"You were pregnant?" His voice was almost pleading with her to tell him otherwise.

"Yes." Her fingers felt his body tense and pull back slightly. "It wasn't planned and he didn't want marriage, and I wasn't about to have a baby like that. So...I aborted it behind his back. And I might as well tell everything; I shut him out and when I dumped him for you, it was by email. I couldn't face him after that."

"But you could face *me*," he growled, though his tone held glaring pain. His hand was on his chest. "You could be with me day in and day out knowing you did that shit and act like it was all good?"

"E.J., you have no idea the torment I was going through at that time! When I was alone, I cried my eyes out. I knew back then that wasn't the way to handle it, and the guilt ate me up. You were my bright spot. I was thrilled to be with you, and over time, everything that happened with Dane just...faded out."

The light went out in his eyes. She saw it the moment it happened.

"E.J..."

He removed her hands from him, pushing his body off hers. His expression was empty as he stared at her.

"Baby, please don't..." Natalia sat up herself, covering her mouth with her hands before reaching for him. He moved his hand, evading her. "I'm still the same person. I fucked up, again. I get it. But-"

"So that week or so when you wouldn't sleep with me, that was right after the abortion, wasn't it?" E.J. verified, remembering. "You said you just weren't feeling well but that was bullshit too, right?"

"I should've told you."

"Yes. You should've."

"Would it have mattered?"

"Fuck yeah it would've mattered, Natalia, are you serious?!" he exploded, making her jump. "You don't think I would have wanted to know that I was sleeping with a woman who was carrying another man's baby??"

"Dane and I were *over* by then!" Natalia cried, sitting up on her knees. The cover fell from her bare body and her hands mashed against her chest. "I didn't even know I was pregnant at first...I just, I was having my doubts about Dane, anyway, and was already pulling back from him after he told me he didn't want to get married."

"So how do you know the baby wasn't mine?"

"Because I realized I was pregnant a week after we met. And it freaked me out. I actually tried to forget about it, like that would change anything. It was my sister that finally convinced me I needed to do something; she went with me to the clinic."

He scoffed, looking away momentarily before his marveled eyes swung back to her, his hands on his hips. "Wow, Natalia."

"I was young and stupid and scared but I absolutely was wrong with how I handled everything, with Dane *and* with you."

"Yeah, I've been hearing that a lot from you lately." His words were biting. "You seem to be allergic to being straight with people."

"That was *then*, E.J., not now."

"Let's not act like you didn't let us go ten years with me thinking that you wanted a baby when you didn't. Or that you haven't lied or kept other things from me since I found out about *that*. Don't try to act like all this shit was back then."

"Can you not understand how hard it had to have been for me to deal with all this? You know me and the kind of person I am; there's not much I hold my tongue about. For me to have been *so* afraid to admit to all this...can you please try to see my side?"

"See your side? Is that a joke? How 'bout you try to see *my* side? My wife keeps hitting me with secret after secret ten years into our marriage, and I'm supposed to just get over it and move on because you're crying about it?"

"I didn't say that, baby. I expect you to be angry and you have every right to be. What I'm asking is that you please try to be gracious enough to realize my position, that's all. Be mad at me but don't start thinking I'm a horrible person because you found out about another mistake I made."

"Why are you telling me about this now?" he asked, folding his arms as he looked at her suspiciously. "Are you trying to tell me that guilt *alone* is making you reveal all this? I never would've found out about it, most likely. What made you decide to bare your soul now?"

This was one time she hated how perceptive he was. Natalia should have known that E.J. would have smelled something fishy. And it wasn't like she'd had the best track record for being up front about major things lately.

"Okay...Dane came to my office the other day talking about wanting to get back together. I told him to go to hell, then he tried to push up on me. When I clocked him, he got in his feelings and threatened to tell you everything."

"I see. So not only did you not tell me about him coming to see you...now I know you likely *wouldn't* have told me all this if he hadn't threatened to tell me himself. Got it."

He got off the bed and Natalia scrambled to follow him, her legs momentarily getting tangled in the sheets. "E.J.-"

"You might wanna leave me alone right now, Natalia."

"I don't want us to do this again. We were just getting to a good place-"

"Well you shot that to hell, didn't you?" He went in the bathroom, slamming the door in her face. She recoiled, but quickly recovered and tried to open the door, both relieved and fearful to find it unlocked. E.J. was leaning over one of the sinks in the double vanity with his head down. He didn't even look up when she entered. "Get out of here."

"No, E.J. I'm not gonna let you shut down on me. We've come too far to go back to that."

The look he gave her when he raised his head sent a chill straight down to her toes. She took a step back.

"You have a lot of damn nerve, demanding *anything* of me right now," he grumbled. "Maybe if you had told me about all this when you were confessing your *other* lies, I could have dealt with it better. But no, you keep throwing them out like breadcrumbs, letting me pick at one then the other then the other, waiting for the next one to fall at my feet. What am I gonna hear from you next, Natalia? What other lies or revelations are you sitting on? Just go head and get them all out now so I don't have any more damn surprises."

"There's not anything else, I swear," she sobbed, her eyes blurring with tears.

"Right." He stood upright, snatching a towel from the rack and wrapping it around his waist. "Whatever you say."

"E.J.-"

"If you'll excuse me, I need to take a shower." His voice had turned stiff, as if he was talking to a stranger. There was no warmth to be found. "I'm late getting to the gym before I go to work."

"B-but...I thought we were spending the day together."

"No thanks. I've changed my mind." He moved over to the door and looked at her pointedly.

Getting the message, Natalia eased backwards out of the room. As soon as she was over the threshold, the door closed in her face. She heard the shower start mere seconds later.

Knowing it was pointless to try to talk to him when he was still so upset, Natalia decided to give him some time to calm down, as much as she didn't want to. She was sure that once he was thinking rationally again, he'd realize that while what she did was far from honorable, it didn't change anything in the big picture, when it came to them.

But she was wrong. E.J. barely looked at her for the rest of the day, or in the days after. He only spoke when he absolutely needed to, and his words were always short and clipped. Natalia tried everything she could think of to melt the ice that had formed around him, but nothing worked. He had nothing to say to her.

E.J. wasn't enjoying this. But every time he thought he was ready to finally talk to Natalia, he remembered the times they spent together with her knowing she was still with another man. And when he remembered the part about her carrying another man's baby, *knowingly*, while she still hugged and kissed on him, his rage flared like water on a grease fire.

His head wanted to get past it but his heart was weary. Yes, what she did happened years ago. But part of him felt like he didn't even know his own wife anymore, and it wasn't a good feeling. It angered him that she would do this to them. If the roles were reversed, she would have put him out already. He didn't know how she expected him to just let this go.

He went through the motions at work, barely engaging in meetings or with his staff and zoning out in his office for hours on end. There were several times Roland found him just staring out of the window at the 845 office, not even aware that anyone had entered. Roland knew something major must have gone down, and after a couple of days of E.J.'s standoffish behavior, he asked him about it.

"What's going on with you, man?" He nudged E.J.'s shoulder as he stood at his usual spot by the window. "You've been acting strange."

E.J. just shook his head, his eyes still on the cars moving up and down the street below.

"E.J., come on. I'm not trying to pry, but something is clearly messing with you. You don't have to hold everything in; you know you can talk to me."

"I know." He finally turned his eyes to his little brother, who was looking at him with clear concern. "And I appreciate it, brother. But I'm not to the point where I can say it without getting pissed off again. I need to get a handle on this anger first."

"I'll respect that. Look, if you need to take some time, I got you covered. Go get your mind right."

"Nah," E.J. immediately refuted, shaking his head. "Being here is what's keeping me from flipping out."

Roland didn't bother asking if this mood was because of something with Natalia; that was the only thing that would have E.J. like this. He just hoped that it was something they could work through.

"All right," Roland conceded, clamping a hand on E.J.'s shoulder. "Whatever you feel is right. I'm here if you need me."

E.J. just nodded, his eyes back on the street. As soon as he heard the door close behind Roland, he closed his eyes and sighed, his forehead meeting the cool glass.

• • • •

USUALLY, E.J. LOOKED forward to spending time with his mentees. And he had hoped that they would help take his mind off of what was going on at home, if only temporarily. But it was only marginally working.

"You good, Mr. B?" Teddy asked after E.J. had Nigel repeat himself yet again. "You're zoning out like I do in Calculus."

Forcing a slight chuckle, E.J. told himself to get it together. His boys deserved his full attention.

"I'm sorry, fellas. I have some stuff on my mind but it's nothing y'all need to worry about. So," he rubbed his hands together. "You said you had some news, Nigel?"

"I do," the boy grinned, his leg bouncing excitedly. He whipped an envelope out of his jacket pocket and waved it in the air triumphantly. "I got into college!"

"For real??" E.J. grabbed the envelope holding Nigel's college acceptance letter, his grin spreading as he read it. He shot out of his chair, giving his excited mentee a loud clamping handshake and yanking him out of the chair for a hug. "I'm *so* proud of you, man!"

"Thanks, Mr. B. I know it's just community college, but-"

"Uh-uh, don't do that," E.J. immediately corrected, pulling back and pointing a finger at him. "Don't downplay it. There's nothing wrong with community college. Be proud of yourself."

"And you can always transfer later," Teddy offered, throwing an arm around Nigel's shoulder. "My cousin went to community college and he's making major bank now."

"It's all about what you do with it," E.J. stated.

"Thanks, y'all," Nigel said, his back straightening a little at the encouragement. He and Teddy slapped hands and bumped shoulders before they all retook their seats. "I'm pretty excited about it. My girl wants to go out to celebrate. She was talking about going to some fancy restaurant so we can get dressed up. Good thing you got me that suit, Mr. B."

"Oh yeah, I love mine," Teddy piped up, smoothing his hand over his hair that was cornrowed into a tiny bun and sliding his fingers around his faint mustache. "I can't wait to wear it to the prom."

"Yeah, I saw all those pictures you posted in it," E.J. chuckled. "You trying to be a model or something?"

"I'm handsome enough. But I'll stick to the plan of being an architect."

"And I'm gonna be a weatherman," Nigel added. "Between getting accepted to college – and with a scholarship – and getting my license the other day, me and my girl have a lot to celebrate."

"Are you two gonna..." Teddy's voice trailed off, wiggling his eyebrows pointedly.

Nigel cleared his throat, glancing at E.J. "We might. She wants to."

"And you don't?"

Nigel eyed E.J. again.

"You can admit it," E.J. assured him. "I'm not gonna come down on you."

"Mama has been on my back about it," Nigel admitted, slumping in his seat in mild relief. "She keeps telling me over and over that I'm not ready for sex and that I need to wait until I'm married, blah blah blah. I think she's more worried about me getting my girl pregnant and making her a grandmamma."

"That's real, though. Even if you strap up, she could still get pregnant. And you do know you should *always* wear protection, right?"

"Even if she's on the pill?"

"Doesn't matter. Wear it anyway. I don't know your girlfriend and I mean no disrespect, but plenty of girls *say* they're on the pill when they're really not. Hell, grown women do that. Cover all the bases you can."

"Well, I'm not trying to make any babies but if we did, it wouldn't be the worst thing in the world," Nigel declared. "I love my girl and we've already been talking about getting married. We've both got our lives planned out; I've got my sh-*stuff* together. We'd be all right."

"You're barely eighteen, man," E.J. reminded. "Don't be in a rush to get into grown shit before you have to. If you and your girl really love each other, great, but let that be enough for now. Both of you should experience some more life first before you try to take it to the next level."

"So...no sex, then?"

Unable to resist a laugh, E.J. clamped a hand on the boy's shoulder. "I'm realistic enough to know you're probably only gonna wait so long on that. I was the same way at your age. I'm just saying, if you do, be as careful as you can. But there's nothing wrong with waiting. Sex isn't something you should do just because your friends are or because you think it'll make you feel like a man. It should mean something, to both of you."

Both Nigel and Teddy pondered his words.

"That's real talk," Teddy finally muttered, scratching his head.

"I appreciate that, Mr. B," Nigel commented, nodding as he rubbed his arm thoughtfully. "Mama just tells me what to do. I appreciate you leaving it up to me."

"Hey, it's your life," E.J. reminded him. "You have to decide what to do with it. *And* live with the consequences of the decisions you make."

The three of them hung out for a while longer before E.J. took them to get something to eat, promising they'd go out and celebrate Nigel's college acceptance and Teddy's new part-time job. After he dropped them off at home, he headed to Barfly, since it was closest. Once he got there, though, he didn't get out of the car; he just sat in the almost-full parking lot, hearing the music from inside and watching people go in and out. He knew Roland was in there, overseeing things.

When a text came in from Natalia asking where he was, his thumb hovered over the screen to respond, but he ended up dropping the phone in his lap. He squeezed his eyes shut in frustration, rubbing them with his thumb and index finger.

Everything in him wanted to push past this latest hiccup with his wife. And maybe if this was her first revelation, he would've let it go by now. But it had been one thing after another since their anniversary, which had barely been seven months earlier. He didn't like feeling he couldn't trust his own wife. And for the time being, he was just out of energy for her drama.

Still, he couldn't make himself flat-out ignore her text, so he simply responded "Barfly" before clutching the phone in his fist, his other hand rubbing his chin in thought. He could agree with Natalia on one thing; they *had* come too far to go backwards.

He perked up slightly as a thought occurred to him, and he scrolled through the contacts on his phone. Expelling a relieved breath that he had the number, he placed the call, hoping he didn't get voicemail.

"Hey, it's E.J.," he greeted once they answered. "I know this is sudden and unexpected, but do you have some time to meet up? I promise I won't take up too much of your time." He listened to their response, his head falling against the headrest in relief. "I appreciate it. Is the coffeehouse over on Blanchard okay with you? Good; I'm on my way."

E.J. started the car and pulled out of the parking lot, his energy renewed.

Chapter 15

• • • •

"GIRL, YOU *really* know how to put your foot in it."

Natalia sighed, lowering her head to the wooden table in her mother's kitchen. "Mama, can we not?"

"You're the one that came over here crying about this latest fuck-up with your husband," Florence Gaines reminded her, in a demonstration of where Natalia got her sharp tongue. "It's not like *I* brought it up."

"I get that, but I feel bad enough. You rubbing it in my face isn't helping any."

"That's not what I'm trying to do," Florence insisted, joining Natalia at the table with a tall glass of fresh lemonade. She pushed it towards her daughter. "Here."

"Unless it has liquor in it, no thank you."

"You don't need liquor. You just need to make better decisions."

"I'm aware of that. But unfortunately, I can't go back in time and change anything. I just need to figure out what to do from here. Where's Horace?"

"He's working. Had to be in early today." Horace was Florence's second husband, who she married about five years earlier. They were living out of state for a while before they moved back to the area, as Florence wanted to be closer to her grandchildren. Natalia liked him all right but they weren't terribly close. Part of her still felt weird about her mother being with any man other than her dad, but she was just glad Florence had found someone to make her happy after so many years of struggling raising her and her siblings while grieving her late husband. "Why?"

"Just wondering. Wouldn't want him to come in and see me all jacked up. I feel stupid enough as it is."

"If I could take all this away for you, you know I would." Florence reached over and ran her hand over Natalia's arm. "It's no fun time when your man is pissed at you."

"Especially when I brought it all on myself." Natalia lifted her head, brushing her bangs from her face with both hands before dejectedly grabbing the glass of lemonade and sliding it closer, looking down into it. "There have been a few times when it seemed like E.J. wanted to say something to me but stopped himself. I hate that I've pushed him to where he can't even talk to me."

"He'll come around. E.J. might be stubborn but at the end of the day, he loves you. And he made a vow. From what I know of my son-in-law, he doesn't just give up on those."

"I can only hope so."

"For the record, I don't blame y'all for putting Kira out," Florence stated, adjusting the sleeve of her housedress over her large arm. She was a big woman who had no issue with the weight she'd put on over the years. "That child called me trying to tell on you, but I just laughed when I found out the real deal. I kept telling her she was gonna cross the wrong one sooner or later."

"Where is she staying now?" Natalia felt compelled to ask.

"One of those motels you rent by the week. It's a good thing you got her that job."

"I'm surprised she's taking advantage of it."

"She doesn't have a choice. She's either screwed over or worn out her welcome with whatever friends she has left, and your brothers and sisters told her not to even bother coming to them, especially after they found out what she tried with E.J. It's on her to get her shit together and she knows it."

"Hmph." Natalia was still mad at Kira and wasn't in the mood to try to gather any sympathy for her. Just like Natalia, Kira brought her situation on herself with a string of bad decisions. Natalia didn't love that they had that in common.

"So how are you gonna fix things with your husband?" Florence asked her. "You can't let things keep going on like this forever."

"I know, but I'm honestly not sure what to do, at this point. I'm worried that E.J. is getting to where he doesn't even care one way or the other. Everybody has their limits."

"Well, what does your therapist say?"

"We, um...we never went," Natalia admitted, slumping slightly in her seat. "I cancelled the appointment when I changed my mind about having a baby."

"Damn, girl," Florence sucked her teeth. "I swear I don't know where all your common sense done went to."

"I figured since that was our main issue-"

"Well, clearly, you were wrong. Maybe you need to go to one by yourself to figure out why you can't seem to be straight with your man that you claim to love so much."

Natalia frowned, taking offense. "I *do* love E.J., Mama."

"That's what you *say*. But you keep lying to him. So maybe I should say you don't respect him, then."

"Mama-"

"I don't wanna hear no denial, 'cause your actions have been proving it these past few months," Florence snapped with an upheld hand. "Being married – hell, being in a committed relationship – isn't just about sharing a mortgage and a last name and getting to have hot sex with the same fine man every night. It's about going through the trials and tribulations together. And you've been so busy trying to hide everything that you haven't let E.J. show how he'll stick by you through the tough times."

Natalia knew there was nothing she could say to that. She was so afraid of E.J. leaving her if she was honest with him about so many things...maybe that should have told her something about herself more than it did about E.J. She used to be so proud of how brazen and honest she was, and it was embarrassing that she'd gotten away from that.

And all because of fear. Natalia didn't used to be afraid of anything. Except rodents.

Maybe her mother was right; maybe it *would* benefit her to go see a therapist solo.

But Natalia wanted to put her energy towards how things were now instead of continuing to torment herself about how she got there. She didn't even think E.J. would bother with a couple's therapist at this point. So she'd have to come up with something else to hopefully save her marriage.

• • • •

EVEN THOUGH HE HADN'T had any words for her recently, Natalia was anxious for E.J. to get home that night. When she got home from her mother's, he was out and, of course, hadn't left her any messages letting her know when he'd be back. She decided against calling or texting him, opting to be patient. He always came home regardless, which was something she was grateful for, considering.

It was after eleven that night when E.J. finally got home. Natalia was on their bed wearing nothing but a t-shirt and panties, more for comfort than anything else. She knew better than to expect E.J. to get enticed by it, given the attitude he still had.

She stifled a yawn when he walked into the room, putting down the copy of *Essence* she'd been half-reading. "Hey. I'm glad you're home."

His eyes only barely flicked in her direction. "Hey."

Hesitating, she finally pushed out, "Where've you been?"

E.J. took his time answering as he unbuttoned his shirt. "Out."

Natalia chose to let it go, since she knew his anger was driving that vague response. She didn't believe for a second that he'd been out doing anything shady; he just wanted to make her suffer.

"Look," she rubbed the bridge of her nose before leaning her head against the headboard. "I know you're still pissed. But I'd like for us to please talk. This is making me miserable, E.J."

He cut his eyes at her before wordlessly going into the closet. Natalia's shoulders slumped in disappointment.

But he came back out moments later, stalking straight over to the bed and leaning his knee on the corner of it. His gaze didn't acknowledge her smooth legs that were stretched out towards him and crossed at the ankles, or the red-painted toes he liked to suck on so much. She might as well have been wearing a snow suit.

"If you were me, what would *you* do?" he quizzed. "If you found out about lie after lie I'd been telling you over the years, would you stay?"

Natalia held his gaze, chewing her bottom lip. "I'd like to think I would."

"But we both know you probably wouldn't."

"E.J., I meant those vows I said to you. Just like you meant yours. Yes, I'd be pissed and would probably need some time, but at the end of the day, we'd still be together."

"Uh-huh. And there goes your subtle way of trying to tell me how to deal with this. Thereby implying that I'd be in the wrong if I decided I was fed up."

Her brow furrowed. "That's not what I was doing."

"The hell it's not, Natalia."

She sat forward, running her hands down her face. "E.J., if you're gearing up to tell me you're done, just do it. Don't make me suffer. It's already been hell for me these past few days."

"Like I've been walking on air with this shit."

The tears were already stinging. Natalia readied herself to hear what she'd been dreading ever since her latest confession. Apparently the hope she'd been hanging onto that she and E.J. could work things out was for nothing.

Sighing, E.J. stood and glared at her for a moment before his shoulders slumped and he leaned over, resting his fists on the bed and hanging his head. A few torturous moments passed before he finally spoke.

"I don't want to leave you," he admitted, anguish weighing down his words. He lifted his head high enough to look at her feet. "But I'm also tired, Natalia. Tired of forcing myself past the anger and betrayal of being lied to only to have to summon up the energy to do it again. Then again. Then *again*."

Releasing a shaky breath, Natalia crawled across the bed, kneeling in front of him. She leaned forward on her elbows, her hands just shy of touching his.

"I'm so sorry," she expressed.

"Yeah, you've mentioned that." His eyes met hers. "Are you sure there aren't any more secrets you need to unburden yourself from? *Anything* else you need to get off your chest? If there is, I wanna know right now; no more of this one-revelation-at-a-time shit."

"E.J. baby, you've already asked me this. I told you there was nothing else."

"Surely you don't think I'm just gonna take your word for it at this point."

"E.J..." She hedged, hesitating before sliding her hand over his. "If you want to leave, I...I won't try to stop you."

He didn't speak for a moment and she wondered if he was actually considering it.

"What did I just say, Natalia?"

"I know you said you didn't want to. And believe me, I don't want you to. But I get that a person can only take so much. And if you felt that's what you needed to do...I get it."

"I'm no quitter."

She sat up slightly, peering at him in realization. "Is this about you genuinely wanting us to work things out, or about you just not wanting to admit defeat?"

"Excuse me?"

"You've never liked to lose. And we all know how stubborn you are. How much of you're not wanting to leave is just about your refusal to fail?"

Standing upright, he folded his arms. "Does it matter?"

"Yes. *Hell* yes, it matters." She straightened herself, standing on her knees on the bed. "I want this to be about your love for me and for what we had. Because we said this was for life. Not because you just don't like anything getting the best of you."

"Natalia, I don't think you have any idea how hard it is for me to even be standing here in front of you right now," he barked. "I'm battling all these...emotions at once and I'm trying my best to deal with it. I said I'm *in* this. Regardless of how pissed and hurt I still am..." He swallowed, his frown melting some. "...And how I don't quite see you the same anymore, I'm willing to stick it out. And now that I apparently won't be blindsided by another bombshell, I believe we can finally move forward."

Natalia couldn't even let herself get excited about his assurance that he wasn't going anywhere. Only one part of his statement stood out to her.

"You don't see me the same anymore?"

His arms fell. "How could I, Natalia? After all this...how could I possibly still look at you the same way?"

They just continued to stare at each other before she sank down hugging her knees and he walked out of the room.

• • • •

"HEY, YOU GOT A MINUTE?"

E.J. glanced over at Roland as he leaned against the bar at Barfly, looking over the new menu suggestions their chef Hive had given him. "Yeah, what's up?"

Just then, Roland's phone rang and he glanced at the screen. "I have to take this, but meet me in the office in ten. I have something I need to rap with you about."

"All right."

They had just wrapped up their daily staff meeting and E.J. was proud of himself for managing to keep his mind on things. It wasn't easy, given how his thoughts strayed to Natalia every few minutes. What she'd said a couple of nights earlier about his motivation to fix their marriage stuck with him. He was the first to admit he hated to lose, but he didn't think that was all that was behind his refusal to throw in the towel on him and his wife. He loved Natalia, despite her flaws. And while he *had* considered leaving when his anger and hurt was at an all-time high, the thought of his life without her wrenched his gut. This wasn't a pride thing.

At least, it *mostly* wasn't a pride thing.

He spoke to Casey for a minute about the open mic event that was being held there later that night before heading to the office. Roland entered a few moments after he did, tucking his phone into his pocket and closing the door behind him.

"Everything okay?" E.J. asked him, taking a seat at the desk.

"Yeah, it was Lovey. Everything's good. Mama Elyse is gonna watch Xavier so she can come hang for open mic night tonight." Elyse was Desiree's mother and was like a mother to Lovey, especially since both Lovey and Roland's parents were deceased. She considered little Xavier to be another one of her grandchildren. "You know that was one of our first semi-dates."

"Yes, I know, man. I was right here through all of y'all's stuff."

"Anyway, I wanted to talk to you about this." Roland opened the leather folder he was carrying under his arm as he perched on the edge of the desk. "I've been looking over the terms of this offer from Barber his people sent over and there's a couple of things that's making me pump the brakes a little bit."

"Yeah?" E.J. had only taken a cursory look at the terms himself, and that was the day they were presented with them. Since he had no intention of accepting, he hadn't bothered with digging into it too deeply. To him, it showed Barber's arrogance that he would even disclose those plans to them. Barber was probably counting on him and Roland to be so entranced by the amount of money he offered that they wouldn't care so much about what he'd do to their clubs. "What's that?"

"I already know you barely looked at this, but did you happen to see this section about the changes he would make, namely over at 845?"

"No. But he mentioned he'd want to change some stuff."

"Yeah, and apparently one of those things is the clientele."

"What?" E.J. looked up from the computer monitor he'd been looking at. "What are you talking about?"

"Dude wants to transform it into some exclusive members-only lounge with a sky-high fee. And from what I know of Barber, he'd likely have some approval process where folks have to jump through hoops. So there goes most of our current customers."

"Hmm." E.J. wasn't surprised in the least. "Anything about what he'd do to Barfly?"

"Looks like he wants to turn Barfly more into what we have going on at 845. Get rid of the casual vibe and make it more upscale."

"I see. Well," E.J. threw up a hand and turned his attention back to the computer monitor. "That's your boy."

Rolling his eyes, Roland shook his head. "Man, for real. Have you told Natalia about these new developments yet?"

"She knows. About the offer, at least. With all our shit we've got going on, keeping her updated on this has been the last thing on my mind."

"She's still saying she's down for whatever you want to do or has she changed her tune?"

"If she's changed it, she hasn't told me."

"I think we should have a sit-down with her and Lovey to discuss all this."

"What's to discuss, Roland? My position hasn't changed."

"I'm aware, but even though we're the owners, this doesn't just affect us. This is major and our wives should be involved."

"Fine, man," E.J. conceded, wanting the conversation to be over. "But I don't see what there is to talk about. I told you it wasn't going to be as easy as it seemed with Barber, with him offering up that kind of money. And I'm willing to bet the stuff in this folder isn't even the totality of it, or that he wouldn't switch up and do something totally different altogether once everything was finalized. And he'd be well within his rights, regardless of how we felt about it."

Roland's eyes drifted to the open folder, considering E.J.'s words. "True."

"But we can discuss everything with our wives, if that's what you want."

"Good. 'Cause this changes some things for me." Roland closed the folder and tossed it on the chair in front of the desk before peering at his brother, who was focusing on the email he was reading. "So what's up with you?"

"Looking at the sales from the last merch drop. Folks really love those Barfly hoodies."

"Dig that, but I was talking about you and Natalia."

E.J. glanced at his brother before sitting back in his seat. "Oh."

"I know you didn't want to talk about it before and I'll respect it if you still don't. I'm just trying to make sure you're good, that's all."

Tapping his thumb against the arm of the chair, E.J. shook his head. "Can't say I am."

"What's going on? You haven't seemed like yourself for a while now."

E.J. wasn't eager to talk about his issues with Natalia, but figured Roland might be able to give him some insight he hadn't been able to find on his own.

So he told him about the latest round of drama with his wife, the words bringing more dejection than the usual anger. Roland sat there listening, slack-jawed.

"I don't even know what to say to all that," he finally managed, clamping a hand on the back of his neck.

"I had plenty to say about it. Not that it changed anything."

"Please don't tell me you've been ignoring her since you found out about this."

"As tempting as that is, no. Not really. I know nothing is gonna get fixed that way. But I keep grappling with feeling gutted and still refusing to give up on us."

"I thought y'all were going to counseling."

"She canceled the appointment when she decided she wanted to have a baby after all. Which I admit I didn't totally believe when she said it. But her actions since then seem to back that up."

"So, let me ask you, brother...do you *really* want to be with Natalia after all this?"

E.J. looked at Roland with a slight frown. "What?"

"You know I love Natalia so this isn't about me downing her. But she's hit you with a lot these past few months. And it's okay to admit if you need a minute."

"I don't need a minute. I'm fine."

Roland sucked his teeth. "You're *not* fine. You just said you were feeling gutted. There's nothing *fine* about that."

"Are you about to tell me I should leave my wife?"

"No, I'm telling you that you should examine why it really is you think you want to stay with her."

"Because I love her. And I made a vow to her."

"I get it but if that's all you've got, you're in for a long road, brother. 'Cause to me it sounds like the time you refused to come out of that football game back in the day, even though you had gotten knocked in the ribs and was clearly in pain. Or when you kept challenging Dad at chess until you beat him. Or when the bank initially denied us for a loan."

"Your point?"

"I just wonder if your marriage has become a challenge you refuse to lose more than anything else."

E.J. eyed him. "You know, Natalia said something similar to that. It was almost like she *wanted* me to leave, the way she kept pushing it."

"Maybe you need to take some time to figure all this out."

"What do I need time for? I already said I was staying. I want to work this out."

"How, though? Y'all have had one issue after another since your anniversary with barely any time to recover in between. It's been a merry-go-round of bullshit and you clearly don't know how to stop it. It wouldn't be the worst idea to spend some time – alone - deciding what it is you really want. Then, if you decide that you *sincerely* still want to be with Natalia, go from there."

Pondering Roland's advice, E.J. folded his arms over his chest. Maybe there was something to what he was saying. E.J. had been so focused on convincing himself that he was going to stay that he hadn't taken the time to figure out how they could possibly move forward once he did.

"I see your point," he finally admitted, begrudgingly. "I guess that *is* something I need to think about."

"It is."

"On another note, Lyric has been reaching out to me."

Roland's brow arched. "For what?"

"Said she just wants to stay in touch. I've tried to be polite, but the last thing I need is to be entertaining ex-girlfriends. You see what happened when Natalia started back talking to Dane. It unleashed a whole other round of bullshit."

"Do you and Lyric have secrets or something that Natalia doesn't know about?"

"No. I just don't need the headache. Would you still deal with Desiree if she and Lovey weren't best friends?"

"Probably not. But Lyric didn't do anything shady like Desiree did, unless there's something you haven't told me."

"No, she didn't." E.J. sat forward and rested his elbows on the desk, tapping his fists to his forehead. "I'm just tired, man."

Roland looked sympathetically at his older brother, seeing the weariness. E.J. might've seemed like his usual self to everyone else but Roland could see the emptiness in his eyes, the tension in his gait, and the usual vigor missing from his voice. E.J. didn't have his same motor, and Roland knew his situation at home was draining him. He wished he could tell him exactly what to do to fix things, because he missed his brother at his usual self.

He reached over and gave him an encouraging pat on the back. "Man...take some time off. Don't worry about work; I've got it covered. Go get a hotel or something and just clear your head. It's okay to admit you don't have it all together right now. As strong as you are, brother, you're still human."

• • • •

E.J MANAGED TO GET his mind right enough for the rest of the day, though he ended up leaving a little earlier than usual, at Roland's insistence. He knew his brother had a point with what he told him, as far as needing to step away. E.J. had never been a man that enjoyed down time, but clearly, something had to change. And he and Natalia hadn't been doing a very good job of figuring things out so far.

Apparently Natalia was on the same page. When E.J. got home, he found her in their bedroom, in a fitted hunter green romper and thick grey socks, tearfully tucking clothes into a suitcase.

She looked up at him when he appeared in the doorway, sniffling. "Hey."

He slowly entered the room, feeling his chest tighten. "What's going on?"

"I'm gonna leave." Her voice was barely above a whisper. A fresh wave of tears appeared with her words. "I think that's best for us right now."

He swallowed, feeling like there was a baseball in his throat. "You're leaving me?"

"No," she quickly verified, her red eyes snapping to him. "I'm not leaving you, baby. I'm just leaving the house for a while. I know being around me isn't easy for you right now so...I'm giving you some space."

E.J. felt the quiver in his brows as he watched his wife pack suitcases to move out. Even if it was just temporary, the sight was like a knife in the gut. He squeezed his eyes shut and looked away, unfamiliar tears hitting him like a mack truck.

"This is the *last* thing I wanna do," Natalia continued, slowly and haphazardly folding a sweater to press into her suitcase. "But I know I at least owe you this. And you'd probably never ask me to leave on your own. So I'm..." She sighed, gathering herself. "I'm gonna fall back."

"Natalia." His voice was thick with emotion. "I..."

"Baby, just...let me do this, okay? I brought it on myself. And maybe once you've had some time, if you want, we can revisit the counseling option I so stupidly hit the stop button on because I thought I had this all figured out."

"Natalia, baby, stop." He hurried over to her, grabbing her hand as she started to reach for one of the dresses lying next to the suitcase on the bed. "You don't have to do this."

"No, I do. I think we need it." She couldn't even look at him.

"Okay, fine. Maybe we do. But you stay here; *I'll* go."

Her eyes wide, she looked up at his pained face. Seeing the glassiness in his eyes broke her heart. How in the world had they gotten here?

"Okay," she whispered, knowing there was no changing his mind.

"All right." His hold on her hand loosened, but he didn't let go of it. His thumb stroked her skin, already hating the thought of being away from her. Even with all the anger and tension that had filled their house the past few months, E.J. always knew he was coming home to the woman he loved. Knowing he wouldn't be seeing her for days on end didn't sit well with him, despite him knowing it was necessary.

Natalia turned to face him, the hand that was encased in his rising to rest on his chest. They stood there looking at each other, as if taking in last looks. Suddenly, she reached her other hand behind his head, pulling him to her for a kiss. He immediately responded, wrapping an arm around her and pulling her closer, their kiss going from mild to desperate in seconds.

As soon as her arms slid around his neck, he grabbed the back of her legs and lifted, and they fell onto the bed on top of Natalia's clothes as her legs encircled his waist. They moaned and gasped against each other's mouths as their deep, sloppy kisses intensified, immediately starting to move against each other as soon as he was on top of her.

"This probably isn't the best idea," she panted, holding his head between her hands. Her eyes fluttered closed as he began kissing down her neck and chest.

"You want to stop?"

"No! Please don't stop."

They pulled at each other's clothes, their movements growing jerky and erratic as they undressed each other. Their limbs occasionally got caught in the clothes they were rolling around on, and Natalia's suitcase ended up on the floor with a thud, its contents spilling onto the light gray carpet.

It was all grunts and moans and hisses as E.J. pounded into her, a deep scowl marring his gorgeous face. He was angry at his wife, angry at the situation they were in, angry that he was even thinking about sex when he was about to leave the house they shared for who knows how long. But he couldn't help it; he needed this last taste of her.

Natalia held his body close to hers, willfully taking the punishment he was giving her. His arms were braced on either side of her head as he went harder than he had, probably ever. She couldn't form any words; her mouth hung open as breaths escaped with every stroke he gave her. Her fingers dug into the back of his head as he buried his face in her neck, his own voice breaking as he felt the release coming.

"E.J.!" she finally breathed, her legs tightening around him.

Taking a handful of her hair, he reared back and looked down at her, his bottom lip between his teeth.

Their eyes stayed locked until E.J. began to growl as the orgasm hit him, gritting his teeth as his head fell back. Natalia reached down and grabbed his ass, pulling him into her as she readied herself for her own release.

"Give it to me," she urged through clenched teeth. "Make me feel it."

And that he did. He grabbed one of her legs and pushed it to where her knee touched her shoulder, holding it in place with his strong hand as he gave several more hard thrusts before yelling at the top of his lungs, releasing everything he had into her.

He didn't even give himself a break as he looked down at Natalia, a light film of sweat plastering her bangs to her forehead. His hips continued moving as he grabbed her breast with one hand and strummed her clit with the thumb of the other. Her body seized immediately in pleasure.

"Yes..."

"Get yours," he ordered, his voice a low rumble. "I'm not stopping until you do."

It didn't take her long. In the next few moments she was screaming as loud as he just had, every nerve in her body like a live wire. She jumped at the slightest touch, chest heaving and actually feeling a little dizzy.

She reached for him, and they shared a leisurely kiss, taking their time since they each knew what was coming next and was in no hurry to get there. E.J. didn't even extract himself from her; he just savored these last moments, her face cupped in his large hand and his sweaty body on hers.

"I'm sorry," she whispered, the tears firing back up.

He nodded, his forehead against hers. "I'm sorry, too."

Reluctantly, he pushed himself up and off of her. The longer he stayed in his wife's arms, the longer he'd have to concoct some rationale that neither of them needed to go anywhere and they could figure something else out. And, as hard as it was, he knew this was what needed to be done. So he had to make himself move.

He took a couple steps away from the bed before stopping and hanging his head, his hands clasped in front of his chest. Moments later, he felt Natalia's arms slide around him from behind.

"I can't watch you leave," she whispered. "You're still here and I miss you already. I love you, E.J. *So* much."

With one more kiss to his back, she stepped around him, grabbing her bathrobe from the ensuite before hurrying out of the room, unable to look at him.

E.J. stood in that spot for several moments before finally starting to get his things together, his body feeling like it was trudging through sludge. He did nothing about the tear that rolled down his cheek as he pulled out his own suitcase, his heart breaking.

Chapter 16

• • • •

NATALIA DIDN'T KNOW how in the world she was going to get through this.

It had only been two days and she missed E.J. so much it hurt. She almost didn't even want to be in their house without him. Going home knowing he wouldn't be showing up eventually brought the tears every time.

She knew she needed to stop beating herself up for all the mistakes she made that led them to this point, but she wasn't quite there yet. Because of her, her husband was staying somewhere else. They hadn't discussed how long he would be gone; she figured he'd let her know when he was ready to come back.

Work was the last thing she was interested in, and she was glad that she had turned down that new project they'd dangled in front of her. Bonus or not, she was in no mood or mindframe to deal with anything extra, as it was taking all of her strength to go to work at all. She thought about taking a few days off, but figured there was no point; she'd just sit around moping. Might as well stay productive.

One thing that did serve to momentarily take her mind off things was a call from her sister, Kira. They hadn't spoken since Natalia kicked her out of their house the night Kira made a move on E.J.

"What the fuck do you want?" Natalia snapped, wasting no time with false pleasantries. She still hadn't gotten over what her sister had done.

"Guess I don't have to ask if you're still mad at me," Kira grumbled.

"No you do not. Now, what?"

"I was hoping we could meet up and hash this all out."

"We don't have nothing to hash out. You pushed up on my man and I kicked your ass. I'm not over it. I'm damn sure not apologizing for anything. So as far as I'm concerned, you can go to hell."

"Wow, really, Natalia? I know I messed up but I'm still your little sister. The *least* you can do is talk to me."

"That's what I'm doing now, isn't it? Be glad I even answered the phone for your trifling ass."

"Don't you care where I am, how things are going, anything?"

"You're doing well enough to call me from the phone you clearly still have, so you can't be doing too bad."

Kira sighed. "Can I please just get ten minutes? I'll come to your house; you won't even have to go anywhere."

"Kira, I swear if you even come on my *street*, I'll knock your braids out."

"Fine, then!" Kira exclaimed, fed up. "I was hoping if I gave you some time, you'd be more open to listening but I guess you're still as stubborn as you always were."

"Call it what you want to."

"I saw Dane around town the other day. Maybe I'll hit him up, see if he'd let me stay with him."

"I don't give a fuck."

"Don't act like you wouldn't care if I got with your ex," Kira sucked her teeth. "You were too into Dane back in the day. I don't care how long it's been or if you've moved on, you'd be pissed if I jumped on that."

"Jump all the way on it. Maybe then the both of you will leave me alone." Natalia hung up.

. . . .

NATALIA WAS GRATEFUL for Desiree, Lovey, and Lovey's sister Liz coming by to keep her company. She hadn't done a very good job of handling being in the house by herself yet. Trying to distract herself with books or movies or online shopping hadn't worked so far.

"You don't look good, girl," Desiree noted once they were all congregated in the den. Bottles of wine and several orders of various types of sushi were crammed onto the huge stuffed ottoman in front of them.

"Desiree!" Lovey admonished.

"It's all right, Lovey," Natalia waved a tired hand. "I know I look a mess."

"If this is what you call a *mess*, I need to get on your level," Liz commented, noting Natalia's plain fitted tee and blue leggings. A colorful scarf was on her head since she hadn't bothered to do her hair, though she still donned some diamond stud earrings. Her face was makeup free. "You should see Lovey when *she* gets depressed. She has these tired gray sweats-"

"Liz! Do you mind?" Lovey interjected, though a good-natured smile tugged at her lips. "We're supposed to be here for Natalia."

"I *am* here for Natalia. I'm letting her know that she still looks great even when she's down in the dumps."

"Well, that's something, I guess," Natalia gave a dry chuckle. She grabbed a spicy tuna roll. "What's going on with y'all?"

"Girl, stop. You know we're over here to talk about you," Desiree chided. "I almost thought you were joking when you told me E.J. left."

"How are you holding up?" Lovey asked, rubbing Natalia's shoulder. "I know I'd surely be a mess if I were in your situation."

"Yeah, but you *wouldn't* be in my situation, Lovey, because you wouldn't have lied to Roland like I've lied to E.J.," Natalia noted. "I caused all of this."

"Damn," Desiree shook her head, looking at her friend sympathetically. "I thought things would've surely gotten better between y'all when you changed your mind about having his baby."

"Wait, you changed your mind?" Liz halted with a slight frown and a raised hand. "I know I'm a little behind, but last I heard you were dead-set against having kids. Please don't tell me you gave in just to get on E.J.'s good side. Or that you let him talk you down."

Natalia shook her head. "That wasn't the reason. E.J. wouldn't want me to agree to something this major just to appease him. He'd want me to be as all in as he is."

"And now you are?"

"Yeah." Natalia didn't have the energy to explain her reasoning to Liz at the moment. "But unfortunately any happiness about that was wiped out by the fact that I had even more secrets I'd kept from him. When he found out I got with him while I was still technically with Dane, *and* that

I was pregnant with Dane's baby at the time, all hell broke loose. And it didn't help that I aborted the baby behind Dane's back and then dumped him in an email."

Liz hissed. "Ouch."

"I know, it was foul. It's embarrassing that I was such a punk in so many ways back then. I couldn't tell Dane *or* E.J. the truth."

"Is everything out in the open now, though?" Lovey asked. "Or is there more that E.J. doesn't know about?"

"No, this is it. This is plenty."

"Then maybe this is what you all need; some time apart so E.J. can process all of this. You've hit him with a lot these past few months."

"Yeah." Natalia stuffed another spicy tuna roll into her mouth. "I guess I should be thanking God that he hasn't packed all his shit and left for good. I know most men would have."

"I'm sure once he calms down, you two will be as good as new," Desiree assured.

"I don't know...he admitted he doesn't look at me the same anymore. And I can't blame him. Even if we stay together, I know things will never be the same."

"Maybe not, but that doesn't mean you can't still be happy together," Lovey countered. "You just both have to put in the work and the effort. It wouldn't be realistic to not expect some shifts after all this. Secrets are just poison to relationships."

"If I didn't know that before, I surely know it now."

"Forgive me for harping on this," Liz spoke up, "But are you sure that you didn't change your mind about the baby issue just for E.J.? I know how it is being a woman that doesn't want kids and constantly getting pressure and guilt trips from men; some have broken up with me when they found out I don't want kids while others tried to make me feel like some kind of horrible person. If you truly don't want to be a mother, that's valid and I'd hope your husband would be able to accept that."

"Liz..." Lovey warned.

"It's okay, Lovey," Natalia assured tiredly, accepting the glass of chardonnay Desiree had poured for her. "Liz, I get where you're coming from. But I assure you that the decision to change my mind was based off of my own realizations, not anything else."

"You're *sure*?" Liz clearly wasn't convinced. "I'm not trying to be a nag about it but I know how much you love E.J. and...let's just face it, you might be desperate enough to do anything at this point, given how things are between you."

"I'm not desperate. Hell, it was *my* idea to separate; I knew he probably wouldn't have done it on his own because it would be like admitting defeat, and E.J. doesn't do that."

"So if you found out you were pregnant tomorrow, you'd be happy about it?"

"Honestly, yes. Because it would be E.J.'s child and regardless, that's something to be happy about."

"Even if you end up raising it alone?"

"Liz!" Desiree exclaimed. "Will you chill out?"

"I'm just trying to get her to see the less-rosy side of all this," Liz defended. "I'm not trying to be a bitch but what if you've changed your stance only to end up being a single mother if he ends up leaving you, anyway? E.J. is cool and I'm not trying to say he's wrong for wanting a child-"

"Liz, my husband has his flaws but let's be clear, *I'm* the one that fucked everything up here," Natalia said strongly. She plunked her half-empty glass on the wooden tray on top of the ottoman. "I'm the one that lied to him about what I wanted and didn't want. I'm the one that made him wait ten damn years for something I didn't plan on giving him. I'm the one that kept secret after secret and told lie after lie. So whatever comes from that, whether it's our relationship being forever changed or him leaving me altogether, I'm willing to accept it. Because he didn't deserve any of that shit I did. So spare me, all right?"

Pursing her lips, Liz held up her hands in concession. "I apologize if I overstepped. I'm just worried about you in all this."

"Well, I'm worried about me too but I'm also worried about my marriage. And getting pestered isn't helping. I didn't need that before I changed my mind and I damn sure don't need it now."

"Understood. I won't mention it again."

"Have you heard from E.J.?" Lovey asked Natalia after a few tense moments. "Are you communicating at all during this separation?"

Natalia winced at that last word. She still couldn't believe things had gotten to his point and any reminders that E.J. was no longer staying in the house with her caused an ache in her gut. "Not really. We've exchanged a couple of texts but it was mostly just him letting me know where he is.

I said I was giving him space and that's what I'm trying to do, even though it's killing me."

"Where is he staying?" Desiree asked.

"We have some investment property across town. The people that were renting it just moved out a couple weeks ago so he's staying there for now."

"And I don't guess he's given any indication of how long this is gonna last?" Liz carefully spoke up, grabbing her wine glass.

"No. It hasn't been that long but I don't wanna rush him. Of course, I want him to come back today, like now."

"Maybe you should use this time for you, too," Lovey suggested. "I know it's tough on you, but you'll drive yourself crazy if you just let yourself sit around here and pine over your husband."

"Yeah, maybe you should talk to someone on your own to work through why you have trouble with tough conversations," Desiree added. "Or find something else to focus on other than the fact that E.J. isn't here, especially if you have no idea how long he'll be gone. This is a chance for you *both* to work on some things, girl."

Natalia chewed her lip, thinking about that. She honestly hadn't given much thought to exactly what she'd do once E.J. left. She was just flying by the seat of her pants, getting up every day and wishing E.J. would change his mind and come back, and keeping herself marginally occupied in the meantime. But she couldn't deny that some self-examination couldn't hurt. She'd played around with the idea of solo therapy before but maybe it was time to stop playing.

So the next day, she made two appointments; one with a therapist and one with her OBGYN.

Chapter 17

• • • •

E.J.'S JAW CLENCHED as he stood in front of his parents' graves, his hands jammed in his jacket pockets.

"I wish y'all were here," he mumbled. "Y'all would know what to do."

He'd gone out to visit their graves and get things off his chest, something he did when things were heavy on his mind. His parents, Dennis and Nora Bell, had been gone for years and this was definitely a time when E.J. missed them the most. He didn't have anyone he could go to for marriage advice or guidance like he wished he could; at least he could come and talk to their graves.

"This is so crazy," he continued, rubbing his forehead. "I feel conflicted about my marriage, and y'all know how much I hate feeling conflicted. Not knowing what to do about anything makes me itch. But this is a position I never thought I'd be in; feeling like I can't trust my wife, like I don't know her as well as I thought I did. I'd like to just...*get over* all the things she's done but...how can I? I still love her with everything in me but I'm also pissed at her for doing this to us. I get that I have my issues, too, but I haven't lied to her about anything or kept any secrets. I'm just...I don't know how I'm supposed to move forward at this point. Or...if I *want* to."

Admitting that last part burned his throat. Part of him felt ashamed for even contemplating throwing in the towel, but the other part felt relief at the admission.

E.J. stood out there for a while longer, talking to his parents and musing about his situation. He felt lighter after he unburdened himself, though he still wasn't clear on what he wanted to do. It had only been a couple of days and he missed his wife terribly, despite his anger at her. He'd already almost gone home instead of to their investment property he was staying in a couple of times. Being in the unfamiliar surroundings was just a glaring reminder that he was actually separated, and he tried to stay there the least amount of time necessary.

At least he still had work to focus on. He knew Roland wanted him to take some time off, and E.J. had said he'd consider it at the time, but that was before he and Natalia decided to separate. He felt time off was the last thing he needed now. What would he even do with himself? If there was anything E.J. hated, it was sitting idle.

His phone vibrated in his pocket, and he immediately pulled it out and checked it. Part of him hoped it was Natalia, despite how strained things were between them, and the other part of him hated that he wanted anything to do with her after everything that happened. He just wished he didn't miss her so much.

"Yeah?" E.J. grunted, answering the call.

"Hey, where are you?" Roland asked immediately.

E.J. stopped pacing the small circle in front of his parents' graves. "Why?"

"Because we had a meeting this morning about the hot sauce line, remember?"

Gritting his teeth, E.J. cursed himself and rubbed his eyes. "Sorry about that, man."

"You set the meeting up, E.J."

"I'm aware of that. Did you reschedule?"

"No, I handled it. I'll get you caught up but we need to talk about this, man."

"Look, let's not turn this into a huge deal," E.J. sighed. "I get it, I messed up. But-"

"I'm not talking about that. Everybody slips up here and there; I'm not tripping off that part. Again, where are you?"

"Visiting the folks."

"Come by Barfly when you leave there."

"They're putting in the new sound system?"

"Yeah, they're here now. They'll probably be done by the time you get here; they got here early this morning."

"All right."

E.J. hung up and banged a fist to his chest, angry at himself for missing that meeting. Thankfully it wasn't one that he absolutely needed to attend, but it still wasn't a good look. The one thing E.J. could hang his hat on was how he handled his business, regardless of what was going on in his personal life.

After a few more minutes talking to his parents, E.J. turned and headed for his car. He knew Roland was probably going to give him grief about forgetting the meeting, regardless of what he'd said. E.J. certainly didn't tolerate people flaking unless there was an extremely good reason, and 'just forgetting' wasn't one of those.

When he got to Barfly, Roland was talking to the men who had just finished installing the upgraded sound system. E.J. started to join them, but Roland waved him away, indicating he had it covered. Tamping down his frustration,

E.J. just headed back to the office to look over the previous night's numbers.

Roland joined him a few minutes later. Closing the door, he looked at E.J. with a stern expression.

"Do whatever it is you need to do and hurry up, because you have exactly two hours before I'm cutting you off."

E.J. frowned. "Excuse me?"

"You heard me. Since you clearly won't take time off on your own, I guess I'll have to kick you out of here myself. I'm suspending you for a week."

"Have you lost your mind? You can't *suspend* me!"

"I can and I am. And you might as well not even bother trying to argue with me about it."

"Look, if this is about the meeting this morning-"

"It's not about that. Not *just* about that, anyway. The fact that you missed it at all says a lot, man. You're going through some real shit and you need to deal with it."

"I *am* dealing with it. But that doesn't mean I can't work."

"You don't need to work, E.J. I told you I got it. You never take any time off, you never take a vacation...you and your wife are living apart and you're trying to act like everything is everything. That's not healthy."

"And just what am I supposed to do for a week if I'm not working?"

"Figure it out. But you don't need to be here. Or at 845."

"Roland..."

"You and I both know you mainly go to our parents' graves when you need to unleash. You're weighed down emotionally and mentally, and there's nothing wrong with stepping back and reevaluating. You can't do that if you're wearing yourself out getting up at the crack of dawn to work out then working twelve or fourteen-hour days so you're too tired to do anything else but sleep when you finally leave. You're not *really* dealing with it and until you do, you're just gonna stay on this treadmill you're on, tiring yourself out going nowhere. And I bet you're not even taking care of yourself like you should. Have you eaten today?"

E.J. released a frustrated breath. "No."

"Did you eat yesterday?"

"I...ugh, I don't know, man."

"See what I'm talking about?"

"Roland-"

"Save it, bro. This is because I love you. I'm gonna go have Hive make you something. Wrap up whatever it is you're doing, eat all of whatever Hive makes, and then I'm clearing your calendar and kicking you out. Don't bring your ass back here until this time next week."

E.J. just glared at him.

"If it'll make you feel any better, when you come back we'll make a final decision on the buyout offer," Roland said, undeterred by his brother's ire. "We'll sit down with our wives, hash things out, and then give an official answer to Barber and get this off our plates."

Figuring it was pointless to argue anymore, E.J. just threw up his hands. He realized he didn't even have the energy to keep going back and forth with Roland, which he had to grudgingly admit was an indicator that he wasn't himself. His usual stubborn relentlessness and unyielding nature was temporarily lights out.

"Fine, whatever," he conceded.

"You'll thank me for this later," Roland insisted, turning for the door. "Trust me."

"Uh-huh. Right."

Actually chuckling, Roland walked out of the office.

• • • •

BARELY ONE DAY INTO his forced time off and E.J. was already restless.

He could only work out so much. He tried reading but couldn't concentrate. Fiction audiobooks sounded like garbled noise that grated his ears. He didn't have any other hobbies to speak of. And when he tried to just shut everything else out and sleep, he couldn't.

It was a mild shock to him that there wasn't much left in his life when his wife and work were off the table. He'd been so consumed with both for so long that he hadn't noticed. Natalia had said something to that effect a while back, and it looked like she wasn't far off.

He wondered what was going on at Barfly and 845, and pulled up the security footage on his phone, but made himself stop watching after a few minutes. This wouldn't be much of a break if he spent his time silently overseeing what was happening at work. It would only make him want to go in. And if he was going to do this 'taking a break' stuff, he would give it the same energy he gave everything else he committed to.

He wasn't about to fail at *this*, too.

Hobbies. He needed hobbies.

Since Roland was handling everything at the clubs, E.J. didn't want to bother him for suggestions. He bought a 1000-piece puzzle, wanting the challenge, but found himself getting frustrated that it was taking him so long to find the right pieces, and started pounding them with his fist and getting angry when the pieces he tried to force together wouldn't go. The whole thing ended up in the trash.

Movies. They'd never really been his thing but he figured, what the hell. He tried a comedy but thought the humor was idiotic. Musicals annoyed him, with all the spontaneous singing. The suspense movie bored him once his mind ran away with the plot and came to its own conclusion. The thriller, yawn. The drama put him to sleep. Superheroes, nope. Westerns, sci-fi, and horror weren't even considered. And he didn't even watch animated movies when he was a child.

Baking? He couldn't even make decent brownies from the box. Not that he ate a lot of sweets, anyway.

Maybe he could take some kind of class, but once he scrolled through the options of dance, pottery, drawing, playing some kind of instrument, photography...none sparked even the tiniest bit of interest.

Irritated, E.J. ran his hands down his face and looked at his watch, hoping somehow six days had almost passed just like that. This was torture.

He wondered what Natalia was up to, and if she was having as hard a time without him as he was without her. He missed her like crazy, but that sting of anger still flared when he thought of her. But still, his body ached for his wife. His mind recalled their last time together before he left the house, and he groaned at the automatic tightening in his groin. It had taken all of his strength to pack his bags and leave the house he shared with her. They'd picked that house out together, both falling in love with it after weeks of searching. E.J. didn't realize just how much he missed going home to his wife until he was no longer doing it.

But then he wondered if he truly missed Natalia or if he just missed the familiarity of his routine.

Couldn't it be both?

This was making his head hurt. Glancing at the time, he decided to check on his mentees. He called Nigel first.

"Mr. B, I was just about to call you," Nigel answered, his voice strained.

E.J. immediately sat up. "What's going on?"

"My girl..."

Once a couple of moments passed, E.J. urged, "Yeah?"

"I should've asked you how to put a condom on right."

Blowing out a breath, E.J. briefly dropped his head. "So you had sex. And what, the condom came off?"

"Yes, sir," Nigel admitted, his voice shrinking slightly. "We realized it after..."

"Nigel."

"She brought the condoms and didn't know what size to get. We figured it wouldn't matter; that I'd just hold it in place. But we got caught up and..."

"Yeah." E.J. sighed and ran a hand over his head. "I get it."

"What if I knocked her up, Mr. B?" Nigel asked, his voice sounding timid. All the bravado he sported when he was declaring it would be no big deal if he and his girlfriend ended up expecting was nowhere to be found. "She's been freaking out and I'm trying to hold it together, but I started thinking about diapers and formula and daycare and all that...babies cost a lot."

"I know they cost a lot. That's what I told you and Teddy. You knew this was a possibility when you laid down with her, son."

Nigel sighed. "You're gonna lecture me, aren't you?"

"No need for that. You've done the deed now."

"Mama is gonna *kill* me if Karlotta is pregnant. If she is and Mama puts me out, can I come stay with you? I won't be any trouble. I can work at your club cleaning up or something. Or I can cut your grass or detail your car-"

"Nigel, calm down," E.J. ordered. "Just take a second and breathe, man. You've gotta keep your head together. When did this happen?"

"Last night."

"You've heard of the Plan B pill, right?"

"I...oh!"

"Go to the CVS down the street from your place and get it for her. If she takes it within seventy-two hours, it'll knock the chances of her getting pregnant down big time. You have any money?"

"Yes, sir. But what if Mama sees it?"

"Then she sees it. I'm not advocating you keeping it from her. You remember what I said about living with whatever came of you getting down with your girl? Well, dealing with your mama is part of it. You're still a teenager in her house and if you father a child, a lot of that is gonna fall on her shoulders, too."

"Yeah," Nigel acknowledged, glum. "I guess I didn't think about that."

"I know you didn't. But try not to panic without even knowing what the deal is. Just go get the Plan B, give it to your girl, and go from there. Keep me posted, and let me know if you need anything. However things turn out, know that I've got your back regardless, okay?"

"Okay. Thanks, Mr. B. I appreciate it."

"No problem."

E.J. hung up the phone and sighed. Now he had Nigel's situation to worry about on top of everything else. But he meant it when he said he loved him and Teddy like sons so he'd absolutely be right there offering support (and any necessary admonishment) if Nigel ended up being a teenage father.

He leaned back on the couch, glancing around the professionally designed living room that he felt no attachment to. There was no warmth to it; it was just white walls and hardwood floors and strategically-placed artwork and modern furnishings. He didn't even care for the things the designer picked out, but, as she had to remind him a few times, he wasn't going to be living there so it wasn't about his tastes, but what would make people want to choose to rent there over an AirBnB or a hotel. E.J. took her word for it because she knew more about this than he did, and it turned out she'd been right; they'd had a string of renters since they made it available. E.J. never once thought he'd be staying there himself.

Not in the mood to try to decide what to do next, E.J. decided to just go to bed. Part of him hoped he could just sleep for the next few days.

But when he woke up the next morning at four o'clock as usual, he groaned. Usually he sprang out of bed, ready to get his day started. But he made no move to get up, in no hurry to begin another day of no real plans other than going to the gym.

He rolled over and put the pillow over his head, hoping he could go back to sleep. But lingering in bed was no fun without his wife, so he threw the covers off of him and trudged to the bathroom, cursing under his breath the whole time.

After extending his workout as long as he possibly could without hurting himself, E.J. showered at the gym before going to run some errands. Everything in him wanted to stop by Barfly, especially since he knew Roland was at 845, but he needed to be a man of his word. He had agreed to this forced vacation, and as much as he hated it, he would stay away from his clubs, as promised.

While he was out, he decided to stop at Best Buy to get some laptops for his mentees. Neither Teddy nor Nigel had a computer at home, and they always had to wait until they got to the school library or the community center to use one. He actually started to feel some excitement when he pictured how hyped they would be upon getting their own laptops.

"Can I help you, sir?" an eager employee asked as he entered the store.

"No thanks, I got it," E.J. assured, not in the mood for any sales spiels. "Just looking for some laptops."

"Oh, sure. They're right over there," the employee directed, pointing.

"Thanks." E.J. headed in that direction, his brow already furrowed in determination. He took his time perusing all the options, reading the spec cards and internally debating which ones he thought would be better for his boys. He already knew he'd be getting them both the same one, to avoid either thinking they got the short end of the stick.

"Good afternoon, Mr. Bell."

Glancing over his shoulder, E.J.'s frown cleared when he saw Lorenzo standing there.

"Hey, what's up?" E.J. greeted, touching his fist to Lorenzo's extended one. "How's it going?"

"I can't complain. You look like you're in deep focus over here."

"Oh, yeah..." E.J. glanced at the row of displayed laptops in front of him. "Thought I'd come get some computers for my boys."

"That's funny you said that, because I was planning on surprising mine with that very thing for their graduation gifts," Lorenzo stated. "One of them has been dropping some not-so-subtle hints lately."

"Yeah?"

"Yes, they have one in the household but between his three sisters, he doesn't get much time on it, he says. I know he'll be thrilled to have one of his own, especially since he just found out he got accepted to college. I'm taking him out to celebrate that this weekend."

"That's great, man," E.J. stated, nodding. "It's something else, watching them make plans for their lives like that. Both of my boys are headed to college and I couldn't be prouder."

"You and me both. You know which one you're gonna go with?" Lorenzo asked, turning his attention to the laptops himself.

"I've got it narrowed down."

"Need some help?"

"I'm good."

"Ah, I see," Lorenzo smirked, folding his huge arms across his chest. "You don't like to accept help from anybody."

E.J.'s head swung around, his slight frown returned. "What?"

"Between Desiree, Roland, and to a quite lesser degree, Lovey, I've heard a lot about you over the last couple of years. And two of the most common descriptors have been 'driven' and 'stubborn.'"

"Hmph," E.J. grunted. "I've been hearing that last one a lot lately."

"You put everything on your back and don't like to let anyone help you carry the load, even if it's killing you," Lorenzo continued. "It's like accepting help is some kind of admission of weakness."

E.J. eyed his fingers as he traced the outline of the spec card in front of him, conviction pricking his chest. "They said that, huh?"

"In so many words."

"I guess I can't deny that. I'm just used to taking the lead."

"And finishing what you start, come hell or high water, even if it's to your own detriment." Lorenzo nodded as if he understood. "I get it. Matter of fact, I used to be the same way. You should've seen how bullheaded I was after I passed the bar; trying to take on everything I could at work so I could prove myself, not to mention handling everything for my sick mother despite having siblings who were willing and able to do their part. Drove the lady I was dating at the time crazy."

"Can't say my wife loves it, either."

"Thankfully I got past that. I realized I was wearing myself out when I didn't have to. And I was doing more harm than good not only to myself, but to my loved ones. Didn't even realize I was hurting them, trying to be superman. I was so busy trying to take care of everything and everyone myself that I wasn't actually enjoying anything."

Roland's words about loosening up and how life was to be lived rang through E.J.'s mind. And Natalia's pleas about them taking a vacation together that he'd brushed aside. Yes, he'd put it back on the table right before she revealed her latest batch of secrets, but he now regretted being so dismissive in the first place. Just like he'd been dismissive of taking time off, of the deal from Carlton Barber, and of countless other things, just because it didn't fit into his set-in-stone plans.

"I can make a suggestion, if you want," Lorenzo told him, placing a friendly hand on his shoulder and nodding towards the laptops.

Snapping out of his musings, E.J. nodded, casting a quick glance at him. "Sure, yeah."

A half hour later, E.J. was armed with two new laptops as he strolled out of Best Buy, the anticipation of giving them to Teddy and Nigel returning. He wished he could head over to see them right then, but they were still in school.

"You wanna grab something to eat?" Lorenzo asked him, folding the receipt for the new refrigerator he'd just purchased and sliding it into his pocket. "That omelet I had earlier is already a distant memory. Unless you have somewhere you need to be?"

"Oh, I have to..." E.J. paused, remembering he didn't have *anywhere* he needed to be. All he had was time. He shrugged in concession. "Actually, what the hell. All I've had is a protein shake, anyway."

"Yep, that sounds familiar, too," Lorenzo chuckled. "Wanna follow me?"

Resisting the automatic urge to suggest *he* lead their lunch excursion, E.J. forced himself to say, "That's cool." It didn't matter who picked the restaurant, he told himself.

They headed to their respective vehicles, and E.J. followed Lorenzo's steel gray Escalade out of the parking lot.

E.J. was pleasantly surprised when Lorenzo turned into the parking lot of Hot Jam, a popular brunch spot that E.J. had always been curious about but had never taken the time to actually go to. There was a bit of a wait and he was relieved when Lorenzo didn't try to engage him in a lot of small talk. They each checked messages on their phones, only speaking occasionally. When Lorenzo broke out into a smile and began furiously swiping his thumbs across his screen, E.J. figured he was probably responding to Desiree. Which only made E.J. think about Natalia, thus waking up the ache of missing her he'd managed to temporarily suppress. He wondered what she was doing right then.

When they were finally shown to a table, they placed their drink orders and E.J. tried to focus on the menu instead of pining over his wife. Thinking about her when he couldn't see her would only frustrate him, and he didn't want his mood to sour. Or to have to explain why it did.

"I've only been here once but the croquet monsieur was so good I ended up getting one to take home, too," Lorenzo commented, his eyes scanning his menu. "You eat pork?"

"Occasionally. I'm gonna go with the crab cakes and sweet potato hash," E.J. decided, closing his menu.

"You're decisive. That's good. I usually am, also, but there are so many tempting things on here it usually takes me a minute to decide."

E.J. just gave a little shrug and mindlessly checked his watch. He hadn't even looked at the whole menu; he just saw something he liked and went with it.

After another minute or so, Lorenzo signaled the server over and ordered the croquet monsieur plus crème brulee French toast with drunken strawberries, with a side of chicken sausage and crispy home fries.

"You hungry or what?" E.J. semi-joked after he'd placed his own order and the server scurried away.

"I have a big appetite," Lorenzo shrugged, sitting back in his chair. "I'm mindful but I still indulge here and there."

E.J glanced at Lorenzo's huge arms. "Did you used to be a bodybuilder or something?"

"Nah," Lorenzo chuckled, clearly no stranger to that question. "I've just always loved weights. Especially when I got to law school; it's how I handled my stress. It's wild how surprised people get when they hear I'm an attorney and not on someone's football team. Guess that's not expected for someone 6'5 and built like I am."

"I get that a lot, too." E.J. himself was around 6'4.

"You played back in the day?"

"In high school. Didn't have an interest in playing in college. Just wanted to focus on my studies."

"I had a football scholarship but it was a means to an end; I had no desire to go pro. I've wanted to be an attorney since I was a kid."

"What kind of law do you practice?"

"Family law. I run a firm with my dad. What about you? How are things with your businesses?"

"Ugh," E.J. exhaled, feeling some of his tension return.

Noticing, Lorenzo questioned, "Not good?"

"No, it's not that. Business is fine. Great, actually. I'm just on vacation from it for a few days."

"Let me guess; you don't know what to do with yourself and are counting the hours until it's over, right?"

E.J.'s eyebrows shot up. "You're pretty perceptive."

"Comes with the job. Plus, as I mentioned, I used to be the same way. How have you been keeping yourself occupied?"

"Working out. Errands. Sleeping."

"Doesn't sound like much of a vacation."

"I'll admit I'm not very good with doing nothing," E.J. said. "Both my brother and my wife think I don't know how to have any fun and if these last couple of days are any kind of indication, I guess they're right. But working is what I love to do."

"I get it, man. You've established a routine and you're disciplined about it. Nothing wrong with that but it's when you let it constrain you so much that you can't function outside of it that it becomes detrimental. There's something to be said for letting loose."

E.J. didn't even think he'd know how to do that if he tried. He hadn't felt anything close to carefree since his high school days. His father was a successful businessman and E.J. always emulated him. Dennis Bell was a great father and he was always quick to proclaim how proud he was of his boys. It only made E.J. want to work harder to make him even prouder, and apparently he still was years after his father's passing.

He and Lorenzo continued to talk as they ate their meals, with E.J. feeling more comfortable with Lorenzo as the time passed. He let himself ask how things were going with Desiree, and Lorenzo's face brightened when he reported that they were doing really well, having gotten past the whole scene at her birthday party. When Lorenzo asked about Natalia, E.J. had to fight to keep his expression from faltering, but it was apparent that it wasn't a subject he was eager to get into. Thankfully, Lorenzo sensed it was a touchy subject and dropped it.

"So what do you have on deck for tomorrow?" Lorenzo asked, wiping his mouth with his napkin before dropping it onto his empty plate.

Scoffing, E.J. downed the last of his water. "Other than the gym, not a thing."

"Good. You're hanging with me tomorrow."

E.J.'s brow lifted warily. "To do what?"

"You won't be able to plan for this one, man," Lorenzo informed him, actually chuckling. "Come ten o'clock tomorrow morning, just be ready to hear from me."

Chapter 18

• • • •

E.J. KNEW HE SHOULD have demanded more details.

Lorenzo had somehow used his persuasion skills to get him to blindly agree to spend a day doing who knows what. And not only that, E.J. wasn't even driving himself; Lorenzo had insisted that he pick E.J. up. It wasn't lost on him that E.J. would make a break for it at the first opportunity, especially when he saw what Lorenzo had planned for the day.

"Why are you turning in here?" E.J. questioned, frowning at the building they were approaching. "This is a spa."

Lorenzo chuckled as he put his truck in Park. "I'm aware of that."

"Why are we here?"

"We have an appointment."

"What?"

"Man, this is where I need you to start opening your mind; let yourself be open to things outside of your norm. I have a feeling I know the answer to this, but have you ever *been* to a spa?"

"Just to drop my wife off."

"I figured as much." Lorenzo opened his door. "Come on, let's go."

E.J. sat defiantly in the passenger seat for a few moments before finally grudgingly pushing open the passenger door. He looked anything but pleased as he stood and looked at the brick and glass building, his hands on his hips. The wariness was evident.

"You look like you're ready to make a run for it," Lorenzo joked as he rounded the truck.

"I don't know about this, man…"

"Don't make it into a big deal. Don't overthink it. It's just a spa."

E.J. watched as Lorenzo turned towards the building, and made himself move his feet towards the door. He'd never in his life considered going to a spa and wasn't exactly thrilled about spending his morning like this.

But he figured it wouldn't be that bad. Maybe they wouldn't even be there that long.

"Try to clear that frown, too, man," Lorenzo muttered as he reached for the door handle. "Wouldn't want to scare the young lady at the desk."

E.J. hadn't even realized he was frowning. He tried to neutralize his expression; no need in walking around looking evil.

After Lorenzo checked them in, they had a very short wait before they were shown to their respective rooms. E.J. was surprised to learn Lorenzo had booked a full spa day for each of them that included a 90-minute deep tissue massage, a hot towel facial, and a men's manicure and pedicure. It took all of E.J.'s restraint not to scoff when he learned that.

But he found himself undressing and putting on the provided plush white robe, anyway, feeling ridiculous. When the massage therapist entered the room, he could barely look at her; all he registered was that she was tall and her skin was almost as dark as his. He hated feeling so awkward.

Thankfully, she didn't try to engage him in a lot of conversation; she just asked him a couple of questions about any pain points or areas he didn't want massaged before instructing him to get on the table face-down. He reluctantly removed the robe and climbed onto the table, feeling exposed in nothing but his boxer briefs (he refused to get totally naked) and put his face in the cradle, hoping this ninety minutes shot by. At least the cushion was comfortable.

When she re-entered the room and began the massage, E.J. immediately tensed up, feeling funny about another woman touching him like this. The only massages he'd had were from Natalia.

"You okay?" the woman asked him, her voice warm and soothing. He hadn't even bothered remembering her name. "You're *so* tense..."

"Oh, um...sorry." E.J. cleared his throat, feeling silly.

"Not used to getting massages, huh?"

"Is it that obvious?"

"A little," she replied good-naturedly, her thumbs sliding up the back of his neck. "Just close your eyes and try to relax. Clear your mind."

Easier said than done for E.J., but he figured he might as well try, since he was there.

Between the warm oil, the massage therapist's soft hands, the scent of lavender in the air, and the calming music, though, E.J. felt his ever-present coils of tension unfurl. He stopped worrying about how much time was left or other things he could be doing and just gave in to the relaxation.

There was no denying how good the massage was. He felt as if he was melting onto the table.

The hot towel facial was another pleasant surprise; E.J. actually felt like he could go to sleep in the chair.

A tiny bit of his tension returned with the manicure and pedicure, but it wasn't as bad as he thought it would be. E.J.'s previous versions of mani/pedis just consisted of nail clipping and lotioning. But he had to admit; this was significantly better.

The experience was capped off by a light lunch of crab salad sandwiches, fruit salad, and cucumber and mint-infused water. By the time he and Lorenzo strolled out of the spa over three hours later, E.J. was feeling like liquid.

"How'd it go?" Lorenzo asked him, unlocking his truck. "I made sure to schedule you with Dru, the best therapist there."

"Oh, that was her name? Dru? I admit I didn't remember it but she surely knows what she's doing."

"So not too bad, huh?"

E.J. couldn't deny it. "Nah, it wasn't. It was actually really relaxing. I don't think I've ever felt this..." He shook his head, searching for the right word. "*Loose*."

"I can tell. You're even moving differently. And you're not scowling."

E.J. chuckled. "You must think I'm mean as hell."

"Nah. Just intense. I've been around you enough to know you're a good guy at heart. Your loved ones certainly speak highly of you."

"Even Desiree?" E.J. asked, though he didn't exactly consider her one of his 'loved ones' despite them being cool now.

"Yeah, even her. She respects your hustle and your loyalty, and how you handle your business. I haven't heard her say anything negative about you since I've been around."

"Hmm." E.J. glanced out the window as they headed out of the spa parking lot, sinking against the back of the passenger seat. "That's nice to know, I guess."

They rode in relative silence for a while, with E.J. not even thinking to ask where they were going next. He really did feel more relaxed than he had in years, which was a welcome change from how he'd been since his forced vacation started.

His zen was interrupted when Lorenzo pulled into a trampoline park.

"Are you nuts??" E.J. exclaimed, turning to him.

Lorenzo laughed loudly, unfazed. "Not even a little bit."

"What the hell, Lorenzo?"

"We're letting loose today, remember?"

"I did that with the massage and the facial. You didn't say anything about jumping around on trampolines."

"I know. That was intentional."

"Man..."

"Don't start talking yourself out of it. Just roll with it. That's the motto of the day."

"Just roll with it." E.J. shook his head, but made himself get out of the truck. He just hoped no one he knew was in there.

As much as he wanted to adopt Lorenzo's carefree mindset (at least for the day), E.J. couldn't help feeling ridiculous as he and Lorenzo paid for an hour's time on the trampolines. He didn't usually worry about what others thought, but he couldn't help but imagine how it looked; two grown men on trampolines in the middle of the day.

"At least you came in and didn't lock yourself in the truck," Lorenzo quipped as they removed their shoes. "I count that as a win."

"Hmph." E.J. again shook his head as he placed his black Nike Air Max sneakers into one of the cubbies. "Of all things in this city you could've chosen..."

"I knew exactly what I was doing. It's okay to be silly sometimes, man. Everything doesn't always have to be so serious and structured. Doing stuff just for fun keeps you young."

"I'm young enough."

Lorenzo laughed. "Watch what I tell you; you'll feel even younger when this hour is up."

E.J. just grunted as he headed over to the sea of trampolines, separated in squares by padded dividers. He didn't want to flat-out disagree with Lorenzo's declaration, even though part of him did.

But Lorenzo's spa suggestion had been on point, so E.J. told himself to try to keep an open mind.

He hopped on the trampolines, feeling weird instantly. He hadn't been on a trampoline since he was a child. But the more he hopped around, the more he let himself enjoy it. Lorenzo was already doing his own thing, having soared across two trampoline squares and bounced off the trampoline wall, grinning at a couple of nearby little kids who looked to be in awe of the hulk of a man bouncing around them. E.J. watched as Lorenzo indulged in a game of chase, letting the kids tail him across the expanse of the trampolines. E.J. couldn't help but smile at how happy the kids were, laughing and squealing every time Lorenzo slowed down enough to let them get close, only to bounce away at the last second.

Before E.J. knew it, he had joined in on the fun. It became a large game of tag, with more kids joining in on trying to catch the two men. E.J. laughed more than he had in recent memory, loving how much joy the children were having just from playing with him. A couple of them even convinced him and Lorenzo to join a game of dodge ball, though it didn't take all that much convincing; by that point, E.J. was up for just about anything.

"That's our time, man," Lorenzo informed him after the third game of dodge ball.

"Already?" E.J. panted, his hands on his hips. He hadn't even been thinking about the time.

"Yep. It goes fast."

"It really does. All right, then."

E.J. reluctantly said good-bye to the kids they'd been playing with, giving them high fives. One of them hugged his right leg, looking up at him with a toothy grin.

"Thank you for playing with us, mister," the little girl said, displaying her missing tooth.

E.J. grinned, gently cupping the back of her head. She had two huge afro puffs. "My pleasure, sweetheart."

"Jeanie, oh my god; let that man go!" A nearby woman hissed. E.J. figured it was the girl's mother. She looked at E.J. apologetically. "I'm so sorry about that...she's not as shy as I wish she was sometimes."

"It's no problem at all; she's fine," E.J. assured, smiling down at the girl. He wanted to pick her up, but resisted. He felt the tiny pang of yearning hit his chest, but he forced it away; he wasn't about to let his marriage issues sully his good mood.

He knelt down to where he was eye-level with the girl. "You caught me a couple of times out there; you're pretty awesome, you know that?"

Jeanie beamed, proud. "Thank you! I always catch my brothers, too!"

"I bet! If I see you here again, can I get a rematch?"

"Deal!" Jeanie eagerly agreed, holding up her little hand. E.J.'s smile widened as he held up his palm for her to give him a high five before she threw her arms around his neck. Melting a little, he returned her hug, almost hating that he probably wouldn't see this adorable little girl again.

"So E.J. Bell has a soft spot for kids, huh?" Lorenzo commented as they headed outside a little while later.

"Something like that," E.J. admitted. "I've always loved kids."

"I can tell. You were almost like a different person out there, once those children joined us. If I didn't know better, you almost looked disappointed when I told you it was time to leave."

Part of E.J. *had* been disappointed, as he was sincerely having fun. He knew the kids played a large part in that; if it had just been him and Lorenzo jumping around for an hour, he didn't think he would have enjoyed it nearly as much.

"I enjoyed myself," he admitted, securing his seatbelt after getting into Lorenzo's truck. "I can admit when I'm wrong. You're two for two."

"Glad to hear it."

"Though I kinda wish we'd done that *before* the spa. I was all languid and chill before and now I'm wired from those kids chasing me around and hurling balls at me."

Chuckling, Lorenzo pulled out of the parking lot. "I've got you covered, man. I'm kinda hungry after all that; what about you?"

"Actually, yeah; that small sandwich at the spa only went so far."

E.J. wasn't expecting them to pull into Five Guys. He looked over at Lorenzo, who just held up a hand.

"Before you tell me you don't eat fast food, remember the motto for today. Just roll with it. One meal of a burger and fries won't kill you."

Knowing he was right, E.J. just shrugged and got out of the car. He loved a good burger, though he didn't eat them terribly often. And his stomach certainly wasn't protesting the delicious smells that hit him when they entered the restaurant.

"Do you always eat this much?" E.J. asked jokingly after Lorenzo ordered two burgers with various toppings and a large order of fries.

"Takes a lot of fuel to keep this tank going," Lorenzo responded with a grin, waving a hand along his huge body.

"I just love food. And sweets. Thankfully I learned how to make vegan desserts so I don't feel deprived."

"Oh yeah, I've heard the ladies raving about those. I'm surprised you're not a full-fledged vegan, then, in that case."

"Tried it and hated it. I'll go meatless for a few days here and there but I'm not giving it up completely."

"Another thing we've got in common."

E.J. thought they were going to eat their food there, but Lorenzo told him they were taking it with them, as he had one more place for them to go. E.J. just settled into his seat and went along for the ride, actually curious instead of wary of what was next on the agenda. He also had to resist the urge to pull a few fries from the bags in his lap.

When they arrived at a park, E.J. couldn't help but ask, "Don't tell me we're having a picnic. I might have to draw the line at that."

Lorenzo shook his head, snickering. "It's not a picnic. We're just eating outside."

"That's a picnic, man."

"Whatever. Get out of the truck 'cause I know you want to dig in as much as I do. I saw how you kept eying those fries."

Chuckling in concession, E.J. exited the truck and followed Lorenzo over to one of the iron benches facing the lake. They sat on opposite ends and devoured their food, E.J. actually grunting at how good it tasted. He didn't even care about how many calories he was consuming with the huge amount of greasy hand-cut fries they'd put in the bag; he just shoveled them in, enjoying the indulgence.

"So now what?" he asked Lorenzo once he was done, sliding down slightly on the bench and placing a hand over his full stomach.

"Now, nothing. We're just gonna sit here for a while."

"And do what?"

"Just sit. It's a beautiful day; we're not cooped up inside somewhere working and letting it pass us by." Lorenzo gazed out towards the water, resting his elbows on his knees and taking a contented breath. "We're gonna take advantage of that."

E.J. started to protest, but he clamped his mouth shut and just leaned against the back of the bench. His eyes took in their surroundings; the expanse of green grass, the calming lake, the trees, the occasional bird flying and chirping overhead, the gentle breeze flowing around them. It was all very beautiful and serene. E.J. couldn't remember when he last visited a park, or when he let himself just sit and do nothing like this; he always felt it was a waste of time. But he realized he didn't hate this. It was nice to just...be.

They sat out there for a while with very little conversation, each enjoying the quiet time and break from their busy and demanding careers. E.J. wasn't thinking about his marriage or his clubs or the buyout offer or any of the other hundred things that crammed through his mind like a rush hour traffic jam every day. He just sat and appreciated the moment he was in, without thinking about the next thing on his regimented schedule. For once, he didn't feel like he was carrying the burden of everything; he felt weightless. Leaning his head back and letting the sun hit his face, he let out his own contented sigh.

He didn't even know how much time had passed before Lorenzo cleared his throat. E.J. looked over at him in mild alarm, almost having forgotten he was there.

"How are you feeling, man?" Lorenzo asked him, stretching.

Sitting forward, E.J. shook his head. "Man...you really showed me something with this. *All* of this today. I appreciate you pushing me out of my comfort zone. I can't even describe how I'm feeling right now but it's definitely better than I've felt in years."

Grinning, Lorenzo reached over and gently nudged his fist to E.J.'s shoulder. "Somebody had to do the same for me once upon a time. It was my pleasure, brother. You deserve the credit for being open to it."

"It took me a minute but I'm glad I stopped resisting." E.J. looked over at him with sincere eyes. "Thank you, man. For real."

Lorenzo nodded before standing and holding up his hand. E.J. followed suit, and the men slapped hands before sharing a brotherly hug, their new friendship cemented.

Gathering their trash, they headed for Lorenzo's truck, dumping their empty food bags and cups into a trashcan along the way.

"What do you have going on the rest of the day?" E.J. asked once they were inside the truck.

"Meeting up with Desiree in a couple of hours."

It was then that E.J. realized he didn't know what time it was; he hadn't even thought to check the time all day. He was surprised to see it was almost five o'clock in the afternoon.

"What about you?" Lorenzo asked him, backing out of the parking space.

"I wish I knew," E.J. replied, his face tightening a little. He felt himself frowning and tried to clear it. "My brother will try to kick my ass if I go to work and my wife and I are separated right now, so...it's just gonna be me and that empty house, I guess."

Glancing over at him, Lorenzo pulled over to the side of the road leading to the park exit. Turning to him, he asked, "How long are you going to let that anger consume you, brother?"

E.J. wondered how much Lorenzo knew about his situation. "You know what's going on?"

"I don't know specifics. But I could see the tension between you and your wife at Desiree's birthday party; you barely engaged with each other at all, staying on opposite sides of the room most of the night. Not to mention how angry you looked that night and every time I've seen you since. It's like your countenance has a default setting of 'scowl.'"

Turning his attention to a squirrel scurrying up a tree, E.J. muttered, "Like you said, I can be pretty intense."

"I'm not trying to get in your business. But it's clear that whatever you've got going on at home is consuming you. From what I know of you and Natalia, it must be something pretty major going on to make you two live apart."

"Yeah. You could say that." E.J. ran a hand down his face, not particularly eager to talk about it. "Finding out your wife has a bucket of secrets that she's kept from you the entire marriage is pretty major, I'd say."

"You need me to refer you to some divorce attorneys?"

E.J.'s head whipped around in shock. "What?"

"Have you gotten *any* closer to a resolution since you separated? Have you been communicating? Or have the both of you just been stewing in your own anger or guilt without taking the steps necessary to fix the actual problem?"

Conviction hit E.J. like a lightning bolt. If he was honest, he *hadn't* done anything towards fixing the problems between him and Natalia. They hadn't talked about how long the separation should last; they'd barely communicated at all since he left. E.J. hadn't even let himself think about Natalia that much, not wanting to deal with the yearning and frustration from missing her and also from her indiscretions. His mind had been on the restlessness of being alone and off work more than anything. Truth be told, he had no more clarity on their situation now than when they decided to separate.

"You've got me on that one," he admitted.

"Without even knowing all the details, I can understand how infuriating it is when you learn your spouse has broken your trust," Lorenzo stated. "I see it every day in my practice but I've also experienced it in my own past relationships. And I had to decide if I wanted to stay and work it out or leave. And if I was going to stay, if I'd be willing to make the effort to move beyond the betrayal and let the past go. I'm big on trust so, oftentimes, I couldn't. And that's okay if you can't, either, brother. But you have to have the courage to make the decision and live with it."

Pondering those words, E.J. couldn't do anything but nod. "You're right. I've just been so angry that I got stuck in it, idling on the fact that we were in this situation at all instead of putting that energy towards figuring out how to get out of it."

"Hey, it happens. It's natural to be angry when you're wronged, especially by the person you love the most. But at some point, you have to take action. Otherwise, you just end up bitter and not better. Holding on to that kind of emotion day in and day out can be draining."

"You're right about that. I didn't even realize how mentally and emotionally tired I've been until today, when I managed to put it all out of my mind for a while. And I'm in no hurry to go back to feeling like that."

"So don't. Do something about it, man. I'm not saying it's going to be easy or even the ideal solution, whatever it may be. But you've gotta move forward *some* kind of way."

That advice stayed on E.J.'s mind as they headed back to his rental property and once E.J. was alone again. While he still didn't know what his next step would be, at least it felt he was finally thinking with a clear enough head to figure it out. He'd been way too emotional before, his anger skewing his rationale.

First and foremost, he knew he didn't want to leave Natalia. He thought he might, but realized that wasn't what he wanted. Imagining his life without her in it was too painful to even consider. His mind ran down the list of secrets he'd learned about her and her other indiscretions in the previous months and while they still stung, he didn't think they were so heinous that he couldn't get past them.

It was still true that he didn't see her the same way as he did prior to learning about everything, but he believed she was genuinely sorry, and that there wasn't anything else she was hiding. That counted for a lot.

He tried to imagine his life without kids, if it came to that. Natalia might have changed her tune about having babies but E.J. had yet to let himself get fully excited about it, almost as if he was waiting for her to freak out and change her mind. If it did end up just being the two of them indefinitely, it wouldn't be the most terrible thing. He still had Teddy and Nigel, his mentees who were like sons to him. It wasn't the life E.J. had envisioned but when it came down to it, he'd rather have Natalia and no children than a house full of them with some other woman.

The days' events replayed in his head and E.J. wondered how different things would've been if he had allowed himself to loosen up years ago like he had today. While he knew the bulk of his and Natalia's problems didn't lay at his feet, he was willing to own his part in things. He recalled everything Natalia had told him about how difficult he was to be with, and Roland's words about how stubborn and cold he could be. It wasn't something he was proud of.

He pulled out his phone, mildly surprised when he realized he hadn't touched it in hours. It was freeing, unplugging like that for a while. He needed to do that more often.

Placing a call, he mindlessly perused one of the abstract paintings on the wall as he listened to the phone ring. Relief washed over him when the line picked up.

"Well, this is a surprise. Twice in the same millennium?"

Unable to resist a chuckle, E.J. shook his head. "Hey, Lyric."

"What's up, E.J.? I thought hell had frozen over when you called a few weeks ago; I'm almost *sure* the apocalypse is coming now."

Laughing, E.J. dropped onto the white couch in the living room. He had called Lyric that night after leaving his mentees hoping to get some insight about how he was in their relationship, thinking it might help in his marriage, but ended up cancelling at the last minute. It didn't feel right meeting up with his ex, regardless of the reason. Especially after how he blew up upon finding out about Natalia sneaking off to see Dane without telling him. He'd ended up just driving around the city, thinking. "You're a trip, you know that?"

"I have my moments. To what do I owe the pleasure?"

"I wanted to ask you something, if I could."

"Of course. Anything."

"When we were together...was I hard to be with?"

Lyric paused. "Meaning?"

"Was I a bad boyfriend to you?"

"Oh." Lyric released a long breath. "No, E.J., I wouldn't say that. Overall, you were very good to me. But I can't deny that being in a relationship with you came with some challenges."

Not surprised, E.J. leaned against the back of the couch. "Like?"

"Well, I didn't feel like I could make mistakes with you. You demanded so much of yourself and everyone around you that it almost felt like I was going to the principal's office whenever I messed up. There wasn't a lot that you took in stride."

E.J. grabbed the television remote and tapped it against his leg. "So what made you stay?"

"I knew it wasn't coming from a bad place; that it was more about you just wanting the best for and from everyone and not about you trying to be some kind of dictator. And to your credit, the couple of times I mentioned how stringent you could be, you listened and tried to do better. But it was only a matter of time before things slipped back to how they were before. It wasn't terrible but it wasn't ideal, either."

"I guess I didn't realize I was that bad. It was *never* my intention to make you feel anything less than loved and appreciated, Lyric. I sincerely hope you believe that."

"I do," Lyric assured. "You're not a horrible man, E.J. I knew you loved me, but it always felt like you were holding back; like you couldn't fully open yourself up to me. Especially after the pregnancy incident."

E.J. had almost forgotten about that; it was such a difficult time that he'd forced it out of his memory. "Yeah...I know things changed after that."

"To put it mildly. You were over the moon when we thought I was pregnant and when it turned out I wasn't, that was the beginning of the end. You were never the same with me after that; it was almost like you blamed me. Can't say that didn't hurt."

Wincing, E.J. dropped the remote and rubbed his eyes. "I'm so sorry about that...that wasn't fair to you. I'm ashamed that I didn't realize it at the time."

"Hey, we live and learn. I was disappointed and even angry when we ended up parting ways, but I moved past it. Everything happens for a reason. And we definitely had more good times together than bad, so I just look at our time together as a stepping stone towards who I'm really meant to be with."

"You always did have your head on straight," E.J. marveled. "After how I acted back then, I just appreciate that you don't hate me."

"Of course I don't hate you, E.J. You had your flaws but you meant well and I knew that. You just...feel things deeper than others do sometimes."

"Can't dispute that."

"I know you didn't call to ask me this for no reason," Lyric surmised. "Just like I know you're not going to give me any intricate details about what's going on between you and your wife; we're cool but I'm still your ex. So I hope you're able to work out whatever is going on."

E.J. couldn't help but smile. Lyric always was a sharp one. "I appreciate that, Lyric. Thanks for talking to me."

"Anytime."

E.J. hung up the phone and let it slide out of his hand onto the couch. He actually felt relieved that Lyric didn't think ill of him, despite how they ended. Over the years, he didn't let himself think about her or any of his other exes, choosing to focus on the present instead of the past. But that didn't mean that his time with her meant nothing to him. Their breakup affected him enough to where he didn't even think about dating anyone else for over a year; Natalia had been the first woman to pique his interest in the slightest.

When they met, it was instant sparks. E.J. knew Natalia was it for him, but he didn't doubt that he and Lyric could've been happy if he hadn't gotten in his feelings about their pregnancy false alarm and ended it.

He searched around and found a notebook and a pen before going to sit at the dining room table. He made himself write out everything he was upset at Natalia about, as well as anything else that frustrated him about their marriage. His frown increased as he wrote, and he had to make himself calm down and take a breath when he started bearing down on the paper so hard that he ripped it. He told himself that this wasn't about dredging up repeatedly-rehashed stuff or beating a dead horse; it was about purging. Getting his frustrations out. And the more he wrote, the lighter he felt. He was surprised at just how much he'd had bottled up.

When he was done with that, he flipped to a blank sheet of paper and started writing out everything he loved about his wife and their relationship. A small smile came to his lips as he listed her good points, like how loyal she was or how she always supported him, and how she made him feel like he could do anything. His hand moved furiously as more and more things came to his remembrance, even going back to the early days of their relationship. Thankfully, he didn't let himself focus on the state he now knew she'd been in back then; he kept the light shining on the good stuff. And when he finally finished, his hand aching from writing for over an hour, the pros page was more jam-packed than the cons page. He couldn't help but smile at the realization, feeling even more hopeful.

Pushing himself up, E.J. went to take a shower, his mind whirling over the events of the day. Even though he still had a lot on his mind, he felt a sense of positivity that hadn't been there before; like even though he wasn't sure how yet, he felt everything would turn out all right.

As the hot water ran down over him in the slate-tiled shower, E.J. felt the ache of missing his wife return. Everything in him wished she would appear right then, sliding the shower door open with one of her naughty smiles and joining him. He missed her company, her beautiful bronze skin, her laugh, how she touched him. Yes, they still had some things to work out. And he actually felt like they could, if that's what she still wanted.

Needing to hear her voice, E.J. got out of the shower, hurriedly drying off before exiting the bathroom, not wanting to drip water all over the hardwood floors. He went to get his phone, hoping she wasn't working or out with her friends. She answered after two rings.

"Hey," she greeted, clearly surprised.

"Hey. You busy?"

"I was looking over some work stuff but it can wait; I'll absolutely make time for you. Everything okay?"

"Yeah..." E.J. rubbed the back of his neck, amazed that he actually felt a little nervous. "I, um...I know we still have our shit to work through. But I just wanted you to know that if I'm not sure of anything else, I know that I want us to end up together at the end of all this. Whatever has to happen for that to be the case."

"E.J..." Natalia was clearly thrown for a loop. "You have *no* idea how much I needed to hear you say that, baby. That's what I want, too."

"I'm glad. I know we haven't really talked since I left and I wasn't sure if your feelings had changed-"

"Absolutely not," Natalia insisted strongly. "Hell no. If anything has changed, it's how much I miss you being here, because it increases by the day. But there's no doubt that I want us to be together, E.J."

"Good. That's good to know."

"I hate you not being here, but I've made myself take advantage of this time, instead of just moping around and punishing myself for everything I've done," Natalia told him. "I went to talk to a therapist yesterday."

His eyebrows shooting up, E.J. paused in grabbing the container of body oil he'd been reaching for. "Seriously?"

"Seriously. I wanted to explore my reasons for all the shit I did, and why it was so hard for me to come clean with you and Dane when I should have."

"What about the baby issue?"

"Nothing has changed about that. Everything I've said about being on board to start our family was real. I was actually a little disappointed when I took a pregnancy test and it was negative; I'd been hoping that one of those recent times we were together might have stuck."

"You and me both," E.J. muttered, forcing himself to tamp down his disappointment. At least they were on the same page about it now. "But we can keep trying, though."

"And we will. I can't wait."

A somewhat awkward silence hung between them, neither of them wanting to broach the subject of when he should come back home. Despite how much more positively E.J. was feeling about their outlook, he didn't want to jump the gun too soon. They had already made that mistake when Natalia cancelled their therapy session before.

"Roland and I want to sit down with you and Lovey to discuss the buyout," E.J. eventually commented. "Is that okay with you?"

"Of course. When?"

"In a few days, when I'm done with this time off Roland made me take."

"It's so wild hearing that anyone *made* you do anything," Natalia chuckled. "I can just imagine that you're going crazy over there."

E.J. smirked. His wife knew him well. "Something like that. But today was actually a good one. I hung out with Lorenzo and he made me get out of my own head; it helped me get some clarity about things."

"Really? I didn't know you two were that close."

"We've always been cool but he's mainly been Roland's friend more than mine. But I've run into him a few times recently and once I got to know him a little better, I realized he's pretty easy to talk to. And we have more things in common than I thought. He's a decent brother."

"That's great, baby. I'm glad you two are becoming friends. I've always thought Lorenzo was a great guy. The fact that you're opening up to someone like that says a lot."

"I guess it does, huh? There was something to what you told me that night, about not having any other friends besides you and Roland, and no other outlets besides work. It's still a process but I saw what it felt like to unplug and let loose today and I enjoyed it; I wanna keep that up, even after I go back to work."

"I'm so proud of you for that. That'll be good for you; it's time for you to start enjoying what you've been working so hard for, baby. I don't want you wearing yourself into the ground."

"Same. I appreciate you putting up with me, babe."

"Are you kidding? The fact that we're even having this conversation and not contacting divorce lawyers is enough to have me praising the Lord. After everything I did..." Natalia's voice caught and she took a moment to compose herself. "I'm grateful that you still *want* to work things out."

"I still love you, Natalia," E.J. emphasized, hating that he wasn't with her right then. "With everything in me. That hasn't changed."

"It hasn't changed for me, either," she replied with equal intensity. "You'll always be my heart, E.J. Bell. That's for life."

E.J. smiled, nodding and placing a hand over his chest. "For life."

Chapter 19

• • • •

NATALIA FELT MORE HOPEFUL than she had in months.

Hours after her call with E.J, she laid in bed, her mind recalling everything they talked about. She'd never been more relieved as she was when he assured her that he wanted them to stay together. Part of her feared that his time alone would lead him to the realization that he thought they'd be better off apart; that he wouldn't be able to get over everything she'd done. It meant everything to her that he remained as committed as she was.

She wanted her man to come home, but she didn't have the nerve to ask him to. It would have hurt too much if he'd turned her down, regardless of the reason. So she made herself just be grateful that they seemed to be on good terms and on the road to reconciliation.

Thanks to Lovey and Desiree's advice and encouragement, she'd managed to pull herself out of the funk she was in after E.J. left. She still missed him terribly, but she was taking advantage of the time to work on herself, and she was encouraged to hear that E.J. was doing the same. For the first time since they separated, she had confidence that they would come out of this mess together.

"Twice in two days; you weren't kidding about needing help, huh?"

Natalia blinked, then chuckled. Liz had warned her about Dr. Jacobson's candor when she referred her and Natalia appreciated it, even if she found it jarring at times.

"I absolutely wasn't kidding," Natalia replied, settling into the plush tan armchair in Dr. Jacobson's office. "Though I know better than to think that everything is going to be all hunky dory after a couple of sessions."

"If only, right?" Dr. Jacobson adjusted her fashionable red-rimmed glasses and crossed her long brown legs. Her thick natural hair hung around her shoulders like a fluffy black cloud. "But that wouldn't be very good for business."

"Right," Natalia smiled.

"So when we talked yesterday, you told me about the whole situation with you and your ex, Dane," Dr. Jacobson stated with a glance at her notes, getting down to business. "When I asked you the reasoning behind why you handled things the way you did, as far as ending your relationship in an email instead of face-to-face, you couldn't give me an answer. Have you thought more about that?"

"I have," Natalia took a deep breath, rubbing her hands along her thighs. "At first I thought it was all about getting a clean break; he couldn't try to talk me out of anything if I emailed him. In my head, it was best for both of us, since we didn't ultimately want the same thing, as far as marriage. But I can also admit that I was embarrassed."

Dr. Jacobson sat forward slightly, intrigued. "Explain that."

"I had *so* much anxiety over the decision to end our relationship, especially because I knew Dane wouldn't want me to. There were several times when I started to call him or go see him to tell him in person, but I always chickened out. And that embarrassed me and pissed me off, because I'm not supposed to *get* scared. Not because of a man. That's not what I do."

"Who says?"

"It's just not. I was the one who always got in trouble for talking too much or cussing people out at the drop of a hat; it burned me that I didn't have the spine to let Dane know about the abortion. *And* that I wanted to break up."

"Were you afraid of him?"

"Not in the way you're probably talking about. I didn't want to disappoint him. Despite everything, he'd been good to me. And..."

Dr. Jacobson looked at her expectantly. "Yes?"

"Maybe I feared he'd be able to talk me out of it," Natalia admitted, realizations blasting through her mind like fireworks. "That he'd manage to sweet-talk me into staying together and having the baby and us just shacking up like he wanted. Then I'd feel like I was stuck with him because we had a kid together, and I'd start to resent myself and him."

"And what did you think would happen when you dumped him in an email?"

"Of course I knew he wouldn't appreciate that. But at least I wouldn't be able to see whatever reaction he had. And it was easier to convince myself that he understood where I was coming from."

"Thus relieving your guilt."

Natalia's eyes narrowed thoughtfully. "I didn't think of it like that, but I suppose so."

"What about the part about you seeing your current husband before you and Dane were over? How did you rationalize that?"

"E.J. was my stress relief. I was going through all the emotions over my relationship with Dane not being what I thought it was, and knowing I was going end it...when I met E.J., I was so turned on by everything about him that I didn't want to risk losing him to somebody else. And I told myself it was fine since Dane and I were over in my head and I wasn't ready for anything deep, anyway."

"And you didn't think E.J. would go with that?"

"I wasn't sure and I didn't want to chance it."

"Was there any part of you that felt that if E.J. rejected you, it would be another indication that you should stay with Dane?"

Natalia paused, having never considered that. "I don't think so."

"You sure? It sounds to me like E.J. wasn't just your stress relief; he was your insurance policy. Not only against not being alone, but against giving your decisions a chance to haunt you. You had already justified everything to yourself; any deviance from that would've just increased the anxiety you were already running from."

"Wow...I guess that could also explain why I waited until E.J. asked me to make our relationship official before I finally sent Dane that breakup email."

"It very well could. And you justified apologizing to Dane in a text also, right?"

"I figured it was still an apology, even if it wasn't an ideal one," Natalia revealed with a hunched shoulder. "And I had a feeling he'd probably heard about me and E.J. by then; we weren't exactly being discreet. But I guess I had stopped caring by then."

"Maybe you *wanted* him to find out about you and E.J. so he'd break up with you first and let you off the hook."

Pausing, Natalia considered that and shook her head in wonderment. "Damn, you're good."

"I'd better be, as much as it cost to rent this office space. Was it also embarrassment that kept you from being honest with E.J. about your initial lack of desire to have a baby?"

"In a way, I guess. It was mostly because I knew he absolutely wanted kids and figured he'd walk if he knew I didn't, but a small part also didn't want him thinking of me differently. Some men think women that don't want kids are cold and selfish."

"And you don't think he would have understood and respected your reasoning?"

"Again, I wasn't about to chance it. Even though we were keeping things casual at first, I knew I didn't want him with anybody else but me. Come to think of it, I barely even thought about it when I told him I wanted kids as much as he did; it just came out on its own and I ran with it. Part of me actually thought we'd laugh about it in the long run. I guess I had deluded myself again into believing I hadn't done anything terrible, even if it wasn't totally right."

"You're rather good at that. But it's commendable that you're digging into these issues and owning up to everything, regardless of how many years later you're doing it."

"Yeah. This was long overdue. I've never once questioned my decision to leave Dane and get with E.J., but I know now that the way I handled it was fucked up. I mean, messed up."

"No, you had it right the first time. It was fucked up."

Unable to resist, Natalia burst out laughing. She would have to take Liz out for drinks for referring her to Dr. Jacobson.

Natalia booked more sessions over the following days, eager to keep exploring why she did the things she did. They dug into her marriage with E.J., her relationship with her parents and siblings, her realizations about why she initially thought she didn't want children, even her friendships with Lovey and Desiree. It was fascinating getting a professional point of view and considering things she hadn't before. Even when the discussions got difficult or painful and had her in tears, and Dr. Jacobson wouldn't let her get away with saying 'I don't know' and made her dig for the answer, Natalia left each session feeling better than she did when she arrived. It made her feel accomplished to finally tackle issues she'd spent years running from, simply because she was afraid of what it would reveal about herself.

Yes, she had made some horrible decisions. But at least she was owning them and making amends. And she had certainly learned her lesson about being up front, even if it was difficult or cast her in an unfavorable light.

Natalia wanted to call E.J. She wanted to tell him to come home. But she knew she needed to give him whatever time he felt was necessary. As positive as he sounded when he called her a couple of nights before, he clearly felt it was still necessary to stay separated since he made no mention of coming back. It was easier for her to be patient knowing he wanted them to work through things as much as she did. She could only hope that his continued realizations didn't lead him to rethinking that.

As glad as Natalia was about all the effort she was putting into her therapy sessions, it was also pretty draining, especially considering the fact she'd been going practically every day. She needed to let loose, so she called her girls, asking them to meet up.

"Y'all have no idea how happy I am to see you two," Natalia commented once they were all settled on one of the couches at Barfly. They'd already ordered a round of drinks, along with some appetizers. "It's been a heavy past few days."

"We didn't come here because you're trying to see E.J., did we?" Desiree asked her with a quirked brow.

"No. He's not back to work yet. I'm not sure what he's doing right now."

"Lorenzo told me they hung out the other day. Blew my mind. And I heard him talking to your man on the phone last night. You'd think they were lifelong friends, the way they were going on and on."

"Yeah, I'm still tripping about that myself. E.J. isn't usually eager to open up to people. But that just shows how much progress he's made."

"Is he in therapy, too?" Lovey asked, reaching for one of the pesto chicken sliders on the table in front of them.

"Not that I know of. He didn't mention that when we talked the other day."

"Well, regardless, I'm so glad that it looks like the two of you are making a turn for the better."

"Girl...I can't even tell you how relieved I was when he let me know he hasn't changed his mind about wanting us to stay together. That was the main thing I was afraid of when this whole separation kicked off."

"That's totally understandable. You two are dealing with some heavy stuff. And unfortunately, not every couple would be willing to tough it out."

"I know what you mean, though, Natalia, because I had those same fears with Lorenzo," Desiree chimed in. "I was scared to death that he was going to decide that he couldn't get over my turning down his proposal."

"You think he's going to propose again?" Natalia asked, biting into her shrimp eggroll.

"I hope so. But now I wonder if he hasn't because he thinks I'll turn him down again. I told him that what happened at my birthday party was absolutely a one-time thing but I guess he doesn't buy it. For all I know, he took the ring back and everything. Lovey, where's your wine?"

"Oh...I'm not drinking tonight," Lovey replied, a slight flush coming to her cheeks as she sipped her water.

"Why not?"

"Wait a minute," Natalia hedged, holding up a finger and eyeing Lovey with a cautious smile. "Is somebody pregnant?"

Desiree gasped.

Unable to hold it in, Lovey squealed and bounced her knees excitedly. "Yes! Roland and I found out last night!"

Natalia and Desiree screamed with excitement and dove on their friend in a group hug, drawing curious glances from the people around them.

"Congratulations!" Desiree exclaimed, hugging her bestie around her shoulders. Lovey beamed, grasping Desiree's arm with both hands. "He finally put another bun in that oven, huh?"

"Yes, *finally*!" Lovey replied. "It's so wild how it works sometimes; Xavier was totally unplanned. We thought it would be easy this time, since we were actually trying, but it took longer than we thought. But it doesn't matter now because we have our second little blessing getting ready for us."

"I bet Roland probably did a cartwheel when he found out."

Lovey laughed. "He was definitely thrilled. We both were. Part of me still can't believe it."

Lovey's announcement made Natalia remember her and E.J.'s recent failed attempts at getting pregnant. They hadn't been on a crusade about it like Lovey and Roland were, but Natalia had expected some good news on that front by now. She'd almost forgotten about the doctor's appointment she'd had that morning.

She started to tell them about it, but changed her mind. E.J. needed to hear it first.

The ladies continued to enjoy themselves, stuffing their faces and dancing to the live music. It felt good for Natalia to let go of her issues for a while, since work and therapy and missing E.J. had zapped her of most of her mental energy.

Her phone lit up on the table and she dove for it, thinking it might be E.J. She sucked her teeth when she saw it was just a message from Kira.

"Who's that?" Desiree asked, noticing her expression.

"Something from my dumb-ass sister."

"Kira's at it again, huh?" Desiree chuckled, coming to peek over Natalia's shoulder. "See what she wants; you never know, maybe she's telling you she's sending you money for all the time she spent at your house. Or that she's back in school. Or that she got her own apartment."

"Since we're making up stuff, why don't we go ahead and say maybe she hit the lottery or married a pro football player or invented a magic pill that cures blindness?"

"Just check the message, smart-ass."

Figuring she might as well, Natalia clicked open the message. It was a video and when she played it, both her and Desiree's jaws dropped.

"Is that..."

"What are you two looking at?" Lovey inquired, coming over to join them. "Oh my god!!" Her face got as red as a beet when she saw the video of Kira and Dane having sex. Kira kept shooting sly glances to the camera, and Natalia figured Dane wasn't aware that he was being filmed. "Why would she send you that??"

"Ugh," Natalia grunted, stopping the video and closing out of the message.

"That is too funny!" Desiree hooted, actually laughing. "Natalia, girl, nobody can say your sister is boring, that's for damn sure!"

"Yeah, she's hilarious."

"Oh my god, I can't un-see that..." Lovey droned, her hands pressed to her cheeks as she paced back and forth.

"Can you forward that to me?" Desiree asked Natalia.

"What? No!" Natalia exclaimed, shaking her head. "That shit is deleted and she's now blocked right along with Dane."

"Aww."

"Well, at least I can give her credit for doing something she said she was gonna do. She told me she was gonna try to get with Dane, thinking I'd give a damn. And apparently whatever charm or lies she used on him worked."

"You think he got with her to make you jealous?"

"Don't know and don't care. They can have each other." Natalia put her phone down and chuckled, glancing at Lovey. "Let's try to un-traumatize our girl here before she dissolves into a frazzled mess."

The friends stayed out for a while longer before Roland came looking for Lovey, letting her know it was time to go home. Now that she was pregnant again, he was back in super-protective mode. Desiree started teasing her friend before Lorenzo texted her, asking when she was coming home. When she immediately started gathering her things, Natalia laughed.

"And your ass was clowning Lovey," she teased, giggling. "Now look at you, running when your man calls, yourself."

"Let's not act like you haven't done the same thing," Desiree reminded. "I seem to recall you leaving me at Rocky's when E.J. called one night."

Natalia's smile grew, remembering that. She gave a conceding shrug. "You got me with that one."

"Bye, girl. Love you," Desiree leaned in, giving Natalia a hug and air kiss. "You gonna be all right? I can wait a little while, if you still want to hang. Lorenzo will understand."

"Girl, go home to your man. I'm about to head out, myself."

"All right. I'll call you tomorrow."

Natalia was in her car a little while later, the smile from the good time she'd had with her friends still on her lips. She was so happy for Lovey's pregnancy and Desiree being back on track with Lorenzo. It did her heart good to see her friends so happy.

Of course, it also made her think of E.J. Natalia couldn't deny she'd felt the tiniest pang of jealousy when her friends' men came calling for them, like E.J. had done for her so many times before they separated. She didn't realize how much she appreciated that before; the fact that he cared enough to know where she was and wanted to make sure that she was safe. There was so much she missed about the life she shared with her husband.

Unable to resist, she called him. She just had to hear his voice.

"Hey babe," he greeted, igniting flutters in her chest.

"Hey, baby. What are you doing?"

"Reading. A novel."

"What?" Natalia grinned. "Since when do you read those?"

"It's some paranormal stuff that Roland recommended. I can't say I love it but it's entertaining enough for me to keep reading."

"Wow. Maybe I oughta check to make sure I'm not actually in the Twilight Zone."

E.J. chuckled. "I've actually said the same thing. Are you heading home from Barfly?"

Natalia paused. "How did you know?"

"Roland might have tipped me off that you were there with Lovey and Desiree. He had to bribe me not to come over there."

"I'm almost mad at him for that. I would've loved it if you had."

"He no doubt thought I'd try to do some work if I did. But all I wanted was to see you."

Natalia felt like she was going to explode with yearning. Everything in her wanted to head over to their investment property just so she could feel her husband's arms around her. She ached for it. "I miss you *so* much, baby."

"I miss you, too."

"E.J..." Her hands gripped the steering wheel. "I know I've said it before, but I'm so sorry for everything I did to get us to this point. I'm learning a lot about why I did what I did in therapy. And it was so unfair to you. You've been way too good to me...I just-"

"Babe, stop," E.J. gently interjected. "You don't have to keep apologizing. I know you're sorry. Just like I'm sorry for my part in things."

"You didn't do anything. At least, not on the level of the shit I did."

"Doesn't matter. You were unhappy with how I was."

"One or two aspects of how you were, that's *it*," Natalia quickly corrected. "I was absolutely happy with you and with us overall. The things I pointed out...yes, they were worth mentioning but they were far from deal-breakers."

"Well, regardless, I don't want that to be an issue anymore," E.J. stated, sounding determined. "I just ask that you be patient with me when I slip up, 'cause I'm sure I will."

"You know I will. Just like you've been with me all this time. We have each other's backs."

Their conversation continued as she drove the rest of the way home. She hated going back to that empty house, but being on the phone with E.J. as she walked in helped take her mind off it and made it a little less painful.

Their conversation ended up lasting for another couple of hours, them staying on the phone as they each started winding down for the evening. Natalia didn't even want to get off the phone when she took a shower, putting the call on speakerphone and perching it near the open shower door. Knowing she was naked had E.J.'s voice dropping to that octave that always pushed Natalia's arousal to full-blast. Their banter turned increasingly sultry as she got out of the shower and began moisturizing her body, imagining E.J. there with her. When she laid on their bed, naked and writhing, her hand automatically went between her legs.

"You still naked?" E.J. asked her, his voice a hoarse whisper.

Natalia let out a shaky breath before biting her lip, her eyes tightly closed. "Yes."

"You touching yourself, baby?"

"Yes...and I want you to join me. Stroke that dick for me, E.J."

He groaned, his breaths a little more shallow. "Damn, I want you, Natalia."

"Oh, I want you, too..."

"I can't wait to get back home to you. I hate being away from you, baby. You need to be on top of me right now, riding this dick."

"E.J, *shit...*"

"Then I'll eat you into a coma."

A hard shudder ripped through Natalia's body at his words. Her fingers began circling her clit faster, her hips picking up speed right along with them. "Yes, god yes...keep talking."

They continued their phone sex, bringing each other to much-needed climaxes. Natalia screamed when she came, trying as hard as she could to pretend it was her husband's fingers between her legs and teasing her nipples instead of her own. And he sounded so amazingly sexy that it was unfair.

"You know I'm tackling you as soon as I get the chance, right?" she informed him, breathless and still tingling.

"You read my mind. 'Cause I'm gonna be all over you as soon as I get back there."

"When *are* you coming home, baby?" she finally worked up the nerve to ask. "I need you here with me."

"Soon," he promised. "Believe me, I want to be there as much as you want me there. As much as I hate being away from you, though, I think this time is good for both of us. We're going to appreciate each other and our marriage so much more now, babe."

"Absolutely. Because I damn sure don't want to go through anything like this again."

They talked for a little while longer before reluctantly wishing each other good night, with E.J. reminding her to check the doors and make sure the alarm was set. Natalia was tempted to tell him about her visit to the doctor that morning, but she wanted to tell him in person. She could only hope that it didn't derail the progress they'd made when she did.

Chapter 20

• • • •

E.J.'S VACATION WAS finally over and it was time for the couples to get together to discuss the buyout offer. He was thrilled that they were going to go ahead and put this issue to bed, not to mention that he would be able to go back to work. But he was most excited about finally getting to see his wife.

They'd been in increasingly more consistent contact of late, but he hadn't seen or touched her in too long. He was more anxious about that than he was about the buyout issue, and he took extra care getting ready, specifically selecting a white shirt that hugged his muscles and spritzing on the Polo Black cologne that he knew drove her crazy.

Natalia was equally as excited. She couldn't wait to get over to Roland and Lovey's, where they all were meeting. Her hands actually shook as she got ready, anticipating E.J.'s reaction upon seeing her in her orange minidress. It was a little dressy for what was essentially a business meeting, but she didn't care. She wanted to be extra cute for E.J.

She was the last to arrive to Lovey and Roland's, and her nerves were in overdrive as she rang the doorbell. Lovey swung open the door with a huge grin.

"Hey, girl!" she greeted. "Come on in!"

Natalia smiled at her sister-in-law as she stepped inside the brick colonial house; Lovey and Roland had just moved into it about a year earlier. Natalia was too anxious to notice any of the recent changes that Lovey had made since her last visit, though; she was actually tingling, knowing her husband was somewhere in the house.

"How are you feeling?" Lovey asked her in a low voice, after she'd closed the door behind her. She eyed her knowingly.

"I'm...I'm okay," Natalia replied, releasing a shaky breath. She pressed her hands to her stomach. "It's wild that I'm actually nervous. He's here, right? I know I saw his car outside but I still need to hear it. And do I look all right? How does he look? Oh my god, I'm gonna throw up..."

"Natalia, calm down, sweetie," Lovey urged, gently touching Natalia's face before pulling her into a reassuring hug. "It's gonna be just fine. E.J. is absolutely here; he's off somewhere with Roland. And to answer your questions, he looks great and so do you."

Resisting the urge to run through the house screaming E.J.'s name, Natalia forced herself to stay cool. She could use another moment to get herself together, soaking in the comfort and encouragement from Lovey's hug for a minute before stepping back with a grateful smile. "Thank you for that, girl." She then noticed the aromas in the air. "You cooked?"

"Yeah. I figured since we were all going to be over here, I might as well feed everyone. Especially since it's around dinnertime. It's just chili; nothing fancy."

"Girl, bless you, 'cause I've admittedly been too all over the place to eat. Where's my nephew?"

"Oh, he's sleeping; he spent the day over at Mama Elyse's with the other grandkids so he's good and tuckered out."

"And how is my new baby in there?" Natalia teased, leaning her face closer to Lovey's stomach. "Helloooo my little niece or nephew! Auntie Natalia loves you already!"

Lovey laughed, beaming in her pregnancy glow already. "Everything is great in there. We just went to the doctor this morning, actually."

"I already know you're over the moon, girl," Natalia commented as they moved from the entryway into the family room. "I can't wait until-"

She looked up to see E.J. heading straight for her, having just entered from the den with Roland. His eyes were hungry and laser-focused on hers, and her hand flew to her chest, her heart already pounding with excitement and anticipation. She wanted to faint at how ridiculously hot he looked.

He snatched her to him, sliding his hand behind her neck and laying a kiss on her that knocked her back a few steps. Their arms wrapped tightly around each other as they got lost in the moment, either forgetting or not caring that they weren't alone in the room.

"Umm..." Roland hedged, scratching the back of his neck with a teasing smile.

"Come on, sweetie, let's give them a minute," Lovey told her husband, placing a gentle hand to his chest. Her face was a little flushed but she looked at the reunited couple with a grin before leading Roland out of the room.

E.J. and Natalia were in no hurry to let up, and stood in the middle of the room making out for a good ten minutes. Their hands roamed all over each other, neither able to get as close to the other as they wanted. It was taking all of E.J.'s restraint not to pick Natalia up and take her against the wall right then.

"I've missed you so much, babe," he whispered against her lips. His hands gripped her waist tighter.

"Oh I've missed you, too," Natalia impassionedly concurred, holding his face in her hands. "Oh my god, E.J., you have *no* idea."

"I wish we weren't in my brother's house 'cause...*damn*, babe, I wanna get at you right now."

"You think they'd mind if I rode you on the couch real quick?" She slid her hands up and down his chest, biting her lip as her chest heaved in desire that was growing by the second.

"Probably. And you know Lovey would faint if she happened to come in and catch us."

"Guess we'll have to wait, then. Unless you want to sneak off to the-"

"Are y'all done slobbing each other down yet?" Roland asked, re-entering the room.

E.J. grunted, giving his wife one more sweeping look with a lick of his lips before turning to his younger brother. "No, but since you interrupted us..."

Lovey peeked around the corner with apologetic eyes. "I tried to tell him to give you two some more time, but he didn't listen to me."

"I'm glad you two are so happy to see each other and everything, but we need to get this going before it gets too late," Roland commented, though he was smiling.

"I guess." E.J. held Natalia close by the waist, and her arms were wrapped around him. "The sooner we start, the sooner we're done."

"Oh, I forgot to tell you, Lorenzo and Desiree are coming, too. They should be here any minute."

E.J.'s brow furrowed slightly. "Why?"

"What we decide largely affects Desiree, and she's had a big hand in us being so successful. She asked if Lorenzo could join and I didn't have a problem with it."

Natalia looked up at E.J. pensively, expecting him to go off. Lovey was eying him nervously, too, waiting for him to reprimand Roland for inviting people who were outsiders – from an owner's standpoint – to such an important meeting.

But to everyone's surprise, he just nodded briefly. "Fine."

Roland's eyebrows shot up but he left it at that, not wanting to poke the bear. He could only hope the meeting went as smoothly.

Once Desiree and Lorenzo arrived shortly after, they all enjoyed the meal of chicken chili and yeast rolls before Lovey started practically bouncing in her seat, a huge grin on her face.

"Girl, you all right?" Desiree asked her, eying her friend as if she was losing it. "Or are you still giddy about that bun you've got in the oven?"

"Something like that," Lovey teased, eyeing Roland. He just chuckled and shook his head.

"Clearly, my wife can't wait to tell y'all the good news," he commented, reaching for Lovey's hand.

"What good news?" Natalia asked.

"That we're having twins."

"You what??"

Everyone shrieked or cheered in excitement, jumping out of their chairs and surrounding Lovey and Roland with hugs and kisses of congratulations. Lovey was tearing up, she was so happy.

"We just found out today," she informed everyone as things calmed down. "I couldn't believe it when the doctor said she saw two babies in there."

"Hell, *you*? I thought I was going to faint," Roland added jokingly, even though everyone sensed there was some truth to that. "It took me a minute to process all of that. Once I came down off the shock, though, I was as thrilled as Lovey."

"Wow, that is so awesome, y'all," Natalia commented, placing a hand to her chest. "I am *so* happy for you two."

"So am I," Lorenzo chimed in, lifting his glass with a smile.

"Me, too. Two babies at once??" Desiree marveled. "I'd be losing my mind but that's perfect for you. And you know Mama is gonna wanna throw a party over this."

Everyone laughed. "We were going to wait to tell everyone but I just couldn't hold it in anymore," Lovey admitted. "I'm just so, so excited to be growing our family like this."

E.J. eyed his sister-in-law who was beaming with joy and his brother, who was gazing at his wife with clear love in his eyes, and E.J. felt a rush of emotion hit him. The fact that twins were on the way to the family hit him right in the chest. But it wasn't jealousy he was feeling; it was a surprising sense of peace.

"Congratulations, y'all," he spoke up, briefly raising his glass of sparkling water. "Hearing this news is actually the perfect cue to kick things off about why we're here, if that's all right."

Wariness flashed through Roland's eyes, but he nodded. "Yeah, let's get it going."

"I know we've gone back and forth about this buyout offer for weeks and weeks now," E.J. began, taking a sip from his water glass before setting it on the table and lacing his fingers together next to it. "And I've been adamant about my position. Just like you've been about yours."

"True. But before you go there, man-"

"No, let me say this first 'cause it needs to be said, especially now," E.J. held up a hand. "We can save everyone a lot of time, here. We'll accept Barber's offer."

Lovey and Natalia gasped, and Roland looked as if he was expecting E.J. to start laughing and admit he was joking. But E.J.'s expression stayed neutral; he didn't look angry or resentful in the least. Desiree and Lorenzo glanced at each other warily.

"What's going on, E.J.?" Roland finally asked after a few more moments of stunned silence. "What brought this on?"

"I was thinking about it a lot during my down time," E.J. explained. "Analyzing the hell out of it, wondering if I could really live with that kind of change. I heard you when you told me your reasons for wanting to accept, even though it might've seemed like I didn't. And hearing your news tonight, knowing you have two babies on the way...maybe it's the right thing to do. For you and Lovey."

"E.J..." Lovey marveled, placing a hand to her chest. She was clearly touched.

"Brother..." Roland looked emotional himself. "I can't believe I'm hearing you say this right now."

"I'm really okay with it," E.J. assured, as much to himself as everyone else. "At least, I think I can be. You'll want to be home with your wife and your three young kids, and this is an opportunity for you to do just that for as long as you choose to. Not everybody gets that opportunity. I'm not gonna stand in the way."

"E.J.-"

"What do you think about that, babe?" E.J. asked Natalia, turning to look at her. "I know we haven't had a chance to talk about it yet."

Natalia grinned, having never been more proud of her husband. She rubbed a hand across his back. "You know I'm down for whatever you want to do. I just want you to be happy, at the end of the day."

"And I don't think you will be, despite what you're saying," Roland spoke up, looking at his brother. "I love you for wanting to do this, man, but in a matter of days you'll be kicking yourself and we all know it."

E.J. knew he was probably right, but he still shook his head. "I'll get over it."

Natalia could see how hard E.J. was trying to keep it together. Everything in her believed that he didn't really want to sell the clubs, but he was making a sacrifice for his brother. She admired him for it, but part of her also worried about how it would affect him down the line, because she agreed with Roland's prediction about E.J. kicking himself later.

But this was hard enough for him, and she didn't want to make it harder by challenging him when he was trying to do something selfless. She'd just do everything she could to be there for him at the end of it.

Roland had no problem challenging E.J., though. "E.J., I appreciate it..." His hand landed on his chest with a thump, "More than you know. And I think I can speak for Lovey when I say that it means a lot that you're offering to do that for us. But I'm not gonna let you. We're *not* accepting Barber's offer."

Everyone but Lovey's head snapped to Roland in surprise.

"What?" E.J. marveled, clearly thrown.

"Just like you've been thinking about it a ton lately, so have I," Roland informed. "And I already told you how I was starting to have second thoughts, once I learned about some of the things Barber wants to do. Besides that, Lovey and I have discussed this a *lot*. And I can't deny that she has a point about how I'll probably feel about all this at some point later on."

"I've been telling him that I believe he'd regret it eventually," Lovey added, looking at her husband. "The money is definitely enticing, but some things are just more important. And just like you're thinking about us in this decision, E.J. – which I *so* love and appreciate you for – I'm thinking about the two of you. The money just isn't worth it if you're going to end up unhappy with how you got it."

"And since you said that, Lovey, I'm gonna go ahead and agree," Natalia spoke up. "I said I was down for whatever decision you made, E.J., and I meant it; you and Roland built those clubs into what they are and that's something to be damn proud of. And if you don't *truly* feel selling is the right thing to do, then don't do it." She squeezed E.J.'s arm. "We're gonna be good. We're *already* good; we don't need that man's money."

"And neither do we," Lovey added, rubbing Roland's hand. "We're already so blessed."

"If I may ask a question," Lorenzo spoke up, briefly lifting his hand. His bass voice filled the room. "I take it Mr. Barber doesn't want to do a partnership of any kind, correct?"

"Correct," Roland replied. "He wants exclusive ownership. Which means he can change Barfly and 845 to whatever he wants. There's no guarantee he'd keep our employees, that he'd keep you on as promoter, Desiree; we'd be totally out."

"Forgive me for being late to the party and not knowing any of this, but why doesn't Mr. Barber just start his own entities? He's certainly no stranger to business."

"He's a stranger to *this* industry, though," E.J. emphasized. "His name doesn't have the same pull in our world as it has in the real estate and tech arenas. And he pretty much wants something ready-made so he can hit the ground running."

"I see." Lorenzo rubbed his chin, frowning slightly in thought.

"Why, what are you thinking?" Desiree asked him, placing a hand on his leg. "I know that look."

Lorenzo glanced at her before his eyes slid around to everyone else. He shook his head, clearing his expression. "It's nothing. Sorry to interrupt."

"No sweat. But as I was saying, E.J., I'm serious about declining this," Roland stated. "I've prayed on it. My wife and I are on the same page. And I *know* that's what you really want to do. So go ahead and admit it so we can end this and get on with our lives."

E.J. peered at his brother, feeling his wife's warm encouraging hand on his back and the urging eyes of the other people in the room. The smile tugged at his lips and pretty soon he couldn't hold it anymore, and broke out into an uncharacteristic grin. In seconds, everyone at the table was following suit.

"Enough said, then," E.J. concluded, sitting back in his seat. Relief washed over him like a cooling shower. It had pained him to agree to sell the clubs, but he was willing to make the sacrifice for his brother. He would've tried his hardest to live with it, but he was thrilled that he didn't have to. "I'll contact Barber tomorrow and let him know our answer."

"Good. And now that we've decided this, I'm even more amped to take our shit to the next level," Roland said. "I want us to keep this going, brother. I want a legacy for my kids. Our name means something in this city and like you said, nobody can buy that."

"You're right. And believe me when I tell you, when those babies come, you'll be able to spend whatever time you need or want with them," E.J. assured, looking at Roland

and Lovey. "Like *you* said, family is more important. And I recognize that."

The six of them talked a little more before they began clearing the dishes, ignoring Lovey's claims that she could do it herself. They were all talking and joking in the kitchen, enjoying the lightened mood.

"I appreciate you all inviting me to be here, even though I really don't have a say in all this," Desiree commented, stacking the dirty bowls next to the sink. "That's much appreciated."

"It's affects you, too," Roland shrugged.

"You've helped us a lot over the last few years, Desiree," E.J. added. "Your work has brought a lot of people through the doors. We don't discount that."

"Babe, stop," Roland gently admonished, stopping Lovey as she started to lift the crock pot insert for washing. "You know better than that. Go sit down; we've got it."

"Roland, I can help. I'm not going to break in pieces from washing some dishes," Lovey insisted.

"Girl, hush and relax over here," Natalia fussed, guiding Lovey to one of the stools in front of the kitchen island and brushing down an errant lock of her long hair. "You want some ice cream or something?"

"Oh, Natalia, not you too," Lovey whined. "I'm totally fine, y'all."

"And you're gonna stay that way," Desiree insisted, sliding a bottle of water in front of her friend. "Now shut up."

"Gosh, are you all going to be like this through my entire pregnancy??"

"Yep," everyone chorused.

Lovey chuckled as she shook her head. "I love you all for caring so much, but I cannot just sit around for the next seven months. I'm following all of my doctor's orders. Y'all know I wouldn't do anything to jeopardize my babies."

They heard Xavier on the baby monitor and Roland went to go check on him. The rest of them continued to talk and nosh on the vegan cheesecake that Lorenzo had brought and everyone had been too preoccupied to notice, marveling at how good it was.

"You know I think it's mad sexy that you can bake like that," Desiree flirted, siding up to him as he washed dishes. "That's part of how I knew you were the one for me."

Lorenzo smiled down at her. "Oh yeah?"

"Most definitely. It kinda blows my mind that you're still putting up with my crazy ass two years after we met."

"Hey, you put up with me, too." Lorenzo kissed the top of her head. "I meant it when I said I believed we were meant for each other, even if I had to be patient for you to be fully ready for that level of commitment."

"What if I said I'm a hundred percent fully ready now?" Desiree asked, looking up at him with anxious eyes. "What if I said I wouldn't be mad if we left here and hopped a plane to Vegas or wherever so we could get married *tonight*?"

Lovey and Natalia gasped as everyone whirled around to look at Desiree in shock. Her eyes were fixed on Lorenzo, though, as she gripped his forearm with both hands and nervously bit her bottom lip.

"Are you serious?" he asked her.

"What's going on?" Roland asked, re-entering the kitchen and seeing everyone's stunned expressions. Lovey just pressed a finger to her lips and waved him over, grinning at his confused look as he came to stand next to her.

"Baby," Lorenzo hedged, his whiskey-colored eyes searching Desiree's pleading ones. "Are you proposing to me?"

"Yes," Desiree replied without hesitation. She stepped closer to him. "I was stupid to not accept when you asked me the first time."

"Well, Desiree," Lorenzo wiped his hands on a dish towel as he turned to her. "I can't let you do that. So in response to your suggestion, the answer is no."

Desiree's face fell. "Wh-what?"

Natalia's hands flew to her mouth and Lovey's eyes were already shining with tears. Roland and E.J. shared a pensive glance.

"You're too special for some impersonal Vegas wedding," Lorenzo told Desiree, taking her hand. "I love you too much to give you less than you deserve, which is the beach wedding I know you want with our family and friends there, and your dad walking you down the aisle. And that's what you're going to have. But you're also not going to deprive me of the privilege of asking you to be my wife and hearing you say yes."

When Lorenzo pulled out his wallet and produced the same engagement ring he'd presented to Desiree on her birthday, the ladies all shrieked in excitement and the brothers broke out into relieved grins. Natalia and Lovey clasped hands, practically jumping with excitement while

Desiree looked like she was about to hyperventilate as Lorenzo lowered his huge frame down in front of her to one knee and took her left hand in his.

"Yes!" she exclaimed before he could say anything else.

"Baby, will you let me propose to you, please?" Lorenzo admonished, grinning, as everyone laughed.

"Okay, okay, sorry." Desiree was already bouncing on her toes excitedly, grinning and crying. "But you *know* I'm about to explode so please don't do a super long-"

"Desiree, shut up!" Natalia practically screamed.

"Sorry!"

"Desiree," Lorenzo chuckled, shaking his head. "As soon as I laid eyes on you at Lovey and Roland's dinner party a couple of years ago, you've enthralled me. And once we had our first date, I was sure I wanted to be in your life for as long as possible. I know you've been through a lot, and you were scared the last time I asked you. But the way you fought for us after that meant a lot. I'm honored to be the man you trust with your heart. Desiree Mashburn..." He slid the ring onto her finger. "Will you marry m-"

"YES!!" Desiree screamed, unable to hold it in. She jumped into Lorenzo's arms as soon as he stood, wrapping her legs around him and kissing all over his face as everyone laughed and cheered. She cupped his face in both hands and pressed her lips to his before sliding her arms around his neck.

"I love you so much," she whispered as he rocked her side to side.

"I love you, too," Lorenzo muttered against her neck. He closed his eyes, the moment hitting him. "More than anything."

"Oh my god, that is so beautiful!" Lovey exclaimed, happy tears streaming down her face. She grinned up at Roland. "I'm so happy right now!"

"Me too, babe," Roland agreed, wrapping an arm around her and kissing the top of her head. He hugged her close as she leaned against his chest, sliding her arms around him. "We're all extremely blessed, like you said."

Natalia looked over at E.J. and he was already gazing at her, unleashing immediate tingles all over her body. She smiled as she returned his gaze, wishing more than anything that they were alone right then. It wasn't just her body that missed his; she missed everything about E.J.; his presence, his touch, his conversation, the warmth and security she felt when he was around. She hated being in that house without him. Natalia needed her husband back.

• • • •

AS HAPPY AS E.J. WAS for his friends, he was happier to be home with Natalia.

He followed her there after they left Lovey and Roland's, and Natalia grabbed his hand and went straight upstairs to their bedroom. They each kicked their shoes off and climbed on the bed, E.J. pulling Natalia to him.

"It feels *so* good to lay with you like this," she sighed, resting her hand on his abs. "I almost can't even believe you're here."

"Me, either." E.J.'s hold on her tightened. "I hate being away from you. What do you think about me coming back home?"

She sat up to look at him. "I love it. You know I want you back here. But I need to tell you something first."

His eyes immediately narrowed, and she hurried to place a reassuring hand to his cheek. "It's not what you're thinking. This isn't a secret or something I've been hiding from you. I promise there aren't any more of those."

E.J. looked relieved. "What is it?"

"I went to the doctor a couple of days ago," Natalia began, her voice wavering slightly. "I wanted to talk to her about what I could do to increase my chances of getting pregnant."

"Yeah?" E.J. sat up and took her hand, sensing this wasn't good news.

"After she ran a few tests, she told me that I'd developed uterine fibroids. I had no idea because they hadn't given me any pain or bothered me in any way. But because of the placement of them, they basically changed the position of my cervix."

"So what does that mean?"

"It means it'll be more difficult for us to conceive, because not as many sperm can get to my uterus. It's not impossible, but who knows when it'll happen, if it ever does."

She looked down, not wanting to see the disappointment that she was sure covered her husband's face. It hurt her to have to give him more bad news, even if it wasn't as bad as it could've been. She just hated that this was yet another hiccup between them.

"Babe..." E.J. lifted her chin. "Look at me."

She lifted her eyes to his.

"What's with the face?"

"Because I know this isn't what you wanted to hear. I was hoping we'd be able to just make a baby like we're supposed to be able to do, but of course, nothing can ever be that easy when it comes to us. No *wonder* nothing happened after those times we went raw. It's like we just can't catch a damn break."

"Natalia, stop," E.J. admonished. "Baby, this isn't the end of the world. I'm not thrilled to hear about it but at least there's still a chance. I'm just relieved it's not worse than it is."

Her eyebrows rose in surprise. "Really? You're not upset?"

"No. After everything we've been through these past few months, this isn't going to sway anything. At least, not for me."

"Oh my god, E.J.," Natalia breathed, throwing her arms around his neck. "You have no idea how relieved I am to hear you say that. I was expecting you to go through the roof."

"For what? For you getting something that a lot of Black women get? Hell, my mother dealt with fibroids."

"So does mine," Natalia recalled. "Clearly hers didn't stop Daddy's iron man sperm, though, since they still ended up with eight of us."

Laughing, E.J. rolled on top of her. He lowered his mouth to hers, giving her a series of leisurely pecks. "Thank you for letting me know. But I don't want you to stress, okay? We're going to get through this together just like we've gotten through everything else."

Natalia grinned as her hand gripped the back of his shirt. "Absolutely."

"And as far as I'm concerned..." His hand slid to her breast and squeezed before he began strumming his thumb across her nipple through her dress, earning a gasp from her. "That just means I need to send more sperm through there."

Moaning, Natalia clamped her legs around his waist. "I don't disagree. And I think we need to get a jump on that *right now*."

It didn't take long for the intensity to go from zero to sixty. They clawed at each other's clothes, tossing them aside uncaringly, eager to be joined together. Natalia's head was partially off the bed when E.J. entered her, giving her that smooth firm stroke that she'd been missing.

"I'm gonna fall," she breathed as E.J. began to go harder and his thrusts started inching her further off the bed.

"No, you're not. I got you." E.J. slid his arm under her and pulled her to him, holding her close. He buried his face in the crook of her neck, the emotion from being with her again gripping him like a vise. "I've always got you."

Chapter 21

• • • •

NATALIA PADDED BAREFOOT into the kitchen, little Xavier perched on her hip. She and E.J. were babysitting for the weekend.

"I'm hungry, Auntie," Xavier informed her.

"I know, baby, just one second..."

E.J. entered the kitchen, phone in hand. Natalia glanced at him as she opened the refrigerator.

"Let me guess; Lovey called again?"

"Yep." E.J. chuckled. "You know she can't resist. But at least this was only the second time today."

"She's getting better."

"Uncle E!" Xavier exclaimed excitedly, reaching for E.J.

"See how he forgets about me every time you come around?" Natalia joked as E.J. took the toddler from her arms. "Men."

"Don't hate." E.J. tossed Xavier into the air, grinning when his nephew squealed with laughter. "I can't help that I'm his favorite uncle."

"You're his *only* uncle. He has a gang of aunties." Natalia cut up some turkey meatballs, avocado, and baked sweet potato and put it on Xavier's sectioned plate. E.J. grabbed it and sat at the table with Xavier on his lap.

"You know he can sit by himself, right?" Natalia asked, smiling. "There's a high chair right there."

"So he's sitting on my lap. He's still feeding himself."

"Gosh, you're a softie for this boy." Natalia pulled out the chair next to E.J.'s, dropping onto it as she handed Xavier his blue fork. "I can't believe Lovey is almost seven months. This pregnancy is flying by."

"I'm just glad that she and Roland could get away before she gets shut down for traveling. Did she tell you about any complications or anything?"

"Oh no, it's nothing like that. It's just precaution because she's carrying multiples in her late thirties, that's all. She insists she feels great."

"Good. Our niece and nephew will be here before we know it."

They continued to talk while Xavier ate his dinner, then E.J. gave him a bath, declining Natalia's help. He tended to hog Xavier when they were babysitting, but Natalia thought it was cute. E.J. was practically a different person when he was around his nephew.

"He's finally down," E.J. announced a while later, entering their bedroom with the baby monitor in hand. "He wanted me to read the same book to him like three times."

Natalia giggled. "And I bet you read it three times."

"Of course. You know I love me and little man's quality time."

"Can *I* get some attention from you now?" She stood from the bed, dropping her robe from her shoulders. Her freshly-showered nude body made E.J.'s eyes tighten in arousal. "I've been waiting for my turn all day."

"Umph." E.J. placed the monitor on the dresser and pulled his shirt over his head before crossing over to his wife. He took her into his arms, laying a languid kiss on her. "I'm all yours."

Natalia eagerly returned his kiss as she began untying the string of his sweatpants. She pushed them and his underwear down and ran her hands over his hard buttocks before sliding them up his back. Their kiss deepened as they inched towards the bed, E.J.'s hand tangled in her hair.

"How do you want it?" he asked between kisses.

Tearing her mouth from his, Natalia climbed onto the bed and got on all fours, looking over her shoulder at him lustfully. E.J. wasted no time pressing his groin against her, giving her backside a slap.

"You know you can't be too loud, right?" Natalia reminded him, only half-joking.

"You should be telling yourself that." E.J. reached around, fondling her clit as he placed wet kisses to her back, making her arch and hiss in pleasure. "Wanna challenge me to see if I can make you scream?"

"We both know you can. *Fuck*," she whispered, her eyes closed. She wound against E.J.'s hand. "Come on..."

E.J. was in no more of a mood for teasing or lengthy foreplay than Natalia was, and he stroked his hardness a few times before sliding inside of her. They both tried to keep their voices down as they enjoyed each other, Natalia's hands gripping the sheets and E.J.'s gripping her hips.

They'd been like animals for each other since they reconciled, even more than before their separation. Even though they both still wanted a child, they had agreed to just go at it as they always did and let nature take its course. Neither of them wanted their intimacy to become all about trying to get pregnant. If it happened, it happened. E.J was content knowing that they were finally on the same page and everything was out in the open; anything else was out of their control.

And he absolutely *loved* not having to use condoms anymore.

· · · ·

"MY SISTER CALLED ME today," Natalia told E.J. as they sat across from each other at Rocky's a few days later. They'd each been working from home and were taking a break for lunch, neither in any particular hurry to get back to work. "Apparently Kira is still with Dane. She's moved in with him and everything."

"Wow," E.J. shook his head. "Interesting turn of events."

"She thinks she might be pregnant."

"Of course. Everyone else is."

Natalia eyed him but he was wearing a good-natured smile. She was relieved to see the subject didn't upset him. He'd been a lot more at ease lately, not just about having a baby but in general. He was still disciplined and about his business, but he now also took time for leisure, too; delegating more to his employees so he could spend more time with Natalia, getting regular massages to relieve tension, and going to the park when he needed to clear his head. They made a point to have date night at least once a week, even if it was just a romantic dinner at home. E.J. would go all out and hire a personal chef, and they'd get dressed up in separate rooms, meeting downstairs for dinner and dancing. There were times when Natalia couldn't believe this was her husband.

"You're actually eating fried fish?" she marveled once E.J. got his order.

"It's my indulgence for the week," E.J. shrugged.

"You had a cupcake last night."

"You my nutritionist now?"

"Hey, don't get me wrong; I'm not complaining. You're still fine as fuck."

"Glad you're pleased," he smiled, winking at her.

"I'm more than pleased. And I hope *you're* pleased with what we have planned for your birthday next week."

"Ugh. I told you we don't have to make a big fuss, babe. I'd be just fine just spending the evening in bed with you."

"Oh, we're doing that. After."

"You know I don't love parties. Especially ones where I'm supposed to be the main focus."

"Remind me what business you're in again?"

He tossed one of his fries at her, making her giggle. "I don't know why y'all like doing this to me."

"What, celebrating the man we all love and respect so much? Turning forty is a big deal, baby. There's no way I wasn't gonna do it up for you."

"Well, I appreciate it."

The night of the party came quicker than E.J. would've liked. While he appreciated the love, he wasn't exactly eager to party. The last time he had acquiesced on that was for his and Natalia's ten year anniversary, and he couldn't help but remember how everything started changing after that night.

But, as he had many times over recent weeks, he pushed those negative memories from his mind. All of Natalia's secrets and the turmoil they caused in their marriage were in the past. They were in a great place now and he was grateful for that.

This time they were having the party at Barfly, since Natalia knew E.J. would prefer something more laid back. Most of the same friends and loved ones that had been at their anniversary party were there, including Roland and a very pregnant Lovey, and the newly married Desiree and Lorenzo. Natalia was excited to surprise E.J. with a trip to Jamaica, which was where they'd gone on their honeymoon.

"You good, Lovey?" Natalia asked, noticing her slight wince.

"Oh yeah, I'm fine. My back is just a little sore, that's all."

"I'm surprised Roland loosened up the leash for you to come out tonight," Liz commented, rubbing her little sister's back. "You know he's been watching you like a hawk since he put those twins in you."

"Believe me, I know. It's only because it's for E.J. that he let up for tonight. Where did they go, anyway?" Lovey asked, glancing around the room. They were holding the party on Barfly's off night, and E.J. had managed to convince Natalia to keep the guest list under thirty people. It became a negotiation, because he had initially requested just twenty, at the most.

"I don't know; him and E.J. have been acting kinda weird tonight," Natalia commented, looking around, herself.

Desiree floated over, her seemingly ever-present grin in place. Natalia chuckled.

"Well, here comes the glowing newlywed."

"Please tell me you and Lorenzo weren't off somewhere having quickies in the bathroom or something," Lovey pleaded, only half-joking.

"I don't know what you're talking about."

"Desiree Mashburn-Wade..."

"Nobody saw us so it doesn't count!"

"Oh my god."

"All y'all are some horny asses," Liz shook her head, smiling. "And Natalia, don't think I didn't see you and E.J. coming out from the back looking good and satisfied earlier."

The ladies turned teasing eyes to Natalia, who grinned as her face flushed with convicted heat. She sipped her pinot noir and flipped her hair over her shoulder. "I had to give him the first part of his birthday gift."

"It must be his birthday *every* day, then, the way you two are all over each other all the time."

"Well, hell, can you blame me? I'm so grateful that we're in the great place we're in right now, after the hell we've been through this past year. Not to mention, he's fine as fuck."

They all laughed. Moments later, Roland and E.J. appeared from wherever they had gone and Roland called for everyone's attention.

"If I can have y'all's ear for a minute, I just want to say a couple of things," he announced, rubbing his hands together. Once the talking and the music quieted down, he continued. "I know we're all here to celebrate my brother's fortieth birthday, and we're absolutely doing that; I certainly don't want to take any shine off him. He's an awesome brother, husband, uncle, friend, business partner and we all love him, blah blah blah."

E.J. shook his head good-naturedly as everyone laughed. "Get to the damn point, man."

"Still impatient in your old age, huh? Fine. This time I'm as anxious as you are to finally come out with this. Lovey, Natalia."

The ladies looked at each other in surprise before glancing towards their husbands. Since Lovey was so pregnant and nursing a sore back, the men moved over to where she and Natalia were seated near the bar. Everyone gathered around them in a loose semicircle.

"We've been working on something," Roland began, looking at his wife anxiously. "And now we're finally able to tell you about it."

"You remember that deal from Carlton Barber that we turned down, right?" E.J. asked, drawing a curious nod from the ladies. "Well, he's back in the picture now."

Natalia's eyes widened. "He made another offer for the clubs?"

"Not exactly. I know we all agreed to decline his initial offer and haven't regretted that, but even I can't deny that associating with someone like Barber would be a good business move, in the right capacity."

"Then Lorenzo hit us with an idea a while back," Roland continued. "Long story short, we're going to be partnering with Barber on another venture. A high-end cigar bar and lounge. We're majority owners. And Barber secured a prime location."

"Are you serious?" Lovey shrieked excitedly. Natalia's jaw was on the floor.

"We're all the way serious, babe. E.J. and I had already been kicking around ideas for what we wanted to do next, and when we sat down with Lorenzo and Barber and our respective business people, we came up with this."

"This way we get our new venture, Barber gets to have his hand in this arena without having to build something from the ground up himself, and we get to use each other's names and reputations to make it the hottest thing in town. Everything is already in the works." E.J. sported a proud smile.

"So that's why you've been holed up in the office on your phone and on those secret Zoom meetings so much these last few months?" Natalia marveled, grinning as she nudged E.J. in the shoulder before giving him a congratulatory peck on the lips. "This is wonderful, baby!"

"And we definitely want the most important women in our lives to have their stamp on it," Roland added, taking Lovey's hand. "So we're naming the place Natavey. A combination of your names."

Several people gasped, most loudly Lovey and Natalia.

"If that's all right with you," E.J. concluded with a wink.

The tears were already springing to Lovey's eyes as she opened her arms for Roland, who grinned and gathered her up into a firm but careful hug. Natalia wrapped her arms around E.J.'s neck, resisting the urge to wrap her legs around him, too. Her eyes slid closed as she thanked the Lord for the millionth time for this man she had the privilege of being forever committed to.

"Thank you, baby," she whispered, pressing her cheek to his.

"Thank *you*," he countered. He pulled back slightly and rested his forehead to hers. "You keep me going, babe."

"Oh, E.J...I love you. For life."

"I love you more. For life."

The party continued for a while longer before Roland wanted to get Lovey home and E.J. was ready to ride out the rest of his birthday alone with his wife. Of course, that had to include another round of birthday sex, which began in the car.

"You can't be doing that to me while I'm trying to drive, baby," E.J. breathlessly scolded as they screeched into their driveway. "As much as I love when you give me head-"

"Did you think I was done? I only paused so you wouldn't keep almost running off the road." She gave him a naughty smirk as she reached for his still-hard dick that he hadn't yet tucked back into his pants. "Now I can *really* get it in. Let that seat all the way back."

It was another twenty minutes before they finally went into the house, E.J. grabbing her as soon as they were through the door. She squealed when he picked her up and spun her around before carrying her over to the couch, sitting with her on his lap.

"I have something I wanted to run by you," he told her.

She laced her fingers behind his neck. "Yeah?"

"What would you think about leaving ModCode to come work with us? Over at Natavey?"

"Really??"

"If you want. I know you haven't been hyped about your job for a while. You could manage it-"

"You don't have to try to sell me on it," she interjected, placing a finger to his lips. "I'm putting my notice in at work *tomorrow*."

"Wow, I thought I'd have to do some more convincing," E.J. joked.

"As much as I'd enjoy whatever you'd do, it's not necessary. Like you said, I haven't really cared about my job; I don't hate it but it's turned into just something to do. But getting to work side by side with my husband? I'd *absolutely* love that."

"I'm glad to hear you say that, babe. And I'm glad that you and Lovey were so happy about it; Roland and I were a little worried how you'd react about us moving forward with another business without running it by you."

"I'm sure I can speak for Lovey when I say we trust you two and your judgment. You wouldn't enter into something like this unless you'd done all the due diligence. I know nothing is a sure thing, but y'all know what you're doing. And we all know Carlton Barber doesn't associate himself with bullshit."

"You're right about that."

"Are we done talking now or can we get back to being mannish?"

Laughing, E.J. leaned in and kissed her. "What do you think?"

He slid her off his lap before easing off the couch and kneeling in front of her, licking his lips as he slid his hands up her smooth legs, taking the hem of her cream halter dress with them. She was already whimpering and writhing in anticipation as he dragged down her panties, tossing them aside before licking up the inside of her thigh.

"Open wider for me," he ordered, gently biting her skin.

Immediately doing as instructed, Natalia's head fell back when E.J.'s tongue hit her clit. She panted loudly as he got her back for the taunting head she'd given him during their ride home, feeling the orgasm coming way too soon but knowing there was nothing she could do to stop it outside of pushing him away, and that wasn't happening.

"E.J.!" she screamed, gripping the back of his head with both hands.

"That mannish enough for you?" he asked, gently blowing on her before giving her a slow lick, just like she loved it. "'Cause my birthday isn't quite over yet."

Natalia gave him a sex-drunk grin. "We haven't done it in the kitchen in a while. You know I like it on the counter."

· · · ·

A WEEK OR SO AFTER his birthday, E.J.'s alarm went off at four in the morning as always, but instead of rolling out of bed to get ready for the gym like he usually did, he rolled to the other side of the king-sized bed, lowered the top of his sleeping wife's thin nightshirt, and helped himself to her pretty bronzed brown breast, moaning as he traced her nipple with his tongue. He'd always loved her skin color.

"Umm," Natalia stirred, arching into him. Her eyes were still closed. "Good morning to you, too."

"You don't mind, do you?"

Her hand slid to the back of his head as his hand began fondling her other nipple. She moaned loudly, finally easing her eyes open. "Hell no."

E.J. continued savoring his wife's breasts, bringing her to a cursing, panting orgasm. He gave her a brief kiss before reluctantly easing out of bed. As much as he wished he could've lingered in there with her longer, he had a lot on his plate that day and he had to get his customary early start.

Natalia rolled over, watching him as he started preparing to go to the gym. She rested her head on her hand, her elbow propped on the pillow. "Meetings all day, huh?"

"Yeah. And both clubs are rented out for tonight so we need to double-check to make sure everything's on point for that, especially since it's the mayor that's gonna be at 845."

Natalia's eyebrows shot up. "Really?"

"Yeah. Holding some kind of fundraiser."

"That's amazing. That place stays booked."

"And I'm not mad at it."

"I've got a good amount of stuff to do today, too. I'm still in the middle of hiring the Natavey staff, and I've gotta get with Desiree on the promotion. It's a whole different vibe from Barfly and 845 and she's like a salivating Doberman looking at a raw steak, as excited as she is about the things we've got lined up."

"I bet she is," E.J. chuckled, grabbing a pair of socks from the drawer. "I'm looking forward to seeing it, myself."

"Are you gonna have to pop in on the mayor's thing? Nigel and Teddy's graduation party is tonight, isn't it?"

"Yep, and I'm not missing it."

"Is Nigel still walking on air about his girlfriend not being pregnant?"

"You know he is," E.J. chuckled. "I've never seen that boy so relieved."

"We would've been right there for him as honorary grandparents but you know I had to smack him upside the head for being so careless."

"Trust me, you weren't the only one. He got that and more from his mama once she found out. But he learned his lesson; him and his girl both wanna chill on the sex for a while after that. In answer to your question, Roland is mainly handling the mayor's event, but you know he hates leaving Lovey since he's paranoid about her going into labor at any second. He's already assigned Liz to keep an eye on her while he's gone and will be right back home to her as soon as he's able to be."

Natalia smiled and shook her head as she flopped onto her back. "Sounds about right. That man is gonna drive Lovey crazy."

"If he hasn't already. But he's just excited about those twins getting here. Little Xavier is looking forward to being a big brother, he said."

"Aww, that's so sweet! With his cute self. I can't wait for him to come back over here."

"It'll be soon enough, I bet, especially once the twins are born. Three kids barely under three years old at once is gonna be a lot."

They continued to talk about what else they had on deck for their respective days as E.J. moved into the ensuite to brush his teeth and wash his face. He grabbed one of his hoodies from the closet and slipped it over his head as he strolled over to the bed, leaning down to give his wife a kiss.

"I'll see you later?" he asked, taking another peck.

"Can't wait."

He headed out to the gym and Natalia curled up and hugged her down pillow, still feeling a slight buzz from her morning orgasm. She was glad that she no longer had to worry about going to ModCode and could structure her own day. Getting to work with her husband, managing and interacting and engaging with people was way more up her alley than being stuck in front of a computer all day, and she was extremely excited and grateful for the change. Grinning contentedly, she closed her eyes and let herself doze back off.

She got up a couple of hours later, stretching languidly before rolling out of bed. The house was quiet; she knew E.J. had likely showered at the gym and gone straight to work. Natalia tried to tamp down her yearning for him as she went about fixing herself some breakfast, taking a shower, and calling to check on her mother before going into the home office. She wanted to work on the app idea she was playing around with for a while before getting ready to head over to Natavey.

When she had to go to the restroom a while later, she noticed one of her pregnancy tests she'd bought a while back when she looked under the sink to get more soap. She'd stopped testing herself when she and E.J. decided to not focus on getting pregnant and just enjoy each other and let the chips fall where they may. Since it was the last of the tests she'd bought, she felt compelled to go ahead and take it right then, more to get it from under her sink than anything else.

"What the hell," she muttered, opening the box. She tossed the instructions aside, well familiar with the process by then. Several minutes later, she had taken the test, relieved herself, washed her hands, and set the test stick near the sink. When her phone rang and she saw it was Desiree calling, she answered and fell into a conversation that went on for close to thirty minutes, the test in the bathroom forgotten.

The front door opened, and she rushed out of the office to see E.J. heading up the stairs.

"Hey, I didn't expect to see you back here so soon," she said as he gave her a quick peck to the lips. "Everything okay?"

"Yeah, everything's fine. I just forgot the projection binder I was looking over last night," he muttered, clearly frustrated with himself. "Thankfully the ten o'clock meeting got pushed back."

"Did you eat? And I'm not talking about that raggedy protein shake."

"Yeah, I had a sandwich a little while ago."

"Good."

Natalia went to their closet to choose what she was going to wear before strolling back into the bathroom to do her hair and makeup. It was then that she remembered the pregnancy test sitting on the sink. She grabbed it, fully expecting to see the usual negative result so she could toss it in the trash, but she actually screamed when she saw the word 'Positive'. She blinked, rubbed her eyes, and screamed again when the word was still there.

"What's wrong??" E.J. exclaimed, running into the bathroom ready to handle whatever it was that was freaking his wife out like that.

Unable to speak, she just held the test out to him, her hand shaking. E.J. froze when he saw the result in front of him, several moments going by before he snapped out of it and looked up at Natalia.

"Please tell me this is for real," he croaked.

"It is, baby," Natalia confirmed, breaking out into an excited grin as the reality started to hit her. "E.J...we're pregnant!!"

He placed a hand to his chest and stepped back, momentarily feeling like he'd gotten the wind knocked out of him. Emotion slammed through him like an offensive line as he processed this, running his hands down his face. E.J. rarely cried, but the tears started coming and he didn't try to stop them.

"Baby..." Natalia put the test down and rushed over to her husband, swiping his tears with her thumbs. E.J. grabbed her face in both hands and kissed her eagerly and urgently, hoping to high heaven that this wasn't some dream he was about to wake up from.

He fell to his knees in front of her, pressing his face to her stomach and clutching her nightshirt in his hands. The happy tears continued to flow, soaking through the shirt's thin material, and he quickly lifted it so he could plant kisses all over her bare stomach. Natalia smiled and cried right along with him, holding his head in her hands.

"Thank you," she heard him whisper, over and over. She wasn't sure if he was talking to her or to God, but it didn't matter. Natalia had plenty to be thankful for, too, and it certainly wasn't going to stop any time soon.

Standing to his feet, E.J. grabbed her around the waist and picked her up, breaking out into a grin as she laughed while he spun her around. He set her down on the counter next to the positive test, standing between her legs and keeping his hold on her waist. His eyes looked at her in adoration.

"I'm the happiest man alive right now," he informed her. His hands started lovingly roaming her back.

"Believe me, I'm as thrilled as you are. I feel like we just hit the lottery."

"And I'm gonna do whatever I need to do to keep you feeling that way," he assured, sounding as determined as ever. "Just like I promised."

"I know you will. I trust you more than anybody, baby. This is it; you, me, and our latest blessing," Natalia grinned, pressing a hand to her stomach. "For life."

"Damn right. For life."

Thanks so much for reading! It was so much fun writing E.J. and Natalia's story. I've got more coming from this batch of characters...can you guess who might be getting their story told next?

• • • •

IF YOU ENJOYED THIS (even if you didn't), please consider leaving a review. And if you want to show *extra* love, share that you read it on social media! ☺

• • • •

YOU CAN FIND ME ON Instagram and TikTok at @authorjessicaterry and on Twitter (I'm not calling it that other name) at @itsJessicaTerry. And don't forget to subscribe to my email list at jessicaterry.com.

Also by Jessica Terry

Some Like 'em Thick
It's All Right...Now
Not By a Long Shot
Get Right
Decisions and Consequences
Take One For the Team
When You Share Too Much
Backtalk
Emasculated
Restless
The Beginning of Again
Always and Nevers
She is Me
Split By the Bell
The Karma Call
Forehead Kiss
All Because of Ava
Love Intolerant
Mr. Time Waster

• • • •

The Introvert Series
An Introvert's Christmas
Wooing the Introvert
The Introvert Roast
I, Take Thee Introvert
The Introvert Series Compilation (paperback only)

• • • •

Discussion Questions

• • • •

1. Do you feel there was *any* justification for Natalia lying about wanting a baby?

2. After E.J. found out that Natalia had led him on for ten years regarding the child she knew he wanted, did you feel he was foolish for forgiving her?

3. The Bell brothers were split about the buyout offer from Carlton Barber. Do you think they should have sold, or is no amount of money worth giving up what you worked hard for?

4. E.J. was very stubborn and disciplined, and often unyielding. How big a part do you think he played in the distress his marriage was in?

5. Do you think guilt was a good justification for Natalia letting Dane back into her life? Was that just another way she disrespected E.J., even though she told him they were back in touch?

6. Natalia cut her sister Kira off after what she tried with E.J. Was Natalia a hypocrite for not forgiving her, considering all the things she'd done herself?

7. Did Liz overstep her boundaries with the way she questioned Natalia about wanting a baby?

8. What did you think about the outing Lorenzo took E.J. on? Did you think it was silly or did you understand what Lorenzo was trying to do?

9. Did you feel E.J. should have mentioned to Natalia that he ran into Lyric, or was it no big deal? Was it comparable to Natalia's situation with Dane?

10. After everything Natalia did, do you think she deserved to get her husband back? Or did she learn enough of a lesson?

Did you love *The Stubborn Kind*? Then you should read *Mr. Time Waster*[1] by Jessica Terry!

For most women, getting dumped on their birthday – and *not* for the first time – would be enough of a lesson.

But for Claire Hutchinson, letting go of Montrel Burns is easier said than done, despite his pattern of dissing her, missing her, and then dissing her again. She tries to move on with the respectful and romantic good guy Warner, but there's something about Montrel that keeps sucking her back in...

---

1. https://books2read.com/u/47WyB8

2. https://books2read.com/u/47WyB8

Montrel swears he's not a monster. He loves Claire and is sure they'll end up together eventually; he just needs time to be ready. But seeing Claire with anyone else in the meantime drives him crazy.

Will Claire wise up and focus on Warner, or will she let Montrel waste her time one time too many?

Read more at https://www.jessicaterry.com/.

About the Author

Jessica Terry caught the writing bug at a young age and loves little more than holing up at home in Douglasville, GA, cranking out contemporary novels. And eating. www.jessicaterry.com

Read more at https://www.jessicaterry.com/.